D1024785

SILENT
THUNDER

Peter Tasker is also
the author of:

*The Japanese: A Major
Exploration of Modern Japan*

SILENT THUNDER

A NOVEL

PETER TASKER

KODANSHA INTERNATIONAL
Tokyo • New York • London

Distributed in the United States by Kodansha America, Inc., 114 Fifth Avenue, New York, N.Y. 10011, and in the United Kingdom and continental Europe by Kodansha Europe Ltd., Gillingham House, 38-44 Gillingham Street, London SW1V 1HU. Published by Kodansha International Ltd., 17-14, Otowa 1-chome, Bunkyo-ku, Tokyo 112, and Kodansha America Inc.

92 93 10 9 8 7 6 5 4 3 2 1

Library of Congress Cataloging-in-Publication Data

Tasker, Peter
Silent thunder/Peter Tasker. — 1st ed.
p. cm.
ISBN 4-7700-1685-9
I. Title.
PR6070.A65S57 1992
823. 914—dc20

91-45468
CIP

For Nadine

1
:
:
.

THERE was pandemonium outside the Seikyu Hotel. Yumi-chan, Japan's favorite teenage idol, had just emerged from the press conference called to announce the end of her latest romance. Outside, the traffic was locked solid. Security people were bellowing through megaphones. TV cameramen were jostling for position. Hundreds of rain-sodden fans were chanting her name, then surging against the rope barrier when the slim seventeen-year-old finally came out into the night air.

She was wearing a velvet beret, a strapless microdress with a padded bust, and a confused, slightly scared expression. For an instant, she stood there transfixed, like a small animal caught in the headlights of an oncoming truck. Then she remembered her training and smiled her famous snaggletoothed smile. Instantly, she was raked with strobe lights. Camera motors were buzzing like insects. Journalists from the scandal sheets were yelling out questions:

"Tell us what happened. . . ."
"Are you happy, Yumi-chan? . . ."
"Are you sad? . . ."

A thousand pairs of eyes were on the girl's blank, puppylike features. No one was looking upward into the indigo sky, so no one saw the man tumble from the twentieth-floor window. No one saw the bundle of arms and legs flailing in the air. What with the jostling and yelling and general hubbub, no one even heard the primal wail of fear and anguish that sprang from his lips.

There was a crump of metal as the body bounced off the hood of a parked car and flipped onto the gravel pathway. The crowd turned and gave a single gasp of horror and excitement.

The man was lying on his back, arms and legs flung wide in the relaxed pose of a sunbather. The top of his head had cracked open, and pink-and-white matter was leaking onto the path. Instinctively, the crowd surged forward, forming a circle around the body. The megaphone voices rose to a frenzy. A couple of free-lance photographers started flashing away, but the TV crews didn't budge from their positions at the hotel entrance. They kept their cameras trained on Yumi, who was being hustled toward her limousine, waving and smiling brightly all the while.

2

.
.
.

MORI gazed at the rice paddies and bamboo groves sliding southward past the train window. It wasn't often that his work brought him to such an unspoiled part of the country. After half a year of chasing runaway teenagers and stalking unfaithful spouses, he could do with a few days of good clean air and fresh seafood. But it wasn't going to be a few days. Just a few hours, then back to Tokyo and an investigation that promised to be as depressing as his last divorce case.

The train was in character with the remote area it served: wheezing brakes, hard wooden seats dented and polished by decades of use, a conductor with an impenetrable local accent. As they juddered toward the end of the line, the only other passenger left was an old man with a hen under his arm. The train pulled into a tunnel and the carriage was plunged into roaring, rattling darkness. The conductor yelled an unintelligible joviality. The hen squawked and flapped its wings impotently. When they emerged on the other side of the mountain, it was into a different world. The browns and dark greens of the valleys and forests had disappeared. In their place was the glinting blue of the long flat sea.

The station was tiny, little more than a wooden shed and a wicker gate. It was unmanned, a sign of the steady drift of depopulation. Indeed, looking around the dusty streets and shops of the small town, Mori was struck by how few people there were between the ages of fifteen and fifty: schoolgirls chattering away in their singsong north country accents; middle-aged men with gnarled weather-worn features; old ladies shuffling along bent almost double, the heritage of a lifetime's work in the fields; but no trendy teenagers, no sharp-looking career women, no corporate samurai striding to appointments. It was like entering the simple, heartwarming world of an Ozu movie.

But the reason for Mori's presence was far from heartwarming. He recognized the Haras at once by the dull, grief-stricken expressions on their faces. Two old people who had just lost the pride of their lives. They greeted him politely, invited him back to their large wooden house, offered him any number of succulent local specialties, but they looked and sounded terribly tired.

What must it have been like for them, he wondered? Probably, old Hara had expected his only son to follow him on to the fishing boats, to grow big and strong enough to heft the portable shrine at the annual festival. At first he would have been disappointed that the boy was skinny and pale and spent all his time reading books. Then pride would have been restored as he passed every examination at the top of the class. It would have been replaced by awe when the parents realized the scale of the boy's abilities. Triumph when he won a place among the nation's elite at Tokyo University, redoubled when he was accepted into the Ministry of Finance, the most prestigious and powerful bureaucracy in a system that made bureaucrats into gods. Yet triumph mixed with sadness, for they must have known that their little fishing village had lost him for ever. Probably, they had only the vaguest idea of what his work actually meant.

And now shock. Finally, their boy had disappointed them in the most comprehensive way possible. Two weeks ago he had booked into the Akasaka Seikyu Hotel, as he sometimes did when he had been working late. After eating a three-course French dinner he had settled down in his room to watch a video, an American comedy according to the police report. Then halfway through, he had gotten up, opened the window, and jumped out into the Tokyo night. Death had been instantaneous.

"It's so strange," said old man Hara, cracking his knobbly knuckles one after the other. "We can hardly believe what has happened."

"He never inconvenienced anyone before," added Mrs. Hara, apologetically. She was smiling as she spoke, but a handkerchief was twisted tight between her hands, tight enough to turn her fingers white.

Mori listened to their story, which was one he had heard many times before. The boy had been happy, satisfied in his work, married to a good woman. Not once in his life had he suffered from depression or emotional distress. In fact, he had always been the picture of stability, his life a steady progression from one goal to the next. Then suddenly this one act which was so shockingly out of character as to be inexplicable. Why had he done it?

Mori didn't know the answer, but he did know that the personalities that people constructed, the faces that they showed the outside world, often hid something completely different. And when the thing that lay beneath the surface, unknown even to their family and closest friends, suddenly manifested itself, it was useless to try and connect it with anything else. Half his business was created by people acting in ways that no one would have believed possible. Adoring wives who killed their husbands for insurance; loyal servants of the company who suddenly embezzled millions of yen; well-brought-up daughters who decided to finance their life-styles by offering their bodies to four or five men a night. In Mori's experience, anyone was capable of anything, given the right kind of stimulus.

"He didn't phone much," the old man was saying. "But he did call three nights before. He told us how pleased he was about the promotion."

"Promotion?" asked Mori.

"He'd been nominated to some important committee or other. He said he was looking forward to the challenge."

"Did he seem nervous about it, or excited in any way?"

"You didn't know him, Mori-san. Our son never once failed in anything he attempted. He was absolutely confident."

The old man couldn't disguise the pride in his voice. He smiled and glanced at the photo of the young man in graduation robes that stood on top of the television.

"Do you have any details about this new job?"

"It was very important, he said. But other than that . . ."

The old man's gaze became distant again. The inner workings of the Ministry of Finance were obviously not something in which he took a close interest. He was looking out of the window, at the fishing boats bobbing on the tide.

Mori chewed his way through some freshly caught crab, slowly savoring the tang of the sea. He would take the case, find out as much as he could, write a five-page summary of potential scenarios, assigning a probability factor to each one. And afterward how much better off would anyone be? If he discovered that the brilliant young man had been a secret alcoholic, or that his pretty wife had taken a lover, or that he had gambled away his future in mah-jongg parlors, would that help the old man sleep any better?

But the Haras wanted an answer, something that would clear up all the uncertainty. That was the yearning in their eyes. The dreadful uncertainty—it makes you feel stupid and powerless. Mori understood that.

He asked a few more simple questions, but there was little to add. When he had explained his system of charges, the old woman went to a mahogany dresser at the side of the room and took out a thick bundle of notes. Mori repeated that he would be sending his bill on completion of the investigation, but the old woman was adamant.

"We humbly entreat you," she said, slipping the money into a white envelope. "It will make us feel much better."

"The truth," said the old man, with vehemence. "We want the truth." As they were driving back to the station along the coast road, Mori noticed a group of gravestones between the rice fields and the sea. One of them stood out, its white marble gleaming in the sunlight.

"That's where he's resting now," muttered the old man, half to himself. "He's with his ancestors."

Mori said nothing. They wanted the truth. He thought about that again as the ancient train rattled back toward the hole in the mountains. The truth! That was a commodity that, like cheap fresh lobster, might be easily obtainable in a North Japan fishing village. But in Tokyo it had to be patiently hunted through grid-locked traffic, seething crowds, warrens of nameless alleyways, and thousands of elliptical conversations.

At noon the next day, Mori met Deputy Inspector Kudo on a bench in the middle of Hibiya Park. It was convenient for Kudo, because Marunouchi Police Station was just across the road. It was good for Mori because he had spent the morning in the national library and because he liked the brass band music and the scent of the grass.

"What's the interest in the Hara case?" asked Kudo, as he handed over the photocopies.

"It's for the parents," replied Mori.

Kudo nodded his head thoughtfully.

"I know," he said. "They want to know why it happened, why their beloved son should do something so completely out of character."

"You spoke to them yourself?"

"Never met them, but I can guess how it is."

Kudo was a solid cop, twenty years in the force. He had the stoic look, stoic but still generous, of a man who had become a policeman not because his body was built that way, but because he had once had ideas about responsibility and community service. Mori had been trading favors with him for almost ten years. Sometimes, it was Mori's turn to call in a favor, sometimes it was Kudo's. It didn't really matter. Showing documents from police files to civilians was absolutely prohibited, but that didn't matter either.

"Sometimes I'm glad I'm not smart," said Kudo. "The pressure on these elite people is really something. No wonder they're always cracking up."

"It's tough at the top, that's for sure."

"There seems to be a spate of it these days. It must be the examination system."

"More than usual, are there?"

"It's a real boom. A guy from the Bank of Japan just slit his

wrists in the bath last week. Then there was that executive at a
big insurance company who hanged himself. Another one, a guy
from one of the big banks, did exactly the same as Hara. Left his
hotel room without using the door."

Kudo shook his head from side to side, as if the world had
once more defeated him with its sheer perversity.

"By the way," said Mori, "How's your son doing at school
these days?"

"The same as before. Bottom third of the class."

"Perhaps you should be thankful," said Mori, and clapped
him on the shoulder. They both laughed.

They parted company outside the head office of Dai-ichi Life
Insurance, one of the few buildings in the area that had remained
standing through the bombing raids. After the surrender, the gray
concrete castle, with its narrow windows and Doric pillars, became the headquarters of General Douglas MacArthur, Supreme
Commander of the Allied Powers. Now it was back in the hands
of Japan's second largest insurance company, a major supplier of
capital to the American government.

Mori walked back across the park. Already, the crowds of
shirt-sleeved salarymen were drifting back toward the office
buildings of Marunouchi and Yuraku-cho. Not for the first time,
he wondered what it would be like to be one of them. That's how
it would have been if fate hadn't intervened.

Mori's university had been prestigious enough to get him into
a top-class company. He was the right age now to be a section
leader, perhaps even a deputy department chief. He could be there
in the midst of them, wandering down the pavement with a
toothpick in his mouth and pack of Mild Sevens in the breast
pocket of the shirt. In the evenings, he would stride down the
Ginza in his Burberry raincoat, a couple of admiring juniors on
either side. They would laugh at his jokes, stop taxis for him,
pour his beer, usher him into elevators. After plenty of food and
drink and gossip, they would go off to some Ginza club, where
the girls would clap their hands at his *karaoke* performance and
call out, "Bravo, deputy department chief!"

He would be on a salary of six million yen, plus semiannual

bonus, with steady increases every year. He would have a fat expense account and company housing. There would be a couple of kids in middle school, the youngest just the right age to get out of the educational system right before he retired. Everything would be fixed, everything taken care of.

But twenty years ago a different Mori, an angry young man in a face mask and a hard hat daubed with slogans, had done something which had made all that impossible. Together with a group of other radicals, he had smashed his way into the university offices and torched the files that were kept on students. Someone in the group had gone to the authorities, or perhaps had been a spy all along. That kind of thing happened. Anyway, the result was expulsion. And after that, it would have been a waste of time even to attend any job interviews. He was marked down forever as a troublemaker, a man with no respect for consensus and group harmony. It had been a pretty random affair. Some of his friends had been sent to jail, and some got off with just a warning. It all depended on what amount of influence your family could bring to bear. In Mori's case, it had been negligible.

Soon afterward, the Americans handed back Okinawa, the Vietnam War ended, and all the rest of it started to seem pretty pointless. What had happened to all the others? The ones who had gotten away with it could well be in the crowd wandering back for another afternoon in the office. The ones who had gotten the same treatment as Mori had been dealt out of the system for life. They had gone and found work as free-lance teachers and coffee-bar owners and the like. Compared to that, being president, department chief, section chief, and sole employee of an investigation agency came pretty close to success.

Interviewing widows was only slightly less grueling than interviewing bereaved parents. Mori sat by the open window, the sunshine hot against the side of his face, and listened to Mrs. Hara punishing herself for her husband's death. It was only a week since the all-night wake had been held. She was still wearing black, and her eyes were red-rimmed.

The ministry obviously didn't believe in pampering its staff.

The apartment was small, just two rooms in an ivy-covered concrete block. The outer wall of the building was a spider's web of fissures, the legacy of thirty years of earth tremors. There was even one large crack above the radiator in the Haras' main room, a putty-filled scar that ran from the door to the window. An attempt had been made to cover up the worst part with a large flower arrangement.

"Can you tell me about his work, any special ambitions or worries?"

Unlike the parents, Mrs. Hara had a fairly good understanding of what her husband's work involved. They had been married five years ago, and the go-between who had brought them together was a senior ministry man. "My husband was a very determined man," she said. "He believed that he had the ability to take much more responsibility than he was given. He believed that he understood Japan's interests better than anyone else."

An ideal bureaucrat, thought Mori.

". . . Naturally, there were tensions in the ministry. He talked about them quite a lot."

"What sort of tensions?"

"Do you follow international monetary policy, Mr. Mori?"

"Not all that closely, but I keep up with the major trends."

Mori tried to sound casually confident. In fact, the subject bored him stiff, and he usually skipped any newspaper articles that discussed it. Charts, tables, jargon, acronyms that signified mysterious agencies—it all swam in front of his eyes, defying comprehension.

"Well, you may know that Japan has played a great role in the international financial system, recycling money to the third world, funding the American deficit and so on."

The words came out automatically, as if she was reading from a script. Which in a way she was. Mori could almost see the intense, bespectacled husband sounding off over dinner about comparative inflation rates, currency intervention, and so on. The wife would be nodding as she sipped her soup, the words and phrases and the assumptions behind them sinking into her consciousness.

"You mean the current account surplus," said Mori, trying desperately to remember what a man in a dusty classroom had said twenty-five years before. "That's right, the surplus."

There was a slight faltering in her voice. She doesn't understand it much better than I do, thought Mori with relief.

"Anyway, there are two factions in the ministry. One supports all this intervention and recycling—and that's what my husband thought. He said Japan should take the lead in building up a new system of international cooperation, with the yen at the center of it. The other faction wants Japan to be much more aggressive, to demand something in return for all the money we're providing. They were always battling away, trying to one-up each other. Sometimes, it got quite heated. He would still be angry when he got home."

"What about the promotion? Did that worry him at all?"

"Absolutely not. It would have given him the chance to put his ideas into practice. You see, he would have been adviser to the vice-minister on currency policy. He would have had direct responsibility for contact with Washington."

Her voice dropped a register, as if she were awestruck by the prospect. Perhaps she had repeated those words in the same hushed tones when her husband had first told her the good news. He would have been studiedly offhand, hiding his pride and excitement; the wife cautious, unsure what it all meant.

"I'm very sorry to have to ask you this. . . ."

This was the worst bit: prying into the marriage bed, looking for quarrels, neuroses, suspicions of unfaithfulness. A married man who spent two nights a week in a city-center hotel? He could have been up to anything. Mori had seen it all before, and from people just as outwardly diligent and respectable as Hara.

But this time there were no clues. According to Mrs. Hara, her husband had been a paragon of virtue. He didn't drink, had no interest in clothes or expensive food, was easily embarrassed by vulgar television programs. She even gave a strong hint that he had been a virgin at marriage. She was tired, defensive, slightly angry, but Mori believed her. The husband she had known had been dutiful, abstemious, 100 percent serious.

"If only we had had more fun," she said, sobbing slightly. "If only we could have laughed together more. I don't know why, but I think I failed as a wife. . . ."

Mori mumbled a few words of condolence, and they sounded more inadequate than usual. He got up and let himself out.

He walked through the small overgrown garden where a group of children, no doubt the offspring of the men steering Japan's financial policy, were busy making mud pies. A couple of butterflies were fluttering about like scraps of newspaper. Or they might have been a couple of scraps of newspaper fluttering about like butterflies. The heat was heavy on his shoulders and neck.

Mori thought about the ambitious bureaucrat working late into the night on a new yen-dollar agreement. Then he thought about the single man in the hotel room watching an Eddie Murphy movie. It was a variation from type, a small inconsistency that just might signify depth.

Mori got back to his office in Shinjuku at two o'clock. He had two rooms halfway up a ramshackle five-story building that shuddered in earthquakes and rattled and banged in typhoons. Mori often speculated about the psychology of the architect who had planned it. He was obviously a man who didn't like windows much, because there were none at all facing the street, and the ones at the back had a view of two feet to the concrete wall of the building behind. There was no elevator, and to save space the staircase had been tacked onto the outside of the building. The whole structure had been set on an area just about large enough to park a Toyota Lexus.

The ground floor was occupied by an enterprise called the "Magic Hole." From what Mori gathered from the garrulous old man who ran it, it was one of the highest-margin businesses in the district. Inside was a semicircular arrangement of dark, curtained booths equipped with TV screens. Customers would come in, select the pornographic video of their choice, and stand in the booth watching it.

So far, so simple. The place's main attraction was the small hole, the "magic hole," in the far wall of each booth. For an added fee, customers could, while still watching the videos, employ the services of the woman who sat in the small room on the other side of that wall. She was a diligent worker, and, when business was booming, could attend to two customers at a time. The manager proudly insisted that once she had even managed to cope with three. Mori sometimes saw her coming to work in the mornings—a squat, cheerful woman in her mid-fifties.

The second floor was taken by a specialty import company. It was nearly always closed for business, perhaps to avoid follow-up inquiries about some of the specialties on offer. Every so often, details of new products would appear on stickers on the door:

"Baldness Remedy X—As Used by Tens of Millions of Chinese"

"Endurance Cream—Transport Women to the Peak of Ecstasy"

"Special Vitamin Mix—Guaranteed for Energy and Longer Life"

In the opinion of the manager of the Magic Hole, the only thing that distinguished any one of these products from any other was the container it was put inside. But even he had no idea who owned the company or who bought its products.

Mori's own office was small, but comfortable. There were two rooms—a kitchen-bedroom-lounge and a toilet-storeroom-shower. Together, they contained everything he required to conduct his trade—a solid desk, a whiny refrigerator for beer and fruit, a battered sofa to snooze off hangovers, a tape recorder, and a battleship-gray filing cabinet stuffed with old newspaper clippings, bills, and letters from long-forgotten clients.

He knew he should get a personal computer. With a laser printer and the right software, he would be able to create his own junk mail, instead of just being on the receiving end. That was what his first and last secretary had said on her first and last day at work. A nice girl, but typical of the "new human" generation that the media were always talking about. She had announced that she was quitting immediately after using the toilet, which was Japanese-style, not Western-style.

Anyway, there were too many other things to think about.

First, there was a routine premarriage investigation, the sort of work which had kept him in cigarettes and whiskey for the past ten years. The bride's parents had received an anonymous letter claiming that the groom's aunt had suffered from mental illness in her youth. The bride's family, respectable owners of a sake business in Kyushu, wanted that story cleared up. If it turned out to be true, then the wedding would have to be canceled immediately.

Then, there was the case of the psychiatrist's wife. Mrs. Nishida, an elegant woman in her late thirties, was getting worried about her lover, an actor in samurai movies. He was spending too much time away on location, and there were rumors that he was planning an arranged marriage with the daughter of a powerful film producer. Now he was asking her for a loan of fifty million yen. It was an interesting case, with plenty of potential for expense claims.

The telephone rang. The voice at the other end was fussily precise.

"Mr. Mori? Am I correct in thinking that you are investigating the death of Keisuke Hara?"

"Where did you get that idea?" said Mori cautiously.

"I heard from Mrs. Hara. Let me explain. I am Kaneda of Mitsutomo Insurance. I've been a good friend of Hara's ever since university. We used to meet every month and discuss economic and monetary policy."

"Really?"

More economic and monetary policy! This was going to be a tough case.

"In fact, we had a discussion just three nights before he died. I need to talk to you about some of the things he said."

"Go on. I'm listening."

The man's voice dropped to a whisper.

"It's too sensitive to discuss here. Please meet me at six-thirty tonight. The noodle stand on the platform at Tokyo Station. I'll be reading the *Stock Market Daily*."

Here was a man, thought Mori, who had been watching too many TV dramas. The noodle stand on a railway platform— what a ridiculous place to arrange a meeting. But before Mori had time to object, the line went dead.

When he got to Tokyo Station, it was close to the peak of rush hour. The platforms were liquid with moving bodies—bustling grannies, junior-high-school archery teams, office ladies on the way home, hostesses on the way to work, salarymen, salarymen, salarymen. Mori's ears filled with the bellowed announcements, often three or four at the same time, the squealing of train wheels, the hissing of doors and buzzing of bells and shrieking of whistles.

Half a dozen men were huddled around the noodle stand, slurping passionately at the large china bowls they held between their hands. When the next train arrived, five of them thrust the bowls onto the counter, wiped their mouths, then darted into the scrums forming around the train doors. The last man continued to shovel noodles into his mouth with his chopsticks, looking warily from side to side as he did so. There was, Mori noticed, a newspaper on the counter in front of him. Mori just managed to squeeze alongside, ahead of a group of salarymen who had gotten out of the train.

The newspaper on the counter of the noodle stall was *Japan Investment News*.

"Good paper," said Mori. "Easier to read than *Stock Market Daily*."

"I couldn't get *Stock Market Daily*," his neighbor muttered with embarrassment. "I tried everywhere, but it was sold out. I'm terribly sorry."

It was the same voice, albeit more agitated than when Mori had heard it on the phone. Its owner was a small, thin-faced man, with hair raked over his bald patch in the style known as "moon through the bamboo screen." Being a university friend of Hara's meant that Kaneda was in his mid-thirties, but he could easily have passed for fifty.

"That's no problem," said Mori. "Anyway, now that we've met up, shall we go somewhere a little quieter?"

"No, this is fine. No one can overhear us with all this racket going on."

That was true enough. Neither could they hear each other, unless they bent their heads together like a courting couple.

Kaneda, Mori couldn't help noticing, had a bad case of halitosis. There was a sprinkling of dandruff on his jacket collar as well, and an unhealthy pallor to his complexion.

Kaneda leafed through the newspaper, occasionally pointing out sections with his forefinger, as if summarizing the writer's argument.

"Let's pretend we're discussing this article," he went on nervously. "We've got to be careful. I think I'm being watched, you see."

He gave a furtive glance down the platform. It was as jam-packed as before.

"Watched? By who?"

"I don't know. Probably the same ones who killed Hara. That's what I need to talk to you about."

Mori looked at the man a little more closely. There was a small but rapid tic in his left eyelid, no doubt the product of night after night of long overtime. As Kudo had said, these elite types had a tendency to crack up under the strain. After all the years of being crammed with facts and figures, their minds seemed to lose the capacity for common sense.

"Hara committed suicide. That was perfectly clear from the police investigation. All I'm doing is trying to find out why."

"Hara was a close friend of mine, " said Kaneda. "I've known him since university, and he was the last man in the world who would commit suicide. He had too much of a sense of mission."

"But why should anyone want to kill him?"

Kaneda brought his face so close that Mori could feel the heat on his cheek. The tic in the eyelid was rippling away furiously.

"Dangerous information," he hissed. "Last time we met, he told me he was expecting a crisis in the financial markets. Powerful forces are working toward one."

"What on earth gave him that idea?"

"They knew he was going to get the job on the currency committee, so they asked him to join them. At first, he played along, just enough to find out what they were up to."

"'They'? What do you mean, 'they'?"

"There's a network. Not just in the Ministry of Finance, but in the other ministries, the mass media, the big financial institutions, in my company as well. They're everywhere, you see. They're probably watching us right now."

Kaneda was shaking slightly as he spoke. The man was a bag of nerves. He had hardly touched his special pork cutlet noodles.

"Interesting," said Mori soothingly. "And did he say any more? Did he tell you exactly who approached him?"

Kaneda shook his head, then glanced up and down the platform again.

"We'd better split up now," he said. "Just in case they notice anything suspicious. If they found out I was talking to a private eye . . ."

He levered himself off the tiny stool, tossed a few hundred yen onto the counter, and disappeared into the stream of people moving down the platform.

"Your newspaper," shouted out the noodle man, a plump fellow in a stained apron. "You forgot your newspaper!"

"Keep it," advised Mori. "There may be some good tips in it."

It had been a strange encounter. Kaneda was clearly an unreliable witness, as twitchy as a squirrel, probably suffering from all sorts of "elite" complexes and phobias. Still, he didn't look like the kind of guy who would make up the whole story for fun. It would have to be checked out. The noodles were good and spicy, the way Mori liked them. He finished them down to the last mouthful, then made his way to the stairs that led to the exit. He was nearly at the top when he heard a high-pitched shout, then the alarm-bell cutting through the hubbub of the crowd. An incoming train squealed to a halt halfway down the platform, squirting a shower of blue sparks into the air.

Mori understood at once what had happened. Normally, he would have shrugged it off in a moment and continued on his way. This time, however, something told him to take a closer look. He clattered down the steps and pushed his way through the throng of people being herded away by station officials. The doors of the train were still closed, and the faces pressed against the glass seemed possessed with a strange excitement. The loudspeakers were blaring out a stream of instructions, warnings, apologies at earsplitting volume.

The body had been thrown several yards forward by the impact. One leg had been severed above the knee, and the suit jacket had been ripped in half. There was a large pool of blood by the side of the rails, and some crimson spatters had reached right across the platform. The face was flat against the tracks, but Mori recognized him instantly from the hairstyle—the long strands over the moonlike bald patch.

"What happened?" he asked one of the station officials.

"Another crazy," said the man tersely. "Jumped straight in front of the train."

"You sure he jumped? You saw him do it?"

"No, but I heard all right. Strange how they often scream out something at the last moment. Anyway, why do you want to know? Was he a friend of yours?"

There was a stiff, peremptory tone to the man's voice. He was enjoying his moment of authority. Mori paused, and gazed once more at the broken body by the side of the rails. Suddenly, Kaneda's story seemed worthy of more respect.

"Never saw him before in my life," he answered, and turned back toward the staircase. As he passed the noodle stall, he was only vaguely aware of a man in a white T-shirt talking quietly to the stall owner.

About a mile from the Imperial Palace, down a narrow lane overshadowed by ginkgo trees, there stands a fine example of the deep-eaved Sukiya style of tearoom. It houses a restaurant that has no sign nor menu outside and accepts no credit cards. Within its mottled wooden walls, two hundred trillion yen was gathered around a human table.

As usual, its interests and priorities were represented by a group of elderly gentlemen who spoke slowly and softly about matters of mutual benefit. As usual, the forum had been chosen by Land-san, who owned the building, the street, the district, indeed most of central Tokyo. As usual, the table had been supplied by Information-san, a man who always took a fatherly interest in the young actresses at his television company. Tonight's

role was an undemanding one for the girl on the tatami mat, requiring her just to lie still while the men picked slices of sashimi
and other delicacies off her naked body.

"The wind from the east seems a little weaker these days,"
observed Diplomacy-san as he chewed on some bream, the fish
of good fortune and long life. "The Americans have confidence
in our new man."

"A good politician," said Heavy Industry-san. "He uses words
like a squid uses ink."

Votes-san seemed a little put out to hear his craft so
disparaged.

"Minakawa has his points. Foreigners like him because he
talks smoothly, but he's not respected in the party, not even by his
own faction members. He's too much of a rationalist."

He uttered the word as if it were the ultimate condemnation,
then lifted an octopus tentacle with his chopsticks and brushed it
back and forth over the girl's left nipple. It distended visibly, and
she gave a practiced sigh.

In the alcove, a wooden statue of Hotei, the god of prosperity,
looked on with an expression of the profoundest enjoyment, one
hand rubbing his ample belly, the other clutching his sack of
coins. Not everything he had witnessed in that room, with its
creaking rafters and acrid tatami smell, had been in such close
accordance with the energies he represented in divine form.

One snowy night in February 1936, the restaurant had been
commandeered by the rebel officers whose tanks had sealed off
central Tokyo. Here, their leaders had bolstered their spirits with
drafts of hot sake, hoping against hope that the emperor and the
army would sanction their audacious move. Heavy Industry-san
had been one of those rash young men who had roistered
together for the last time on that chilly night. Whenever he came
back, he drank a silent toast to the others, lost half a century ago
on the steppes of Manchuria and the jungles of New Guinea.

Eight years later, the squat wooden building had been miracu-
lously spared from the huge bonfire lit by the B-29s. Leaders of
the great *zaibatsu* conglomerates met here to discuss the surrender
that they, unlike the fanatics of the military, had always known

was inevitable. After the war, much the same group gathered to plan how to outmaneuver the Occupation authorities and their dangerous liberal reforms. In this room in 1955, the "black curtain men"—so called for their similarity to the faceless puppeteers of *bunraku* theater—negotiated the merger of the Liberal and Democratic parties, thus starting off a political ascendancy that had yet to be broken.

Since then, many dramas had been played out under Hotei's beatifically jovial gaze. He had seen dying industries killed off, new technologies planned, scandals hushed up, takeovers, marriages, and trade pacts arranged, company presidents dismissed while they caroused in nearby nightclubs, prime ministers chosen who had no idea that they were even running. He had witnessed the secret life of a nation struggling with its own history.

Next to speak was Regulations-san. A man who had devoted his life to managing the nation's affairs, he had little time for politicians and their petty intrigues.

"My people are by no means optimistic about the situation. In trade, we have made concession after concession, but the grumbling of foreigners knows no end. We can no longer manage our currency due to the activities of speculators. Our population is aging, and our trade surplus is declining too fast. As for the younger generation—pah, you can hardly call them Japanese."

"The people have become rich," said Wheels-san. "They want to ride in luxury cars and enjoy their lives. This is natural."

He took a slab of red tuna and slid it down the girl's belly and out of sight. It was known as the most succulent in Tokyo, taken from the tender behind-the-neck region of the largest, freshest fish.

"Japan has no assets other than its workers," went on Regulations-san. "And now they are becoming selfish and weak."

"Not in my company," said Wheels-san.

"Furthermore, we are losing control of certain sectors of the economy. Large accumulations of power are being built up which do not respond to our guidance. This is unacceptable."

Regulations-san stopped to drain his sake cup. The sweet, heavy aroma was spreading into his chest and head, fueling his resentment. "You know who I'm referring to," he said emphatically. "A certain insolent, loudmouthed individual who without question will bring shame on Japan."

Diplomacy-san was carefully peeling a lark's egg. He glanced at the bureaucrat's pudgy features, now blazing away like the setting sun.

"We must consider matters from an international perpective," he said smoothly. "This is an interdependent world in which foreign peoples and Japanese have many complex relationships. We can monitor and suggest. We can use our skills to overcome crises. But we can no longer control."

"The nail that sticks out should be hammered in," said Regulations-san, his voice suddenly too loud for the small room. "That is the wisdom of our ancestors!"

Diplomacy-san removed the last fragments of shell from the glossy white oval, then rolled it underneath his palm down the girl's stomach and between her thighs. She opened her legs and shifted herself slightly off the ground. When he removed his hand, it was empty.

"You know," he said thoughtfully, "there is an English proverb which advises us to distinguish between a mountain and a molehill. The individual you refer to is objectionable, certainly, but the world is full of objectionable people."

The girl maneuvered herself over to his place, then squatted before him, hands resting on his shoulders. With a conjurer's flourish, Diplomacy-san slipped his hand between her legs, and suddenly the egg was back in his palm, slightly glossier than before. He sprinkled it with black pepper and popped it into his mouth.

"The old man would not condone this laxness," said Regulations-san, shaking an agitated finger in Diplomacy-san's imperturbable face. "He would strike now before matters get out of hand."

Diplomacy-san swallowed the last traces of the egg, smacked his lips in satisfaction, then lifted his right hand for the girl to wipe it with a hot towel.

"If you believe this trifling matter is worthy of the old man's attention," he said casually, "then may I suggest that you inform him of it yourself."

"I already have!" cried Regulations-san.

There was a moment of silence while the others gazed at him blankly, then he bowed slightly and gave a self-deprecating smile. Immediately, Diplomacy-san steered the conversation onto less contentious issues. Regulations-san made a point of agreeing with everyone enthusiastically, but the damage had been done. By acting before a consensus had formed, he had broken the unwritten rule of the group. And yet he did not regret it.

Two hours later, Diplomacy-san was entertaining a ballerina and an oil prince. Wheels-san was busy approving production schedules for his plant in Spain. The table, now equipped with a Chanel suit, was guessing the price of Tibetan yak cheese on a TV quiz show. Regulations-san was sitting in a Ginza bar, working his way through a bottle of the Scotch whiskey whose import he had reluctantly liberalized six years before. Everything was upside down, he grumbled to himself. Everyone had grown so complacent and soft, just as he had always feared. It seemed that the only ones who were still vigilant were he himself and the old man in his lonely mountain temple.

His mood would have been darker still if he had known what was happening on the top floor of a building on the other side of the Imperial Palace. In an otherwise deserted room, a man was tapping away at a computer terminal. Thanks to the stream of commands that flowed from his fingertips, a few short sharp tremors passed through the electronic interchange of pluses and minuses that makes up the international financial system.

On dealing screens all over the world, fuzzy green numbers were breaking into dance. A couple of minor currencies tangoed up, then down. Three leading shares in three different countries dropped roughly the same amount. Gold rose and fell five dollars in the space of five minutes. The price of options to sell index futures suddenly surged. Then it was over.

Regulations-san sat watching the neon colors refracting through his whiskey glass. The god Hotei sat in a darkened room, the occasional headlight beam flashing across his mad wooden smile.

3

⋮

IN London, it was a quarter to two on a wet Thursday afternoon. Amid the hustle and din of the largest dealing room in the City, a Japanese man in his early forties was watching the numbers dancing on the screen in front of him. The sudden burst of movement intrigued him. Someone was shifting big money around, and it was his job to keep track. But then his attention was caught by a sharp rally in the French franc, something he had been waiting for all morning. He started rapping instructions into the microphone on his headset in fluent, cockney-tinged English.

The man's name was Tsutomu Kono, but most of his English friends called him Tom. His Japanese colleagues considered him eccentric. They didn't like the way that he took his lunch in the pub together with the local staff, or the way he went home to his wife at six o'clock. He drank real ale, and knew the different types. He sent his two sons to a local school, where they would fall years behind their friends at the high-pressure Japanese school. He even went to cricket matches on Sunday afternoons!

Tom was a problem, but his foibles had to be tolerated, even by the new branch manager. That was because Tom was quite simply the best futures and options trader Sumikawa Bank had ever had. He had spent years refining his own computer models of market movements, and the strategies he had developed had earned the bank billions of yen. Only Tom himself and a few key directors knew how much he had contributed toward

Sumikawa's rise to the pinnacle of world banking. His "book," the trading position that he ran, was by far the largest in the Euromarkets. When word went round that Tom Kono had decided to go long or short of something, prices started to swing around. Almost every day, his name would buzz down phone lines from Geneva to New York to Singapore to Sydney, and his deepest thoughts and intentions would be discussed in German, Arabic, Spanish, and Mandarin Chinese.

The new branch manager had been sent out from Tokyo only a few months before. He had distinctive ideas about how the business should be run. He installed a time clock to be used by all grades of local staff, and corrected what he considered sloppy forms of address among the Japanese staff. The proper honorifics had to be used when addressing superiors, and the ordinary polite forms were forbidden when speaking to juniors. In Branch Manager Yamaguchi's view, Japanese companies had beaten the Westerners precisely because Japanese people knew instinctively how to meld their energies together in organizational form. Any signs of laxness or informality or what he called "individualism" were treated with a bawling out from point-blank range.

Tom was not the type to throw his weight around. In fact, he had been so preoccupied with the straddle play he was running on French bonds that he hardly noticed the changes that were taking place. When Yamaguchi called him in for a private meeting that morning, he was more surprised by the man's tone of voice than anything else. He had snapped, like a headmaster reprimanding a naughty schoolboy.

"This is a highly distasteful matter," said Yamaguchi when the door was closed. "But it is my duty to tackle it sincerely. That is exactly what I intend to to."

Tom's mind was still on the French yield curve. He was having difficulty in concentrating.

"Distasteful? What's distasteful?"

Yamaguchi's stare bore into him. For a moment, the only sound was the drumming of raindrops on the windowpane.

"You have been in this country too many years, Kono," he said softly. "You lack respect. Have you forgotten the

Japanese way to address a superior?"

"Please forgive my rudeness," stammered Tom, suddenly confused.

Yamaguchi smiled his thin little smile and cracked a knuckle.

"Better, Kono, but too late I'm afraid. You will not disturb the harmony of this branch office much longer."

"I'm sorry, but I don't understand."

"An internal investigation has been taking place," said Yamaguchi. "Certain suspicions have been raised about your market activities."

"Suspicions? What suspicions?"

Yamaguchi raised a querulous eyebrow, and Tom improvised a short bow of contrition.

"That's better. Yes, suspicions. You have close relations with some of the local people, don't you?"

"Yes," said Tom doubtfully. "I suppose so."

"That was probably your big mistake. They are not trustworthy partners. One of these fine fellows has confessed to being involved in an insider trading ring. He and his friends have been making hundreds of thousands of pounds front-riding the positions you take on your book."

"Impossible," said Tom. "Who is this man?"

"For the moment we are keeping his identity a secret. The interesting point is how he was able to know of those trades in advance. Do you have any idea how he knew, Kono?"

Yamaguchi leaned forward so that his face was no more than six inches from Tom's. An odd little smile was playing over his lips.

"No, of course not," said Tom.

"Well, you should. He says he knew about the trades in advance because you told him."

Tom jerked forward in his chair as if he had been stung by a wasp.

"This man's a liar, whoever he is!"

Yamaguchi nodded sardonically.

"If word got out, it would be a criminal matter. You enjoy the company of the local people so much—how would you like five years in a British jail surrounded by British thieves?"

"This is ridiculous."

Tom's mind was reeling with the absurdity of the accusation. Insider trading rings, anonymous confessions—none of it made sense! Incongruously, Tom thought for a moment about Lewis Carroll, one of his favorite English writers. Is this is what it's like to fall down a rabbit hole?

"Luckily for you, Kono, we can't allow it to be known that our chief dealer has been engaging in insider trading. We have booked a seat home for you on the Saturday JAL flight." Yamaguchi couldn't keep the note of triumph out of his voice. "At my request, the personnel department has found a suitable position for you—assistant manager of general affairs in one of our smaller Hokkaido branches. Not what you're used to, I'm afraid, but it's better this way for everybody. Don't you agree, Tom-san?"

The sarcasm that Yamaguchi invested in that last phrase was savage. He leaned back in the revolving chair, spat noisily on his spectacle lenses, and began to polish them.

Tom gazed out of the window at the ash-gray buildings and the slate-gray sky. Rain was slanting down on the black taxis and the grimy double-deckers. Even the dome of St. Paul's, nestling between two skyscrapers, looked wet and forlorn.

"You have an hour to clear your desk," said Yamaguchi, putting on the spectacles and taking a sheaf of documents out of a file.

The dull boom of the great bell sounded twice. Tsutomu Kono got up and left the room in a daze.

It was just after ten when Mori got to the Seikyu Hotel. The manager was busy with the late check-ins, but confirmed that there had been nothing unusual about Hara's behavior that evening. He had checked in at eight o'clock, as he did twice a month, carrying his overnight bag and attaché case. He had looked reasonably cheerful and relaxed, had even swapped a few remarks with the bellboy about the Giants game.

The bellboy was a tall handsome lad, who wore a crisp white

tunic with a plastic badge that read, "Ohmae."

"How do I know you're a detective?" he said suspiciously. "You could be a confidence man."

Mori showed him his business card.

"That doesn't mean anything. Anyone could have one of those printed up."

"You'll just have to take it on trust," said Mori, and showed him a couple of thousand yen notes.

"I don't need that," said Ohmae angrily. "It's just that I don't want to be made a fool of. Actually, I'm thinking of training to become a detective myself. I know I've got the right sort of skills."

"Have you?" said Mori. "What sort of skills are those?"

"Observation, diligence, good powers of logic."

"I see. You've got pretty well everything you need."

Ohmae beamed at the compliment. Mori gave him a friendly smile and a pat on the shoulder.

"If you're as observant as you make out, you should be able to tell me quite a lot about Hara."

"Of course. I tried to tell the police, but they didn't have the slightest interest. But then, they never do, right?"

"Right."

Ohmae nodded sympathetically.

"Anyway," he said. "Hara-san was wearing a blue polyester suit and a Burberry raincoat. He had one of those polyethylene umbrellas, but he was still pretty wet, especially his trousers. I was amazed when I heard he was an elite bureaucrat. He always looked so shabby."

"Well done," said Mori. "That's extremely impressive. By the way, . . ."

Here he dropped his voice to a conspiratorial whisper.

"Did you ever get the impression that Hara was entertaining lady friends during his stays? I mean, that does happen, doesn't it? Even at a fine hotel like the Seikyu?"

"Happens all the time. Some of the the things I've seen while I've been working here—unbelievable!"

The boy compressed his lips in an expression of mixed aston-ishment and admiration.

"And what about Hara?"

"Oh, Hara-san always checked in alone. Went straight to his room."

"And no visitors?"

"I don't know; there could have been. The elevators go right up to the guest floors, you see."

Mori was well aware of that. One of the Seikyu's main points of attraction, never mentioned in any brochure, was that guests could go from street level straight to their rooms without passing through the first-floor lobby. For a hotel situated within five hundred yards of Tokyo's premier nightlife district, that was no accident.

"Would anyone else have noticed? One of the maids, perhaps?"

Ohmae seemed slightly put out.

"Impossible," he frowned. "It's hotel policy to keep staff out of the corridors in the evenings. The guests don't like it."

Mori shrugged and nodded his thanks. He hadn't expected much enlightenment. If anything, it was the bellboy who seemed the more disappointed.

"Wait a minute," he said as Mori walked away. "I've got an idea. Let's examine all Hara-san's bills and see if he took any wine from the liquor cabinet. If he took wine, that probably means there was a woman, right? How about that?"

So this was Ohmae's logical faculty in action. Mori didn't think much of it. Still, it would do no harm to check.

He went to sit among the rubber plants and potted palms in the dimly lit bar at the side of the lobby. It was empty except for a couple of businessmen staring into space and a greasy-haired bartender, who was shaking a cocktail as if he loathed it. Loudspeakers somewhere were putting out "The Sound of Silence" played on a Hawaiian steel guitar.

After a few minutes, Ohmae arrived clutching a wad of bills. There seemed to be at least twenty of them. Mori looked through them slowly, trying to find inconsistencies. They were, however, almost exactly the same. Basic room charge, bottle of Kirin beer, in-house movie—all paid in cash the next day.

"No wine," said Ohmae apologetically.

Indeed, no wine. But there was one feature that caught Mori's attention. Every time, Hara had made a single, minimum-rate phone call. Home to his wife, perhaps? Mori thought of prim Mrs. Hara sitting at home with her flower arrangement. Perhaps not.

"Outgoing phone calls," said Mori. "The operator must log them in a book somehwere."

"No book. Phone calls go straight into the exchange's memory bank. We access the data when we print out the bill."

"So you've got computer records of Hara's phone calls."

"That's right," said Ohmae proudly. "The system was developed by Seikyu Software, our subsidiary. It holds three months' information—just in case we get any complaints."

"Can you get me a printout? There might be a clue there somewhere."

Mori used the word "clue" deliberately, and it had the desired effect. It took Ohmae less than ten minutes to supply the telephone record of Hara's last four stays at the hotel. Each time, he had called the same central Tokyo number. Mori wrote it down in his notebook. Ohmae gazed at him with obvious admiration.

"You've found the murderer!" he exclaimed.

"Murderer? Who said anything about murder?"

"Come on," said Ohmae. "I don't believe everything that's in the papers. If Hara-san had been going to kill himself, he wouldn't have been so interested in the Giants lineup for the next game. That's pretty obvious, isn't it?"

Mori looked at Ohmae more closely. The boy was nodding his head confidently. Maybe he had some potential after all.

Mori's apartment was a couple of rooms above a rice shop on the outskirts of Shinjuku. Across the street was a dingy snack bar which extruded the woozy strains of karaoke until well after midnight. Farther along was a *juku* cramming school. It opened for business early in the mornings, before regular school started. Mori treasured the brief hours of tranquillity after the last strains of "North Country Spring" had died away and before the chanting of English irregular verbs started up. The croaking of the frogs in the paddy field next to the school, the trucks on the nearby overpass, the wind rattling the window in its frame—these were the lullaby sounds that soothed him to sleep.

He clattered up the steps to the second floor and unlocked the door. He sensed the presence of the other person just as his hand reached for the light switch, but by then it was too late. An arm reached around his neck, pulling him down, and a fist thumped into his kidneys. Mori grunted with the impact.

"Shut up," said a voice. "Another sound and I kill you now."

The words were spoken with too much emphasis, as if the speaker were trying to convince himself.

"No, don't hurt me," gasped Mori, then drove his elbow back into the man's stomach. The grip loosened immediately. Mori span round, in one movement driving his knuckles into cheekbone and his knee into groin. There was a howl of pain, then a crash as the weight of the man's body went through the sliding door that partitioned off the bedroom.

Mori yanked the light cord in the center of the room, sending the heavy lamp swinging back and forth. The man was attempting to crawl toward the door, muttering incoherently under his breath. Mori grabbed him by the collar, slammed his head against the floor a couple of times, then hauled him to his feet. He was a small man in his early forties with a curly "punch perm" hairstyle and a flabby, sallow complexion.

"What happened to Kaneda?" demanded Mori.

"Don't know."

The man looked dazed, slightly frightened. Mori grabbed him by the windpipe and squeezed. The eyes bulged open, revealing Tokyo subway maps of thin red veins.

"Kaneda," hissed Mori. "You people killed him. I want to know why."

"Whaah?"

"Come on. Who sent you?"

Mori gave a final squeeze, turning the face puce, then relaxed his grip. The man shook his head like a dog shaking off rain.

"Doctor Nishida," he said faintly. "He found out you've

been seeing his wife."

It was Mori's turn to look confused. Nishida was the psychiatrist whose wife was jealous of her samurai lover.

"What are you talking about?"

"He knows all about it. I was supposed to give you a warning,
that's all."

They had indeed met a couple of times over the past month,
mainly in coffee shops and hotel bars. And Mrs. Nishida was an
elegant woman, tall with long hair sweeping down over her
shoulders. Mori had frequently pondered what she might look
like underneath the Italian dresses and blouses. Silk underwear,
probably—black against the creamy skin . . .

"That's nonsense," said Mori. "Anyway, who are you?"

"I am Kawada of the Kawada Group," said the man
haughtily.

Mori knew most of the *yakuza* groups and their numerous
offshoots, but this was a new name.

"What kind of group is that?"

"Independent. We're just starting up—me and my brothers
and my eldest son. He's only eighteen."

"Well, you go and tell Doctor Nishida that he's got the wrong
idea completely. I haven't touched his wife."

Kawada stared at him. Blood was dripping out of his left
nostril onto the tatami mat.

"And if I come across you again, or your brothers, or your
eldest son for that matter, there's going to be trouble, all right."

"The Kawada group must protect its honor," said Kawada.
"We fear no one, alive or dead."

"I need to sleep," said Mori wearily. "Either you get out of
here now or I throw you down the stairs."

The little man left, holding a handkerchief to his nose. Mori
cleaned up some of the mess, then collapsed into his bedroll. He
was just slipping into unconsciousness when he heard the sound
of footsteps in the corridor outside, followed by a gentle rap on
the door. Mori sprang to his feet and grabbed a baseball bat
from a cupboard. The Kawada family obviously needed a few
lessons in elementary courtesy—such as the importance of

knowing when you're not wanted.

He silently eased the latch, then shoved the door open with his foot. It swung on the hinge and banged against the outside wall. He sprang out into the corridor, muscles tensed, ready to bring the bat crashing down on the first Kawada in view. When he saw the woman's figure, he stopped himself just in time.

It was Lisa. She was still wearing her working gear, a tight satin dress slashed to the hip and a pair of stiletto heels. There was a cool breeze, and her nipples were pressing out of the thin material like cherry stones. She was swaying on her feet slightly. Her eyes were large and shiny, as they always were after she had been crying.

"You look funny," she said in a slurred voice. "Been having a nightmare about the Giants, or what?"

"Come in," said Mori, bringing the tip of the bat down to the ground. "I'll get you a pancake and syrup."

"Bourbon . . . I need bourbon."

"Pancake and syrup," said Mori firmly, and tugged her gently by the wrist.

It had been a long time since he had last seen her, almost a year, but she looked exactly the same. The same free-flowing curtain of hair, the same little-girl pout, even the same musky perfume. There had been no conscious decision to split up, just longer and longer gaps between seeing each other. Then, for both of them other people came along, and suddenly they were making excuses over the phone, talking like strangers.

Mori watched her shovel the pancake into her mouth. She would never eat when she was working, and afterward she would be too drunk to have a proper meal. "What happened?" he said finally.

"Big Steve, the sax player. He threw me out of his car in the middle of the expressway."

"Why'd he want to do that?"

"I don't know. Because I bit his arm, I suppose."

"So why did you bite him?"

It was a silly question. Why did Lisa do anything? The first time they had met was the result of a similar incident. It was in the parking lot of a Yokohama nightclub. The band had just finished their last set, and Mori had been enchanted with the frail-looking singer with the deep, smoky voice. He heard the voice again just as he was getting into his car, this time spitting out obscenities in English and tough-guy Japanese. When he went to investigate, he found Lisa backed up against a pile of beer crates, struggling with a big black guy. He had lifted her off the ground, and she was flailing at his chest with her fists and his shins with her feet.

Mori turned the man around and punched him hard in the side of the neck. He was built like a bull. He just stood there half-stunned, the whites of his eyes rolling. Mori took a step back and hit him in the stomach with a full-speed *mawashi-geri* reverse kick. The black guy went down in a heap, taking half-a-dozen beer crates with him. Then Lisa started kicking, driving her sharp toe-caps into the inert back.

"Eighty thousand yen, you dumb creep," she yelled. "It was eighty thousand yen!"

In the motel afterward, Lisa gave the background to the disagreement. The black guy was a sax player, a great sax player, apparently, and generally a nice guy. The only problem was his arithmetic. He had promised Lisa eighty thousand yen for three nights' work. Now he was saying sixty, just because she had been fifteen minutes late on the each of the first two nights. It was a clear breach of contract.

Lisa was dangerous, which was why she was fun. There was no saying what she would do or say next.

She finished her pancake, and licked the syrup off the aluminum spoon like a little girl. Suddenly, she looked wide awake, full of spirits. Mori glanced at the clock on the wall. It was two o'clock, or just four hours before the English irregular verbs would be starting up again.

Lisa crawled toward him on all fours, eyes gleaming, hair falling across her face. Raindrops were pattering against the window. In the paddy field next to the school, the croaking of the frogs rose in celebration of the rainy season.

In Washington, it was still early afternoon. Max Sharrock's stretch limousine pulled into the leafy driveway that led to the sprawling, Frank Lloyd Wright–style bungalow. He slipped the charts he had been reviewing back into his attaché case, stubbed out his cigar, and waited for his chauffeur, an Englishman whose presence was costing him one hundred fifty dollars a day, to open the door.

The chauffeur was one of Sharrock's most prized possessions. He had a uniform with buttons that were polished every day, and an accent out of one of those television dramas about butlers and chambermaids. He was so polite it was almost rude. Some men in Sharrock's position might go for private helicopters and racing yachts. Some might go for movie-star wives. But as far as Sharrock was concerned, when Bennett opened the car door and gave him that dignified but utterly subservient bow, he lacked for nothing.

Sharrock was at the top of his profession, one of the most successful pollsters in the United States. His firm, Sharrock Associates, had developed a range of unique sampling techniques which provided its clients with segment-by-segment snapshots of public opinion. How were middle-class black women responding to the administration's drug policies? What did skilled workers in a certain district think about the ethics investigation into their congressperson? To what extent were reports of torture and other human rights abuses in a friendly third world country hurting its image among heads of households with incomes over one hundred thousand dollars? Sharrock Associates sliced up political issues like meat loaf, using complex statistical techniques to monitor the undercurrents that usually went unnoticed, then presented its clients with a computer-generated strategic plan designed to optimize approval ratings.

While working for many different clients, both domestic and foreign, Sharrock had made one simple but brilliant discovery which had established him as a leader in the field. Among all the highly contentious and divisive issues that dominated political life, there were a number that could be characterized as "zero downsiders." On most issues, such as abortion, or welfare mothers, or the Middle East, winning support from one segment of the public would usually mean sacrificing support from another segment. In the case of zero downsiders, however, the loss would be negligible or nonexistent. This might be because, as in the case of flag-burning or school prayer, the issue appealed strongly to one particular segment of the public and the rest hardly cared at all. Alternatively, as in the case of the rain forest and the case of Saddam Hussein, all segments might perceive the issue the same way. Sharrock had concluded that the successful politician would emphasize as many zero-downsider issues as possible and forget about the rest.

It was this discovery, or rather its latest manifestation, that brought Sharrock to the meeting in the bungalow. Zero-downsider issues were usually quite short-lived. There was a disappointing tendency for segments of the public to alter their perceptions of an issue once their attention was drawn to the balance of costs and benefits. The war on drugs and environmental protection had both begun as zero downsiders, but had soon developed into ordinary "confrontational" issues. Recently, however, Sharrock's analysis had identified a new zero downsider. It was, he believed, potentially the most rewarding he had ever come across. It provoked powerful nonrational responses from an enormous band of the public. Best of all, although the responses were complex, the issue itself was beautifully simple—Japan and the Japanese. He had known it was a winner, right from the start.

They were waiting for him in an oak-paneled drawing room lined with oil paintings of American presidents. Although it was early summer, there was a log fire blazing away under the white marble mantelpiece. The temperature in the room was freezing cold, since the air-conditioning system was on full blast. That was how John Johansen liked it, and nobody was going to argue with John Johansen about what he did in his own home, or anywhere else for that matter.

Johansen greeted Sharrock with his usual crushing handshake and gleaming cemetery of a grin. The others sitting around the big mahogany table were the same ones who had been present at the last meeting three months ago. There was Murdoch the lawyer, Gluck the media consultant, Tirani the tax accountant, and Zager the professor of political science. It was a grouping of some of the best strategic thinkers in Washington, but Johansen dominated proceedings right from the start. Murdoch and the others were men of great influence and talent, but Johansen was on another level. The CEO of a top Wall Street firm by the age of forty, he had gone on to become an adviser to presidents and a lobbyist for whose services the oil and auto industries had been willing to pay tens of millions of dollars. Johansen was one of the most powerful men in town, and he didn't like people to forget it.

"Well, gentlemen," he began smoothly. "I have excellent news for you all. Our client has evaluated the preliminary study very highly. He agrees with our probability analysis and is eager to move into the second phase—implementation. Before going any further, though, I want to remind you of the secrecy clauses we all signed. Believe me, our client doesn't play games. If word of this project leaks out, the person responsible will incur severe penalties."

Johansen looked around the room. One by one, the others nodded their assent. Sharrock thought about asking what the penalties would be, then decided against it. There had been an edge to Johansen's voice that suggested that they weren't just financial.

"Right, let's get down to business. Today, we're going to draw up a detailed plan for the next six months. I want to hear any new ideas, good ideas, that are going to build up the momentum we need. Remember, our client is making big money available. He's expecting to spend it."

"John, can we just clear up one simple point?"

The speaker was Zager, a mild-mannered academic whose work on the psychology of political choice had turned conventional thinking upside down. Johansen answered with the indulgent smile which he reserved for the only man in the room who didn't have a seven-figure salary.

"Sure. What is it, Lewis?"

"Well, I just want to know, and I guess the others do too—I mean, who is this mysterious client of yours, exactly?"

Johansen's smile switched off like an electric light. He was a silent for a full thirty seconds, his cold blue eyes boring into Zager's confused features.

"Lewis," he said finally. "You should have known that question was out of order. This is the biggest project you, or anyone else in this room, will ever be involved in. Our client is making available as much funding as we need. He is offering us a front-loaded fee package which guarantees that none of us will have to work again for the rest of our lives. All he requests—no, insists on—is anonymity. If these conditions are unacceptable to you, you'd better haul ass out of here right now."

The air-conditioning was raising goose bumps on Sharrock's back, but Zager suddenly looked flushed.

"Okay, okay," he gulped. "If it means that much . . ."

"It does."

Johansen kept his gaze on Zager for another few seconds before turning to Sharrock.

"Over to you, Max," he said, the affable grin back in place. "Let's have an update on the latest street feelings."

Sharrock handed around a sheaf of charts that illustrated some of his recent analytical work.

"All the trends we identified are still intact," he explained. "Indeed, in several cases they've strengthened. The Japanese security-threat question, for example. Unskilled workers in three major Eastern cities have swung five points on this one in the past three months. 'Japan is unfair,' 'the Japanese are taking advantage of Americans,' 'Japan is planning to dominate the world economic system'—assent/dissent ratios on these are rising nicely in every single segment. 'Japanese investment undermines American prosperity'—California is still very weak on this, but we've seen some good pickup in the Midwest and the South—"

"Conclusions, Max, conclusions. We don't have all day."

"The conclusion is exactly as I stated in the preliminary report. This issue is strong enough and deep enough to build an entire campaign around. It allows people to articulate a whole range of worries and fears about the future. The appeal is extraordinarily broad. From the fundamentalist Right to liberal intellectuals, from autoworkers to environmentalists, from Houston to New York, it's the same story everywhere. Blacks, Hispanics, women, gays, young professionals—everybody's on board."

"Except the Japs, of course," said Murdoch.

"And they don't vote in U.S. elections," said Sharrock with a smile.

There was a brief ripple of laughter around the table.

"Good work, Max," said Johansen. "I'm sure Steve here can provide all the media reinforcement we need."

Gluck nodded. "No problem," he said. "With a budget of this size, I can really make some sparks fly. Still, before I make any specific plans, I'd like to know where we stand on candidate selection."

"That's a fair question," said Johansen, glancing meaningfully at Zager. "And the answer is that selection has been finalized."

He picked up a remote-control handset from the table and pressed it twice. The lights dimmed and a projection screen slid down the wall above the fireplace, covering up a murky depiction of Teddy Roosevelt astride a white horse. Johansen turned around to the opposite wall and clicked the handset at a slide projector mounted on a shelf.

The first picture on the screen was of a man in blue jeans and check shirt loading bales of hay onto a truck. It took Sharrock a few seconds to recognize the boyishly handsome features with the square jaw and carefully tousled blond hair. The second slide showed the same man in evening dress at a fund-raising dinner, and this time Sharrock was left in no doubt. It was Senator Robert Reckard, a rising star on Capitol Hill. The next slides showed him, in succession, leading a Veteran's Day parade, on his knees in church, playing softball with some black schoolkids, deep-sea fishing, chatting with Arnold Schwarzenegger, playing a banjo, and carving a turkey.

When the lights came on again, there was a murmur of collective approval.

"Brilliant choice," said Gluck. "Absolutely perfect. With

that kind of material, we can't fail."

"I thought you'd agree," said Johansen smugly. "That's why I took the opportunity of inviting the candidate to meet us here today."

He twisted around in his seat and flicked on the intercom on the wall.

"Jenny, please send in the senator," he rapped.

The man who came through the door looked a little shorter than his image on the screen, but he had the same deep tan and modest, slightly sheepish grin.

"Gentlemen," said Johansen, getting to his feet. "I would like you all to meet the next president of the United States."

He started clapping, so, a split-second later, everyone else did the same.

Later that afternoon, a strange rumor spread through Wall Street. Japanese investors, it was whispered, would not be taking up their usual 30 percent of the next auction of U.S. treasury bonds. Instead, they had decided to make some heavy disposals. Afterward, dealers in New York said the story originated in Tokyo. Dealers in Tokyo said it started in London. Some dealers in London said it started in New York and some said it started in Tokyo. Whatever its source, the effect was dramatic. The American bond market fell sharply, and long-term interest rates shifted upward all over Europe. All the major Western stock markets fell between 3 and 5 percent in a matter of hours.

The following day, major Japanese institutions went out of their way to deny the rumor. Their appetite for U.S. bonds, they emphasized, was as great as ever. The markets, however, failed to make any sort of recovery.

4

$\vdots$

THE telephone number on Hara's hotel bill led Mori to a place he had come across once before—an establishment called "Love Oasis" in the back streets of Akasaka. It was a garish "cabaret club" with a limited selection of not-very-attractive girls. Many of them were new arrivals from the country-side, trying to save up the deposit for an apartment in the big city.

An elite bureaucrat like Hara could have had his pick of the most elegant, sharp-witted hostesses in the Ginza. Instead, he had chosen the radish-calved, heavily-made-up denizens of Love Oasis. Not for the first time, Mori found himself wondering whether human personality really existed, or whether it was just a reflection of whatever patterns were thrown onto it, like scenery floating on the surface of a lake.

The manager of the place was a flashy thug called Yokohama George who prided himself on his fluent English. Once upon a time, he had lived off the foreign businessmen who flooded through the area at night, fastening on to them in the street and hauling them up into the warren of cubicles, each one containing an airbed and a shower. That was when the yen was 280 to the dollar, 350 to the pound, and foreigners were worth pursuing. Since then, Love Oasis had restructured its business to cope with the changed economic environment, bringing in new ideas and softening the marketing pitch. It was now totally reliant on domestic demand, and a good proportion of revenues came from

specialty services at nearby hotels. The main gimmick was uniforms. Jaded salarymen on business trips to Tokyo could enjoy
the attentions of JAL stewardesses, high school girls, nurses, dom-
inatrixes in black leather corsets, or whatever other female type
took their fancy.

Yokohama George was lolling against the entrance in a
Hawaiian beach shirt and white slacks with a crocodile skin belt.
There was a thin gold chain around his neck, and a fat Rolex on
his wrist. It was another dull, drizzly day, but he was wearing a
pair of steel-framed aviator-style sunglasses, just the same as when
Mori had last seen him five years ago. Evidently, no one had had
the courage to tell him they had gone out of fashion.

He recognized Mori instantly.

"What you want here?" he growled. "I've had enough trouble
from you already."

"Lucky I'm a nice guy," said Mori. "If I wasn't, you'd be in
Abashiri prison making bamboo dolls. And it's much too cold up
there for a beach boy like you."

He lifted the shades off the bloated lizard face. George blinked
in surprise, then swung a fist that featured a chunky brass ring on
the middle finger. It was a lazy, ostentatious attempt at a punch.
Mori caught the wrist half way up, jerked it to one side, then
sunk his fist into the man's ample midriff. He exhaled like
someone blowing out the candles on a birthday cake.

"No sense of gratitude," said Mori.

George tried to say something, but failed. He had gone pale
underneath his tan. Mori grabbed him by the elbow and dragged
him inside. A young salaryman carrying a briefcase was coming
down the creaky staircase that led up to the cubicles. He stared at
the two of them, panic-stricken.

"Sincere thanks for your honorable patronage," said Mori rev-
erentially, and gave a slight bow. The man scuttled outside into
the daylight.

When George had recovered sufficiently, he slumped down in
his seat behind the counter and poured himself a glass of Suntory
White whiskey. He hadn't changed much in the years since Mori
had found the fourteen-year-old runaway working under his

expert tuition. The father, a schoolteacher in Niigata Prefecture, had wanted the place shut down and George slung in prison. Mori had convinced him that a court case would do more harm than good. He didn't mention that the beloved daughter had been Love Oasis's star attraction, admired by dozens of regular clients for her enthusiasm and natural talent.

"What is it this time?" said George shakily. He picked up an ice cube and popped it into his mouth.

"I need a favor," said Mori. "I want to spent some time with the girls."

"Which girls?"

"How many have you got these days?"

"Same as before. Ten regulars."

"They'll do fine. It won't take long."

George held the ice cube between his teeth for a moment, then crunched it in the side of his mouth. He gazed at Mori quizzically.

"All ten at once?" he said. "We don't have the space."

"One after another."

George leaned back in his chair and narrowed his eyes so much that they almost disappeared into the fleshy folds around them. His nostrils, meanwhile, grew larger and rounder. A couple of gleaming black hairs were coiled inside them like springs.

"You're after something, aren't you?" he said softly.

"I'm after a little variety," said Mori.

"It'll cost you."

Mori turned around and slammed the glass door shut with his foot. He flipped over the cardboard open/closed sign to read "Closed."

"It'll take about twenty minutes," he said. "And that's what I'll pay for."

George looked sullen. His jawline tightened. Sacrificing twenty minutes right in the middle of the day, when all the salarymen were on lunch break, was a difficult idea for him to handle. There were people higher up the Akasaka economic hierarchy who were relying on him to maximize turnover. They were bad people to disappoint. On the other hand, unlike Mori, they were not standing in front of him right now threatening trouble.

"All right then," he muttered finally. "But no rough stuff. These are the best girls in Tokyo."

Mori made his way upstairs. At the top, a dozen girls were sitting on the other side of a one-way mirror. Some were watching television, some reading magazines, a couple shoveling down cup noodles. Mori went into one of the cubicles and sat down. He took a ten-thousand-yen note out of his pocket and placed it on the airbed.

The first girl who appeared was dressed up as a cheerleader, with pigtails and a pleated miniskirt.

"My name's Lemon," she said. "I'm humbly grateful to be at your service."

She completed her self-introduction with a high kick which revealed a complete lack of underwear.

"That could be yours," said Mori, pointing at the money on the airbed. "To earn it you've just got to answer some questions."

"Dirty talk?" said Lemon brightly. "That sounds like fun."

"No dirty talk. Just tell me about this guy." Mori took out a photograph of Hara and flashed it in front of her face. The sexy-pouty expression disappeared from her face at once, and she became a plain, skinny twenty-year-old.

"Are you police, or what?" she asked in a tiny, nervous voice.

"It's okay. I've cleared it with the big boss downstairs."

But she didn't know Hara. Nor did the Chinese peasant girl who succeeded her, nor did the four after that. Mori had almost given up, when he caught a flash of recognition on the face of the seventh girl, who was wearing a nun's habit over stockings and a garter belt.

"You know him?" he asked.

"Mmmm. Maybe, I'm not sure. It's the same kind of face."

She had a tough Osaka accent that evoked the greasy black waters of the Yodo River.

"Same as what?"

"Same as over at the Seikyu, about three months ago. He rang through."

"What else?"

"He was a regular. Not for me, for Midori. It was because—

well, because she couldn't that night—that I went instead. When I got there, the bastard took one look and sent me back."

The nun looked bitter. Evidently, her professional pride had been stung.

"Where's Midori today?" asked Mori.

"She quit last week. I think she got a boyfriend or something."

Mori picked up the ten thousand yen and replaced it with a five-thousand-yen note.

"Halfway there," he said. "Find me Midori's address and you get the big one too."

She hitched up the habit and tucked the banknote into her garter belt. She was back two minutes later holding a little notebook. Mori wrote the address down on a slip of paper and handed her the ten-thousand-yen note.

"Good girls," he said to Yokohama George on the way out. "You ought to be proud of them."

George had his tasseled white loafers up on the desk. He seemed genuinely pleased by the compliment.

"They do their best. Actually, I taught them everything myself."

He grinned his reptile grin and took a swill out of his whiskey glass.

"Everything?" said Mori. "Including all that heavy tongue work?"

"Sure."

"In that case, I better try you out next time too."

The sound of Yokohama George choking on his whiskey was music to Mori's ears.

The address that the nun had given Mori was of a ramshackle apartment block in Nippori with a funerary ornaments shop on the ground floor. The old man in long johns and clogs who sat among the bronze Buddhas and incense burners was also the caretaker of the apartments.

"She's gone from here," he said with a nostalgic leer. "Left last week."

Mori said that he was Midori's uncle, up from the country,

and that he hadn't seen her since she was a little girl. The old man brooded over this information while polishing a thirty-armed statue of the Goddess of Mercy.

"She had lots of uncles, that girl," he said finally.

Mori laid a five-thousand-yen note on top of one of the incense burners.

"It means a great deal," he said.

"That much, huh?" The old man sounded impressed. "All right, if you want to see her, she's probably still working evenings at the Seikyu Store. And say best wishes from me, will you?" He was leering away in the gloom as if he were in a blue-movie theater.

"Certainly will," said Mori.

The people at the store weren't as suspicious. They told him straightaway that Midori was working on the central elevators. It wasn't difficult to find her, since all the staff wore square lapel badges with their names on. She was a pretty, sharp-eyed girl of around twenty-two. The dowdy blue uniform, white gloves, and little cap that said "Seikyu" on the front couldn't quite suppress the natural vivacity of her manner.

"Welcome, dear people," she said in a clear monotone. "Our humble store is greatly honored that you have spared the time to visit us today. On the first floor are umbrellas, ladies' and gentlemen's shoes, accessories, and travel goods."

She spoke well, but the clogged vowels of the north country were still present in the background. Mori waited until the elevator reached the top floor and the last pudgy-faced child had tugged its mother off into the toy department.

"Time to descend, dear people," she said brightly. Mori was the only other person in the elevator. Did she go through the same routine when there was no one there at all?

"I have a message from Yokohama George," said Mori quietly.

She stopped in midflow and darted a contemptuous glance into his face.

"That creep! What does he want?"

"Meet me at Dogen Shrine after the store closes. I'll

tell you there."

She looked as if she was about to say something angry, but then the elevator door opened at the fifth floor and her features were once more suffused with an expression of radiant self-abasement. She bowed at the dozen bag-wielding housewives who squashed into the elevator.

"Thank you very much," she trilled. "We are sincerely grateful to have had the privilege of receiving your honorable patronage. The fourth floor contains sporting goods, gentlemen's coats, and lingerie."

Mori got out at the second floor, bought himself a couple of business magazines, then made for the shrine.

Seven o'clock in the evening, and Shibuya is seething with human traffic. The pavements are rivers of faces, Hachiko Square an ocean of shuffling bodies. Long lines form suddenly at the telephones, at the ticket machines, at the toilets, then mysteriously dissolve. The air is thick with the smell of coffee, the smell of fried squid, the smell of urine. Trains go thundering by, overhead and underground. Nothing is at rest.

The daylight world of concrete and glass has been replaced by a dimensionless neon scroll. Solid department stores have been transformed into names that flash, rotate, or slowly unpeel themselves. Every line of sight, every surface, every corner, is laden with messages. The glass walls of the telephone booths are plastered with stickers from massage parlors and pink salons. A couple of old men wander through the crowds carrying billboards advertising love hotels. Salesgirls are standing around handing out free tissue paper and leaflets. Stall owners are bawling out their bargains. The centuries-old street cry of the baked-yam seller repeats itself again and again on a loop of tape.

Information overload—unless you know how to blank it out. The young men and women who work in the nearby boutiques and fast-food joints blank it out by instinct. Their faces are calm, their eyes empty. They walk quickly, without seeming to hurry. They don't see anything, don't hear anything. They swim like fish through the sea of events.

It was a long time since Mori had been nineteen, so the effort of blanking it out made him feel tired. He went over to the shrine, where at least the noise was reduced to an echo, and skimmed through a couple of magazine articles on financial policy.

Why was the dollar so strong? That seemed to be the great topic of the day. Japanese money was surging into the American financial markets, pushing up asset prices and the value of the dollar. The experts, bankers and economists and so forth, had all sorts of different reasons why this should be happening, none of which seemed to be particularly convincing. Some said it was because interest rates were going to stay high. Some said it was because interest rates were going to fall. Some said it was because of renewed confidence in the American economy. Others said it was all to do with Eastern Europe, or the oil price, or the U.S. election. Mori was starting to get the picture. Once you stripped away the jargon, what you had left was a bunch of people sounding off much like taxi drivers did about the Giants.

Midori arrived at the shrine an hour later, when it was already pretty dark. There was a courting couple cuddling up on one of the benches, and a tramp sprawled under a stone lantern in a pool of urine. Mosquitoes were everywhere. It wasn't ideal, but at least it was quiet.

She was wearing a smart print dress and swinging a Louis Vuitton handbag and looked well-off, healthy, normal—just another of the modern girls you see around the place, being modern. Can't blame her really, thought Mori. Probably came to Tokyo with no friends, nowhere to live, then having to pay key money, gratitude money, and three months' rent just to live in a tiny concrete box. You couldn't kick that off on an elevator girl's wages.

"Okay, what's the problem?" she said abruptly. "I told George I was quitting."

The accent was more noticeable when she was wasn't using her Seikyu Store training-manual voice. Mori placed it as Akita Prefecture, not far away from Hara's hometown.

"No problem," said Mori, holding up his hands in a placatory gesture. "I just need information, that's all. I heard you might be qualified to help."

Before she had time to protest, he took out the photograph of Hara and handed it to her.

"I know you knew him," he said. "Let's not bother with how or why. I also know you were with him the night he died."

She flinched as if he had thrown a cup of coffee over her smart new dress.

"Who are you? What do you want with me?"

"I'm an investigator retained by the Hara family to clear up the facts surrounding his death. I operate independently and under total confidentiality."

"I don't need to talk to you. I had nothing to do with that incident."

She wanted to play it the difficult way. Fair enough.

"This job you have at Seikyu," he said. "It must pay well."

"Not too bad," she said warily. "But I'm just part-time for the first three months."

"I don't suppose they're gotten the references from your last employer yet."

"What do you mean?"

Mori took out a flier for Love Oasis, the kind that was put into people's mailboxes in the middle of the night. It featured a drawing of a girl in a negligee eating a banana, under the legend "Your Little Lover for Ninety Minutes—Anywhere in Central Tokyo."

"I hate you," she said in a tiny voice, then sat down heavily on the bench.

"Fine," said Mori. "Now let's take it from the beginning."

She took a deep breath and started talking in a low monotone. Mori interrupted only when necessary, letting her tell the story in the way she knew best.

Thirty minutes later, they walked down the stone steps that led from the shrine, leaving the place to the lovers and the tramp and the whining mosquitoes, and went their separate ways. Midori disappeared into the flood of young office girls pouring down into the subway. Mori took a cab back to

Shinjuku. He needed time to think.

According to Midori, she had been meeting Hara at the Seikyu Hotel for the past year. He would ring through to the Love Oasis, usually on a Tuesday or Wednesday, and ask for her by name. When she got to his room, he would be watching television, dressed in a cotton robe. She would stay for two hours; sometimes longer, if he requested.

It was after the first couple of sessions that he asked her to bring the junior high-school uniform. That hadn't surprised her much—it was a popular routine with several Love Oasis clients. But from then on, the sex just stopped. She would change into the uniform in the bathroom, and when she emerged he would already be tucked up in bed. She would sit down in the bedside chair, and they would talk—about her friends at school, about the first time she wore makeup, about his attempts to play baseball, about shoveling the snow from the roofs, about the autumn festivals, about the colors of the setting sun over the Japan Sea. There were more than fifteen years betweeen them, but for a couple of hours a month they were ruddy-cheeked, village schoolchildren, without a care in the world.

He never asked her what she was doing in Tokyo, where she lived, how long she had been there. He didn't want to know, it seemed. Similarly, he never talked about his work. In fact, she had no idea what he did until she read about his death in the paper.

She had gone to the hotel that evening at eight o'clock. Hara was already wrapped up in bed when she arrived. He seemed relaxed, slightly more talkative than usual. He told her about the time he had been caught stealing rice crackers from the local shop. He had been so scared that the shopkeeper would tell his father that he had promised to give the man's son free lessons in history and mathematics.

Less than twenty minutes had passed when the telephone rang. The conversation was brief, but when Hara put the phone down, his mood had changed completely. He was clearly distracted, angry. Something important had cropped up, something to do with his work. Some people would be coming up to the hotel room to discuss it with him in a couple of minutes.

Midori would have to leave instantly.

So she did, without even changing out of the school uniform. A couple of men were coming out of the elevator as she was getting in. They stared at her, but that was not surprising—she must have looked like a pretty mature fifteen-year-old. Mori interrupted to ask what they looked like, but she hardly remembered. One had been a big hefty fellow wearing, she thought, a white raincoat. The next day when she read about Hara's death in the paper she immediately got suspicious and a little scared. She didn't believe Hara had killed himself. He simply wasn't the type.

That was an observation that Mori was hearing again and again. He turned the matter over in his mind as his taxi nudged through the end-of-the-month traffic jam; Kaneda, Midori, the yen, the dollar, the little fishing village in North Japan. At the Shinjuku Park junction, his reflections were disturbed by the blaring of a loudspeaker van parked right in the middle of the road. It was manned by a group of rightists, and one, a young fellow in paramilitary uniform and dark glasses, was standing on the roof shrieking through a bullhorn at enough volume to rival a heavy-metal band. The left-hand side of the intersection was blocked off, and the traffic behind it was frozen solid. Some passersby were covering up their ears, some were grimacing, others were trying to do the impossible and pretend that nothing was happening.

"Sincere apologies to the workers of Shinjuku," roared the metallic voice. "Please forgive us for the inconvenience, but our message is important. It is time to throw out the corrupt, money-oriented Minakawa government which is bringing shame on our motherland. Minakawa and his lackeys take bribes from big business; they bow down before the Americans who tested their atom bomb on our cities; they trample on the great spirit and traditions of Japan. We will endure no longer. We will have revenge."

The man's voice, cracking with rage, rose to a climax, then was replaced by martial music played at a similar volume. Mori glanced at the van as the taxi edged past. It was heavily fortified, with wire mesh instead of window glass and metal shields covering the tires. The fiery red characters on the side of the van spelled out the usual rightist slogans—"Defend the Emperor System," "Destroy the treacherous Teacher's Union."

There was one, however, which Mori had never seen before. Fluttering from a pole attached to the radiator grill was a red-and-white pennant which read, "Defend Asia against the Western Conspiracy."

It was a strange idea. What Western conspiracy? It reminded Mori of some of the semihysterical ideological discussions he had taken part in twenty-three years ago. One of his friends, a Trotskyite who played electric guitar in a folk-rock band, had openly laughed at the idea of a conspiracy of multinational companies. The others went to his apartment in the middle of the night and accused him of slandering the struggle of the masses. They held a mock trial and found him guilty. The sentence was carried out immediately. After gagging him with a mikan orange and a handkerchief, they used steel pipes to smash his wrists. Mori knew exactly what had happened because he had been standing by the door at the time, making sure that no one interrupted.

"Crazy," grunted the taxi driver.

"What's that?"

"These rightists, blocking up the road like that. I don't know what's going on. The whole world's going crazy."

Finally, they got past. Mori heaved a sigh of relief as the martial music grew tinnier and quieter behind them. What the taxi driver said was true. There was too much irrationality around. Everybody was restless, on edge.

Seiji Terada gunned his red Ferrari Testarosa up the mountain road. He had been on edge recently too, although no one would have guessed it from his manner, which was as calm and dignified as befitted a distinguished graduate of Keio business school, the owner of Japan's finest collection of Toulouse-Lautrec prints, and the third in command of Tokyo's largest gangster syndicate. He was perhaps a little sharper with his subordinates than usual, a little rougher on the Testarosa's gearbox, but that was all.

Terada was the unofficial leader of the *intelli yakuza*, the faction of the gangster world that specialized in large-scale white-collar crime. He had always had complete contempt for the traditional yakuza, the type that he referred to in private as "the primitives." Loan-sharking, extorting money out of construction workers, running prostitutes—it was all so hopelessly vulgar and outdated. Terada had been the first to see the potential of pornographic video, now one of the Kawashita Organization's most profitable businesses. He had developed cash-laundering systems in the Eurobond market that were too complicated for most of his colleagues even to understand. Now he was involved in a far more delicate and lucrative project, one that was so secret that he had spoken of it to only his most trusted aides.

The Ferrari turned into a long cedar-lined driveway that led to a wrought-iron gate. A dark-suited man carrying a walkie-talkie rapped on the window with his knuckles. He had seen both Terada and the car dozens of times before, but the correct procedures had to be followed. Terada wound down the window and identified himself formally. Seconds later, the gate lifted and the car swished up the driveway toward a large modern bungalow. There were bars on the windows and metal plating on the front walls. Two carbon copies of the man at the gate directed Terada into a large tatami room in which a dozen men in kimono were gathered around a table. On the wall above their heads hung a scroll emblazoned with the powerful characters of the chief, who was an accomplished calligrapher.

"Benevolence is the Mother of Power," it read.

"Late again," grunted the huge, bull-necked man at the head of the table. It was Aga, the leader of the traditionalist faction.

"Sincere apologies to the deputy chief," said Terada smoothly, and gave a low bow.

"We are discussing the ceremony to mark the imminent release from prison of my younger brother. It is appropriate for one senior officer to lead the group outside the prison, and you are the obvious choice."

Terada groaned inwardly. He hated ceremonies, oaths, tattoos, and all the other nonsense. He had even managed to avoid lopping off his little finger. He had seen what that could do to a golf handicap.

"I have to go to Hawaii next week," he said. "Our resort development plan is meeting with some problems."

"Most unfortunate," said Aga with satisfaction. "What kind of problems?"

Aga had always opposed the Hawaiian project. His vision of aggressive expansion was limited to intimidating pachinko parlor operators in Osaka.

"As you know, dollar interest rates are moving against us. I'm planning to switch some of the short-term bank borrowings into subordinated debt, probably with an equity option. That could lower our financing costs by as much as thirty percent."

Aga glared at him silently. The kimono hung loose around his neck, revealing the swirling pattern of serpents and lion-dogs that covered his upper body like a singlet. The man belonged in the 1950s, along with his appalling suits and the white Lincoln Continental he cruised around in.

"That is a shame," said Kubota, Aga's right-hand man. "Aga-kun has suffered in prison for five years on behalf of the organization. We must show him our respect."

Respect indeed! The man was an utter buffoon. In comparison, the elder brother was an intellectual genius. Anyone stupid enough to attempt to smuggle a hand grenade through Narita Airport deserved five years in jail at least.

"I'm sure the chief would expect you to be present," said Aga icily.

"Really? Last time I spoke to him he specifically asked me to give the Hawaiian project maximum attention."

That conversation had taken place three months ago, but Terada knew that no one would attempt to check what the chief thought now. The old man was lying in a hospital ward connected to a life-support system. Everyone in the room knew that the cancer was in its final stages. The doctors were too scared to operate.

"In the chief's absence, I am responsible for all group affairs. I want you to lead the ceremony."

There was a sharp tone to Aga's voice that Terada didn't like.

"The financing problem is urgent," he said. "Any delay will cost us hundreds of millions of yen."

Aga lost his temper, as Terada had suspected he might. His fist bashed down on the table, upsetting the sake cups.

"You will be present," he roared. "You will honor the rules of the organization!"

Terada nodded, half-smiling. At the other end of the table, a few of his allies were trying to suppress their smiles as well.

"Of course, deputy leader," he said.

He remained silent for the rest of the meeting. It was Aga who had lost face, not Terada. Anyway, the project he was now involved in would put him in a position to dispense with the Aga brothers anytime he wished.

Two hours later, as the Ferrari sped down the winding road that led back to Tokyo, Terada was absorbed in thoughts of what he would do after all of East Japan had been brought under his control. When the call came through on his car phone, at first he didn't recognize the voice that came crackling through the static.

"Ah, sensei," he said finally. "How is your American trip proceeding?"

"Everything is going according to plan. What about your side?"

"No problems," said Terada.

"And that cleaning contract we discussed? Did you manage to complete it?"

"All stages are now finished. Everything is sparkling clean and good as new."

"That was quick work. Well done!"

"I'm a perfectionist, sensei. When I take on a cleaning job, I don't like to leave any specks of dirt at all. By the way, did you try that restaurant I mentioned, the one in Greenwich Village?"

Suddenly, Terada felt content with life. It made a pleasant change to be working with a man of intelligence and refinement instead of oafs like the Aga brothers. And when the project was complete, he would stand shoulder to shoulder with the sensei, one of the progenitors of the new Japan.

5

∴

BRRRING, went the telephone.

Six-thirty already? Impossible! There was a dead slug in Kenji's mouth, which was his tongue. His head was a bottomless well of pain. His eyelids couldn't keep out the twin shafts of red light that were boring into his skull.

He passed a hand over a brow slippery with sweat. His face felt like someone else's.

Brrring, brrring . . . Brrring, brrring . . .

Clips of the previous evening were being shown in a screening room in the back of his brain. There he was, bowing down in apology, his forehead pressed against the carpet. There was the client glaring down at him. Then afterward at the restaurant, . . . the giant abalone writhing like a muscle as it baked on the open fire, the steaming hot sake, the cold beer . . .

Brrring, brrring . . .

Then reeling through the streets of Kawasaki arm in arm. The girl's soapy body slithering above him. The client roaring a ballad into a microphone. Whiskey, brandy, more beer. Being shaken awake by the railway guard at the last station, his own stop somewhere far behind. Then clinging to a telegraph pole while his stomach heaved . . .

Brrring, brring, click.

"Good morning, Okada-san. This is Sachiko. Are you feeling well today?"

The phone was set up so that her voice lisped out of speakers at the foot of the bed. Kenji mumbled a reply through the microphone hanging from his dresser. "Noooo . . . I feel ill. . . ."

"Bad luck! Last night, I went to a disco with my new boyfriend, the tall one from the Medical School."

"Another one?"

"He wanted to get to C on the first date, but I only let him have A and B. He'll have to give me lots of presents before we get to C! Anyway, I've just had a shower and my hair's all wet. Do you want to know where my finger is?"

"Where is it?" His eyes were wide open now.

"It's in my ear. But I am going to put it between my legs like this. . . ."

A sea of sighs came rolling out of the speaker system. He sat bolt upright, suddenly wide awake.

"Oh, Okada-san . . . oh, Okada-san . . ."

Who was Sachiko, what did she look like, where did she live? He had no idea, but for three minutes every morning she was his best friend alive, well worth the ten-thousand-yen membership fee.

Sa . . . chi . . . ko . . .

Five minutes later, Kenji rolled up his bedroll and stuffed it in the cupboard. From above, below, and both sides came the water music of humanity waking up—tanks boiling, pipes gurgling, stopcocks groaning, flushes flushing. From the corner where he did his cooking, he could hear the couple next door wrangling over the week's budget. From the wall opposite came the buzz of an electric razor and the wail of a baby.

Another installment of reality for the denizens of Royal Garden Heights, a reinforced concrete "mansion" block located in the semi-industrial, semiresidential sprawl just outside Chiba City. The rent was steep and the daily commute long and tiring, but the place was paradise compared to the four square yards Kenji had inhabited in the Maruichi Securities dormitory for single males. There the doors were locked at midnight. No female visitors were allowed at any time. He ate his meals at the long wooden table in the main hall, together with several dozen other employees of Maruichi Securities. He bathed in the big bath with four or five Maruichi men. When he used the toilet, there would be a Maruichi man straining away in the next stall. All the time, Kenji would have to adjust his attitude, his tone of voice, to the people around him, depending on their status within the organization. Twenty-four hours a day, seven days a week, he was the property of Maruichi Securities.

After three years of that, he had moved out, a decision that had cost him eighty thousand yen a month in rent and untold damage to his promotion chances. Several of his seniors were still at the dormitory, and they felt personally insulted. Kenji Okada is a man without true company spirit, he could imagine them muttering behind his back, an unreliable individualist. Still, the sacrifice had been worth it. Small and cramped though it might be, Number 809 Royal Garden Heights was a sanctuary, a place where Kenji Okada could be himself.

The station was a ten-minute bicycle ride away. After parking in the vast tangled forest of bicycles that surrounded the north entrance, Kenji bought a *manga* comic book and a health drink, which he promptly swigged down. According to the ads, this concoction of caffeine and nicotine with a spicing of pickled adder had remarkable effects on male stamina. It was also a useful hangover cure.

The train journey was the worst part of the day. Fifty minutes pressed into a solid mass of flesh, eyes inches from another human being's nostrils, nose inches from another human being's mouth, wrist caught in a liquid armpit, high heels stepping on toes, knees thrusting into his groin, other human beings' sweat soaking into his shirt. Silence, as dozens of eyes strained to avoid each other.

The train braked, and the multiheaded monster staggered for balance. There was a surge as the doors hissed open. Kenji expertly maneuvered into a vacant seat just as a middle-aged man was about to plant down his square buttocks. The man quickly looked away, unable to hide his mortification. More human beings were surging into the car now, levering the man's crotch forward into Kenji's face. It gave off a sour, wet-cardboard odor.

The girl sitting on Kenji's left began to slump against his upper arm, sound asleep. The Walkman was totally invisible under the curtain of hair that covered her face, but Kenji could hear the English lessons squeaking away: "Please repeat after me. . . ." Slowly, steadily, her head slid down his chest, until it was craning down into his lap, bobbing with the rhythm of the train. Embarrassed, he turned to one side and opened his manga comic book.

Kenji liked manga. Not the stories, which were too bizarre to have any impact, but the flow of images, the expressions and situations. Exaggerated, maybe, but the living city creates its own caricatures. Sitting in this train, for example, he could identify several faces straight out of the pages of *Big Spirits Adventure*. His colleagues at work as well—most of them behaved more like manga than real people. Even his own experiences, his triumphs and embarrassments, often felt as if they had the flatness and distorted edges of manga. Nothing had any depth any more. There was "*ero-guro* nonsense" all around.

He glanced up at the fliers for the weekly news magazines which were flapping from the ceiling. Teen idol Yumi-chan was rumored to have started a new love affair. A press conference would be held next week. The Giants were about to sack their manager. Two billion yen had been found in a garbage bin. Nothing like as convincing as the pages of *Big Spirits Adventure*.

As the train snaked across the rooftops, Kenji watched his destination drawing closer. Already, you could read the bold red characters that spelled out "Maruichi Securities." It was the only real skyscraper in the financial district, dominating the jumble of smallness that surrounded it. The morning sun flashed off the steel-and-glass apex, forcing him to look away.

Kenji was proud to work for the largest securities house in the world. It was good to know that Maruichi controlled a third of Japan's personal financial assets; that it had at its disposal the most advanced satellite communications, data banks, and supercomputer modeling that money could buy. It was good to know that its influence was felt in every policy-making institution in

Japan, that the Ministry of Finance was helpless without its approval, that even the IMF and the World Bank had been known to bend to its will.

Maruichi began life in the late Meiji era, when a bankrupt horse dealer called Ichiro Maruoka began selling government bonds door-to-door. Many smooth-talking young men had the same idea at the same time, but none came close to Maruoka's legendary feats of salesmanship. He worked from dawn to dusk, traveling from village to factory to temple, equipped only with a briefcase of simple leaflets and a burning sincerity.

The secret of his success lay in his fervent patriotism. He strongly believed, and transmitted the belief, that the interests of his customers and the Japanese nation were identical. He spoke rhapsodically of how the government would invest the money subscribed—on roads and universities and shipyards that would put Japan ahead of the West. Illiterate silk weavers, impoverished ex-samurai, the new bourgeoisie with their top hats and parasols—all felt happier with themselves for buying Maruoka's bonds. Maruoka instilled the same obsessiveness in the staff of the securities house that he founded. It was never enough to do better than last year. The target was to do better than everyone else combined, to raise market share until Maruichi actually became the market. The authorities soon recognized the firm's value, and Ichiro became an important string-puller in the political world. He established his own Patriotic Society, called Silent Thunder, which financed and carried out secret projects in Manchuria and China. In recognition of his efforts, he was decorated by the emperor.

In the 1930s, Maruichi became identified with the antibanking, anti-zaibatsu ultranationalist faction that was creating mayhem in the business world. It was widely believed, though never proven, that Maruoka sponsored the assassination of the chairman of Yasunaga Bank, a man who had suggested cutting off credit to the upstart securities industry. Even within Maruichi itself, there were factions that opposed the president's ideas. Maruoka's younger brother, a brilliant stock market strategist, was ousted from the board for trying to rein in the company's expansionist policies.

After the war, Maruoka was one of the two thousand business leaders purged by General MacArthur's Occupation regime. His name was taken off the list of Class A war criminals after he supplied U.S. intelligence with information on secret funds set up by the zaibatsu. But when the stock market reopened in 1949, he was already dying of cancer. Within Maruichi, the initiative was seized by a group sympathetic to his younger brother, who remained a senior adviser to the firm. Branches were set up in London and New York, and promising young men were dispatched to foreign universities. Overseas, nobody took much notice of the gauche, badly dressed Japanese who watched and smiled and asked question after question in painful English.

Back at home, Maruichi used what it learned to establish itself as one of the "Big Five" brokerage houses, but it was still viewed with contempt by the business establishment. Trading conditions were tough, and in 1966 the company nearly went bust, only surviving through the political clout of Ichiro's old chums. The price of the rescue package was decades of obligation to the rightist faction leader who had arranged it. Profits soon recovered, but the Maruichi was still far from Japan's top one hundred companies. Naturally, it was unable to recruit graduates from the big-name universities. The meek, overtrained "elite" flocked to the safety and high status of the banks and insurance companies. Maruichi attracted a different brand of Japanese—less conformist and far tougher, both physically and mentally.

It was well known that Maruichi salesmen traded clients' accounts without permission; that Maruichi's investment trusts were used as "trash cans" for stocks that it couldn't get rid of anywhere else; that it shamelessly manipulated stock prices to benefit important clients; that it used insider information on a daily basis. And yet its market share grew and grew. Maruichi people were simply the sharpest, the most aggressive, the fastest with the excuse and the smile, the most persuasive, the most bullish, the most everything. They were impossible to ignore.

The internal politics at Maruichi remained full of tension, a basic equilibrium being kept among the three main factions. The internationalists, inspired by the now retired younger Maruoka, stressed the interdependence of world capital markets and the necessity for Maruichi to build up a strong overseas operation. The nationalists, headed by Ichiro Maruoka's disciples and upholding his faith in Japan's mission to lead the world, believed in concentrating on the home market, which they would dominate with blitzkrieg sales offensives. The pragmatists had their eyes on respectability and places for Maruichi executives at the top of Japan's economic federations.

In the 1980s, all three groups were to see their goals achieved in spectacular fashion. By now, financial deregulation and the communications revolution had created a huge "symbol" economy, an alternative universe in which time and distance had been abolished. Capital flows many times larger than the trade of real goods flashed from country to country in an endless search for the best return. Windows of opportunity opened and closed in seconds. New information was discounted as soon as it appeared; profits were taken on investments that businessmen hadn't even begun to plan; computers bought and sold options and futures contracts in response to other computers doing the same thing on the other side of the world.

It was a system too vast and complex for any one man to grasp, let alone control. And, as became ever more apparent, it would not tolerate stability. Once upon a time, the greatest worry of statesmen was military attack, and they devoted themselves to analyzing the machinations of diplomats and the dispositions of armies. Now their careers were one continuous negotiation with an invisible, invincible empire whose existence the masses who voted for them barely understood.

At seven fifty-five, Kenji walked into the largest dealing room in the world, containing over eight hundred work stations. Each had fingertip access to Globewatch, a proprietary information system developed by Maruichi Computer Services, Japan's largest software house. At the end of the huge hall was a forty-foot screen on which were flashed up graphics and videoclips giving the Maruichi line on important industrial and economics topics.

All this came courtesy of MRI, Maruichi Research Institute, a think tank containing the best, and most obedient, brains that Japan could produce.

Kenji sat down at his work station, checked the overnight news, then reviewed his client list. As usual, it made dismal reading. The collection of real-estate developers, dentists, and pachinko parlor owners whose accounts he looked after were all losing serious sums of money on Maruichi recommendations. The reason was simple. For the past six months, the Tokyo market had been wriggling sideways like a wounded snake, so the profits that Maruichi could generate for its clients had to be strictly rationed. Top of the priority list were important politicians and industrialists. Next came helpful banks and insurance companies, then large foreign investors. Kenji's department came near the bottom.

Several of Kenji's clients were so angry that he didn't have the courage even to call them. They bellowed at him, using the disrespectful o-*mae* form of address, and banged the phone down when he was attempting to apologize. The situation was getting desperate.

What he really needed was information that the other salesmen didn't have, something that would put him one step ahead. And he had a good idea how to get it.

"Where's the section chief today?" he asked. "Golf again?"

"Bangkok," answered the salesman sitting alongside. "He's entertaining a group of dentists."

Just then, the familiar features of the head of trading appeared on the giant screen at the end of the room.

"Today we begin the Dainippon Steel campaign," he barked. "For the glory of Maruichi Securities, it is vital for us to buy more shares in the market than all other securities companies put together. I want to see the Dainippon stock price soaring. I want to see the competition crushed. All Japan is watching us with high expectations. You know what to do, now *get moving*!"

They got moving.

There was a plump, rather plain girl in the computer services department called Noriko. She was twenty-nine, already "leftover goods" by conventional standards, and, according to the gossip, had been through over forty arranged marriage meetings. Noriko had a thing for Kenji. She had sent him St. Valentine's Day chocolates two years running and always smiled at him in the elevator.

"Let's go out for a drink sometime," she would say. "Sure, sometime," Kenji would reply, meaning never.

Well, now the time had come to show some interest. He dialed her extension and invited her to lunch. She accepted at once.

The place Kenji chose was a cheap sushi bar where the day's fare went round and round in front of the customers' noses on a small conveyor belt. All dishes were priced the same, and tasted much the same as well. At first, Noriko seemed a little tense. There was a smear of lipstick on her teeth, and her perfume was overpowering. Still, after a few glasses of beer, they were swapping gossip like old friends. They talked about arrogant bosses, bonus prospects, suspected pregnancies, jealousies and scandals. The plates piled up by their elbows.

The promise of a weekend date was enough to get Kenji what he wanted. Early in the afternoon, Noriko rang through with the section chief's personal password to the Globewatch system. That was the secret weapon that Kenji had been looking for. He knew that the section chief dealt for several high-priority clients. If he could find out what stocks they had been buying, he could use the information for the benefit of his own clients. He would be on the inside track.

Kenji lost no time in accessing the section chief's files. First he scanned the dealing records of the major clients, then he searched for the largest single deals. Disappointingly, there was nothing unusual. The section leader was buying the same stocks as the junior salesmen, just three or four days earlier, before Maruichi's dealers had started to "ramp up" the prices. That was only to be expected.

He was just about to log off when a small detail struck his attention. Although the menu had told him that the section leader was managing twenty-five accounts, he had only seen twenty-four. He went back and looked again. Yes, there should be twenty-five. It was probably an input error, but he decided to check all the same.

Each account was given a separate code in the index, made up of a six-digit number followed by the first two letters of the client's name in Roman script. It was immediately obvious that one number was missing from the sequence. The letters would take time to puzzle out, since there were roughly sixty different possibilities. Kenji looked up at the giant screen at the end of the room. The Nikkei Index was drifting sideways on thin volume. There was nothing else to occupy his interest. In fact, it took only fifteen minutes for Kenji to discover the existence of Account 890519NA. Immediately, he flashed it up on his screen, then spent the next few moments gazing half mesmerized at the columns of figures that oscillated gently before his eyes.

The first thing that he noticed was the size of the trades. They were huge, much bigger than anything else the section leader was doing. The second, more startling point was the size of the profits. The pattern was the same every time. Gradually, over the course of several days, the account would feed money into an obscure second-line stock. Within a matter of weeks, the same stock would be sold at double, sometimes even treble the price. Either 890519NA was one of the greatest financial geniuses the world had ever seen, or the account was being used to wash billions of yen through the financial system.

Kenji scribbled down a few notes on a piece of paper, then exited the system. The last stock the account had bought had yet to move. Here was his chance to win back his clients, impress his colleagues, and secure the kind of summer bonus he knew he deserved.

He grabbed for the phone. There was still plenty of time left before the market closed.

At three o'clock, Mori was lying naked on a cold wooden floor, while a stout woman in her mid-fifties walked up and down his back. The weight of her body drew clicks and creaks from his vertebrae. Her toes dug into his shoulder muscles like steel pegs. When she finished, he felt great.

Mori had first sampled Okubo-sensei's massage techniques

five years before, when he was recovering from being stomped by three Hiroshima yakuza. After breaking three of his ribs, rupturing his spleen, and dislocating his left shoulder, they had taken the trouble to kick him into a mess of bruises. It had been a thorough, methodical going-over, just what you would expect from the city that produced Mazda cars and the Carp baseball team. Okubo-sensei had not only corrected the spinal curvature that resulted, but managed to ease the muscular tension that made him walk around as if he were carrying a sack of cement.

It wasn't just physical. By tracing the energy flows, she was able to gauge the psychological condition that molded the body's posture. In another life, Okubo-sensei would make a good detective.

"All wrong," she frowned at him. "You're holding your head too far forward, twisting your spine into that S-shape again. Old problems are returning. Have you been seeing that strange woman again?"

"What strange woman?" mumbled Mori.

"I thought so," said Okubo-sensei triumphantly. "She's no good for you. Your *ki* is trying to hide away from her."

Okubo-sensei was very big on the concept of *ki*, meaning "spirit" or "universal force." Mori didn't really believe in it. It was too vague, too irrational.

He closed his eyes and started to think about the Hara case. The man had been murdered, that much was clear. The reason— well, Kaneda's conspiracy theory was becoming increasingly plausible. Who had done it? Probably the man in the white raincoat whom Midori had seen in the elevator. And how could he be traced? He couldn't. No one had had a good look at him. It was a dead end.

Suddenly, Okubo-sensei seized his head, and lifted and twisted in one sharp movement. There was a loud click in the joint of his neck. It was a technique that, if clumsily performed, could result in permanent paralysis from the neck down.

Next, she maneuvered him upright, and started pressing her thumbs into the stress points on his shoulders and chest. He was dimly aware of the television set on the shelf above the sofa. It was showing a banal, show-biz-scandal program. A panel of experts were discussing the Yumi-chan story. What was the real reason she had broken up with her lover? Was it true about the abortion, about the midnight date with the movie star?

In spite of himself, Mori glanced up at the screen. Immediately, he was transfixed. The scene shown was of Yumi-chan being hustled out of a press conference, photographers and fans clustered around her. But what grabbed Mori's attention was not the noise and activity, but the surroundings. It was unmistakably the lobby of the Seikyu Hotel. And in the background, walking toward the house telephones, was the clearly visible figure of a man in a white raincoat.

"What's happened?" said Okubo-sensei. "Your *ki* has suddenly grown strong."

"You've worked wonders," said Mori.

This *ki* business, he thought as he pulled on his shirt—maybe it makes sense after all.

An hour later, he was down at the TV station attempting to extract information from a polite young staffer in the publicity department.

"That's right," said Assistant Manager Sada. "The press conference finished at eight o'clock. We had three crews there—one in the hall, one in the lobby, and one out in the parking lot."

"So the whole thing's on tape?" asked Mori.

"That's right. What's your interest, anyway?"

Sada's soft, pudgy face displayed only mild curiosity. He was obviously used to fielding all sorts of strange requests.

"It's Yumi-chan," said Mori blankly. "I've got all her records, seen all her movies. She's—she's so fresh and lovely. Sometimes I dream about her, you know."

Sada looked at him thoughtfully. "Yes," he said. "She's got a lot of fans in the upper age bracket."

"So the tapes—could you let me see them?"

"Difficult," said Sada, shaking his head. "They've probably been erased by now. Still, if you're really interested, you should get in touch with her managers. They've got copies of everything."

"I am really interested," said Mori. "Thank you very much for all your help. By the way, could you give me your business card, just in case?"

Yumi-chan was managed by a large production company headquartered in a mirror-plated building in Harajuku. Inside the building, she was ubiquitous. There was a life-size, natural-color statue of her in the center of the lobby. Her face beamed from posters on the wall and badges on the staff's lapels. Her voice trilled out her latest hit song in the elevator.

Mori handed Sada's card to the receptionist. She bowed respectfully, showed him into a small side room, and brought him a cup of green tea. After a while, a bored-looking woman appeared. They had never met before, but Mori recognized her instantly. The hair was tomboy-short now, the mouth wider, the set of the jaw much harder. She could only be in her late twenties, but the edges and angles of her face hinted at a long stretch of difficult, tired living.

It must have been twelve years ago that the same face, then cutely dimpled and padded out with adolescent baby fat, had appeared on the nation's TV screens. The Peach Sisters—Rumi and Koko. For a brief eighteen months, they had been the hottest property in Japanese show-biz, with their own program five nights a week, movies, cartoons, number one records, dozens of commercials. The squeaky voices chanting out the nonsensical words, the semaphoric dance routines, the ever-waggling butts and ever-jiggling breasts—they had been, in their own way, unforgettable.

Then what had happened? Mori remembered vaguely a "farewell concert" and a tearful press conference at which they had announced their intention of retiring to become normal girls again. At the time, they must have been around nineteen, which was verging on veteran status for idol singers. The large entertainment company which had marketed them obviously preferred to put its energies into a new product range. A failed comeback with a new "adult" image, a couple of talk-show appearances, some marriages and divorces noted in tiny paragraphs in the sports newspapers—there wasn't much more than that.

The woman introduced herself as Yumi-chan's manager. Mori smiled his most ingratiating smile.

"Aren't you Rumi from the Peach Sisters?" he said. "I was one of your biggest fans."

"Koko, actually," she answered.

"Oh, I'm sorry. Anyway, you were always my favorite. I've been wanting your autograph for the past ten years."

That prompted a wry, heard-it-a-thousand-times-before smile. Mori pressed on.

"Still, how's Rumi doing these days? I liked her too."

"No idea. The last I heard she was doing striptease in Fukuoka."

"Is that right? Next time I'm there I'll watch out for her."

Koko looked at him quizzically.

"Is there any problem?" she asked. "The program went on all right, didn't it?"

"No problem," said Mori casually. "We've probably got the highest ratings of the afternoon. I just need to check some background for next week's show."

She was puzzled, but couldn't refuse. A representative of a major TV network, even a humble assistant manager, had to be treated with due deference if Yumi-chan's career was to proceed according to plan.

She led Mori to a small office piled with magazines and photos. In the corner, a young man was gazing at three TV screens mounted on his desk. On one, Yumi-chan was playing the part of a geisha in a costume drama. On another, she was singing an advertising jingle about rice crackers. On the third, she was bashfully answering questions about her sexual preferences.

"This is Suzuki-kun," said Koko. "He'll give you anything you need. I'm sorry, I've got a strategy meeting to attend. . . ."

Mori found Suzuki-kun to be perfectly cooperative. He set up an extra video machine for Mori to watch the press conference and gave him a dozen albums of still photos to browse through. One photo was of such particular interest to Mori that he spent several minutes scrutinizing it, then slipped it into his pocket.

In the foreground, Yumi-chan's features were slightly blurred as she swept through the hotel lobby. In the background was the bank of house telephones. Two men were standing in front of them, their faces reasonably clear. One was a middle-aged businessman with round, owlish features. The other, younger and uglier, was wearing a white raincoat.

Max Sharrock watched the blonde strip off her evening gown and dive into the swimming pool. She was giggling stupidly, probably flying high on the cocaine that Mitchell usually provided to help break the ice. Mitchell was always the perfect host.

The girl was bobbing in the water now, her large breasts jouncing up and down. She yelled at him to come on in. She was there for the taking, which was no doubt why Mitchell had invited her. Sharrock grinned and shook his head. These days he was too busy for sex, just as he was too busy for golf and squash. The next phase of the Reckard project was taking up all his energies.

He lifted a glass of champagne off a waiter's tray and went back out onto the lawn. A Dixieland jazz band, authentic guys from New Orleans, was playing on a makeshift stage, and several people were dancing jerkily in front of them. Nearby, a small crowd was watching a troupe of mime artists go through their stuff. There was a fleet of vintage cars to ferry the guests around, and a string quartet in the woods. Mitch was certainly giving himself a fortieth birthday party to remember. That was fair enough. After all, he was probably the second best pollster around.

"How's it going, Max? Everything to your satisfaction, I trust."

It was Mitchell, as smooth as ever.

"Great," said Sharrock.

"Seventy-six percent of the sample say they're enjoying themselves, ten percent are undecided, and the rest wouldn't understand the question."

Sharrock smiled dutifully.

"Come over here, Max. There's someone I want you to meet."

Mitchell grabbed him by the elbow and steered him toward a tall brunette standing on her own.

"I want you to meet Susan, my new sister-in-law," said Mitchell. "You may recognize her. She's been getting a lot of publicity these days."

Sharrock took in the sensual mouth, the glossy hair teased into a curtain of ringlets, the lively, amused eyes. Mid-thirties, but superb legs and a great neck. Sharrock always took special note of women's necks.

"I thought maybe you two would have plenty to talk about," went on Mitchell. "You both make a living pretending you know what's going to happen in the future."

The face was certainly familiar. What was she—a weather forecaster, an astrologer maybe? No, she looked much too straight for that.

"Hi," she said, flashing a no-nonsense smile.

"Susan's worth getting to know," said Mitchell. "She's been voted the top technical analyst on Wall Street for the past four years. She called the crash in eighty-seven, called the bottom of the market last year. If you'd done what Susan said, you'd be twice as rich as you are now."

Sharrock remembered now. Susan Zavaroni—she'd been pro-filed in the *Journal* just last week. They called her the "Cher of Wall Street." That was unfair. Physically, she was a lot better pre-served than Cher. She had the blend of overt sexuality and arro-gant intelligence that Sharrock always found particularly irresistible.

They swapped opinions about the stock market, a subject on which Sharrock prided himself on his expertise. He'd started investing in stocks in high school, and by the time he finished law school he'd already made a quarter of a million dollars.

Susan was gloomy. She spoke of a financial system that had completely lost touch with the real world; of unprecedented levels of debt—national, corporate, and personal; of huge risks being con-tinually deferred; of mindless complacency and political paralysis.

"I'm advising my clients to sell everything," she said flatly. "My indicators tell me that the crunch is coming soon."

"Get out of here," said Sharrock. "America's on the way back to the top. The market looks in good shape to me. What in hell is there to knock it down?"

Susan's answer to that was long and complex, but could be summed up in one word: Japan. In her view, the long period of economic expansion that the world experienced in the 1980s had been funded by Japanese savings. Now the constant pressure on the Japanese to liberalize their markets and increase consumption was having two effects. First, the amount of savings had fallen sharply. Second, the Japanese authorities could no longer control what happened to it.

"The stabilizing force has gone," she said. "The system's about to pull itself to pieces. You know, just like Yeats said—'Things fall apart; the center cannot hold.'"

"W. B. Yeats? Is he one of the newsletter guys?"

She laughed for the first time, a nice wide laugh that made her brow wrinkle.

"Come on," Sharrock went on. "We've got the Japanese running scared on trade and takeovers and everything. They wouldn't dare do anything to escalate the situation."

"Don't you bet on it," said Susan. "My contacts are telling me there's a whole new attitude over there now. They don't respect us anymore. They're getting tired of being pushed around. And this stuff that Reckard is coming out with—it could be the last straw."

Susan was referring to an interview with Reckard in the latest *Newsweek*. In it, he had called for across-the-board tariffs on Japanese goods, a total ban on Japanese acquisitions of U.S. companies, and mandated targets for purchases of U.S. products by Japanese consumers. Failure to comply would be met by a freeze on Japanese financial assets. Sharrock knew the proposals in detail because he had helped draft them.

"We froze Iran's assets when they were out of line. We froze the Iraqis' assets. Why shouldn't we freeze Japanese assets now? The Japanese are a much bigger threat to our future than the Arabs ever were."

"That's exactly the point. Iran didn't have the ten biggest banks in the world, and it wasn't holding 200 billion dollars of

U.S. government debt. Come on, this whole thing's a disaster—
you must see that."

She was dead serious now, quite angry in fact. Sharrock liked
that. He liked the way her eyes flashed and her jawline tightened.

He offered to drive her back to her hotel. She turned him
down flat, as he expected. Still, he had put down his marker. With
proper tactics and timing, he would get there in the end. He
always did.

As Bennett steered the stretch through the traffic, Sharrock
thought about what Susan had said. Maybe he ought to liquidate
some of his investments, just as she been advising. After all, he
knew something that she didn't: that the Reckard phenomenon
was only just beginning.

That reminded him. There was a news item he was anxious to
catch. Gluck had promised them it was going to be good. He
switched on the TV that was set into the back of the chauffeur's
seat. After a few minutes of drug busts and serial murders, the
news anchor got around to the special report that Sharrock was
waiting for.

The scene was the street outside a dilapidated factory building.
There was Robert Reckard, standing on a wooden packing crate
addressing a crowd of about two hundred men, some of whom
were waving placards. The camera zeroed in on one which read,
"Just Say No to Jap Job-busters!" then followed with a close-
up of the big rusty padlock that was sealing shut the factory's
main door.

"You men got the shaft," he was saying, "because Washington
failed to protect your interests—American interests—against
unfair trade. Well, I for one figure we've had just about all we can
take. What I'm demanding is American jobs in American companies making American products for American families."

"Right on, Bob."

"Stick it to them, buddy."

Some of the men were cheering, others waved their caps in the
air. They obviously liked what they were hearing.

"We gave them our aid, we helped them build their industries,
we taught them democracy. What did we get in return? They took

our markets, they took our jobs. Now they're trying to buy up the whole darn country. Not a word of gratitude, not even an 'excuse me'! Well, I'm giving due warning: It's no more Mr. Nice Guy."

Reckard's words were drowned in a roar of approval. He stopped and nodded his head, the boyish grin showing surprise at the intensity of the response. Against the crowd of burly, unshaven men in heavy coats and shapeless denims, he looked almost unreally handsome, a being from another planet.

At this point, an assistant rushed forward and set up a trestle table in front of him. On it he placed a radio-cassette player, a stereo, and a couple of video cameras. Next, he brought out a small sledgehammer and handed it to Reckard, who swung it a couple of times to test the weight.

"Let me tell you people," he drawled into the microphone. "This here's an American sledgehammer. I made darn sure of that. And this is what it can do."

Crunch. The radio exploded under the impact, causing some of the men standing nearby to shield their eyes from the flying fragments of plastic.

"One down!" bellowed Reckard. The crowd erupted into a frenzy of cheering.

Crunch. The stereo became a mass of twisted metal and mangled wiring.

"Two down."

Crunch.

"Number three. That one was especially for you good people at this plant. Don't let 'em get you down, folks."

The program cut back to the anchor, who gave a vapid smile before moving on to the next item. Sharrock switched the set off. It had been just as good as Gluck had predicted—a dramatic enhancement of the message they wanted to get across. Doubtless, it would be shown that day on every news program in the country. And Gluck would ensure that the shot of Reckard lifting the sledgehammer, the American sledgehammer, would be kept fresh in people's minds for many months to come.

6
.
.
.

Hot city. The rainy season is nearly over, and days of constant filmy drizzle alternate with painfully blue skies. Today Tokyo trembles in the haze, as if the atoms that compose it are excited by the heat. It is the end of the month, so the millions of men and women who labor in the invisible labyrinth of the Japanese distribution system are out collecting bills and receipts from each other. They sit patiently in their bright new cars and light vans, waiting for the gridlock of traffic to melt for a few seconds and allow them to edge forward to the next red light. Fumes rise from thousands of exhausts, making the world wobble a little bit more.

Hot city. The streets fuller than usual, people moving faster. A second's pause to mop the brow with a handkerchief, or lift a sticky shirt from the shoulders, but no time to break the uniform pace of the crowd as it surges onward like a stream of electrons. Noodle boys on bicycles weave between the cars, steaming trays held high in the air. Hordes of sailor-suited schoolgirls swarm over the station platforms. The great stores are filled with people ordering summer gifts. Clouds of dust blow from construction sites where dingy corner shops and snack bars are being demolished and replaced with "intelligent" office buildings.

Hot city, overflowing with noise. The whir of helicopters overhead. The shopkeepers bellowing "welcome, welcome, welcome." Traffic signals bleeping out "Greensleeves." The tape song of a newspaper collector. Loudspeaker announcements, warnings, advertisements. The thunder of pneumatic drills. The pounding of hammers on metal poles. The manic music blaring from the pachinko parlors. The crash of the silver balls, obliterating everything, like the crash of the sea.

Hot city. On and on it goes, a mighty tangle of baking concrete where thirty-five million human engines live and work and have their being. The concentration of energy, the sheer density of phenomena, overwhelms, exhilarates, saddens. You get seasick walking through a crowd, lose your balance when the lights change. Locked tight, you meet yourself going down on the other escalator.

The city is an amoeba, shapeless, incredibly strong; always growing, always dying. It is memoryless, centerless, boundaryless. It excludes nothing, transforms everything. The city is a god.

Mori first became absolutely sure he was being followed when he was walking across Hibiya Park, on his way to meet Kudo. He'd been watching out for it, so he wasn't especially surprised. He turned around sharply, glancing at his watch, as if he'd just remembered an urgent appointment. About a hundred yards behind, a man in a white T-shirt and jeans melted into a group of tourists. Earlier, the same man had been sitting in a car outside his office, then standing at the other end of the subway platform in Shinjuku. He was tall, easily recognizable. He looked pretty amateurish.

Kudo was standing by the usual bench, smoking a cigarette and watching a gaggle of office girls wandering across the grass. They were chatting and eating ice cream. One of them was laughing loudly, her mouth wide open.

"Good weather," said Mori, slapping him on the shoulder.

"These modern girls," said Kudo. "Look at the way they laugh. No modesty anymore."

He shook his head. Mori handed him the photograph he'd taken from Yumi-chan's managers and pointed to the man in the white raincoat.

"Any ideas on this guy?" he asked.

"Toru Nakamura," said Kudo immediately. "Right-hand man for Terada. Very nasty piece of work."

Kudo's knowledge of the genealogy of the yakuza syndicates was encyclopedic. He even had a wall chart in his office that laid out in full the complex hierarchy of alliance and allegiance. Still, that identification was swift work, even for Kudo. Mori had been expecting him to take the photo back for checking against file material.

Kudo was looking at him keenly.

"What's the interest?" he asked.

"Nothing certain yet," said Mori. "I just need to talk to him about the Hara case. Are you watching him?"

"We're always watching him. He's a killer. There were two hits down in Osaka last week he's rumored to have been involved in."

"What happened?"

"Don't know. Could be the start of a gang war. Could be a grudge. Could be anything."

A new group of office girls drifted past. Kudo took the cigarette out of his mouth in order to grin at them. They ignored him.

Mori pumped Kudo for more information, then took the subway back to Shinjuku. Once or twice, he caught a glimpse of the man in the white T-shirt ducking belatedly out of sight.

He got back to his office in the early afternoon. A couple of students were emerging from the Magic Hole, talking in deliberately loud, jokey voices. On the second floor, the specialist importer was closed for the day again. There was a new poster stuck on the window glass: "Glamour Cream X—Guaranteed to promote paler skin and larger breasts."

Mori poured himself two inches of Suntory Red whiskey and settled down on his thinking couch. The Hara case was disturbing. It was too large, too indistinct. Every piece of information led off in another direction. The more he discovered, it seemed, the less he understood.

His thoughts were disturbed by a scrabbling sound from the corner of the room. Next to the ancient, groaning refrigerator, he had placed a cockroach trap. "Happy Cockroach Motel" read the lettering on the roof of the tiny cardboard building. Inside, two medium-sized roaches were squirming on the adhesive sheet, tearing away their limbs and bellies in order to get a little closer to the sachet of sex essence in the middle.

Mori picked up a sheaf of unopened mail from the table. There was an invitation to a seminar on electronic surveillance from the Association of Research Consultants, a couple of bills, and a hand-written envelope, one of the few he had received recently. Inside was a letter from old Mrs. Hara thanking him for taking the trouble to visit their village. Headed with a formal seasonal greeting, it read as if it had been copied from an old-fashioned style book. Only toward the end did the succession of stiff, standardized phrases break into something simpler and more heartfelt.

"I cannot forget the last telephone call from my son. We know that all this talk of his suicide is a big mistake. Please do your best."

But he couldn't devote all his time to the Hara case. There were so many other things to think about—Mrs. Nishida and the samurai, two more pre-wedding investigations, another runaway teenager.

The phone rang. At first he didn't recognize the excited voice at the other end.

"Mr. Mori," it bubbled urgently. "You must hurry up, or you'll lose your fee."

"Sorry. I didn't catch your name."

"It's me. Ohmae from the Seikyu Hotel. Surely you remember."

"Of course. What's that about my fee?"

"The police have been here again. They've questioned everyone and taken all our records. Hurry up—they'll soon be on the murderer's trail."

Mori thanked him and put down the phone. In a way, it would be a relief if the police did take over the case. It would give him time to concentrate on more profitable business. Still, it was strange that Kudo hadn't said anything. He was usually pretty generous with that kind of information.

Mori called him up, pretending to be angry.

"I understand you people have reopened the Hara case," he said. "Are you trying to put me out of business, or what?"

Kudo laughed.

"Don't blame me," he said. "I haven't heard anything."

"Could you check it out for me? Just see if they've made any more progress."

"I'll see what I can do," said Kudo. "I'm all in favor of preserving endangered species."

Mori thought about that afterward. Perhaps he really was an endangered species. Certainly, his financial position was shaky enough. The rent for the building was due to go up another 15 percent, and the owner would be happy to see him leave. New developments were going up everywhere, handsome marble-fronted office buildings and posh apartments. Where there used to be noodle bars and men in headbands grappling with huge blocks of ice, there were now fitness clubs and shops selling computer software and Swedish furniture.

It's the same thing everywhere, thought Mori. Junior high schools take their yearly trips to places like Hawaii and Bali. Small businessmen buy antiques on live TV hookups with Europe. People are changing; they don't even look the same. Everybody's paler, taller, thinner. Teenage girls have their hair dyed and curled. Students don't look like students anymore—they look like mannequins. Middle-aged ladies who ought to be wrapped up in dark kimono are wearing Italian dresses.

You get rich, and something happens. Reality falls away. Regrettable, perhaps, but good for business. After all, in a world of honest businessmen and happy families, private detectives would have a pretty thin time.

A large roach appeared out of the wainscoting, a sleek slab of gunmetal black with two inches of waving antennae. It scuttled toward the Happy Cockroach Motel, paused at the entrance, and peered in at the severed limbs and twisting bodies.

"Stop, you stupid bastard," muttered Mori. But, after a few moments' scrutiny, the insect scuttled inside. When it found itself stuck fast, it started buzzing frantically, flapping its wings in a vain attempt to pull free.

Mori thought it would do Mrs. Hara good to get out of the lonely apartment with the crack in the wall and the memories of her husband. The meeting place was her idea, a classy coffee bar in Harajuku. She wasn't there when he arrived, and he immediately felt as welcome as a caterpillar at a flower arrangement class.

For a start, he was the only male customer. There were a couple of middle-aged housewives steadying their nerves after a hard day in the boutiques and beauty salons. There was an elegant, remote-looking woman in her mid-thirties, the type that abounds in expensive Tokyo coffee shops, smoking a cigarette and staring into space. Three younger girls, students perhaps, were leafing through glossy fashion magazines. Over in the corner, Nat King Cole was crooning to the rubber plant. Nobody was talking. That would have spoiled the atmosphere.

There were dozens of different types of coffee to choose from, and some mountains of cream, fruit, and trifle. Mori ordered a cup of Kilimanjaro, a Strawberry Soft Paradise, and a packet of Mild Sevens from the robotic waiter.

When Mrs. Hara arrived, Mori didn't recognize her at first. She was wearing slashed culottes in bottle-green corduroy, a billowy print blouse, and high heels. Her hair was flossed out in a coupe sauvage style that made her look ten years younger. She smiled breathlessly and apologized for being late. Mori attempted to reconcile the person sitting in front of him with the tired, red-eyed woman who had talked about her husband in such awestruck tones. It was impossible.

They chatted around the subject for a while, Mori trying to draw her out on her husband's habits and interests. He didn't learn much. Finally, he showed her the photograph.

Mrs. Hara took the photo from him and squinted at it from a range of about six inches. She obviously needed glasses.

"When was this taken?" she asked.

"Some time ago," said Mori evasively. "Did your husband know that man?"

"Why, of course," she said, and looked at Mori curiously. "He's my younger brother."

"Your brother!" said Mori, astonished. "What, this man standing here?"

He pointed at the figure in the white raincoat.

"No, not him," said Mrs. Hara. "The other one, the man standing on the left."

It was the round-faced business man holding the brief-case. Mori peered at the face. Indeed, there was a slight family resemblance.

"What does your brother do?" asked Mori.

"He works for Nippon Infosystems," said Mrs. Hara with a certain measure of pride. "He's chief of the president's office. He reports directly to Iwanaga-sensei. You have heard of Iwanaga-sensei, haven't you?"

"Of course," said Mori. "Everyone's heard of Iwanaga-sensei."

It was too much of a coincidence. Mori asked a few casual questions about her brother, trying not to arouse her suspicions, then went back to the office. When he arrived, there was a message waiting for him on the answering machine. It was Kudo.

"You don't need to worry," he said. "The Hara case hasn't been reopened. You'll survive for a little while yet."

That gave Mori a bad feeling, a sort of prickling on the back of the neck.

Of course Mori had heard of Iwanaga-sensei. You couldn't really avoid hearing about him these days. There were articles about him in the press and features about him on TV almost every day. Suddenly, the man was big news, and he obviously loved the attention.

As Mori remembered the story, Iwanaga had started Nippon Infosystems when he was still a student at Tokyo University. Originally it was a small company publishing magazines that specialized in job advertisements. It had grown slowly at first, then faster as the job market grew more active. Iwanaga was, by all accounts, a brilliant businessman. He diversified boldly into real estate, finance, software, and other areas that now dwarfed the original publishing business. Nippon Infosystems had become one of the fastest-growing companies in Japan. Its distinctive black offices could be seen in cities all over the country, and it owned a casino in Las Vegas, two hotels in Manhattan, a golf course in Scotland, and a chateau in the Loire valley.

The personality of the founder was just as remarkable as the growth of the company. Tall and thin, with no epicanthic fold over his deep-set eyes, he didn't even look Japanese. Occasionally, he would turn up for interviews or business meetings in a lemon-and-rust-colored kimono, sporting a large ruby on his left hand. While still a student at Tokyo University, he had published a book of haiku which had created a sensation, outraging purists with its tough, nihilistic style. He practiced Zen meditation. He rose at five every morning to practice karate. He drove a 750 cc. motorbike and piloted his own helicopter. He spent ninety million dollars on a blue-period Picasso. He dropped five million in a single weekend in Las Vegas. He produced and directed movies and slept with the starlets.

That was Iwanaga—impossible to ignore. The media called him "the neo-Japanese," because he was as far from the traditional, self-effacing Japanese businessman as it was possible to get. One other thing about him that Mori remembered was the nationalistic fervor of his views on the world economy. In magazine articles and speeches, he had been calling for the formation of a yen-based economic bloc in Asia. That was something that chimed with Hara's work in the Ministry of Finance. It deserved further investigation.

The man Mori decided to check with was an occasional drinking companion and information source called Taniguchi. Taniguchi was a free-lance journalist who wrote for the weekly scandal rags. He had once been a star reporter for the *Gendai Shimbun*, the largest-selling daily paper in the world. Then he had made the mistake of writing a story about the financial dealings of a certain powerful politician. The facts had been long known to every member of the press corps assigned to the politician's faction, but no one, except Taniguchi, had the urge to put them into print.

What happened next was predictable. The story was killed, Taniguchi was expelled from the press club by his fellow journalists and then fired from his job. The man who had once been whisked to international summits in limousines marked with the *Gendai* flag was now reduced to grubbing around the weekly magazines for a living.

But he had the talent for it. Taniguchi was adaptable, if nothing else. He switched effortlessly from reviews of "fashion massage" parlors to in-depth accounts of boardroom coup d'états. When a jumbo jet crashed in a remote part of central Japan, killing two hundred people, Taniguchi was on the mountainside even before the rescue services got there. In the cold foggy dawn, he scrambled miles through dense undergrowth. The photos he took were printed in glorious color in *Thursday* magazine. Mangled bodies, severed limbs, a lone hand spiked on a tree-branch—it was a sensational scoop.

Mori found him in the tiny apartment in Ikebukuro that also served as his office. His wife had left him when he lost his job, and the place made Mori's living conditions look luxurious. The table was a heap of beer cans and cigarette stubs, many of them smeared with lipstick. The floor was almost covered with pages of a manuscript he was writing about a scandal at a major trading house. Taniguchi was not the kind of man to use a word processor.

"They'll never live this down," he grinned, waving at the paper. "They offered me ten million to shut up. You should have seen their faces when I refused. They couldn't believe it!"

Taniguchi was never happier than when he was getting even with corporate Japan. Offering money had been a mistake. It would only convince him that they were running scared and encourage him to hit harder.

He offered Mori a glass of whiskey, put on a recording of Mahler's Fifth, and they settled down to talk.

"Nippon Infosystems," said Mori. "The president of the company's in the news a lot these days. Is there anything special there?"

Taniguchi nodded slowly.

"Iwanaga? He's a dangerous man. A friend of mine was doing a story about him, checking into his background and family and so on. One night he was walking home late after a few drinks when a motorcycle gang caught up with him. The neighbors heard him yelling and tried to call for help, but the telephone wires had been cut. His body was found under a bridge ten miles away, hardly any skin left on the stomach and legs. They dragged him there, you see."

Mori let out his breath in a short whistle.

"Could have been a coincidence," he said.

"That's what I thought at first. Then I did a little investigating myself. Another gang of bikers told me that a couple of yakuza had been offering money for the job. Apparently, my friend was only supposed to be frightened off, but they got carried away with the fun of it all."

"And you think Iwanaga set it up?"

"No proof, of course, but the man has a furious temper, and he's completely ruthless. What's more, he's highly sensitive about his background." Taniguchi looked at Mori meaningfully.

"What, you think he's from a minority group?"

It would not be the first time that a prominent Japanese had tried to hide his origins. Korean blood or membership of the outcast groups was still something that it would be better to keep quiet.

"Probably," said Taniguchi. "One thing's for sure—he's not who he says he is. My friend searched for him in the school and district records. Most of them were destroyed in the war, and some of the rest looked like they'd been tampered with. No one remembered him at all—not the teachers, not his classmates, not the people in the neighborhood."

Taniguchi drained his whiskey glass. The majestic sounds of Mahler's Fifth were swelling from the loudspeakers. Mori glanced at the record sleeve which Taniguchi had tossed onto the floor. It was a recording made by the Gendai Philharmonic, the orchestra maintained by his old employers.

"What about the name—Iwanaga?" asked Mori.

"There was an old couple called Iwanaga who ran an umbrella shop next to the junior high school he claims to have attended. Their son attended it for a couple of years."

"Well, couldn't that be him?"

"The boy was hardly Tokyo University material. He left school at the age of ten to help them make the umbrellas. The next year, the whole family was killed in a firebomb raid."

"Strange."

"Everything else about Iwanaga is strange too. A brilliant student, but no real friends at college. A top businessman, but he claims to hate politicians and bureaucrats. Where did the money come from to build up the company? Not from the banks, that's for sure."

"What do you think?"

"I don't know. Maybe someone else is behind him—a politician, or maybe one of the new religious groups. Anyway, I can tell you one thing. Iwanaga's a man it's wise not to cross. I don't know what you're working on, and I don't even want to know."

Suddenly, Taniguchi looked very serious. Mori was surprised.

"You're not scared of this guy, are you Tani-san? After all, he's just another businessman."

"That's what he's not. Businessmen play the game by the rules—their rules, maybe, but rules all the same. Iwanaga is different. He doesn't recognize any rules at all. Be careful, please."

"I'm always careful," said Mori.

As he said it, he felt the prickling at the back of his neck again.

On the way back to the office, he dropped off at the Seikyu Hotel. The lobby was full of elderly foreign tourists and their luggage. Ohmae was looking harassed as he tried to explain himself in English.

"Where's the goddamn bus?" said a man who looked like an ox with a hat on.

Another, a fat man with huge sweat stains on the sides of his T-shirt, was jabbing his forefinger accusingly at Ohmae's chest.

"Yeah. We don't want to wait any longer, pal."

"I think bus soon coming," mumbled Ohmae unhappily. "Bus no problem, I think. . . ."

"Bus big problem," roared the first guy. "Bus must take us shopping before shops shut. . . ." "No, no, this not shopping bus. This night-tour bus. . . ."

Ohmae looked immensely relieved when Mori beckoned him over to the other side of the lobby. Almost at once, a coach pulled up in the forecourt and the foreigners started piling aboard.

"Tell me what you told me on the phone again," said Mori.

There was no mistake. Ohmae was absolutely sure. Two men with police identification had questioned the manager and the desk clerk and taken away the records. They had been polite, efficient, and utterly professional.

"I told them you were already on the murderer's trail," said Ohmae. "They were pretty impressed."

"You said what?" said Mori, incredulously.

"I thought it was only fair," said Ohmae. "Did I do something wrong?"

Mori didn't bother to answer.

Outside, it was already dark. The heat of the city was fading, and a light breeze caressed his cheek. The stars were as sharp as pinholes. Mori decided to walk the couple of miles over to Roppongi, where Lisa was appearing in a small nightclub. He would be able to catch her before the first set.

Roppongi is a video of the future. A place of giant crowds, blurred faces streaming past; of vertical villages of discos and restaurants; of liquid crystal smiles and android eroticism and high definition drunkenness. A place where synthetic Beatles play note-for-note copies of the original hits, where silent couples pose in bar windows, where expressionless disco dancers gyrate in front of mirrors. A digital floating world, where for the few hours before the last train, you can free yourself from yourself.

Lisa was in good voice. She sang some standards and some bluesy ballads she had written herself. Once or twice, she darted a feline glance at Mori as she sang. Could those half-angry, half-regretful lyrics be about him? It was a nice thought. They were sharing a secret in front of sixty strangers.

The audience were mostly women in their early twenties, the kind who do whatever the weekly magazines tell them. They didn't seem to be enjoying themselves much. There had been a brief boom in Lisa's type of music, fueled by TV commercials, but it was now fading away. The young office girls sensed they were doing something that was no longer trendy, and they were vaguely ashamed.

Lisa came to sit with him at the end of the set, and they drank half a bottle of whiskey together. She said she would try to get over to his apartment when she was finished, but Mori didn't really believe her. She only came when something was wrong, and right now she seemed in good spirits.

Afterward, on his way to the subway station, Mori saw something unusual. A middle-aged salaryman in a blue polyester suit was standing in front of a fashionably dressed young couple, shouting abuse. It seemed that the girl had stepped on his foot with her high-heeled shoe.

"Look where you're going," he bellowed. "You ought to be ashamed. Apologize, you little fool."

"Calm down," said the young man. "She said she was sorry."

He tried to get away, but the salaryman was tugging at his jacket. People rushed past, pretending not to notice. The salaryman's voice grew gradually louder and higher, until he finally slipped over the edge of hysteria.

"I hate you! You look down at me—I can see it in your eyes. You're laughing at me, always laughing. It's unbearable. I'm a human being. I'm just as important as you. I have rights!"

He was waving his arms about now, breathing in large shudders. His face was bright red, his mouth a huge hole. Some people stopped to watch, but kept their distance. The girl was pale with shock. The young man finally managed to break free, and hustled her toward a subway entrance. The man continued to scream as they hurried down the steps.

"If I see you again, I'll kill you, you impudent bastards! You're not real Japanese!"

Having delivered the most grievous insult he could muster, the man was suddenly calmer. The fit was leaving him, and he looked around sheepishly at the crowd.

"These young people," he grumbled beneath his breath, then slunk off down the street.

Mori took the subway, then the railway back to Shinjuku. At the other end, he stopped to buy a newspaper at a kiosk and glimpsed the man in the white T-shirt again. In fact, it was difficult to miss him. He was coming up the escalator, a full head taller than the people around him.

Mori took a slightly different route to his office from usual. He went down a narrow winding lane lined with tiny eateries belching out steam of yakitori, chinese noodles, roast fish. There were also a couple of pink salons, a pachinko parlor, and a public bathhouse at the end. Several elderly men carrying towels were ambling toward it, their wooden sandals clip-clopping down the pavement.

At a bend in the road, conveniently set back from the rest of the buildings, was a small love hotel called "Buckingham Palace." It was a cheap place, just 2,000 yen per hour, used mainly by students and married couples from the cramped public housing projects. The building was a squat reinforced-concrete block, with a frontage in the style of a medieval castle, complete with pasteboard battlements and fronds of plastic ivy. Every so often, the proprietors would refurbish it completely. Just six months before, it had been called "The Taj Mahal," and had had a pasteboard facade to match. Before that, if Mori remembered correctly, it had been "Moonbase 2000."

Most guests drove into the underground parking lot at the back and took the elevator straight to the rooms, but there was a small, discreet street entrance dimly lit with a pink lamp. Mori ducked inside and waited.

It didn't take long for the man in the white T-shirt to appear. He was walking fast, looking nervously from side to side. He didn't see Mori standing in the shadows of the love hotel entrance, nor did he hear him coming from behind.

Mori grabbed him round the neck in a choke hold, then slammed his knee into the back of the man's right thigh, knocking his legs from under him, and hauled him into the alley beside the entrance.

The man was struggling, making gasping noises and clawing at Mori's forearm. Mori turned him round, and jammed his knee into the man's groin. He collapsed onto the ground, doubled up and wheezing with pain.

Mori seized him by the elbow and hauled him into the lobby of the hotel. It was completely empty, except for two life-size, natural-color dummies of Prince Charles and Princess Diana. They were smiling and waving benignly at whoever came in through the door. Set into the wall next to the entrance was an automatic vending machine, above it a list of charges for different classes of room.

An optical sensor picked up Mori's presence and an electronic female voice issued from a small loudspeaker set in the vending machine.

"Welcome, dear guest," said the electronic voice. "We offer you our heartfelt gratitude for patronizing our humble hotel. May we remind you that this month there is a twenty percent discount on the Royal Suite for all stays of two hours and above."

Mori glanced at the list of room charges. The Royal Suite cost nine thousand yen per hour. He fed two one-thousand-yen notes into the machine's maw and pressed the appropriate buttons for "Ordinary Room—One Hour."

The strip of plastic that acted as a key appeared at the bottom.

"Thank you very much," said the electronic voice. "We earnestly hope that you will let us offer our hospitality again in the near future."

Mori picked up the key and marched the man into the elevator. His face was white, and he was grimacing with the pain. He looked young, no more than twenty-five.

The room Mori had been assigned was windowless, with a large plastic throne in the center and a mirror-plated ceiling. On the shelf above the bed was a video camera, a pair of handcuffs, and two papier-mâché crowns. Mori shoved the man onto the double bed.

"You need more practice," he said laconically. "You couldn't even tail my grandmother."

The young man had recovered his color a little. He sat on the bed gazing sulkily upward. Mori grabbed him by the face.

"Come on," he growled. "You're going to tell me what's going on."

"Leave me alone," squawked the man. "I'm Kazuo Kawada of the Kawada syndicate. Our syndicate leader has sworn a vendetta against you."

Mori remembered the little man who had limped out of his apartment that night with blood pouring from his nose.

"You mean your father, I suppose," he said.

"That's right. You insulted him. You made light of the syndicate's honor. Nobody does that and escapes punishment."

The young man glared fiercely at Mori.

"And who's going to punish me? You and your uncle?"

"We will have revenge! You can be sure of that."

He was practically spitting with rage. Mori wrenched his head backward.

"Listen, you young fool," he hissed. "You're in the wrong business. Go out and get a regular job. Do something that you may have a talent for, like delivering pizza or cleaning windows. And, whatever you do, just stay out of my way."

But it was no good. Kawada continued to burble on about revenge and honor and punishment. In the end, Mori handcuffed him to the bedstand and left him there.

Down in the lobby, Charles and Diana were welcoming two new guests, a young businessman carrying a briefcase and a girl with a Louis Vuitton handbag and a Hermès scarf around her waist.

"Welcome, dear guest," said the electronic voice. "We offer you our heartfelt gratitude for patronizing our humble hotel. May we remind you that this month there is a twenty percent discount on the Royal Suite for all stays of two hours and above."

"The Royal Suite!" breathed the girl excitedly. "How romantic! Go on, let's take it."

Mori hurried past them, his gaze fixed on his shoes. Leaving a love hotel was always a slightly uncomfortable experience. Leaving on your own was pure embarrassment.

7

S OMETHING was going on at the top of Maruichi Securities, that much was clear. Josen Suzuki, the man who had built up the New York branch into one of the most successful investment banks in the United States, had suddenly been recalled to Japan. He was now deputy chief of domestic sales, a job which required him to rule the sales force with a fist of iron. A dapper little man with a taste for fine wines and Italian suits, he sat all day long in his glass-sided office, staring wearily at computer printouts.

No two Maruichi men could have been less alike in personality than Suzuki and the man he had to report to every day. Rei Takeda had never been out of Japan in his life, a fact of which he was hugely proud. He wore a crumpled blue suit, bellowed out orders in a hoarse Osaka accent, and had a mountain of Mild Seven butts in his ashtray by ten o'clock every morning. His temper was ferocious. Once he had forced a young salesman who had failed to reach his monthly quota to crawl around the dealing room ten times on his hands and knees.

Kenji Okada well remembered Takeda's performance during the crash of 1987. At the end of the morning session only one-tenth of all the stocks on the Tokyo Stock Exchange had traded. For the rest, there were plenty of sellers, but no buyers at all. In the dealing room, the usual hubbub had been replaced by a deathly quiet, and salesmen, dealers, and analysts stood around with stunned expressions on their faces. The mood was near suicidal when Takeda's face appeared on the huge screen at the end of the room. The words he uttered were relayed live to every one of Maruichi's 130 branch offices.

"You will remember every detail of this day," he had barked. "You will tell your children and grandchildren that you were here at a turning point in history, the day in which Japan's strength was revealed. The Americans are greedy and selfish. Their sickness is spreading through the financial system, but we are healthy and we will not let it infect us.

"Every salesman will call up his best clients, his friends, and family members and appeal to them as fellow Japanese to buy as many stocks as they can. Forget about the banks and insurance companies—they are cowards, and always have been. Ordinary Japanese have faith in Japan, and they will not fail us."

Nor did they. When people heard that Maruichi had decided that the market should be supported, they rushed to their local brokerage offices, in some cases forming lines in the street outside. Every other market in the world was shuddering with visions of 1929, and shares were being dumped like rotten fruit. In Tokyo, the mood was close to a buying panic. And, just as Takeda had predicted, the faith of the buyers was rewarded with a famous victory. Within six months, the market had risen 25 percent, Japan was the world's dominant financial power, and Maruichi Securities was acknowledged as the rock on which the winds of chaos had beaten themselves out.

Much had happened since that momentous day. The nightmare was forgotten, and the markets had moved on. Maruichi had developed a web of financial interests that stretched throughout the world. It had bought merchant banks in Europe, commodities dealers in Chicago, money managers and brokers all over Asia. Takeda had been promoted to the main board, and was spoken of as a future president. His influence was felt everywhere, even in the overseas subsidiaries. Everyone was scared of him, even the other directors.

The study program to send promising young staff members to U.S. business schools was terminated. According to Takeda, the only thing worth knowing about U.S. business practices was how to do the exact opposite. A special shrine to Ichiro Maruoka was built in his Niigata birthplace, and all members of the staff were "encouraged" to make a pilgrimage there once a year. A book of Maruoka's thoughts—on such diverse topics as filial piety, the meaning of culture, and the importance of market share—was distributed to all new graduates, who were then made to shout out quotations from it at morning meetings. Now Josen Suzuki had been recalled to the head office, and one of Takeda's acolytes sent to replace him. Sitting in the glass box like a captured enemy warrior, Suzuki was living proof of the domestic faction's ascendancy.

It was ten o' clock in the morning, and Kenji was sitting at his workstation feeling pleased with himself. Two days ago, he had bought the stock he had found in the secret account for his six largest clients. It was already up 15 percent, and he could tell it was going much further. It was predestined.

Kenji's friend Tanaka was leaning over the workstation, explaining the contents of a book on face-reading he had just bought.

"A bright spot between the eyes," he informed Kenji. "That means she lubricates a lot—like that girl on the reception desk. Large nostrils, they indicate tremendous sexual appetite." Kenji had half his attention on Tanaka and the other half on his stock price screen, so he didn't notice Rei Takeda padding up behind him. He jumped when the Osaka accent resounded in his ear.

"Okada! I must speak to you urgently."

Takeda's voice was even harsher than usual. There wasn't even the hint of a smile. Kenji followed him into one of the meeting rooms. He was surprised to find a group of three men waiting for them. Two of them he hadn't seen before. The other was Sugaya, Maruichi's youngest ever director and a legend within the firm for his ruthlessly aggressive tactics. He was staring at Kenji intently, as if he were a criminal in the witness box.

"So you're Okada," he said quietly. "Sit down and explain yourself."

Kenji made a half bow, then sat down opposite the two men.

"I'm sorry," he muttered. "I don't quite understand."

Sugaya tossed a computer printout onto the table in front of him.

"Perhaps this will help you," he said sarcastically. "It's your dealing record for the past few days. Quite clearly, someone has been feeding you highly sensitive information. I want you to tell us who."

Kenji could feel Sugaya's eyes training on him like a pair of gun barrels. He dared not look up to meet them. Should he admit everything? No, breaking into a confidential computer file—that was a serious offense. It would be better to bluff it out.

"There must be some mistake. I heard about that stock from one of my clients."

"Which client?" said Takeda sharply. Come on, tell us his name."

"I don't remember exactly. . . . It could have been any one of them."

"Liar," roared Takeda. "Tell me immediately, or your career at Maruichi is over. I'll have your salary halved. I'll have you cleaning toilets for the next twelve months."

Kenji looked up. Takeda's bullying tone had hit him like a slap in the face. Suddenly, he was more angry than scared.

"What's the problem?" he said tightly. "Is this stock forbidden to ordinary people, or what?"

There was a moment of silence punctuated by Takeda cracking his knuckles. Sugaya sat there chewing his lip.

"How old are you, Okada?" he asked finally.

"Twenty-eight."

"Are your parents still in good health?"

"Yes, they are."

"They would be upset if anything happened to you wouldn't they?"

Kenji nodded.

"Show some filial piety," said Sugaya quietly. "Make sure your parents are not upset."

Takeda got up and walked over behind Kenji's chair. Suddenly,

Kenji felt a stinging blow on the side of his head. The force of it
knocked him sideways onto the floor.

"We're watching you, Okada," he barked. "We're watching
you every minute of the day. And we'll find out what we need to
know, don't you worry."

By the time Kenji had cleared his ringing head and staggered to
his feet, he was alone in the room.

Back at his place in the dealing room, the more Kenji thought
about the incident, the stranger it seemed. Everybody knew that
the top men at Maruichi manipulated stocks in order to reward
important political and business contacts. That was an accepted
part of a securities company's role in the world. So why were
Takeda and Sugaya so angry? It seemed out of all proportion.
There was obviously something more, something they were
anxious to conceal.

Kenji invited Noriko for lunch in the revolving sushi bar. Her
nostrils, he noticed, were huge, almost like a second pair of eyes.
What would Tanaka's face-reading make of that? She ate with
gusto—tuna, herring, squid, scallop, sweet prawn, salmon eggs—
making a little tower on the counter with the empty dishes. At
first, Noriko did most of the talking. She was, Kenji realized,
highly knowledgeable about the stock market. And when she
laughed, she was quite pretty. After a while, he shifted the conversation to the computer system and its capabilities. Finally, he
got the information that he needed.

Back at his workstation, Kenji tracked through all the stocks in
the secret account. He checked the price movements, the changes
in volume, the share of trading of each of the Big Five brokers.
Then, using the command that Noriko had told him about, he
flashed up all the Maruichi accounts which had dealt in the stocks
for the past three months.

In each case, there were fifty accounts which were buying the
stock, all in roughly the same quantity. And it was the same fifty
every time. So the huge flow of cash which had gone through the
section leader's account had to be multiplied by fifty. Near the
peak in the stock prices, the accounts had sold out, and the only

buyer had been Maruichi's own investment trust. In other words, the general public, by buying units in the Maruichi investment trust, was transferring a mountain of cash to the secret accounts.

No wonder Sugaya and the others had been so excited. Over the course of a year or so, the cash generated by these accounts could run into billions of yen, perhaps even trillions! What was it for? Who was at the other end of it? Kenji fingered the bruise on the back of his head. Those were questions that he wasn't prepared to forget about.

It was the middle of the afternoon when Seiji Terada's Ferrari sped up the winding road that led to the sensei's mountain retreat. As he turned into the drive, he caught a glimpse of Mount Fuji in the distance, rising above the other peaks like an adult among children. Just as in the Hiroshige prints, it looked out of proportion, too massive to be real.

Two shaven-headed young men in black kimono and bare feet opened the wrought-iron security gate. They were members of the elite group of warrior monks who served as the sensei's guards. Steeped since childhood in *senjitsu*, a martial art too dangerous to be disseminated outside a small group of mountain temples, they could take on a small army with just their fists, feet, and staves. In fact, in the seventeenth century their main temple had done just that.

The monks gave low bows of welcome, then led Terada through a side door into a walled garden heavy with the scent of flowers. A couple of red dragonflies were dogfighting over the shimmering surface of a small pool. Immediately in front of him, in the partial shade of a wisteria trellis, a woman wearing just the bottom half of a black bikini lay on her stomach reading a book. Her body was wet, and the dark cleft of her buttocks was clearly visible through the sheer material. When she glanced up at him, Terada recognized her instantly, despite the frizzed-out hair and the mirror shades. It was Sayori Soh, the female lead in a samurai movie that the sensei had recently produced. Long-legged, with a natural pout and frown, she looked a good deal older than her eighteen years.

At a word from one of the monks, she stood up, not bothering to cover her breasts, and left by the same door through which Terada had entered.

The sensei was soaking in the hot spring bath at the end of the garden, submerged to the navel in the steaming water.

"Come on in, Terada," he called out. "Your skin could do with some toning up."

Terada stripped off all his clothes, carefully hanging his lightweight Armani suit on the back of a chair. Then he lowered himself into the water. Try as he might, he couldn't avoid flinching. The water was scaldingly hot. He ignored the frantic instruction from the nerves of his lower body to jump out immediately. It must be at least seventy degrees centigrade in there. His heart was banging like a drum, and the flesh of his thighs and calves was turning lobster-puce.

The sensei sat back, as relaxed as if he were in a child's swimming pool. He was some twenty years older than Terada, but he had the body of a college athlete. Taut biceps, bulging pectorals—there wasn't an ounce of fat on the man. Terada couldn't help glancing down at the dark organ that was floating like a dreadnought just below the surface. It was impressively large and threatening, a true weapon of willpower.

"What's all this middle-aged spread!" said the sensei, slapping Terada on the belly. "A man of your age! You should try what I do every spring."

"What's that?" asked Terada politely.

"The five days of rigor at Koan-ji Temple. It'd make a new man of you."

Terada winced at the thought. He had once seen a television program about the five days of rigor at Koan-ji, an ascetic ritual designed for trainee monks. As he remembered it, the participants were allowed just two meals a day of yam gruel and berries that they had to collect themselves. They rose at five every morning to meditate under a freezing waterfall, then ran naked through the mountain paths for the best part of the day, chanting sutras. Some of them charged through dense thickets, so that their thighs and buttocks were laced with blood. In the nights, they were awakened once every hour by a thump in the stomach from the priest's staff, for which they had to express instant gratitude. It wasn't Terada's idea of a health resort at all.

"It is good to enjoy food," continued the sensei. "But we must never let ourselves be ruled by pleasure. That has been the fate of the Westerners, with their drugs and their wealth. Learn to kill your appetites, then you will cherish them more."

That was typical of the man. The project was now reaching the critical phase. A complex series of events was unfolding which would have to be controlled with the utmost precision, yet the sensei seeemed totally relaxed, more interested in philosophical discussion than in the momentous task ahead.

They soaked for a further fifteen minutes, by the end of which Terada had lost all sensation in his toes and hands. The sensei spoke of history and art and world politics. Terada considered himself a well-informed man, but he was once again astonished by the sensei's range of knowledge—from Lao-tzu to modern jazz, from astrology to catastrophe theory. His mind was encyclopedic.

Afterward, in the operations room in the villa's basement, the sensei was a different man—sharp and utterly business-like. He sat at the head of the table and interrogated Terada closely on the details of the project. Nothing escaped his attention.

When he was satisfied that his requirements had been met, he handed Terada a sheet of paper containing the next set of instructions.

"The preparation phase is complete," he said. "Everything is in place. Now we are moving forward to escalation and destabilization."

As the sensei sketched out how events would proceed to the great climax, Terada once more marveled at the elegance and power of the strategy. The sensei was a master of the game of Go—good enough in his youth, it was said, to have become a professional player. Now, the world was his board. Sometimes he would move a piece seemingly at random. Not till several moves later would the meaning of the move become obvious. Then Terada would wonder how he had failed to appreciate it from the start.

For several years, the sensei had been moving his disciples into position—in the political and business world, in the media, in the bureaucracy. People who he trusted, people who thought like him. The numbers were few, but their influence was growing all the time. Some were brought right into the heart of the organization and acquainted with the grand strategy. Some were informed only of the bare minimum, and had faith that whatever they would be asked to do was in the best interests of Japan. It was a loose but intricate structure—an invisible web of power that responded to every tweak of the sensei's hand.

As the sensei had explained many times, it would be useless to attempt to transform Japan merely by appealing to the people's sense of tradition and pride. That was a mistake that had been made by Yukio Mishima, an old drinking companion of the sensei's. Historically, the great revolutions in Japanese consciousness had taken place in times of crisis, and the catalyst had always been pressure from abroad. This time would be no different. There would be no need to appeal to the Japanese to rediscover their pride as a nation. It would be a natural response, in fact the only response possible, to the international situation.

"This will be a second Meiji Revolution," said the sensei, banging his fist on the table. "You and I, Terada, we are the Saigo Takamori and Sakamoto Ryoma of our generation. Like them, we are hatching our plots for the good of Japan and the honor of our ancestors. The disinterested eye of history will look on us as heroes!"

Terada gave a short bow. As ever, he felt proud to share the sensei's innermost thoughts and feelings. Surely he didn't speak like this to any of the others. They were almost equal partners.

Back in his university days, Terada had reveled in the intellectual atmosphere on campus, the late-night discussions about Dostoyevski and Sartre and sexual liberation, the debating club, the surrealist plays in tiny cellars. Returning to the family profession had come as a huge shock, especially since he had had to start at the bottom, selling speed to truck drivers, beating up pimps, and so on. Even now, at the stage of his life when he owned an outstanding art collection and visited the opera in

Milan twice a year, he still missed the intellectual companionship of his youth. Only when he was talking with the sensei did he feel his mind stimulated once more by the presence of great and noble ideas.

"Of course," the sensei continued. "The heroes of Meiji were successful because they understood how to harness technological developments to their purposes—'Western knowledge with Japanese spirit,' as it was later termed. They used warships, cannon, modern military tactics, whatever they could lay their hands on. In our own way, we are doing the same. We are using the most powerful weapon that the modern world has to offer."

Terada thought about that for a moment. The sensei seemed to be expecting a prompt, so he gave it.

"What weapon do you mean?" he asked.

"Money," said the sensei, rapping his knuckles on the table.

Iwanaga watched from the window of his study as the red Ferrari disappeared from sight. He shook his head and smiled. These yakuza—at least they were sincere, and sincerity was a quality that Iwanaga valued greatly. In fact, he trusted Terada more than he trusted any of the others. But the way the man talked, the way he thought—so utterly lacking in refinement.

Next he would have to deal with the politicians—refined men who couldn't be trusted at all. But before that he needed a little relaxation.

Sayori was waiting for him in the garden. She had changed into a strapless white dress, the same one that she had worn in the last scene of the movie. She turned around to allow him to undo the zipper, then shimmied out of it.

One of the monks brought a rug out of the house and unrolled it beneath the wisteria trellis. Iwanaga drew her down with him, then lay back motionless, gazing at the sky. She worked on him slowly, thoroughly, just as he had taught her.

The young monk stood by the gate, watching impassively. The red dragonflies wove patterns in the air above the pool. Out of the corner of his eye, Iwanaga glimpsed the peak of Mount Fuji, rising above the clouds.

Land-san happened to bump into Votes-san at the Nagoya sumo tournament. He was a couple of rows in front, sprawled out in a special box with a Russian trade official and a female translator. As the two wrestlers hunkered down for the last time, he could hear Votes-san's distinctive voice bellowing out the name of his favorite, a newly promoted champion with the bulk of a young elephant and the face of a baby.

Land-san examined the fellow through his opera glasses. The very biggest wrestlers, it was said, were unable to reach round and wipe themselves in the toilet. They had to rely on the young apprentices who served their elders' needs while training. Looking at the scale of the man, Land-san could well believe the story. He had breasts like sacks of cement, and large folds of flesh hung off his buttocks and thighs. He looked all of his almost 400 pounds. By contrast, the other wrestler was a slender veteran with barely enough hair to tie into the regulation top-knot. He squatted there frowning with concentration as he waited for the moment to come.

The cheering reached a crescendo. The umpire's fan dropped. The bellies met with a crack that resounded throughout the stadium. There was a blur of movement—a dozen slaps to face and chest—the frantic chanting of the umpire—arms grappling for belt holds—feet thumping into the sand—the roar of the crowd echoing off the ceiling—and then suddenly it was all over. The young champion was rolling on his back, felled by a simple leg throw. He had failed to control his momentum, and his cunning opponent had used it against him.

As the hubbub subsided, Land-san went down to greet his old acquaintance. The translator was busily explaining the rules to the Russian visitor, who was nodding jovially and swilling vodka out of a Japanese teacup. Votes-san was looking on with disappointment as the champion's huge rump wobbled off into the changing rooms.

"Not enough power yet," he muttered, after formal greetings had been exchanged. "Wait until he gets his weight up to 450 pounds. He'll be unbeatable!"

Land-san nodded encouragingly. The young champion was the pride of Votes-san's electoral district. "It's a pity about the Minakawa Cabinet," he said. "He was so good with the Americans."

The sudden outbreak of factional infighting which had brought down the cabinet had been an embarrassment. Much had been invested in Minakawa.

"Always too much of a rationalist," said Votes-san, shaking his head impatiently. "He boasts about discussing economic theories with foreigners like Kissinger and Schmidt, but he understands nothing of his own people, absolutely nothing! His arrogance had become insufferable!"

Land-san glanced across at the big blond Russian. He had his arm around the translator, and was trying to teach her a Russian drinking song.

"There'll be a leadership contest, I suppose," he said softly. "Who's got the most support in the party?"

"The situation is very fluid," said Votes-san hesitantly. "The mainstream factions are completely deadlocked, so they may not put up anyone this time. That would leave room for a compromise candidate from the anti-mainstream, maybe someone like Ishizaka."

Land-san blinked with surprise. Ishizaka was a minor figure in a minor faction, a man who had gotten himself in trouble with tactless comments on subjects ranging from the colonization of Korea to American ethnic minorities.

"Ishizaka! Surely not."

"We all feel the same. The man is a complete buffoon. Unfortunately, he is extremely well backed at the moment. He's been doling out cash to all the youngsters, regardless of faction. Why, even the freshmen in my own faction got ten million yen each as a summer gift."

Votes-san didn't sound as confident as usual. He was wondering how the coming of the Ishizaka administration would affect his own position. Ishizaka was still in his mid-fifties. If he started promoting men of his own age group, the factional hierarchies would crumble. The older generation, men such as himself who had waited patiently for decades, gradually working their way to the top, might suddenly be cast aside. For all the talk about loyalty and tradition, Votes-san knew that ultimately it was economics that held the factions together.

"Don't worry," he said without much conviction. "Ishizaka won't last long. The first stupid remark he makes, we'll kick him downstairs."

The next two wrestlers had started limbering up, tossing handfuls of salt into the air and smacking their bellies like drums. The excitement of the crowd was building toward another climax. Land-san walked back to his own box. It was a bout he had been looking forward to all afternoon, the most senior of the grand champions against a young bull of a man from Hokkaido. Land-san wouldn't be satisfied unless the young bull was sent crashing into the front row. After all, the proper order of things had to be respected.

Land-san didn't get home until nearly midnight. It took two hours to get back to Tokyo in the bullet train, then he spent the rest of the evening with the bureaucrat responsible for drafting the new bill on property taxes. They went to the exclusive Ginza nightclub that Land-san had bought for his *ni-go-san*, the "number-two wife" whom he had been sponsoring for almost twenty years now. Their relationship had lost its sexual aspect a dozen years before—these days Land-san found it difficult to muster passion for any woman over the age of twenty-five—but he still enjoyed relaxing in her presence. Furthermore, her wit and cool elegance had their uses. That dull fellow from the Tax Bureau had been totally mesmerized.

Land-san left him there, red-faced and grinning stupidly, surrounded by young hostesses. They laughed delightedly at his clumsy jokes, squeezed his sweaty hands, and stroked his knees, and the stupid grin got wider and wider. The *ni-go-san* would arrange for one of the girls to entertain him properly at a hotel afterward, if he weren't too drunk.

The black Toyota Crown swished up the gravel driveway that

led to Land-san's house. After dismissing his chauffeur, he stood for a moment breathing in the cool night air and surveying the thing that he valued more than anything else in his life—the twenty acres of Japanese space that contained his home. From the quiet street outside, the view was unspectacular, just a high wall topped with broken glass and the traditional eaved gate, with its end tiles stamped with the family crest. There was not even a glimpse of what lay behind—the sprawling wooden house with its teahouse extension, the bamboo grove, the tennis court he had built for his daughter, the complex of traditional gardens.

For a few silent moments, Land-san contemplated the scene with great satisfaction. In itself, it was nothing remarkable—the value of the buildings and the cost of upkeep were quite modest. The whole point was the location—right in the middle of Tokyo's most exclusive residential district. In the midst of the world's densest concentration of economic activity, he was savoring the greatest luxury of all: private space. The newspapers said that the grounds of the Imperial Palace were worth more, at current market prices, than the entire state of California. Well, if that was so, then the market value of his own property would surely be equivalent to that of a medium-sized American town.

Just in front of the main building was a set of ponds laid out in the Chinese character for "heart." Huge, brightly patterned carp, each costing several million yen, patrolled the weeds. Land-san knew each one by its individual markings. Sometimes when he was mulling over a new project or a major acquisition, he would sit in front of the pool for hours, watching them swimming back and forth, back and forth.

It was as he turned toward the house that Land-san noticed the man crouching behind the row of bushes next to the porch.

"Hey! What on earth do you think you're doing?" he growled.

The man stepped forward. He was young, no more than twenty-five, and dressed in a black karate robe. He was wearing a headband emblazoned with Chinese characters. In the dim light, Land-san could make out only one of them: "death."

"I am delivering the judgment of the people," said the youth solemnly.

He slipped his hand inside the karate robe. When it emerged, it was clutching a short sword. The blade flashed once in the moonlight.

"Do you know who I am?" said Land-san.

"I know you," said the youth, with an angry sneer. "You are a devil of greed who has defiled the motherland with your property speculation. Because of what your company has done, ordinary Japanese are doomed to work like slaves for their whole lives. Now it is time for justice to be done."

"Market conditions," cried Land-san, unable to keep the tremor of fear out of his voice. "We were just following market conditions."

But the youth wasn't interested in debating cause and effect. He grabbed Land-san by the elbow and swiveled him around.

"No," shouted Land-san. "Don't be a fool."

The words choked off with the impact of the blow. He felt a flash of searing pain as the knife withdrew, and the hands he clasped to his belly were suddenly full of blood.

"Die, you traitor," snarled the youth, and stabbed again, this time from behind. Land-san felt the blade jarring against his shoulder-bone, then sank to the ground. Apparently dissatisfied with the effect, the youth jerked out the knife and slashed him twice across the side of the neck. Warm blood spurted across the back of Land-san's hand and onto the ground in front of him.

He was dimly aware of the sound of running feet. The youth was escaping. He tried to get up, but found that he couldn't. He decided to crawl. Slowly, without much awareness of where he was going or why, he hauled himself across the gravel drive. The chips of stone bit into his hands and knees, but he felt nothing.

Cold unblinking eyes were staring up at him, gulping mouths. He was hanging over the pool, and blood was dripping into the water. The carp were gathering, as if to feed.

Beautiful stupid creatures, he thought as he hung in the air for one frozen moment before crashing into the water.

8
.
.
.

I T took several days for Mori to track down Hara's brother-in-
law. The telephone operator at Nippon Infosystems had no
extension for him, and the personnel department refused to
answer any queries. Mrs. Hara had given a home address in
Yokohama, but according to the local tradespeople he hadn't
been seen there for over a year.

Mori decided on the direct approach. He had heard from Mrs.
Hara that the wife was a difficult woman, obsessed with fashion
and status. Maybe a little flattery would do the trick.

The Yoshimura family lived in smart new apartment block
with a false brick facade and a collection of European sports cars
in the parking area. The caretaker, a grumpy-looking man in a
blue uniform, would only let Mori in when he explained that he
had come all the way from Tokyo to deliver a summer gift. To
emphasize the point, Mori brandished the cardboard box with a
picture of a muskmelon on the side that he had brought with him
for just this purpose. Since muskmelons of that quality cost about
twenty thousand yen, he had put in a beetroot instead. It made
the same kind of noise when the box was shaken.

He left the box on a window ledge on the seventh floor, then
went up to Room 1103. The woman who answered the door was
in her late thirties, tall, and remote-looking. Mori noted the diamond stud earrings and the Cartier watch.

"This is the Yoshimura residence. May I be of any assistance to you?" she asked.

"Thank you for giving me your valuable time," Mori smirked back at her. "I am representing the Tokyo University Yacht Club Old Boys Society. I have an important message for your husband."

Mrs. Hara had told him how proud Mrs. Yoshimura was of her husband's "elite" educational background. As he had hoped, the mention of the magic words "Tokyo University" got him into the living room immediately.

The inside of the apartment was sumptuously large, though the sensation of space was reduced by the clutter of objects and decorations. There was a Persian rug on the floor, a Chinese vase standing on an ornately carved European-style sideboard, and a couple of abstract paintings on the wall. A tiny terrier, not much bigger than a rat, stood on the black leather sofa emitting short falsetto barks.

"My husband never told me that he was a member of the yacht club," said Mrs. Yoshimura. "He wasn't," said Mori carefully. "However, he was well known to many of our members. He was a very popular student, you see."

"I'm sure he was."

"That's why we are trying to get in touch with him. Our members are very keen for him to attend our next reunion."

"That's interesting. I've always wanted to sail on a yacht . . ."

Mori gazed at the woman. The nose was slightly too sharp and the nostrils slightly too pinched for the saucepan-like flatness of the face. From the front it looked as if it could be natural, but in profile it looked stuck on, like a piece of plasticine. It was an expert job, emphasizing the inherent haughtiness of her features.

". . . in the Mediterranean, maybe. Under a cloudless sky, with the sea calm and beautifully blue . . ."

"Not too calm," said Mori with a smile. "We sailors need a bit of wind, you know."

She looked at him as if she were noticing him for the first time.

"Of course," she said sharply. "Now, what is it you wish to know?"

"I want to get in touch with your husband. If you could give me a telephone number at work . . ."

"My husband is away on an important business project. Any messages for him should be left at the head office."

She spoke as if reading from a script.

"When will he be back?"

"Not for many months, probably. It's a special project entrusted to him by President Iwanaga. Now, if you could just leave your business card and the details of this reunion . . ."

"No, don't trouble yourself," said Mori hastily. "I'll try again at the head office."

Mori could see that she knew more, and also that she wasn't going to tell him. Suddenly, she was on her guard. It was time to go before any inconvenient questions were asked.

After leaving the building, Mori walked around to the back and assessed the possibility of breaking in. The Yoshimuras' apartment was on the top floor. It had a balcony. If he could get onto the roof, it should be quite simple to lower himself down. . . .

"Germ! Dirty smelly germ!"

"We're going to kill you, germ!"

"We're going to flush you down the toilet!"

Suddenly, four uniformed schoolkids raced around the corner of the building. The first, a pale-looking boy of thirteen or fourteen, stumbled on the uneven ground, and immediately the others were on him, kicking and shoving him into the corner where the trash cans were kept.

"You little germ, Yoshimura. You won't get away this time."

"Where's our money, creep?"

The three pursuers looked about seventeen years old. They wore their jackets as long and loose as overcoats and their trousers hugely flared. One had dyed his eyebrows a rusty shade of red. Another had piled his hair up into a heavily greased pompadour that jutted out like the bow of a boat. The third, who had a crewcut, looked as if he had been custom-designed for the sport of judo. He was huge, at least six inches taller than Mori, with shoulders that bulged out of his serge jacket and thighs like tree trunks. He had grabbed the pale boy, and was forcing his head into one of the trash cans.

"Mother," the boy wailed. "Help me, somebody."

Mori walked over toward the tangle of limbs.

"Get off him," he said quietly.

"Drop dead," said Red Eyebrows.

Mori grabbed his elbow, then wrenched his little finger up and away from the line of the body. Red Eyebrows doubled up in pain. Before Mori had time to release his grip, Crewcut had grabbed him by the shirt collar and was lifting him off the ground. He was phenomenally strong. Mori waited for the right moment, then curled his hand round the back of the gorilla neck and butted him crisply on the bridge of the nose. There was a satisfying crunch of cartilage and bone, and Crewcut reeled backward. The center of his face looked like a squashed fruit. Greasy Quiff was trying to grab Mori round the neck and punch him in the kidneys at the same time. Mori thrust a hand back into his crotch, squeezed and twisted. There was a yell of pain. Mori let him have an elbow in the pit of the stomach, and he went quiet.

Red Eyebrows was keeping his distance now. Crewcut was staggering forward, his fists clenched. There was blood all over the front of his uniform, but he didn't seem to notice. Mori caught the first swing at the wrist, then used the momentum to slam his face into the wall. That seemed to stun him. Mori took a step back, then drove his fist into the side of the huge bearlike body as hard as he could. Crewcut gave a muffled groan and sank to the ground.

"Okay," said Mori, sucking in air between words. "Any more problems with my friend here, and you won't get off so easy next time."

There was a dazed silence as they picked themselves off the floor and slunk around the side of the building. It was broken by a high-pitched wail of triumph.

"Hear that, you GEEEEERRMS!"

The pale-faced boy turned to Mori.

"I want you to be my bodyguard," he said. "I'll pay well."

Osamu Yoshimura, Mori discovered, was a strange boy. He hated his teachers, hated his classmates, hated his parents, hated girls, hated sports and music. The only thing he enjoyed was playing computer games. Every night he would spend hours and hours that were supposed to be devoted to homework acting out on-line dramas with fellow players in Europe, America and South-east Asia. The programs were so complex now, and had so many built-in options, that a single game could take up to a year to complete.

"What about your schoolwork?" said Mori. "Don't you want to go to an elite university like your father did?"

"What's the point?" said Osamu. "He has to do exactly what the company tells him all the time. If the boss says 'Go and spend two years at our computer center,' he has to say 'Thank you very much' and go. It's stupid."

"Is that where he is now?" asked Mori. "At the computer center?"

"That's right," said Osamu sulkily. "And he can stay there for the rest of his life as far as I care."

Mori slapped him on the shoulder and told him to learn some karate.

"What about the bodyguard job?" said Osamu. "It's worth five thousand yen a day."

"I'll think about it," said Mori.

The next day, Mori took train and bus to the distant region of the Japan Alps where the Nippon Infosystems Computer Center was located. In the old market town that was the prefectural capital, he rented a light van and changed into the delivery-boy uniform and black training shoes he had brought with him. Stitching on the front of the cap read "Takano Enterprises," the name of a small grocery store near Mori's office in Shinjuku.

The Nippon Infosystems Computer Center was a complex of modern buildings nestling in a valley dozens of miles from anywhere. It was surrounded by dense forest, the only road through which was a bumpy mud track. There was a high perimeter fence, and an electronic gate controlled by two uniformed security men inside a little hut.

Mori drove another two miles up into the mountains, parked the van some way off the track, then worked his way around to the back of the installation. He took the binoculars from his side pocket, and watched and waited.

Nothing much seemed to be going on. A couple of men were playing tennis on an ash court. Occasionally people would walk in and out of the large central building. Mori noted that it had a generator at the back. On the roof was a large satellite dish that peered at the sky like a great metallic sunflower. Every twenty minutes or so, a car would draw up at the gate and, after the two men in the hut had satisfied themselves that everything was in order, be waved inside.

It all looked perfectly normal, perfectly innocent. Mori had to remind himself that Yoshimura had been in the Seikyu Hotel on the night Hara died, standing next to a yakuza hit man. Then, as now, he had been working on a special assignment for Iwanaga, the man who wanted to change the direction of Japan's economic policy. It could be a set of coincidences, or it could add up to something pretty sinister. Mori waited until dusk before moving inside. He used a pair of pliers to tear a hole in the fence, then scuttled behind a long white building that he guessed was the living quarters. Many of the windows were open to the cool evening air, and snatches of conversation floated out with the sounds of televisions and mah-jongg tiles being scrabbled.

"Not long now. It'll soon be over. . . ."

"I'm looking forward to seeing my kids. . . ."

"I've almost forgotten what mine look like."

"Have you got everything ready for the strategy session this evening?"

"The sensei's coming, isn't he?"

"That's what Yoshimura says."

"Yoshimura knows everything."

The voices sounded cheerful, sensible, quite normal for a group of businessmen on a long assignment away from home. Mori felt a twinge of doubt. Maybe he had gotten it all wrong.

Suddenly there was a dull roar overhead and an arc of bright light slicing into the dark corner where Mori was crouched. He scuttled along the side of the building and slid between two parked cars. The noise grew louder and the lights on the roof of the building continued to rotate.

It was a helicopter. It came sweeping over the clump of trees behind Mori, so low that he could see the frown of concentration on the pilot's face. After circling the compound once, he brought the machine down in front of the central building. There was a reception committee of half a dozen men in white uniforms waiting there. When the man on the passenger side stepped down, they all bowed deeply.

"At your command," they roared with one voice.

Behind him, a gigantic bald-headed man in a black robe jumped from the helicopter. Despite his bulk, he landed like a cat, then gazed around warily, as if he were expecting a trap. A third man followed, also in a black robe and with a bald, perfectly round head gleaming dully in the lights. The first man gave a short bow of acknowledgment to the men in uniforms, muttered a few words to the big man behind him, then disappeared through the door of the building. The others followed him in.

He was visible for less than a minute, and the light was bad, but Mori had no difficulty in recognizing him. The taut, slender figure, the deep-set eyes and tall brow, the shock of gray hair, the trademark fan which he rapped against the palm of his hand as if he were keeping time—Iwanaga's physical appearance was familiar from innumerable magazine photos and TV clips.

Suddenly, there were footsteps behind. One of the car doors opened and someone got inside. Mori felt a moment of panic. If the car was moved, he would be completely exposed to the sight of anyone in the main building.

"Yoshimura-san, I can't find the circuit prober."

The voice that called out of the car window was young and faltering.

"Not there, you slow-witted fool. It's in the trunk."

The other voice came from the side of the main building. It was domineering, deliberately brusque.

When he heard the footsteps move round to the back of the

car, he sneaked a look in the direction of the second voice. At a glance, Mori knew that it was the same man who had stood in the lobby of the Seikyu Hotel. This time, he was standing in the doorway of the main building, arms akimbo. He was wearing a white uniform with the NI insignia on the chest.

Mori crouched motionless between the two cars for over an hour. There was a full moon overhead, a hundred-yen coin on a dark blue wrapping cloth. It provided enough light to give him a reasonable view of what was going on. Most of the activity was taking place in the main building, and gradually people were drifting into it from the other parts of the compound. Mori waited until the lights were off in the living quarters and the parking lot and surrounding areas were deserted. Then he made his move.

A spiral staircase bolted to the rear of the building served as a fire escape. It went right up to the roof, passing a yard of the panel of windows on each one of the building's nine floors. Mori slipped on a pair of dark gloves, pulled his peaked hat down over his forehead, then sprinted noiselessly across the lot to the rear of the building.

The staircase was flimsy. It trembled as he stretched away from it to peer in through the second-floor window. The blinds were drawn down three-quarters of the way, forcing him to bend down to the window ledge. Inside was a large well-lit computer room in which a dozen men and women sat tapping at keyboards. At the end of the room was a white board covered with algebraic symbols. A middle-aged man with a pointer was standing in front of the board, presumably explaining the symbols. With the window shut, his words were inaudible.

Mori moved up to the third floor. Here the window was covered from the inside by a white cloth screen. There was a narrow gap at the edge just large enough to allow him to squint inside. The room was smaller, no more than half the size of the one on the second floor. Three people—whether men or women it was impossible to tell—wearing baggy white overalls, hairnets, and face masks were standing at a table. One was scrutinizing the dials on a large refrigeratorlike machine at the side of the room, the other two were peering through microscopes. Both the floor and the ceiling were made up of panels of metal grill. Mori recognized the scene from science programs he had seen on television. It was a small clean room. The three workers were manufacturing high-precision electronic components, probably integrated circuits.

Mori carried on up the staircase. The fourth and fifth floors appeared to be deserted. The sixth contained a giant lecture room filled with rows of desks and chairs. Men and some women were filing in through the door, most of them wearing the Nippon Infosystems uniform. Mori kept to the side of the window, making sure that he was out of the line of sight.

A few minutes after the audience had taken their places, Yoshimura walked into the room. He bowed briefly, then turned to face the open door and began clapping enthusiastically. Instantly, the audience rose to its feet and burst into applause. At that point, Iwanaga appeared at the doorway, where he stood gazing expressionlessly into space, apparently oblivious to the scene around him. He held the pose for over a minute, before nodding curtly at Yoshimura, who stopped clapping at once, and then striding over to the podium. Yoshimura motioned for everyone to sit down and began speaking. From where Mori stood, his words were no more than a faint murmur.

Mori went up to the seventh floor, which was also empty, and tried the fire-escape door. It was locked. On the eighth floor, the lights were on. Next to the staircase was a small room in which four men sat around a table playing mah-jongg. Two of them were security people, one was the helicopter pilot, and the other was the large bald-headed man in the black robe who had accompanied Iwanaga. Although he wasn't playing, he sat completely still, apparently absorbed in the progress of the game. An owl hooted somewhere in the forest, and his gaze darted toward the window. Mori jerked his head out of the line of sight just in time.

Mori waited until they started shuffling the mah-jongg tiles for the next round, then tried the fire-escape door. It was unlocked. He eased it open and slipped inside. He was just a thin wall away from the four men, but the air was filled with the rattle of mah-jongg tiles being scrabbled around for the next game.

The corridor was deserted. Mori made for the internal staircase and crept down to the sixth floor. The door of the lecture room had been left half open. Mori could hear what Yoshimura was saying without moving from the staircase.

"Only a man of the sensei's wisdom and courage could have led us forward to this point. Only the sensei has the vision to see a new way ahead for Japan. Truly, the Japanese people are fortunate that a man like the sensei has risen at this critical hour, ready to sacrifice everything for the good of the nation."

Next Iwanaga spoke. In contrast to Yoshimura's clumsy bluster, his delivery was smooth and rhythmical, with plenty of pauses for dramatic effect. In spite of himself, Mori found himself wanting to agree. Iwanaga was a more skillful speaker than any Japanese politician or business leader he had ever heard.

"Comrades," rang out the deep melodious voice. "We are on the verge of a new phase in human development. Those of you who have labored through the German philosophers may recall that, according to Hegel, the spirit of world history has always proceeded in a westerly direction. It started from the alluvial plains of the Yellow River and the Ganges, then flowed westward to the Greco-Roman cultures of the Mediterranean. A millennium later, it had moved on to the seafaring nations of Northern Europe.

"In this century which is now closing, the westward journey has continued. America has become the center of economic, political, and cultural power. The nations of Europe, the ancient civilizations of Asia—all have became mere shadows in comparison with the material strength of the United States. In Japan too, the people have lost confidence in their own culture, and have tried to turn themselves into imitation Westerners. Our project will ensure that it will no longer be possible to make this mistake."

Iwanaga's voice dropped a tone for emphasis. The audience took the cue immediately, and the room was filled with dutiful applause. He waited about half a minute before continuing.

"If Hegel were alive today, he would see that the long

westward journey is ending. Europe is little more than a souvenir shop. America is a desert of stupefying materialism. As anyone who reads a newspaper understands, it is disintegrating before our eyes. Not just in terms of economic power, but in cultural dynamism and strength of purpose, Hegel's spirit is now flowing across the Pacific. First it has come here to Japan, then it will flow through us to the reawakened nations of Asia. The process of history is coming full circle. The great aim of our project is to hasten it on its way."

Another pause, and again the room resounded with applause. When Iwanaga resumed, his voice was softer, more serious than before. Suddenly, he was speaking to them as friends, not pupils.

"I am describing the historical background because it is important to understand the scale of the enterprise in which we are engaged. Sometimes it is necessary to destroy in order to create. The project that you people have been laboring on for all these long months is a project of destruction. The target is the international financial system. That fine network of bogus cooperation, through which the insatiable appetites of the American middle classes are financed by the sweat of Asian workers, will soon be thrown into chaos.

"In the following months, there will be great confusion, here in Japan as much as in America and Europe. Passions will be at the boiling point. Naturally we Japanese will be blamed, as we always are. That is not only inevitable, it is to be welcomed. The anger aroused will be nurtured carefully and directed to serve our purposes. I promise you that there will be no return to the present era of cowardly dependence and cultural surrender. For better or for worse, Japan will stand alone!"

Just as the applause was breaking out again, Mori heard a sound on the staircase below him. Someone was coming up from the fifth floor. In the corridor, there was nowhere at all to hide. He raced up to the seventh floor, and waited. The footsteps kept coming, hurrying now.

"Kuroda," called out a voice from below. "Kuroda, is that you? It's time to prepare the helicopter."

Now Mori knew he could wait no longer. He turned and

sprinted up to the eighth floor.

In the small room, the mah-jongg tiles were being rattled again. Mori edged past to the door leading out to the fire escape. He twisted the handle and pushed, but the lock was stiff. The door wouldn't budge. He jogged the handle back and forth with rising desperation. Just then the rattle of the mah-jongg tiles abruptly ceased, and Mori froze on the spot, the door handle cocked in his hand.

There was a heavy silence, as if the whole room was straining its ears to catch what was happening outside, then Mori heard the squeak of a chair leg scraping against the floor. The door handle was slippery with the sweat of his hands.

"Kuroda? Come back here at once. The sensei doesn't enjoy waiting around, you know."

The angry voice came floating up from below, followed by the sound of footsteps on the staircase. The helicopter man seemed determined to confront him.

Mori had no choice but to move quickly. He released the door handle, wincing at the click that the spring made, then dashed for the staircase up to the next floor, taking the steps three at a time.

The next floor was the top floor. The staircase led up to a long white-tiled corridor similar to those on every other floor. The only visible movement was the drunken flutter of a couple of large gray moths around a flickering neon tube.

"Kuroda! What on earth are you playing at? You'd better—"

The footsteps seemed to halt just where Mori had been standing a split-second before, and the voice broke off in mid-sentence. Mori pictured the bald monk standing at the door of the little room, a finger pressed to his big fleshy lips.

Mori padded furtively up the corridor, glancing behind him as he went. The first three doors he came to were locked, but the fourth had been left slightly ajar. Mori eased it a few more inches open. The lights were off inside, but the room was illuminated by a bank of video screens. It was unoccupied. Mori slid inside and gently closed the door behind him.

He found himself in what appeared to be an office, containing a leather couch, a large steel desk, filing cabinets, and several computer terminals. Above the desk was a half-open window, through which Mori glimpsed the disk of the moon high over the sea of trees. On the left stood a glass display case containing two ancient-looking samurai swords. On the wall to the right, there was a row of four framed certificates, attesting to the fact that Nippon Infosystems had won the MITI award for product innovation in each of the last four years.

Mori glanced at the bank of screens. There were six of them altogether, two of which were dedicated to stock prices and currencies and the others to video images. There was no sound. Mori scrutinized the strange mnemonics and the winking red and green numbers, but they meant nothing to him. The images on the video screens were comprehensible, though with little apparent connection to Nippon Infosystems business. They had been taken from news programs, some Japanese, some foreign. One sequence was of a fair-haired man with the looks of a movie star smashing up a stereo system with a sledgehammer. Another showed a recent demonstration in front of the French Embassy at which a grenade had been tossed at the ambassador's car. Another showed a group of policemen examining a patch of ground next to a carp pond, then flashed up a file photo of an elderly man with the character for "deceased" in front of his name. Mori would have recognized him anyway. The chairman of Japan's largest real estate company and vice president of the Nikkeiren employers' federation, he was one of Japan's most prominent business leaders.

Mori walked across to the desk and tried the drawers. They were all locked. He peered into the wastebasket. It contained a single scrunched-up ball of paper. Mori took it out and teased it flat. It appeared to be a guard roster, with lists of names and duties set against particular days of the week. Mori scrutinized it for a few moments, then silently screwed up the sheet of paper and replaced it in the basket. He was just turning his attention to the filing cabinet when suddenly he froze. There was a noise somewhere outside. Just a small click, of the sort that might be made by someone releasing a door handle. He looked around the room. There was nowhere to conceal himself.

Another click! Someone was trying the doors along the

corridor, moving slowly from one to the next without the trace of a footfall. Whoever it was would be at the door of the office in a matter of seconds.

Mori moved fast, stepping lightly onto the desk then through the window onto the ledge outside. For a dizzying instant, he looked down to the concrete below and thought of Hara.

The roof of the building was just a couple of feet from Mori's head. A jump of six inches would be enough to allow him to grab onto the guttering. It was made of some kind of white plastic. Was it going to be strong enough to hold his weight? He would soon find out. He tensed himself, took a deep breath, and jumped the highest six inches he had ever jumped in his life.

For a moment he was hanging in space while the guttering seemed to buckle under his fingers. But it was a high-quality product. It held. He swiftly levered himself up—first chin above the roof line, then knees, then feet.

The roof was flat, with the cooling tower and satellite dish at one end. In the center was a pyramidical scaffolding about ten feet high, on which was set a revolving searchlight. The spot took less than a minute to make one sweeping circuit of the perimeter fence, illuminating the branches and leaves of the forest with a deathly whiteness.

Dazzled as the beam arced toward him, Mori crouched down and shielded his eyes, and the light passed a couple of feet above his head. He got to his feet and, still bending low, chased behind the beam to the other end of the roof, and flattened himself against the side of the cooling tower. Just a few yards to the left, he could make out the top of a metal staircase. That, if his sense of direction was correct, should lead down to the fire escape. Mori waited for the searchlight to swing past again, then made for the edge of the roof.

He didn't get far. As he passed by the satellite dish, there was a faint rustling sound behind him, and he felt an immensely powerful grip on his shoulder. He twisted around, and the grip was released. The giant bald-headed man in the black robe was standing there gazing at him with an expressionless stare. He had appeared out of nowhere.

"Good evening," said Mori calmly. "Nice view up here, isn't it?"

The big man said nothing. He was not only completely bald, Mori noted, he had no eyebrows or eyelashes either. "Still, we'd better get going. The sensei doesn't enjoy waiting around, does he?"

Mori smiled apologetically, took one step in the direction of the metal ladder, then swung around abruptly to drive his elbow as hard as he could into the bald man's stomach. The man didn't even grimace. The muscles were like granite.

Mori backed off, fists raised in a defensive posture. The bald man moved sinuously forward, hands stroking the air, his hips rolling like a dancer's. The searchlight came cutting through the air toward them. Mori raised a hand to ward off the glare, and a stunning blow caught him in the center of the chest. There was a loud metallic echo as Mori was sent crashing back against the water tower.

Mori straightened up, sucking in air. The bald man advanced again, his face as expressionless as before. He still hadn't uttered a sound. Mori dodged to the left and aimed a reverse kick at the bald man's belly that lost itself in a billow of empty robe. He tried the same thing again, this time aiming in anticipation, but his foot was swept aside with a flick of a forearm. For a moment Mori staggered off balance, then another blow caught him full in the chest, knocking him backward. He didn't even see whether it was a fist or a foot.

Mori rose to his knees, his head ringing. He knew that he was just a couple of feet from the edge of the building. The bald man sidled forward, moving as smoothly and lightly as a giant cat. The only sounds were the two sets of breathing: one deep and rhythmic, one just a ragged gasp.

Mori managed to scramble to his feet and get sideways on to the edge of the roof. The sight of the long drop down was disorienting, but preferable to the sensation of having it just inches from his back.

The bald man jabbed his foot at Mori's head, almost lazily. Mori pulled back just in time, and felt the tremendous force of the kick skidding past his ear. For a brief instant, there was a gap. Mori slid inside and slammed his fist upward into his opponent's groin. The blow was good, but still the bald man made no sound. His eyes and nostrils widened a little, and his brow furrowed as if with concentration. He feinted another kick at Mori's head, and skipped sideways on the balls of his feet. Mori followed through, jabbing his fingers at the lashless eyes. The bald man moved like lightning. Mori felt a grip on his wrist, a wrenching pain in his shoulder, and then he was being lifted off the ground like a child.

Suddenly, Mori couldn't breathe. The bald man was crushing him in a bear hug. His arms were jammed to his sides, his ribs pressed flat against the huge chest. Two thumbs like pegs of steel were boring into his neck. A little more, and they would burst through the skin and tear open his windpipe. The pressure inside his head was unbearable. There were red flashes in front of his eyes, and a roaring noise in his ears.

Mori flailed out with his feet, but there was nothing there but the empty robe. The huge hairless face was just inches in front of him, grimacing with effort. He could smell the radish on the man's breath.

The face drew closer still, until they were gazing into each other's eyes like a pair of lovers. Suddenly there was an opportunity. Mori thrust his head forward and sunk his teeth into the man's squat little nose, holding the bite until his teeth almost met. There was a howl of agony, and the grip on his neck was released.

Mori stumbled backward, holding his throat and gasping for air. The spotlight came raking across the roof again, and for one vital moment the bald giant was lit up in front of him. He was standing inches from the building's edge, clutching his torn nose with one hand and trying to ward off the beam with the other. The intense glare caught him full in the face, highlighting the rivulets of black blood running down over his chin.

Mori swung in low, landing a full-power reverse kick just above the navel. The jarring sensation that ran from Mori's knee right up to his shoulder told him that the impact was perfect.

The bald man teetered backward, his mouth wide open in an "O" of surprise. For a moment his giant figure was silhouetted against the lucid night sky, the arms flapping in a vain attempt to hold his balance. Then he was gone.

There was a thud as the body hit the ground far below, but already Mori was scrambling his way down the ladder to the fire escape. He jumped the last six feet, and the metal sheet twanged under his weight. He didn't worry about the noise, clattering down the fire escape at such a pace that the guardrail burned his hand. At the bottom, he paused and looked around. The man in the black robe lay slumped by the side of the building. Otherwise, the central area was still empty. Up above, he could hear voices raised in excitement. They must have heard him, had probably seen him as well. There was no time to lose. Not bothering to keep low this time, he sprinted for the hole in the perimeter fence.

Once safely outside, he paused to listen. The shouts were louder now. It sounded as if they had found the body. There was no point in going back to the van. By the time he got onto the mud track, the security people would have blocked it off and be scouring the surrounding area. He had no choice but to go ahead on foot.

He was in a pine forest, with reasonable spaces between the trees and a floor of hard mud. He could jog forward well enough without making much noise, and there was just enough moonlight to make out the shapes of the trees ahead of him. Soon the lights of the central complex had disappeared behind him. A few minutes more and the shouts had also gone. The only sound that interrupted the silence of the forest was the beat of his footsteps on the hard ground.

After a while, Mori stopped and thought over his position. The Computer Center was located in a remote southern region of the Japan Alps. There were dozens of miles of similar-looking mountains and valleys in every direction. Apart from the mud track, there would probably be no roads for miles around, just a few hunters' paths leading farther into the mountains. Every year, the newspapers carried stories about hikers getting lost and dying of exposure in just this kind of place. The best plan would be to get over the high ridge in the distance and follow the next valley down toward where the main road should be. Altogether, it would mean a trek of about twenty miles, but he could probably manage it by dawn.

It was getting cold. Mori zipped the jacket of his uniform right up to his Adam's apple and started to jog.

The ridge was farther away than he thought. He had been going for nearly two hours now, and he was still moving along flat ground. A bad thought—all the constant dodging between trees was starting to affect his sense of direction. He could no longer be sure that he was going toward the ridge. He might even be going back toward the Computer Center. He was just about to stop and examine the position of the moon, when he heard a strange sound floating through the air. It was music, the ethereal plinking and twanging of a Japanese lute. He moved cautiously toward it.

It took him twenty minutes before he saw the lights, then he spent another twenty minutes circling the rambling, single-story wooden structure, satisfying himself that there were no Nippon Infosystems people wandering around. The building was set in a large clearing in the forest which was illuminated by half a dozen bright lamps. In the rear was a lawn laid out with what looked like croquet hoops, and at the front a narrow, heavily rutted track that led down into the valley. Above the front door was a wooden sign whose blurred, weather-beaten characters read "Takayama Senior Citizens Rest Home." The music was coming from a loud-speaker above the door, the same dreamy melody being played over and over again.

The place looked harmless enough. He might be able to get some information there about how to reach the main road, per-haps even the loan of a bicycle or motorbike. The ridge was nowhere in sight now, and if he just carried on through the forest, he might end up wandering in circles for the rest of the night.

He took off his shoes in the porch and put them in one of the lockers. The hasp, he noticed, was rusted over, as if it hadn't been used for years. The canvas slippers for interior use were covered in dust, the soles practically falling off. Inside the lobby area, the small reception desk was empty, as was the green felt notice-board. In the corner was a display case containing a mangy, orange-eyed fox. One panel of glass had been cracked and was stuck over with a sheet of yellow newspaper. Mori's eye was caught by the section of headline: "President Ford Arrives in Japan."

Apart from the recorded music, the place was silent. The lounge was empty. The ashtrays were clean. A long cobweb joined the wooden hatrack to the writing desk, a large hairy spider hanging in the middle, completely motionless.

Mori crept across the lounge and into the dingy passageway that led to the back of the building. He stopped. There was a slight smell in the air, the unmistakable odor of noodles. He continued down the corridor, and the smell grew stronger. At the end was a bookcase with what looked like a large sack leaning against it. Only when it shifted position slightly did Mori realize that it was a human figure. Whoever it was had been watching him from the moment he came in.

"Come on, hurry up. We're all waiting for you."

It was the voice of an old woman; thin and unsteady. The tone was irritable, yet kindly; the sort a teacher might use when reprimanding a backward child.

"What's that?" said Mori.

"Come along at once. You've kept us all waiting long enough."

Mori followed her down a musty corridor and through a sliding door into a large room. There was a low table in the center. Around it, three old men sat in front of bowls of steaming noodles. "He's finally arrived," said the old woman proudly. "I always knew he would come."

By any standards, she looked truly ancient. Her face was a mass of wrinkles, and the skin hung off her cheeks in leathery folds. The eyes were watery, the forehead as blotched as an antique table. Yet she seemed possessed by some febrile inner strength. Her head was upright on her shoulders, and her mouth was set in a smile of rapturous pride.

"Where's your uniform?" she said suddenly. "You should have worn your uniform for a homecoming like this!"

Mori looked at the old men. One of them was gazing into space, his cracked lips moving in silent conversation. Another appeared to be asleep, though his jaws were still moving slowly up and down. The third, a man with a beaky nose and flossy white hair, looked more alert. He smiled gently, and beckoned Mori over to sit down.

"It's a shame," he said gently. "She's never been the same since her nephew stopped coming to see her."

"My husband's battalion," said the old lady in a quavering voice, "contains the bravest soldiers in the entire Japanese army. Their brilliant tactical assaults have put to flight tens of thousands of Chinese bandits. It's all there in the newspapers! You can read it any day."

"I've got nothing to do with her husband, you know," murmured Mori to the old man.

"Of course you haven't!" said the old man, with a cackle of laughter. "She was only married for two months. Her husband never came back from China. Everybody knows that!"

"Everybody? How many of you are there?"

"Well, . . ." The old man's voice began to falter. "There used to be a lot of us, you see. Dozens of us once upon a time. There were lovely games and dances in those days. We had such fun. Then, one by one, they all went away."

"But who's in charge here? There must be a manager and staff."

"Yes," said the old man drowsily. "The owner is a farmer down in the village. His wife comes up every day to make our food. Checks everything. Sees everybody's fine."

"How long have you been here?"

"Many, many years . . . ten years, maybe fifteen. My son doesn't come anymore. It's too far." His eyes were closed now, and his breathing was much heavier.

"Everybody's tired," said the old lady crossly. "You kept them waiting so long, you see. Come on, I'll take you up to your room."

It was no good. He wasn't going to get any help from any of them. Still, there might be a map somewhere of the surrounding area somewhere in the place.

Mori went back to the lounge and started searching through the small bookcase next to the writing desk. It contained a pile of ancient photo magazines, an edition of the works of Akutagawa, and several leather-bound volumes of *Government Regulations on the Provision of Water Services to Outlying Districts*. There was no map.

He was just wondering whether to try the old man with the flossy white hair again, when he heard the sound of a throat being cleared behind him. He turned. A tall man in the black robes of a priest was standing in the entrance. He had a gun in his hand, and a walkie-talkie hanging from his gray belt. He nodded at Mori as if they were already acquainted.

"You must return with me to the Computer Center," he said stiffly.

"What are you talking about?" said Mori. "I came here to visit my mother. It's her eighty-third birthday."

"Your words are stupid," said the monk, with a contemptuous smile. "I tracked you through the forest myself. It was not difficult to follow someone blundering about as clumsily as you were."

"There must be some mistake," said Mori. "Look, ask her yourself if you don't believe me."

He gestured at the old woman, who had just shuffled into the lounge like a sleepwalker. The old man with the flossy white hair was with her. The monk turned around to look at them, and shrugged his shoulders dismissively.

"Your pretenses are useless," he said. "You are the spy who killed my brother. I'm looking forward to observing how the sensei deals with you. He has some interesting methods of handling spies."

The old woman had a look of total bewilderment on her face.

"My husband is no spy," she mumbled. "He has been serving the emperor loyally on the Manchurian front. The brave exploits of the Fifth Battalion . . ."

"Don't confuse yourself, granny," said the monk. "This man is a dangerous criminal and I'm taking him away with me. We'll make sure he doesn't give you any more trouble. Now, empty your pockets onto the table."

Mori obeyed slowly. Behind the monk's back, the old woman was rummaging through a closet. She took from it two croquet mallets, and handed one to the white-haired old man.

"This sensei of yours," said Mori, trying to give himself time to think. "He's completely crazy, you know. This project has no chance of success."

"Oh, really," said the monk, with a sneer. "And who's going to stop us? The sensei knows exactly how to deal with the fools who get in his way."

"I see the president of a certain real estate company was murdered yesterday. I suppose he got in the sensei's way somehow."

"That's none of your business!"

The old woman was standing right behind the monk now. She raised the mallet slowly, carefully, until it was perpendicular above her head. It wobbled slightly as she tried to control the weight. The old man lifted his mallet too, holding it sideways like a baseball bat.

Mori took a pace forward, striving to hold the man's attention.

"Stand still!" said the monk tightly, raising the pistol to chest level.

"It's a shame about your brother," said Mori with a wry smile. "He was such a fine conversationalist. Still, that was certainly an impressive dive he made. Two back-somersaults with a half-spin. Nearly Olympic standard, I'd say."

The monk flushed with anger.

"You will suffer for that. You will beg to be allowed to die as quickly as my brother did. You will . . ."

The old lady brought down the mallet with all the strength she could muster. The sound was sweet, clean, like a hammer on a coconut. The monk dropped the gun and staggered forward. Next the old man swung, striking him on the side of the head between the ear and the eye. The monk fell to his knees clutching his head, blood pouring through his fingers. He was half groaning, half sobbing with the pain.

"Show the traitor no mercy," cried the old woman. "He was

plotting rebellion in the emperor's sacred army."

She struck again, driving her mallet into the fallen man's face. The old man followed up with another mighty blow. This time, the monk fell to the floor and lay there prone, making odd jerky movements with his shoulders. The only sound he was making now was a piglike snuffle.

The old woman stood over him, raised the mallet high, then brought it crashing down on the shiny center of his bald skull. It was a mighty blow, raining flecks of blood on the sofa, on the old woman's shirt, even on the wall.

"He was a bad comrade," said the old woman between deep breaths. She was leaning on her mallet like a crutch. The old man with the flossy white hair was giggling softly to himself. There were a couple of spots of blood on his forehead.

"He won't be missed," said Mori, pulling the walkie-talkie from the man's belt.

He pressed the "communication" button. An urgent voice cut through the static.

"Request latest intruder situation. Repeat, request latest intruder situation."

"No trace of intruder," said Mori in a passable imitation of the monk's high-pitched monotone, then switched the machine off and made for the door. The old woman trailed after him, the soles of her slippers flapping against the tiled floor.

There was a small hut to one side of the main entrance. While the old woman watched blankly from the porch, Mori broke open the rusted hasp and pushed his way inside. It was dark and piled with junk—broken tables and chairs, a lawnmower, rolls of moldering carpet, pots and pans, an ancient television with thick gray glass and heavy knobs. There was also a rusty, rickety-looking bicycle. Mori pulled it free of the rest of the junk, and wheeled it out. The tires were almost flat, several spokes were springing loose, and the brakes were useless, but it would do the job well enough.

"You're not going back to the front already, are you?" called out the old woman.

"I have important work to do," said Mori stiffly. "It cannot be delayed any longer."

He walked up to her and brushed her cheek with his hand. There were tears in the old woman's eyes.

"Then serve the emperor bravely," she said. "But be careful! Recently the war situation has become very grave. The American planes come every night. Listen closely and you can hear them flying past now."

She put a talonlike hand to her ear and cocked her head. The only sound was the soft moan of the breeze through the pines.

"I will do my best," said Mori.

The old woman sat down in the porch, her eyes blank now, her mouth gaping. Mori gave a salute, then mounted the bicycle and set off down the overgrown track that led toward the next valley.

9

$\vdots$

THE first typhoon of the summer was on its way, and they
said it was going to be a big one. Already, a hooligan wind
was tearing through the streets, turning umbrellas inside
out, smashing down flowerbeds and shop displays, grabbing the
litter from the trash cans and sending it flying through the alleyways. Only two in the afternoon, but it was dark enough for
evening.

Mori turned away from the window to watch Lisa pulling her
jeans on. She always wore either black or red panties. Today they
were crimson. It was a sad thing to watch them disappearing
under the stone-washed blue denim.

"So aren't you going to tell me anything?"

She picked up a bottle of perfume and dabbed some on the
fine, creamy skin between her breasts.

"It's better you don't know," he said. "There're some pretty
dangerous people involved."

"I see. You turn up at my apartment looking like a ditch-
digger, wake me up in the middle of my beauty sleep, and then
you won't even tell me why. Typical!"

Mori came behind her, kissed her on the back of the neck, and
cupped his hands over her warm, live breasts. She pulled them
away and turned around and glared at him, hands on hip.

"Wait a moment," she said. "Do you think you can distract
me that easily?"

"I didn't mean that," said Mori feebly. "It's all so complicated, you see."

"Too complicated for a small brain like mine to comprehend. Is that it?"

Mori sighed. She had that steely glint in her eye.

"Is it absolutely necessary?" he asked.

"Absolutely."

She sat down on the bed and listened closely as Mori described all that happened since he had visited Hara's parents in north Japan. When he had finished, she picked up a large plastic comb from the side table and started dragging it through her hair with a force that made Mori wince.

"So now you know everything," she said. "Yoshimura killed Hara because he was threatening to betray this insane plan of Iwanaga's. Tell the police, collect your fee and move on to the next case."

"It's not so simple," said Mori. "Iwanaga won't stop here. He's gone too far to turn back."

"The police can take care of all that."

"Maybe," said Mori. "But I'll have to be careful. He's got people everywhere. Now, am I going to get some sort of reward for giving away all my secrets?"

Without a word, Lisa pounced on him, knocking him flat on his back on the bed. For a moment, she held him down by the shoulders and danced her breasts across his face. Then she quickly broke away.

"Is that all?" said Mori, aggrieved.

He made a grab for her thigh, but she dodged him.

"Got to go," she said. "I can't be late for the rehearsal."

After she'd gone, Mori put on one of her tapes and listened to it as he made coffee. After he'd drunk three cups, he called Kudo and arranged to meet in Hibiya Park the next day. Then he switched on the TV to catch the news.

The big story was domestic politics, not a subject that Mori followed closely. Still, this was important enough to hold his attention. Apparently, the long bout of political intrigue that had followed the fall of the Minakawa cabinet was drawing to an end. Senior faction leaders were holding a final series of meetings in the Hotel Okura. The new favorite for prime minister was Shinsuke Ishizaka.

Mori was startled. He had read that Ishizaka was one of the candidates for the premiership, but he had assumed that someone from one of the mainstream factions would be chosen in the end. That was what usually happened. Surely, they wouldn't choose a man like Ishizaka—unpredictable, arrogant, loudmouthed, everything that a Japanese politician shouldn't be.

As a young man, Ishizaka had written a best-selling novel which was then turned into a hit movie starring his actress sister. Mori vividly remembered the scene in which she was raped by two black GIs, based supposedly on a real-life incident. Back in those days, Ishizaka had been known as "the Japanese Norman Mailer" and his sister, who had died of cancer four or five years ago, as "the Japanese Natalie Wood." Ishizaka had given up writing novels soon after and gone into politics, but his strident nationalism and his desire to outrage hadn't moderated at all. Only last year, he had kicked up a rumpus by claiming that American products would never sell in Japan because the workers who made them were of "low innate intelligence."

Mori switched off the TV and gazed out of the window. The sky was pressing down low, suffusing the city with a dim violet light. Large, heavy raindrops were exploding against the tiles of the balcony.

By the time he got to his office in Shinjuku, a full-scale downpour was in progress. The gutters were overflowing, and ripples of rainwater were coursing over the center of the road. Mori used Lisa's 550 cc. Honda Beat, but he got pretty wet just sprinting from the car to the building.

It wasn't a good day for Magic Hole, either. The old man was standing in the doorway calling out to the few passersby who dashed past:

"Welcome in! Welcome in! New hard-core videos . . . Special typhoon discount!"

Not one of them gave him a glance. He looked beseechingly at

Mori, who just nodded his usual greeting and hurried to the stairs. The problem with a business like Magic Hole, Mori reflected, was the fixed costs. Even if no customers appeared at all, the old man still had to pay the wages of the woman behind the hardboard wall, the leasing fee for the equipment, and protection money to the local gang. Compare that with the business of a private detective. His only fixed cost was the rental on his office. Running costs were pretty low too, for that matter. Just enough pocket money for cigarettes, Chinese noodles, beer and sake . . .

Mori froze. The door of his office was a couple of inches open. Inside, there was a faint snuffling sound, such as a dog might make in its sleep. After a while, it stopped. The only sound was the rattle of the rain on the metal staircase. Mori was soaking wet now. His trousers were sticking to his legs, and rivulets of water were running down the back of his neck.

He waited two or three minutes, then kicked the door open and ducked to one side. Nothing happened. Slowly, carefully, he eased open the grimy fanlight and peered inside. Through the gloom, he made out a man's body lying alongside the sofa, his feet toward the door, his head next to the cockroach trap. Mori went inside and switched on the light. The man was in a bad way. Blood was pouring from his nose and mouth, and his face was a mass of bruises and cuts. A couple of fingers on his left hand had been badly cut. He had obviously taken a heavy beating.

The light seemed to stimulate him slightly, and the snuffling noise started again. It was, Mori realized, the noise a man made when he was breathing through a throatful of blood.

He hauled the man into a sitting position, then heated up some water. It took Mori several minutes to recognize the face, such were the swelling and bruising. The acne on the forehead provided the clue. It was the elder Kawada, proud leader of the Kawada organization.

Hot water on the face seemed to revive him. His eyes flickered open and registered a mix of fear and anger.

"Bastards," he croaked, then closed his eyes again.

Mori cleaned up his cuts, stripped off his blood-soaked shirt, and poured one quarter of a whiskey bottle down his throat. This time he revived for good.

Kawada didn't remember much of what happened. He had come to challenge Mori to a man-to-man fight. He wanted to avenge the humiliation to his son, who had finally been discovered in the love hotel by a cleaner at eleven in the morning. The door to Mori's office had already been open. When Kawada went in, there were four men waiting for him. He recognized the leader immediately—Toru Nakamura of the Kawashita syndicate.

Nakamura had demanded to know where Mori was. When Kawada said that he had no idea, they hadn't believed him. They said he must be working with Mori.

Kawada started to explain, but they weren't interested. They started to beat him up—slowly, methodically. Kawada didn't resist because it was useless and because he thought they would stop after a while. But they didn't stop. Then he realized that they didn't care whether they killed him or not, and he got scared.

Mori gave him an hour to recover, during which Kawada drank another quarter of the Suntory White. He had several broken ribs and his front teeth had gone. Otherwise, there was no lasting damage. Then Mori drove him home in the Honda Beat. He was silent the whole way.

Kawada lived in a tiny wooden house squeezed in between a machinery yard and a huge concrete overpass. The roof was mainly corrugated iron, the garden a narrow patch of mud. It was the kind of place that probably wouldn't have a bath or be connected to the sewer system. His son opened the door. He glanced once at Mori, once at the elder Kawada's battered face, then rushed forward, fists flying.

"Stop it," his father shouted. "It wasn't Mori. Leave him alone."

A middle-aged woman and a woman of about twenty appeared from a back room. Somewhere, a baby was wailing. The young woman's eyes were wide with shock. The middle-aged woman compressed her lips in anger.

"You never learn," she said in a low, bitter voice. "I've told you ten thousand times to get a proper job. You wouldn't lis-

ten. You even turned your own son into the same kind of cheap
hoodlum as you are. You're pathetic, the pair of you."

"It's a question of honor," protested the son, already soaking
wet. "We have to defend the name of the Kawada organization."

"Honor? The name of the organization? Hah! The world is
laughing at you, can't you see it?"

Suddenly, the elder Kawada spoke. His voice was quiet, and
trembled like an old man's through his broken teeth.

"I'm sorry," he said, then limped into the house.

Mori nodded to the others, and walked back toward the car.
He switched on the headlights, catching the slanting rain in
the beams.

Mori's next stop was only six miles away, but it seemed like a
different world. The large ivy-covered apartment block was set in
a wooded space where young mothers could sit on benches and
watch their toddlers charging across the grass on tricycles. Even
today, the air felt cooler, less heavy on the shoulders. The Ministry
of Finance certainly didn't devote much of the budget to its staff
quarters, but there was an atmosphere of tranquillity about the
place, of insulation from the hurly-burly of the city.

Mori stopped for a moment to enjoy the plash of the rain on
the small lotus-covered pond, the chant of the frogs, the smell of
the wet moss. The last time he had passed by that little pond was
several weeks before. Mrs. Hara had seemed so fragile on their
first meeting. Then, the second time in the coffee bar—so cool
and self-possessed. The woman was almost as much of a contra-
diction as her husband had been. When she opened the door, she
looked startled.

"Mori-san, I wasn't expecting you."

Mori stared around the room. It was empty, except for a few
packing crates on the floor. The curtains, carpets, decorations and
most of the furniture had been taken out. The flower arrangement that had perched on top of the radiator was gone, and the
fissure in the wall looked longer and uglier than before. It was
the corpse of an apartment; the life that had once been in it
had been extinguished.

"I'm leaving," she explained with a wave of her hand. "No connection with the ministry any more, you see."

Mori nodded sympathetically. They hadn't given her much time.

"I'm sorry to disturb you," he said. "I just wanted to ask a few extra questions."

"Oh really! What about?"

There was a sense of energy and determination about her, as if she were looking forward to moving out. Mori sneaked a glance at her left hand. The rings had gone too.

"About your husband and about your brother, how they got along."

"What's that got to do with my husband's suicide?"

"Probably nothing," said Mori carefully. "I'm just trying to establish the pyschological background."

Mrs. Hara shook her head and gave a little sigh.

"How about a drink first?" she said. "I've only got beer, I'm afraid."

"Beer's fine," said Mori.

They sat down on the packing crates and popped open a couple of cans of Suntory Malts. Mori offered her a Mild Seven, and she smoked it hesitantly, holding it away from her like a firework about to go off. She sat cross-legged, and as she talked her left leg ticked nervously. Mori noticed that she had painted her toenails, all except the little toe where the nail was too small.

The story was a sad and complicated one, though of a type that Mori had heard many times before. It had been an arranged marriage, with the introductions made by a senior bureaucrat at the Ministry of Finance who saw it as his duty to find a wife for the most promising young man of his year. At first her father had been dubious. A top executive at Japan's oldest, largest, and most highly indebted shipping line, he was not enthusiastic about Hara's humble background. However, after due consideration, he changed his mind. Hara was, after all, an exceptional young man with a great future ahead of him. And it was, after all, his second daughter, his son and elder daughter having already been married off into prestigious families. And the shipping line did need massive financial restructuring. . . .

The marriage was approved, but her family had never really accepted Hara, her brother least of all. Although Hara was a year older, Yoshimura treated him like an inferior and called him "the bumpkin" behind his back. Similarly, Hara didn't bother to hide his contempt for Yoshimura and his work at Nippon Infosystems. At home, just the mention of Iwanaga's name was enough to send him into a dark mood.

"What's the matter with Japan today?" he would grumble. "Lunatics are treated like geniuses, and geniuses like lunatics."

Since relations between them were so edgy, the two brothers-in-law rarely met. The last time they had, Mrs. Hara remembered, was about a year before, and a blazing quarrel had resulted.

"What was it about?" asked Mori.

"It's a long time ago, Mori-san. I'm not sure, but I think it was about money."

"Money? You mean a loan?"

Mrs. Hara shook her head. Her left leg was ticking a little more strongly now.

"No, no. Monetary policy—whether it was right to make it easier or tighter. The value of the yen. That sort of thing."

"What was the point of disagreement?"

"That much I don't remember. I only remember my husband saying that Iwanaga had done nothing for Japan and that any policy that put him in trouble was a good one."

"That must have made your brother angry."

"He was furious. He shouted that Iwanaga thought only of Japan's future and that soon everyone would recognize his genius."

"What did he mean by that?"

"I don't know, Mori-san," said Mrs. Hara. "My brother's always had strange ideas, ever since he was young. You should ask him yourself."

It was time to go. He finished off the can of beer and got up.

"You do understand, don't you?" she said in a low, strangely urgent voice. "We were never that close, and now . . ."

She gestured around the empty room. Suddenly, she looked extremely tired.

". . . suddenly it's all gone. I have to start again and there isn't much time left."

"I understand," said Mori, slipping on his shoes.

He left the thirty-five-year-old woman alone in the room with her packing cases and her spasm of guilt.

The main difference between politicians and yakuza, decided Toshio Iwanaga as he waited in his office for Uchida to appear, is that yakuza generally conduct their factional battles with a sense of honor. Dealing with men like Uchida was always a disagreeable business. He wasn't even a real politician, just a behind-the-scenes fixer who ensured that the right amounts of money got to the right people at the right time. In other words, a pimp.

Iwanaga walked to the side of the room and looked out over the roofs of the city. Rain was lashing against the window, distorting the panoramic view of Marunouchi, the Ginza, and Tokyo Bay. For an instant, several blocks were blotted out by a rush of rainwater down the glass. Suddenly Iwanaga was reminded of his first-ever visit to Tokyo, in the summer of 1946. Tokyo: to the wide-eyed schoolboy from the countryside, the very word had conjured up visions of wealth and power and limitless sophistication. He remembered the sickening feeling of shock and disillusion when his gaze met block after block of burned-out rubble, of nothingness.

The speakerphone on his desk bleeped before delivering its message:

"Mr. Uchida has arrived."

"Show him in," said Iwanaga.

Uchida was a small, thin-faced man with greasy hair swept down over his forehead. He greeted Iwanaga with a deep bow and his usual ingratiating smile. "I bring good news, sensei," he said. "The discussions are proceeding very well. The serious opposition to Ishizaka is disappearing fast."

"What about Takemaru?"

"Takemaru is prepared to support us. The price is five seats in the cabinet, including the Construction Ministry for his son-in-law, and a donation to his Economic Research Institute."

"Another donation? How much does he expect this time?"

"Five large ones should be enough."

Five hundred million yen! The man's impudence was breathtaking. Still, at this late stage there was no alternative but to pay.

Iwanaga grunted his assent, then turned away. He had no desire to swap small talk with the likes of Uchida.

"And exactly when will these discussions end?" he asked.

"In another four or five days, probably. The middle and junior ranks are firmly with us, but we need to create more consensus among the senior figures."

More consensus! That meant more meetings in high-class restaurants, more geisha parties, more lavish donations to "economic research institutes."

"Do what you have to," said Iwanaga. "But the whole business must be settled soon. I want the Ishizaka cabinet inaugurated by the end of the month. That is absolutely essential."

"The end of the month?" said Uchida. "What's the hurry?"

Iwanaga turned sharply on his heel and stared at the man with cold fury.

"You'll find out," he snarled.

As the limousine pulled away from the Nippon Infosystems head office, Uchida glanced up at the twentieth floor and gave a slight shudder. That expression on Iwanaga's face—he had heard stories about what happened to people who angered him. For example, there had been the hotel magnate who had double-crossed him in a big real estate deal. Shortly afterward, the hotel had gone up in flames, and eighty guests had been baked to death in their bedrooms. The blackened shell of the still-empty building provoked unpleasant thoughts in Uchida's mind every time he passed it. Iwanaga had sworn him to total secrecy. Usually, Uchida wasn't overfastidious about matters of discretion. This time, however, he planned to keep his word.

And what was behind it all? There were rumors going around about radical new policies that Ishizaka was said to be considering. He was going to scrap the U.S.-Japan Security Treaty. He was going to sell critical technology to the Russians and Chinese. He was going to authorize a nuclear weapons program. Uchida shook his head in resignation. He had always considered himself a pragmatist, a man who got things done as efficiently as possible. He didn't understand these ideological types.

The rain was coming down hard now, drumming against the roof of the car, sweeping across the city in giant curtains. Uchida couldn't resist a final glance up at the Nippon Infosystems Building. For a brief moment, he caught a sight of a figure at the window. Distorted by the rivers of rain on the windshield, it looked as if it were dancing up and down like a tiny puppet.

By the time that Deputy Leader Aga arrived at the apartment block where Naomi lived, the typhoon had passed on. It was well past midnight. A watery moon was hanging in the sky, thin black clouds scudding across it. Getting out of the Lincoln Continental, he moved a little more stiffly than usual. One leg dragged behind the other, and the effort of walking made him swing his shoulders from side to side. Pain and pleasure—in Aga's world the two were closely allied. Three days before, a ring of black pearls had been sewn into the head of his sexual organ. He hadn't told Naomi yet. It would be her birthday surprise.

Aga was too preoccupied to notice the construction worker sitting in a small truck piled up with scaffolding. There were many things weighing on his mind. The Kawashita Organization was proving more difficult to manage than he had expected. The diversification into cocaine had soured relations with the police. The joint venture with the Bamboo Society in Taiwan was a constant source of problems. Back at home, the *intelli* faction had become much too pushy. Young Terada was getting dangerous. He would have to be squashed.

Aga walked slowly into the lobby of the building, taking care not to put too much stress on the muscles of his lower belly. As he called through to Naomi on the security phone, he considered the possible ways in which he could satisfy her without damaging the surgeon's handiwork. It would be at least another three weeks before the black pearls could glisten with her juices of love.

He noticed them just as the elevator reached the ground floor—three of them, dressed in workmen's overalls. He knew what they wanted from the rapid, purposeful way they moved and the stiff expressions on their faces. He had moved that way and worn that expression many times himself.

He ducked into the elevator, but it was too late. They were on him. Suddenly, the little metal box was filled with the crash of their guns. He staggered against the control panel, fingers jabbing at the Close button. A bullet ripped through the palm of his hand, sending a splash of blood onto the carpeted wall. He wanted to yell with the pain, but there was no time. He was falling back into the corner, jerking with the impact of the bullets that were punching into his chest.

It was a full minute before the doors finally shut. Then the elevator hummed upward to where Naomi was waiting on the sixteenth floor.

Next morning, when the newscaster in the Chanel suit described what had happened, she had a grave expression on her face, though not as grave as the one she employed for really unfortunate events like trade disputes and typhoons. A top-ranking member of the Kawashita Organization had, she said, been shot dead in a residential area of Tokyo. Police believed that the incident was related to a struggle for territory between gangs from east and west Japan. According to initial reports, no ordinary citizens had been harmed in any way. At this, she permitted herself a small smile. Then, she went on to the next story, the continuing surge in the value of the dollar.

10

.
.

MAX Sharrock caught the news about the action in the
currency markets in his Manhattan hotel suite. At the
time, he was simultaneously tying a bow tie, drinking
a vodka and tonic, and glancing through some new poll findings,
so it took a few seconds for what the announcer was saying to
sink in. It was, he decided finally, a good omen for the Reckard
campaign.

When he had finished what he was doing, Sharrock switched
off the TV and spent a few minutes examining the view of the city
from his hotel window. It was still a splendid sight from high up.
On street level, though, it was a different story. Random violence,
festering craziness—they had always been present in the background. Now they were simply unavoidable, no matter how rich
you were. Why, only the other week, Sally Cormack, wife of the
Under-Secretary of Commerce, had been robbed of sixty thousand dollars' worth of jewelry in the corridor of a Lexington
Avenue Hotel. A more exclusive hotel, in fact, than the one
Sharrock was staying in. A well-dressed black guy had produced
a handgun from his sports bag and taken the stuff off her right in
the middle of the afternoon. She was lucky not to have been
raped, sodomized, beaten into brain damage, mutilated and all
the rest of it.

The picture-postcard view was almost mocking. Some of those
towers of steel and glass were fast turning into shells, like the

great department stores that had shut their doors over the past few years. The city's finances were out of control again, and corporations were fleeing the taxes, relocating to the Midwest or Texas or wherever. And the more that went, the heavier the tax burden on everybody who stayed behind. So there were roads like obstacle courses which hadn't been fixed in twenty years. The sidewalks were full of homeless junkies and teenage whores and crazies who could never be kept in line, let alone put right. There just wasn't the money. Some districts had slipped into virtual tribal warfare, with the police leaving the ethnic vigilante groups to dish out their own brand of law and order.

Sharrock pulled on his jacket, then made a quick call to Washington. Yes, everything had gone according to plan. Reckard's Trade and Investment Bill, the one he called his "Fairness Initiative," had passed the House with a two-thirds majority. The president had made it plain that he didn't want to sign, but now he would have no alternative. Reckard was definitely on a roll.

As the limo nudged its way through the constipated traffic, Sharrock thought about Reckard and the waves he was making. The whole thing had picked up more momentum than even he had thought possible. A few weeks ago, Reckard had made a speech calling for an oath of allegiance from heads of corporations and other major figures in public life and a special committee to investigate those suspected of being influenced by "economic interests contrary to American values." Within days, hundreds of thousands of letters and phone messages of support had been received. Hank Jones, Jr., had even written a song called "The Ballad of Big Bob Reckard." It was already storming up the country-and-western charts.

Reckard was looking good for the nomination. Johansen had got a team working on it full-time, setting up action committees, cultivating local party workers, squaring everything with potential rivals. Sharrock had already started looking ahead to the presidential contest. One issue in particular was attracting his attention. What about the running mate? What kind of figure would add power and credibility to the ticket? So far, Sharrock's preliminary research had thrown up two clear leaders.

The first was Frank Giordani, the auto man. He was widely admired by blue-collar ethnics for fighting his way to the top of the corporate tree. His father had been a first generation immigrant who had run a bakery store right here in New York City. The son had supported himself through college, then started in the auto industry as a lowly salesman. From there, through brains and energy and sheer chutzpah, he had risen to the CEO's office of one of America's proudest corporations, previously a WASP stronghold. It was a great and compelling story.

On the face of it, Giordani looked ideal. There were, however, some problems. For one thing, there was the performance of the company he had controlled for the past ten years. It was practically bankrupt. Tens of thousands of workers had been laid off. No one liked the cars. They were always being recalled for design flaws and safety problems. Thousands of the latest model were rusting in dealers' lots all over the country. In fact, the only model that was selling well was the compact that was imported from Korea. Despite all this, Giordani insisted on paying himself a massive salary—ten million dollars the previous year—and since his latest divorce his taste for the high life was starting to attract attention. Sharrock had noted the steady rise of negative responses among unmarried professionals, especially women.

The other possibility was Marvin Hooper. Although not as high profile as Giordani, Hooper had the advantage of not being a Catholic, not being Italian, and not being a regular subject of the gossip columns. A congressman for twenty-five years, Hooper was a moderate with an excellent track record and few enemies. He had come out strongly against the Vietnam War in 1971, and had delivered some fierce attacks on Richard Nixon during the Watergate hearings. Furthermore, he was a Korean War veteran who had lost three fingers from his left hand in a grenade accident. In TV bites, he made a point of gesturing with that left hand. The symbolism couldn't be better. With his silver hair, deep tan, and soft drawl, Hooper spelled maturity and responsibility—exactly what was necessary to help balance Reckard's youthful drive and enthusiasm.

Yet even Hooper came with strings attached. A couple of years back, there had been controversy about a large unsecured loan that his wife had received from a bankrupt Texas S&L. Some muckrakers had tried to tie that in to his long and fierce opposition to government regulation of the industry. Then there had been all those problems with his son—expelled from law school for cheating on his exams, the drug arrests, then sexual battery of a Columbia University comparative literature major. That last escapade had cost young Bill Hooper three months stuck in his Manhattan apartment with an electronic bracelet around his ankle, watching MTV all day and eating delivery pizza.

Interestingly, though, Sharrock's polls showed very little fallout from these incidents. Among middle-aged white professionals, Hooper's approval ratings had actually gone up after each one of his son's appearances in the headlines. In Sharrock's view, this meant that problems with unruly kids were now so widespread that they provoked sympathy, not rejection. And, of course, Hooper had handled it all superbly. The sober, slow-talking press conferences, the news photos of the family "standing together," that two-fingered left hand wiping the tears from Liz Hooper's cheek. The man was a real pro, no doubt about it.

Which was it to be? Giordani or Hooper? Sex appeal or safety? It was an intriguing problem. Sharrock would study the poll trends for another six months before coming up with a final recommendation. In the meantime, he would analyze every detail of the Reckard phenomenon, making sure that, in Johansen's words, "everyone got on the bus."

Sharrock picked up Susan outside her firm's head office on Wall Street. She looked tougher, more professional than the first time they had met. Her hair was swept back into a ponytail, and the severe cut of her gray suit almost hid the curves of her hips and breasts.

"Another new high on the Dow," observed Sharrock as she settled into the back seat. "You bears must be hurting bad."

"No depth," Susan replied curtly. "All the broader indices are down again. It's a bad sign. The only buying around is coming through the program traders in Chicago."

"Hey! Interest rates are at historical lows. Corporate profits are on the way up. The market's got every right to celebrate."

Susan shook her head contemptuously.

"When the market finally cracks, it's going to be savage. Treasuries, the dollar, everything's going in the tank, I've never been more convinced of anything in my entire life."

"All sweetness and light, aren't you! Come on, it's Friday night. Nothing's going to happen till Monday at least."

He patted her lightly on the shoulder. She recoiled instinctively, then smiled. Suddenly, she was human again.

Normally, Sharrock's idea of a night out in Manhattan included cocktails at the Plaza, dinner at the latest leading-edge restaurant, a quick tour of a couple of dance spots where they knew him well, then back to the suite where waited the Dom Perignon in its ice bucket, the caviar and crackers, the jacuzzi, the king-size bed like an empty stage.

Not this time. Susan had accepted his invitation only on the condition that she picked the venue. So they were bound not for the latest Sondheim, not for his favorite jazz spot in the Village, not for flaming sauces and palate-tingling sorbets, but for a lecture at the Nippon Society.

A lecture! Sharrock could hardly believe what he was doing. Still, with women like Susan it was always best to give them their head if you wanted to get the favor returned. She obviously wasn't going to rest until she had proved her point about Japan.

The Nippon Society was quartered halfway up a six-story building in midtown that had once held an English-style gentlemen's club. Some of the furniture and fittings—the leather sofas, the carved walnut mantelpiece—looked as if they had been there since the early years of the century. However, instead of the hunting prints that would have once adorned the walls, there were now woodblock prints, charcoal-brush screens, Zen cartoons of monkeys and snakes.

The evening's entertainment, noticed Sharrock glumly, was a talk entitled "From Rice Paddies to Robotics—Evolving Social and Economic Structures in Modern-Day Japan." On the program, the first speaker was billed as the representative of the Tokyo Institute for International Communication. The second was an American journalist who had lived in Japan for five years. The third speaker, Professor Shinpei Ezaki, was chief of the Sumikawa Foundation, a think tank affiliated to Sumikawa Bank. The audience seemed to be composed of academics, earnest students, hungry-looking single women, and a smattering of businessmen, probably, thought Sharrock, employees of Japanese firms willing to do anything to impress their bosses.

"Ezaki's a brilliant man," said Susan. "He's got some excellent insights into what's happening in the Japanese economy. After you've heard him, maybe you'll understand something about the place."

Sharrock nodded thoughtfully, swilled down his whiskey sour, and grabbed another from a passing tray.

The man from the Institute was even more boring than Sharrock had expected. Bald head gleaming with sweat, he mumbled into the microphone in English so laborious that Sharrock caught only one word in three. The subject seemed to be the nature of decision-making in Japanese companies, the careful building up of consensus, the role of the leader in creating group cohesion. After five minutes, Sharrock's eyelids felt as if they had weights attached.

The free-lance journalist wasn't much better. He told a few feeble jokes, then launched into a long explanation of Japanese management techniques, ending up with a plea for an end to all misunderstandings and the sharing of ideas and resources.

"Who's paying this guy off?" whispered Sharrock to Susan. "He's totally sold out to the other side. We ought to have him investigated."

She looked at him quizzically, unsure whether or not he was joking. He wasn't, but he smiled back all the same.

The last speaker finally appeared at the dais. He was about forty years old, tall for a Japanese, with deep penetrating eyes. He had an almost military bearing. For a moment, he gazed around the room, as if conducting a mental roll call of all those present.

"That's not Ezaki," said Susan.

The man spoke English fluently, with a clipped British public school accent.

"Professor Ezaki sends his deepest apologies for being unable to attend this distinguished gathering tonight. I'm afraid he had to return to Japan on an urgent business matter. I trust that as his replacement I will not be wholly inadequate. My name is Machida. I am the director of the American branch of the Maruichi Research Institute."

Machida's speech was quite different from the brilliant analysis of Japanese economic structures that Susan had promised. Instead, it was a summary of Japan's postwar achievements, pointedly contrasted with the failures of the Western countries. The coming century, Machida continued, would belong to Japan. The Japanese people's intellectual ability was the highest in the world. They were far harder-working, better educated, more conscientious than Westerners. They would lead the next industrial revolution, creating technologies that simply wouldn't exist anywhere else.

"One hundred and thirty years ago, you Westerners came to Japan in your black ships and forced us to modernize at the point of a gun. We swallowed our pride and cast off a thousand years of tradition, but you never accepted us. When we tried to imitate your empires, you destroyed us with nuclear bombs. Then you forced us to bend to your will again, this time with grand ideas about democracy and human rights."

Several members of the audience were shifting uncomfortably in their chairs, coughing, smiling nervously at their neighbors. Machida had the hard eyes and rigid expression of a fanatic, but his words were delivered slowly, thoughtfully.

"But you didn't expect us to be so successful. You didn't expect the pupil to grow stronger than the master. When you found out that we were beating you at your own game, you tried to change the rules. You restricted our exports and investments. You attacked our business methods. You tried to destroy the culture and traditions that give us strength.

"You may think you can slap us down as you did so many times before. But you don't understand that the situation has changed. Your period of dominance is over. Now at last we are strong enough to defend our culture. Now it is your turn to bend to our will."

Afterward Susan looked shell-shocked.

"I'm sorry," she whispered on the way out. "The guy was completely off the wall."

"Don't worry," said Sharrock with an ironic smile. "I learned plenty."

But he hadn't learned enough about Susan. When he instructed the driver to take them back to his hotel, she refused point blank to accompany him.

"I'm going back to the office," she said with an apologetic smile. "I'm doing a big buy program in Tokyo, and I need to see how the market's doing."

Sharrock ground his teeth in irritation. There was Japan, getting in the way of legitimate American aspirations once again.

While Max Sharrock sat alone on his double bed sipping champagne, ten stories below him the hotel lobby was filling with tanned, heavy-chested men in dinner jackets and expensively lean women in long frocks. The big banquet of the evening had finished, and, under the beady gaze of half-a-dozen gum-chewing security men, the guests were preparing to depart. They shuffled toward the revolving door, booming salutations at each other and flashing their dentistry.

In the banquet room, the guest of honor sat alone at his place at the head of the table. He hadn't moved since the meal had ended. The waiters glanced at him curiously as they cleared away the plates and glasses.

"Have you got some bad feeling, sah?" asked one of them, a Korean with a staccato accent.

"Quite all right," mumbled the seated man. "Everything's quite all right."

He picked a half-empty brandy glass off the tray that the waiter was carrying and downed it in one gulp.

"Get me another," he said, thrusting out the glass.

The waiter glanced questioningly at the tall man standing by the window. The tall man shook his head.

"I think maybe you have to go now, sah," said the waiter.

Suddenly, the man at the table stood up and glowered down at the diminutive waiter.

"I don't care what you think," he said through clenched teeth. "You're not paid to think. You're paid to bring what you're told to bring. Got it?"

The waiter took the glass and scurried away. The tall man walked over and put his hand on the other's shoulder.

"Let's leave it," he said. "It's been a long hard day."

"Sorry about the speech, Ben. Seems like everything's screwed up these days. Maybe the papers are right. Maybe I should resign."

"Don't be ridiculous. We've been through worse shit before and come out smelling like roses. Come on, I want you to think positive, think aggressive." The other man nodded glumly and passed a hand through his hair.

"They won't dare go through with it," continued Ben. "We'll use everything we've got against them. There'll be street demonstrations, boycotts, a media campaign like they've never seen before. . . ."

His partner said nothing. He was thinking about the afternoon's meeting in the offices of the Japanese bank. What had gotten to him most was the icy politeness of the little guy who did all the talking, the one who had flown over from Tokyo the day before. He had sounded as if he were giving an invitation to a dinner party, not calling in a syndicated loan.

They had all been sitting in the boardroom, with its heavy oak table and panoramic view of the bay. It was a perfect day, and several tourist boats were clustered around the Statue of Liberty. While the secretary handed out green tea in little cups with no handles, the little guy had small-talked about the Yankees and the incredible heat wave. Then, as soon as she had gone, he had dropped his bombshell.

It was a sneak attack, a total shock. Ben had called it a financial Pearl Harbor to the man's face. Of course, according to the fine print of the deal, they had a right to call in the loan. It was technically in default—but then it had been in default many times before and every time the leader of the lending syndicate had arranged a reschedule. Not this time.

"Not this time, I'm afraid," the little man had said in his imperturbably smooth way. "It's a question of risk. Our analysts have downgraded your credit rating several times in the past few years. We have already arranged one major rescheduling, but evidently you find it difficult to make the repayments as agreed. Under these circumstances, our head office has decided that it is inadvisable to continue with the loan facility. . . ."

"Listen, I'm sorry about the delay. I can promise you it won't happen again. I'll give it absolute priority over every other obligation."

"That's what you promised last time, isn't it?"

The little man had a strange expression on his face, as if he were trying to stop himself from smiling.

"You mean you don't believe me?"

"Sumikawa Bank has been doing business with our American friends for many years. After many experiences, we have learned to trust facts, not promises."

The little man's tone of voice left no room for negotiation. The decision had already been made, a decision that would close down hospitals and rehabilitation centers, turn more homeless out into the streets, that would hurt every ordinary family living in the city.

The Korean waiter brought another glass of brandy on a silver tray. Without a word, he snatched it and gulped down half the measure.

"Come on, that's enough," said Ben gently. "Tomorrow's a big day. We're spending the morning with the legal people, then we go to public relations to prepare a statement. After that, I've arranged a meeting with Robert Reckard's people. They're going to be in on everything we do. Don't worry, we're going to make Sumikawa Bank realize that it just made the worst mistake in its history."

The other man nodded, his expression blank, and took another sip of brandy.

"Good work, Ben," he said. "I don't know what I'd do without you."

He emptied the glass and walked slowly toward the door. Ben picked up the draft of the speech from the table and put it in his briefcase. Then he called out to the two security men waiting at the door.

"Okay, boys, it's time to go home. Get the limos to the back, and make sure there's no press around."

That was important. Ben didn't want to open up the morning paper and see a photo of his boss and old friend looking like something from a zombie movie. Whatever the problems, he was still the mayor of New York City, and he had to maintain his public image at all costs. It would be the most important asset in the fight for his political life that had just started.

In a small town in northern Hokkaido, an assistant manager for general affairs at Sumikawa Bank chose not to go out for lunch with the rest of the staff. He told them he would stay behind in the office. That was hardly unusual. He had only been there a couple of weeks, but it was already clear that he was a difficult, antisocial man. What was slightly stranger was the fact that, as soon as they had gone, he sat down at his secretary's desk and started tapping away at the word processor.

A couple of weeks! To Tom Kono, it already seemed like a couple of years. There was nothing for his wife to do but sit at home all day, and his children were being bullied at school for their "foreignness." As for the job, never in his life had he experienced anything as mind-numbingly dull. It was a major event in the life of the branch when a farmer asked for a loan to buy a new tractor, or when one of the small local firms transferred money to a supplier. Tom had soon found that he could hardly communicate with his new colleagues at all. Apart from the branch manager, they were all locals who had only been to Tokyo once or twice in their lives. And it was quite obvious from the hesitant, curious way they spoke to him that they knew he was being punished for a major transgression.

It was in order to inject some purpose and excitement into his life that Tom kept in regular contact with some of his close friends in the London office. They told him that all aspects of the business were being directly controlled by the new branch manager, the man responsible for Tom's transfer to Hokkaido, who was now ruling the organization with a grip of iron. Hardly a week passed without a new regulation being drawn up—on the right way to address your superior, to wear your company badge, to answer the telephone. The local staff had been removed from all positions of responsibility, and most of the longer-serving Japanese had been recalled to the head office. Tom's replacement as chief dealer was a secretive, morose character called Shimada who hardly spoke any English and had no friends, even among the other Japanese staff.

That had saddened Tom, but not surprised him. Much more worrying, however, was a discovery by Tom's old assistant, a cheerful Liverpudlian called Trevor. Annoyed by Shimada's persistent refusal to show him any of the trades that were being made, he had gone to the computer and run off a printout of all the positions that the bank was holding. At first, he had thought that there was some mistake. The numbers were too big; the risk far too heavy to be sustained. In Tom's day, the bank had been the most aggressive player in the markets, but what Shimada was doing was on a different scale entirely. He was using options and futures, but not to hedge his position. Rather, he was leveraging himself up further into a one-way bet of truly massive proportions. Tom had gotten Trevor to fax him the printouts every evening. He had watched Shimada's position build up to the point where it was irreversible. He couldn't get out now without setting off a collapse that would wipe out not only the entire London trading book, but also Sumikawa's profits for the rest of the century. The man's strategy was pure madness.

Or was it? The more Tom thought about the situation, the more worried he became. For the one-way bet that Shimada had taken was in favor of the U.S. dollar. His buying must have played a substantial part in its recent unexpected surge against all other currencies. When he liquidated his position, the result could only be a massive plunge. The dollar would go into free-fall.

Shimada must surely be aware of that.

In a small office in a small town in Hokkaido, Tom Kono sat at a word processor, typing out the most important letter he would ever write. It was addressed to the ex-chairman of Sumikawa Bank, a man who had been forced into retirement after a boardroom coup two years ago. Tom had never met the old man, but they said he still nursed a burning sense of grievance. For Tom's purpose, that would be enough.

And it was. For the past two years, the ex-chairman had been thinking of little else except how to revenge himself on the former protégé who had schemed away behind his back and then finally deposed him. He would never forget the insolent smile on Yazawa's face at that meeting when the allegations were first presented.

Expense claims! They had had the nerve to question his expense claims! He had almost choked on his green tea. So what if his "number two wife" had traveled alone to Paris and Milan, so what if she had spent a few million yen on clothes and jewelry. As he had tried to explain, the boutique that she ran had been a valuable customer of the bank for over a decade. It was quite reasonable for her to be entertained lavishly!

Then they brought up the matter of the Cézanne, and at that moment he knew that he was lost. Somehow, they had gotten copies of documents from his daughter's art gallery in the Ginza. They knew exactly how many times the painting had changed hands and at what price. They had even talked to the appraiser who his daughter had bribed to sign the last three transactions. They had more than enough information to see that the painting wasn't worth one-fifth of the loan that had eventually been collateralized against it.

Since walking out of that meeting in a daze, to find that his limousine and driver had already been reassigned, the ex-chairman had been dreaming of ways to expunge the humiliation, to wipe that insolent smile from Yazawa's face once and for all. He spread rumors, he gave bitter interviews to weekly magazines, he schemed away tirelessly. His supporters were now a dwindling group, mostly removed from the positions of power he had placed them in. Still, they kept their ears open and passed on what they heard. They told him that Yazawa's new policy of recruiting managers into the bank from outside was sparking huge resentment. They told him of arbitrary promotions and demotions and the arrogance of Yazawa's new favorites. They passed on strange stories of massive, unexplained transfers of funds.

When the ex-chairman had finished reading Tom Kono's letter, he closed his eyes and smiled a smile of pure joy. Then he laughed, a deep throaty chuckle that startled the young woman who was acting as his secretary, driver, and masseuse. "What is it?" she asked, glancing at him anxiously. "Some good news?"

"The best, Kimi-chan," said the ex-chairman, still wheezing with laughter. "The best news for years."

Kimiko looked at him more closely. His normally sallow face was flushed bright red, and the mass of wrinkles had disappeared. Suddenly, he was no longer a disgraced businessman of seventy-five years, but a little boy who had just won a game of hide-and-seek.

"That's good," she said soothingly. "Is there anything I can do to help?"

"Yes, there is," said the ex-chairman merrily. "Take off your shirt and brassiere and come over here."

She nodded dutifully and started to undo her buttons.

By the time the ex-chairman took the rubbery nipple into his mouth, he had already decided on his strategy. There was no need to take risks, no need to be obtrusive. He knew exactly the right people to give the information to. They would take care of everything.

His tongue traced the dimpled circumference of the aureole, then flicked south to north, north to south, teasing the nipple to its full erectness. There was something about his ardor that encouraged Kimiko to slip her hand down into his lap. Yes, just as she had thought. The first time in years.

11

.
.
.

NOT far from the murky waters of Tokyo Bay, halfway between the textile district and the fish market, lies a dusty,
grubby part of the city called Kabuto-cho, or "helmet
town." According to legend, "helmet town" was given its unusual name almost a thousand years ago. One of the warlords
fighting for control over eastern Japan happened to be leading his
army through the area. He pitched camp beside the Nihonbashi
River and prayed to the Spirit of the River Dragon for success in
the coming battle. His prayers were answered, and, returning
home, his victorious soldiers paused to give thanks at the same
spot. As a special offering, the warlord took his most prized pos-
session, his ornate golden helmet, and buried it near the river-
bank.

The shrine built to mark the spot still stands today, overshadowed by highways and the gray concrete bulk of the building
next door—the Tokyo Stock Exchange. The men who stop by to
pray are every bit as ruthlessly determined, as iron-willed in the
pursuit of victory, as their tenth-century predecessors. They are
the foot soldiers of Japan's securities industry, and they have made
the shrine their own. They clap their hands and summon the deity
and beseech his aid in the financial battle ahead. Then they pick
up their briefcases and hurry back into the roar of the traffic.

It was near Kabuto-cho that the rice and textiles markets developed in the centuries when Japan was shut off from the rest of

the world. A sophisticated trading system was created by groups of merchants sprawling on tatami mats in the local teahouses. When prices were strong, traders would spend their winnings in the Yoshiwara pleasure quarter on the other side of the Sumida River. The world of the speculator and the world of the geisha grew up side by side. When traders were looking for a word to signify the end of the day's business, they chose *o-bike*, which meant the closing of the great Yoshiwara gate at midnight. *Gyoku*, an ordinary courtesan, became the slang expression for anything purchased in the market. Both phrases are still used today, though the dealers and salesmen who shout them into phones while scribbling figures on order sheets and squinting into screens don't give the etymology a moment's thought.

After the Meiji Restoration, the samurai class was abolished and its members were forced to cut their topknots and hang up their twin swords. Partly as compensation for this blow to their pride, partly to keep them out of mischief, they were awarded government pensions, which were afterward converted into long-term bonds. The samurai were contemptuous of the new, materialistic civilization that had swept away everything that they understood. Rather than find salaried employment, many of them preferred to sell their bonds and live off the proceeds. Often they were so commercially unsophisticated that they were tricked by unscrupulous brokers into accepting abnormally low prices. Anxious to prevent the creation of an embittered clique of ex-fighting men, the government set up an exchange in Kabuto-cho where the bonds could be traded at publicly quoted prices.

Modern Kabuto-cho pays scant regard to its dignified origins. "The island," as it is known to its denizens, has no time for sentiment or tradition, only for hustling, ramping, cornering, stuffing, and the other activities for which it is renowned. There are no fine facades or tasteful decorations. Crisscrossed by stagnant canals, laced with wafts of carbon monoxide, the area is unashamedly, aggressively ugly. The greater part is situated on a landfill completed three hundred years ago on the orders of the first shogun. Although the ground is firm underfoot, the staff of the world's largest securities companies and banks are periodically jarred by sudden tremors that set lamps swinging and coffee slopping. In the event of a major earthquake in Tokyo Bay, the shock could well turn the loose-packed mud underneath into a mass of churning jelly. However, in a place where "long-term" means "by the end of the week," that is not a prospect which anyone has the time or inclination to worry about.

Right at the heart of Kabuto-cho, in a street of cluttered, dimly lit shops selling handmade fans, doll-shaped candies, and antique but valueless share certificates, stands a noodle restaurant that serves some of the finest handmade noodles in Tokyo. In the back of the shop, there are a number of small private rooms in which exchanges of sensitive information can take place without hindrance or observation.

Kenji booked a room first thing in the morning, using the public telephone in Maruichi's gigantic atrium and a false name. He arrived ten minutes early, and walked up and down the street several times before venturing inside.

Noda was already waiting, a bottle of Sapporo beer half empty on the table in front of him. He looked older than the last time Kenji had seen him. With his hair flecked with gray and his face deeply lined around the mouth, he looked considerably more than his fifty years.

"I'm sorry for being late," said Kenji, and gave a bow of respect that was genuine. "Don't worry," said Noda wryly. "An old has-been like me has nothing better to do anyway."

Kenji attempted to fill up the half-empty beer glass, but Noda waved his hand away and filled Kenji's instead. Kenji felt a pang of shame.

When Kenji had joined Maruichi six years before, Noda had been deputy section chief and the one senior man who he admired without reservation. Noda's knowledge of the market was immense, and, still rarer, he was always willing to pass on what he knew to the younger staff. Still, it had been obvious that he would never rise above the lowly status of deputy section chief. The problem with Noda was that he had his own ideas about investment. Instead of taking part in Maruichi's huge nationwide "campaigns" to drive up the stock prices of politically powerful companies, he would recommend smaller stocks that would actually make his clients money. This made him highly unpopular with the people at the top, and in the end they switched him to a *window-side* job, shuffling papers in the personnel department. Soon afterward, he left to set up his own consulting company. Despite the down-at-the-heels impression he liked to give, Noda had managed to score a considerable success. The accuracy of his market forecasts had won him a huge reputation among the select group of investors whom he agreed to advise.

"So how's life at Maruichi?" Noda asked. "I understand you're having some problems with the Sumikawa Heavy Industries campaign."

"Are we?" Kenji was startled. "What makes you say that?"

The campaign to "ramp up" the share price of Sumikawa Heavy Industries had only just begun that morning. No one at Maruichi could know how it was going, let alone an outsider.

"Oh, I have my sources. They tell me, for example, that Yamamura Securities has orders to sell at least thirty million shares at market. The stock'll be down ten percent by the end of the week."

Thirty million! Down 10 percent! That would mean a disastrous loss of face. Yamamura Securities was Maruichi's greatest rival. Like all other Maruichi men, Kenji regarded everything to do with it with utter contempt. Recently, however, the president of Yamamura had set up an "arranged marriage" between his second daughter and the third son of the chairman of Nikkeiren, the employers' federation. Clearly, Yamamura was mounting a desperate attack on Maruichi's status as leader of the securities industry.

Noda drained his glass and wiped his mouth with a paper napkin. He looked at Kenji with a quiet smile on his lips.

"Be courageous," he said. "No company is worth selling your soul for."

"What do you mean?"

"It's written all over your face. You've got a big story to tell, and you're worried about the consequences. You picked me as the audience because there's nobody at the company you feel you can trust. Am I right?"

Kenji nodded. He looked at the man's face, the strong brow, the skeptical downturn of the mouth. Then he took a deep breath and started talking.

When he had finished, Noda was silent for a while. He chewed some pickled vegetables and slowly sipped at his beer.

"Very interesting," he said finally. "I've heard some pretty strange rumors recently. I didn't believe them at first, but now I'm not so sure."

"Rumors about what?"

"About Silent Thunder. I heard they're planning something big, something that needs trillions of yen in capital."

"Silent Thunder?" Kenji was amazed. "Isn't that the secret society that Maruichi ran before the war?"

The subject was not mentioned in any of the corporate histories, TV documentaries, and biographies that Maruichi sponsored. Kenji remembered the name vaguely from a "black" history of the company that a university friend had jokingly given him before he went for his job interview.

"That's right. Founded by old Ichiro himself in 1928 and kept under his personal control."

"But it can't be—I mean, surely all the secret societies were abolished after the war."

Noda shook his head.

"Some things can never be abolished," he said. "All the records were destroyed and most of the leaders went into hiding, but the tradition has been kept alive. No one knows for sure who the members are, but I've always had suspicions about Sugaya and Takeda. They got to the top too quickly. Someone must have been watching over them."

Kenji stared at him. Could he be joking? With Noda, it was often difficult to tell. He would have the same half-mocking expression on his face when he was explaining why a certain stock price was about to explode. Indeed, he had worn just the same expression when he told Kenji about his sudden transfer to the personnel department.

"So what's going on?" asked Kenji. "And what are we going to do about it?"

"Leave that to me," said Noda. "I'll pass the information on to the right people. As for you, you'd better phone in sick and stay at home for a while."

Phone in sick! At Maruichi, sick days were deducted from the annual holiday allowance, which in Kenji's case was only nine days. He hadn't taken a day off sick since joining the company. He had been to the office with streaming colds and blazing fevers. Once he had even gone back to work after having a hemorrhoid cut out during his lunch break.

"For a while? How long is that going to be?"

Noda leaned forward. For once, the half-smile had completely disappeared.

"Until I tell you it's safe to go back," he said.

After lunch, Kenji phoned in sick, just as Noda had suggested. He spent the next hour in a game center trying to forget what he had heard. There was one game he liked especially. Plastic rats popped up through holes in a circular board, and the player scored points by bashing them on the head with a mallet. Gradually, the pace at which the rats appeared speeded up, until in the end the player was flailing about frenziedly. Kenji was in good form. He thought of every rat as having the face of either Sugaya or Takeda. Soon a small crowd had gathered to marvel at his score, which was the highest of the day. When he had used up enough energy, he watched half a porno movie, had a bowl of Chinese noodles, then took the train home.

From the train window, Kenji caught a glimpse of the new skyscrapers under construction in Tokyo Bay. It was a fine sight, one that still made him proud to be a Maruichi man. The project to redevelop the waterfront area, to take what had been a sprawl of moldering wharves and disused shipyards and turn it into an Asian Manhattan—that whole idea had been dreamed up, publicized, and coordinated by Maruichi Securities. At first, the bureaucrats and even the construction industry had scoffed. Where would the money come from? they had cried. Maruichi

168   PETER TASKER

had given them the answer. The stock prices of selected companies, mainly venerable shipbuilders and warehousers who held land on the waterfront, were driven skyward. Then Maruichi instructed the companies to make huge issues of new shares, which were all absorbed by Maruichi's best clients, and share prices were driven upward all over again. Eventually, all the funds necessary were collected.

At first, there had been a few problems with planning regulations, but Maruichi had tackled them in the boldest way possible. The prime minister of the day was the leader of a small anti-mainstream faction thirsty for political funds. Maruichi told his people exactly what shares to buy and when.

Kenji's father, who had worked all his life in a small machinery company, had opposed his son's decision to join Maruichi.

"Bunch of crooks," he would say. "They cheated our section chief out of his bonus two years in a row! Go to a proper company, like Toyota or Hitachi, that makes real things."

Now Kenji had his answer. The waterfront project showed that the financial markets didn't just reflect the real world of buildings and people and cars. They could create it as well.

The train journey took just over an hour. Kenji spent the time reading his favorite comic magazine, *Big Spirits Adventure*. The hero of the first story, a man called Silver Wolf, had been sent to Britain to guard the emperor's son during an official visit. A beautiful blonde assassin in the pay of the CIA was waiting in his hotel room. Under her fur coat, she was wearing nothing but stockings and a garter belt. They tumbled onto the bed together and she twisted her legs around his waist. Then she used the poison gas in her bracelet. As he slipped into unconsciousness, Silver Wolf fumbled for the gun in the bedside drawer. And then . . . And then the story finished. To find out what happened next, Kenji would have to wait another week.

On arrival, he extricated his bicycle from the bicycle forest that surrounded the station and made his way home. It was a pleasant journey, down narrow higgledy-piggledy streets packed with vending machines, through the smell of roast squid and the chiming of wind bells, past old men in panama hats and housewives with babies on their backs and schoolgirls so dark-skinned they looked like Pakistanis.

Kenji was halfway between the station and Royal Garden Heights when the black Mercedes pulled up alongside him. Inside were a couple of stone-faced men in sunglasses, one of whom was talking into a phone. Kenji kept looking straight ahead, pretending he hadn't noticed.

That soon became impossible. The passenger window hummed down.

"A little early to be going home, isn't it?"

Kenji had to look. Huge shoulders, hardly any space between eyebrows and hairline—the man was a gorilla.

"Er . . . yes . . . I suppose so."

"What's the matter? Feeling ill?"

"No . . . I mean, yes. I have a stomachache."

"Well, let me give you a lift home. It'd be much quicker."

"Thank you very much for offering, but I need the exercise."

Kenji gave the same sincere, apologetic smile that he used with angry clients. This time it didn't have the desired effect. Suddenly the gorilla swung open the car door, thumping it against Kenji's leg. Kenji swerved, lost balance, then skidded to the ground. The impact tore a strip out of his trouser leg and made a similar-shaped scrape on the skin beneath. When he looked up, the gorilla had gotten out of the car and was standing over him, a pained expression on his pockmarked face.

"The door," he said bitterly. "You scratched the paint. Have you got any idea what that'll cost to fix?"

Kenji looked at the gleaming white surface. There was no visible mark on it.

"And this bike is bent too. You're going to need a new one—"

The gorilla picked up Kenji's bike with one hand and hurled it over the fence into the paddy field on the other side. It splatted into the wet soil.

"Right," said the gorilla, wiping his hands with a white hand-kerchief. "We'll take you as far as as your apartment house. In fact, we're probably going to take you a bit farther."

They did. For nearly an hour, the Mercedes rolled through the shopping streets and suburbs and semi-industrialized, semiagricultural hinterland of Greater Tokyo. Kenji soon lost his sense of direction. There was no conversation. The gorilla sat dozing in the backseat next to Kenji and his colleague stared at the road ahead. The only signs of life were the periodic rolls of their jaws around wads of gum.

Kenji tried to convince himself that he wasn't scared, but it was no use. Yakuza were bad people to deal with. Everybody at Maruichi Securities knew the story of the branch manager who had put a big yakuza syndicate into a biotech stock just before it collapsed. That was nine years ago now, but people still swapped theories about what had happened to him. Had he been chopped up and fed to guard dogs, or thrown live out of a plane into Osaka Bay? Was he part of the foundations of the new station building there? The only sure thing was that he was no longer around to make any more recommendations.

Kenji thought about the hundreds of billions of yen being siphoned out of the market, about the expression on Sugaya's face, about his parents waiting anxiously by the phone for news of what had happened to him. Then he decided to act.

He waited until the car stopped at a red light in a crowded shopping street, then snatched at the door handle, pushing the back door open.

"What you doing, creep?"

The gorilla grabbed him by his upper arm. Kenji turned, slammed his elbow into the side of the man's face. He grunted with the impact, but didn't let go. The driver glanced behind once, then let out the clutch. Just as the powerful engine surged into life, Kenji twisted out of his jacket, leaving the gorilla clutching the empty sleeve, and threw himself at the open door.

He heard the tires squealing, saw the tarmac rushing backward, then the impact wrenched the breath from his body and he was rolling uncontrollably toward the curb. There was a red flash in front of his eyes and a searing pain in his arm. For a second, he had to fight for consciousness. Then he pulled himself to his feet and ran into a shopping arcade.

Behind him there were shouts and the sound of a car door slamming. His arm was broken, he felt sure. He had to hold it across his chest to stop the jolts of pain. With his left ankle numb and swelling fast, he wouldn't be able to get far.

"Come back, shithead!"

The gorilla was only a few yards behind. Kenji pushed forward through a crowd of twittering schoolgirls. On the corner ahead was a large pachinko parlor, all flashing lights and blaring march music. He ran inside.

The place was full. There were five rows of a dozen or so machines, and a human being sitting absolutely motionless in front of each one. Students, housewives, taxi drivers in uniform, cooks in soup-stained overalls, blue-suited salarymen between visits to customers—all gazing as if hypnotized at the stream of silver balls cascading through the forest of pins.

Kenji ducked down one of the alleys between the rows of machines. Not one of the players even turned to look at him.

"All right, you little bastard . . ."

The gorilla appeared at the end of the alley. He had a truncheonlike bar in his hand.

Kenji dodged back and into the next row. Again, the gorilla appeared at the end. He was slapping the bar into his palm with obvious relish. Kenji glanced behind. If the gorilla made a rush, he would have trouble getting away.

Suddenly, the middle-aged man at the machine on Kenji's left jumped up from his stool and gave a little dance.

"Jackpot," he squawked.

The players nearby got up and peered at his machine, which was bleeping and flashing and discharging a torrent of silver balls. Soon the tray at the bottom of the machine had filled up. Some one handed him a bucket to catch the overflow.

The gorilla charged forward, but was impeded by the half a dozen people now gathered around the lucky machine, which was still puking ball bearings.

"Out of my way, creeps," he snarled, and shoved a middle-aged woman aside.

She staggered backward, knocking over the bucket. In an

instant, the floor became a sea of silver balls. Then suddenly the gorilla's arms were flailing the air and his knees were buckling under him.

"Bastards," he roared as he fell.

There was a crack as his head struck one of the machines, then a moment of silence. Kenji ran for the exit.

At the corner of the arcade a bus was waiting at the bus-stop. A flock of schoolgirls in sailor-suit uniforms was streaming aboard. Kenji elbowed his way to the front of the line. Inside the bus, every seat seemed to be occupied by schoolgirls as well.

"Just three more," yelled the driver. "No need to shove. There'll be another bus in ten minutes."

There were two girls already standing on the step of the bus, waiting to buy their tickets. Kenji forced himself between them, pushing aside a cute young girl of fifteen or sixteen who was carrying a bonsai in a large pot.

"Wah! Rude man!"

"You poor thing—being shoved by that nasty elder brother!"

"It's impermissible, the cheeky fellow!"

"Stop him! Don't let him get on!"

Hands were grabbing at his shirt, trying to pull him off balance. Something was thumping repeatedly against the back of his legs. It was, he realized, the bonsai pot.

Kenji twisted his head round. To his horror, the front of the black Mercedes was nudging out of a side street not forty yards away. It had evidently circled around the shopping district. If the girls pulled him off the bus, he would be completely visible to the driver of the car.

They were surprisingly strong. The girls in front of him on the step were forcing him back, pushing against his chest with their buttocks. The girls behind him had pulled out the tail of his shirt. They had their fingers in his belt hooks. Their nails were digging into the flesh of his back.

There was no time. He had to act immediately. He thrust his uninjured arm under the skirt of the nearest of the girls who were forcing him back and jammed the first two fingers of his hand upward and inward.

"Yah! Lewd and impermissible!"

"Shameful act!"

Their voices got even higher and louder, but they gave way at once. Kenji was able to squeeze up into the bus, just before the doors hissed shut behind him.

"I'm sorry," he said. "I was in a hurry."

"Beast!"

"Pervert!"

"Unrefined elder brother!"

There were at least thirty schoolgirls on the bus, and Kenji was suddenly the object of all their attention. They rained accusations and insults on him till he blushed deep red. They trod on his toes. They poked him in the buttocks with umbrellas and badminton rackets. But Kenji didn't mind at all, because each jolt of the bus's wheels left the two yakuza farther behind.

When the bus reached the end of its route, Kenji got out and called Noda at his tiny office in Kabuto-cho. The advice was the same as before—to stay out of harm's way until further notice. But where could he go? His own apartment was being watched. They would probably know the addresses of his relatives and close friends too.

He took out his address book and scanned his list of telephone numbers. How about Aiko, the hairstylist he'd met in a disco in Roppongi? Would she put him up in her little one-room mansion in Ikebukuro? Unlikely—he hadn't called her for twelve months now. Rika, the Ginza hostess? She would probably be bringing home clients every night. Satako, Kazuko, Keiko, Reiko . . . all too long ago. There was one name, though, that had been written in quite recently. She wouldn't refuse him, he felt sure.

He reached in his pocket for a coin.

The central Tokyo traffic was motionless, locked tight. Mori sat in the driving seat of Lisa's Honda Beat watching the lights change from red to green, then back to red. It didn't matter. No one was moving in either direction. He put on a Janis Joplin cassette that he found in the glove compartment, lit a Mild Seven, and sat back and relaxed.

The car to his left was a Porsche. The driver was a young guy in his mid-twenties wearing sunglasses and a ponytail. The rap music he was listening to was booming out over the road, causing some of the passersby to turn round. In the passenger seat was a girl with her sunglasses perched on top of her head. She looked across at Mori, and gave a big silly smile. Mori smiled back.

The sun was going down behind Mitsukoshi Department Store, casting a soupy orange stain over the horizon. Janis was belting out "Ball and Chain." Mori glanced up at the news bulletins running across an electronic billboard high on one of the buildings.

"Mayor of Kyoto stable after shooting by rightist . . ."

"Yumi-chan denies abortion rumors . . ."

"Gangland feud expected to escalate . . ."

"Three Japanese tourists beaten to death with baseball bats in Chicago . . ."

It was the white noise that usually passed in and out of Mori's consciousness without leaving any mark. Yet now he found it oppressive. The conflicts and crises and public uproars that made up the world of human events seemed to be growing larger, louder, more incomprehensible. And somehow the tempo was accelerating. Approaching the end of the century, history was switched to fast-forward.

"Dollar continues to surge against all currencies . . ."

"Decision on premiership expected next week . . ."

"Kuwana starting pitcher in Giants game . . ."

"Massacre . . . famine . . . hijack . . ."

No doubt, there was a pattern somewhere in all the apparent randomness. Mori thought of Iwanaga and his speech at the Computer Center. The conspiracy would be gathering momentum, though what was part of it and what was separate was impossible to tell. In any case, that was no longer Mori's problem. He had arranged to meet Kudo later that evening. He would explain exactly what he had heard and seen, then leave the rest to the police.

Janis was singing "Me and Bobby McGee." Mori sat in the motionless traffic watching the news go round and round in endless circles.

It took another hour to get to Lisa's place. She wasn't at home. Mori let himself in, made a cup of coffee, and lay down on the sofa. He had plenty of things to think about. The Nishida case was dragging on, but nothing conclusive had come up. Mrs. Nishida's young lover had gotten the leading role in the samurai serial. Mori had seen the first episode, in which he had single-handedly wiped out a gang of thugs in the employ of an unscrupulous rice merchant. Mrs. Nishida had given him a cashmere overcoat in celebration, but she was still worried about the producer's daughter. Then there was a new missing person enquiry. An ordinary salaryman, married with two children, had failed to appear at work one day. He had been seen getting on the train at seven-thirty in the morning, with his briefcase under his arm, but he never arrived at the other end.

The telephone rang. Mori left it alone, and the answering machine switched on. The voice that came out of the tiny speaker was angry.

"Lisa, this is Ono here. That's the second time you've missed rehearsals this month. What on earth do you think you're doing? This was supposed to be your big chance. Well, if you think you're the only one around that can sing this stuff, you're making a big mistake. I'm already talking to Mari Kobayashi. If you don't get over here by—"

Mori dived for the phone. "Mr. Ono? What's going on? She didn't show up for the rehearsal last night?"

"No, she didn't. I've had all I can take. She's completely unreliable . . . She's—who the hell are you, anyway?"

"The name's Mori. I'm a friend of Lisa's."

"Well, you just tell her that I'm going to—"

Mori slammed the receiver down, heart pumping. He looked in the bedroom. Everything was as he had left it yesterday. The bedclothes were in the same heap, the ball of screwed-up tissues in the same place on the floor.

It wasn't unusual for Lisa to spend the night out somewhere. It wasn't unusual for her to miss an appointment. But this rehearsal—she had been talking about it for weeks. It was her chance to get back onto a major label.

Mori had the prickly feeling on the back of his neck again.

He got over to Shinjuku at six-thirty. It was just possible that Lisa had left a message for him at the office. But there was nothing there but the usual collection of junk mail—from real estate agents, massage parlors, even one from a highly exclusive cemetery. The only message on the answering machine was from Mrs. Nishida asking for a progress report. He called the Roppongi nightclub where Lisa had been working the previous week, but they didn't know anything.

He was on the way to the car when the old guy who ran Magic Hole called out to him.

"Mori-san! Hey, Mori-san! I've got something for you."

Mori looked at him blankly.

"Come inside and get it."

Mori followed him into the tiny office. Inside there were two rickety chairs, a gray metal desk piled high with porno videos, and an electric fan whose blades were thick with the grease of years of noodles and Chinese dumplings. The old man opened the desk drawer and took out a parcel.

"Special delivery," said the old man. "It came early this morning. They told me to give it to you next time I saw you."

"They?" said Mori. "Who do you mean?"

"Two guys. Looked like ordinary salarymen. They were very polite."

Mori's name and address were neatly typed on the label. There was no return address. He cut the string, took off the wrapping paper, and shook the cardboard box. There was something inside, something light but quite bulky.

He opened the box. Inside was a shoe, and packed into the shoe were a pair of red panties and a brassiere. Lisa had been wearing all three items when she had left her apartment the day before.

"Why didn't you tell me?" grinned the old man. "I can get you all that stuff specially cheap. No problem."

Mori put the box under his arm and made for the door.

"Any type you like," called out the old man as he left. "Senior-high-school girls, newlywed wives, office ladies—all of them freshly worn . . ."

But Mori was already halfway to the car, his brain buzzing with fear and hate and anger.

He had arranged the meeting with Kudo in a rooftop beer garden close to the central police station. It had a fine view—in one direction the bustling streets of the Ginza, in the other the leafy grounds of the Imperial Palace. The buildings of the palace itself could hardly be seen, just a couple of low flat roofs. It was an empty space, a timeless zero around which the lines of traffic circulated.

They ordered large pitchers of Suntory beer, fried chicken and dumplings. Kudo took huge swallows of beer, and soon his face was blazing red.

"Well," he said. "What's going on? You told me on the phone that you had important information, big enough to get me promoted. Come on, out with it. Don't keep me in suspense any longer."

Mori pursed his lips, and shook his head.

"The situation's changed," he said. "I can't tell you anything right now. Forget what I said on the phone." Kudo looked at him incredulously.

"What the hell are you doing? Trying to compete with us, or something? You've got information about criminal activity—it's your duty to inform the police. If you withhold it for your own benefit, we'll hit you hard, make no mistake. You private detectives may be an endangered species, but there are no special conservation laws protecting you."

"You've got it wrong. This time it's nothing to do with business. A friend's life is at stake."

Kudo was silent for a moment. He picked up a dumpling in his chopsticks and smeared it with about three times the amount of mustard that Mori would have used.

"It's connected with that Hara case, isn't it?" he said finally.

Mori nodded.

"That's right, but don't ask me any more. When it's all clear, you'll be the first to know. Right now, I need some information from you."

Kudo shook his head, half in wonder, half in resignation.

"You've got a nerve," he said. "You're asking *me* for information! Well, come on then. How exactly can the Kudo Data Service be of assistance?"

"This guy Nakamura and his boss Terada. I need to know what kind of guys they are, how they operate, where they live, everything else about them."

"When do you need to know?"

"Now."

"It's that important?" asked Kudo between mouthfuls of dumpling.

"Life and death," said Mori.

12

:

SHARROCK would never have flown First American if the other flights hadn't been canceled. Still, it was either First American or wait another two hours, and if there was one thing that Sharrock couldn't stand it was waiting around at airports. As it was, he had to wheel his own baggage past a picket line of airline workers waving placards and screaming abuse. Just as he was going through the gate, a large gob of saliva flew through the air and hit his pigskin valise. He tried to shake it off, but it was glutinously adhesive.

"Yeah! Take that home for a souvenir, you bastard!"

Sharrock turned around to look at the pickets. The yell had come from a small red-headed woman wearing a white T-shirt emblazoned with the message "Fight For Your Rights." Her face was contorted with rage. She was practically jumping up and down on the spot.

Conveniently, there was a kid standing behind Sharrock in the line drinking coffee out of a paper cup. Sharrock grabbed the cup out of his hand and flung the contents at the redhead. His aim was good. The first splash got her directly in the face, and the rest ran down the front of her T-shirt.

"Have a nice day!" he said, and walked through the gate.

First American had recently filed for Chapter 11. Under the protection of the court, the company had torn up its union agreement, cut wages by 30 percent, and laid off two hundred workers.

That was what the picket was all about. Sharrock had to admit that it was a pretty smart move. Still, no one in his right mind flew First American, unless there was absolutely no choice in the matter. Since the deregulation started, the company had cut its service to the bone. It had changed ownership several times, and each time the new management had tried to squeeze costs a little bit more before selling the business. Now the booking system was a mess, and there was no telling what city your baggage would end up in. Worst of all, the planes had started falling out of the sky—three major crashes already this year. A junk bond–financed restructuring had left the company with a crushing debt burden, so it was unable to replace its ancient fleet. And now half the mechanics were out on strike, and the planes were being flown by guys that they'd brought out of retirement on special contracts. . . .

At takeoff, Sharrock tried to concentrate his mind on a New York Times op-ed on trade policy. It was no good. The body of the plane was rattling and shuddering as if it were fighting to stay in one piece. A couple of hatch doors banged open and the Fasten Your Seatbelt signs were blinking on and off. After they'd been in the air a couple of minutes, the plane jolted into an air pocket and lost a couple of yards of altitude. Sharrock's stomach leapt like a startled rabbit, then turned icy cold. The newsprint started running before his eyes. The well-turned paragraphs advocating "firmness" and "level playing fields" suddenly filled up with phrases such as "no survivors," "severed limbs," and "wreckage spread over wide area."

He closed his eyes and thought about what he had accomplished over the past few days. The trip had been largely successful, confirming the strategy that he'd recommended to Johansen and the others. He had spoken to a couple of contacts in the advertising industry and their comments had been especially interesting. Comparative ads that denigrated foreign, and especially Asian products and values, were becoming a major new trend. Account executives and marketing managers were amazed by the responses they were getting. Sales figures in the target areas were seeing spectacular increases.

One example stuck in Sharrock's head. It had made him chuckle.

A group of Japanese men are sitting cross-legged in a tiny room drinking sake from tiny cups. One of them attempts to get up, but the ceiling of the room is so low that he thumps his head against it and falls over. The impact causes the walls to cave in and the ceiling to collapse, leaving the group sitting in the open air, covered in debris.

"This is an unpardonable dishonor," the guy who stood up says in a hysterical squeak. "I must take full responsibility."

The others ignore him and carry on drinking. Then comes the voiceover, in a laid-back Western drawl.

"Some kindsa folks may like to live like that, but as for me, doggone it, I prefer to live the good old-fashioned way."

Cut to a square-jawed guy in a Stetson making a campfire with a backdrop of the Rockies behind him. When he's finished, he takes a can of beer from his backpack and yanks the tab.

That beer had been losing market share for years, but after the ad came out there had been a dramatic surge in sales, especially to younger consumers. "This is an unpardonable dishonor," shouted out in the same hysterical squeak, had become a hit catchphrase and was spreading from campus to campus like some new sexual disease.

Something similar had been going on in Hollywood. To start with, there had been plenty of concern about those two Japanese takeovers of movie studios. Reckard had exploited that nicely in his proposal for a foundation to monitor "antidemocratic influences on the entertainment arts." In fact, though, the Japanese presence seemed to have no effect on the actual business of moviemaking at all. On the contrary, Sharrock's contacts in Hollywood told him that the movie writers, as in tune with popular sentiment as ever, had gotten some sharp anti-Japanese references into several of the summer's blockbusters. No more chic sushi restaurants, no more glittering high-tech, no more noble ninja. Instead, creepy businessmen, oppressed womenfolk, and gaggles of dumb, shutter-crazy tourists. And next month *Rambo in Tokyo* was set for release.

Sharrock opened his eyes again. The plane was cruising at twenty thousand feet, absolutely steady in the air. He glanced out of the window at the gleaming wing, the limpid blue sky, the cloud cover far below, and breathed a sigh of relief. It had been ridiculous to worry, he told himself. What were the chances of going down in a plane crash, anyway? A lot less than the chances of being murdered or getting AIDS, probably.

It was when he was gazing around at his fellow passengers, checking to see if any of them were looking as relieved as he was feeling, that he saw the Japanese man in the window seat two rows behind. At first, Sharrock didn't recognize him. Wearing an owlish pair of spectacles, he looked like any ordinary Japanese businessman shuttling from sales office to sales office. Then he took off the spectacles, and Sharrock remembered. It was the guy who had delivered that extraordinary speech at the Nippon Society, the one who had filled in for Susan's favorite guru. The memory of it gave him a sudden surge of irritation.

When they'd been in the air twenty minutes or so, Sharrock got up to use the restroom. The toilet was blocked, the aluminum bowl half full. He pumped the flush a couple of times, but it was no good. The maintenance people had obviously joined the strike too. He positioned himself delicately on the seat and added a small contribution to the mound below, then scattered some tissues over it for aesthetic effect.

When he opened the door, he found an attractive blonde woman in her mid-twenties waiting outside.

"It's broken," Sharrock said apologetically. "You'd better try the other one."

"That one's broken too," she said. "And I'm almost bursting."

Walking back to his seat, Sharrock deliberately stopped by Machida's row. The guy had a sheaf of documents on his knees and was shading passages that interested him with a yellow marker pen. At that moment, a flight attendant came down the aisle carrying a tray of soft drinks. Sharrock squeezed into the row behind Machida to let the attendant past. It was a good position to satisfy his curiosity about what kind of document the guy was reading with such absorption. What he saw gave him the shock of his life. The document was in English, neatly word-processed, with two charts side by side in the middle of the page. He recognized it at once. The last time he had seen it was when he had handed over copies to Johansen and the others three weeks before! As for those two charts, he had produced them on the personal computer in his study at home. They showed the distribution by annual income of anti-Japanese sentiment among households in the key Northern states. Machida was reading the latest report that Sharrock had prepared on the Reckard campaign.

The plane bucked at a tiny air pocket, and Sharrock stumbled forward, his shadow falling across the page. Machida glanced around just as Sharrock was pulling away. Instantly, he snapped the file shut. For a moment, their eyes met.

"Bumpy ride, that's for sure," grinned Sharrock.

Machida's gaze narrowed. He was wondering if he had seen Sharrock before.

"I'm going on to Houston," Sharrock continued. "Hope the next flight's a little smoother, huh!"

Machida grunted dismissively and turned back to the file. He obviously hadn't made the connection.

Sharrock spent the rest of the flight racking his brains for an explanation of how such an appalling leak could have been allowed to happen. The key to the Reckard strategy—in the hands of a senior official of a Japanese company! It was an outrageous breach of security. The whole campaign might be jeopardized. Johansen would be incandescent with rage. He would make whoever was responsible pay for it dearly, that was for sure.

When they touched down, Sharrock's first instinct was to phone Johansen and let him know what had happened immediately. But if he did that, Machida would disappear into the city and they would never discover where the leak was. No, it would be more sensible to follow Machida, find out where he was staying and who he was meeting, then leave the rest to Johansen.

Sharrock stayed a couple of steps behind him as the passengers disembarked from the plane and trooped into the main building. When Machida stopped at a newsstand to buy a paper, Sharrock hung back and fiddled with a shoelace. When Machida disappeared into the men's room, Sharrock went to the information desk and wasted the clerk's time with a string of enquiries.

Machida went out to the pickup area and looked around uncertainly. It seemed he wasn't sure who he was waiting for. Sharrock watched from inside the building, ready to move as soon as necessary. After a couple of minutes, a tall black guy appeared holding up a square of cardboard with "Mr. Machida" written on it in large letters. After passing a few words, he waved Machida toward one of the half-dozen stretch limousines pulled up at the curb. As soon as Machida had been ushered inside by the chauffeur, Sharrock walked out to the pickup area.

"I want a limo," he told the tall black guy. "Which one of these is free?"

"These are all booked. I can get you one in ten minutes' time."

"Screw ten minutes' time. I'm in a hurry, you understand?"

Sharrock peeled thirty dollars out of his wallet and stuck the bills in the tall guy's breastpocket. Then he pulled open the door of the nearest car and got inside. The driver, a Turkish-looking guy with a fat, solemn face, turned around and gazed at him blankly. Sharrock took out fifty dollars in tens and handed them over. The solemn-faced man took them without a word.

"My friend's in that car in front," said Sharrock. "He knows where we're going. You just follow, right?"

The driver nodded briefly, as if it were the kind of thing that happened to him every day.

Contrary to Sharrock's expectations, Machida's limo did not make for one of the big city hotels. Instead, it led them to areas of the city that Sharrock had never even been to before, cruising through block after block of trash-strewn streets, boarded-up stores, and burned-out cars. There had been an ugly riot last year, Sharrock remembered. A cop had shot a young joyrider twice in the head. The place had gone up in flames. One incident he had read about stuck in his mind. Two Swedish students from the Johns Hopkins School of International Studies had been pulled out of their car and beaten to death with tire irons. The girl had first been raped with a beer bottle, and the guy had had his tongue cut out and a rose thrust into his mouth.

That was nearly eighteen months ago now, but from the look of the place it could have been last week. Nothing had been fixed. It was early evening, and there were big groups of black kids on every street corner, watching sullenly as the cars went past. When Sharrock's car stopped for a red light, a couple of girls in fluorescent green hot pants zoomed up behind on roller skates and started tapping on the windshield. They looked about fourteen or fifteen. Sharrock stared through them as if they weren't there.

"Hey, mister! Come on, just ten dollars!"

One of them put her fist to her mouth and made an unmistakable gesture. The other laughed and poked out her tongue.

The lights changed to amber. Machida was a couple of blocks ahead now, almost out of sight.

"Hit it!" said Sharrock to the driver. "We don't want to lose them."

Eventually, Machida's limo stopped in front of what looked like a derelict warehouse. Sharrock ordered his own driver to pull in a couple of hundred yards behind, and watched the dapper Japanese man disappear through the entrance.

What should he do? He could simply go back and report what had happened to Johansen. Or he could sit and wait, then follow Machida to his next destination. Or he could try and find out what the hell was going on himself. For surely Machida had come to the warehouse to meet the contact who was supplying him with confidential information on the Reckard campaign.

Sharrock had never considered himself a man of action, but he was burning with resentment. He couldn't bear the thought of the arrogant Japanese traveling around the world with the report that he, Max Sharrock, had taken weeks of painstaking research to put together. He got out of the car and walked toward the warehouse.

A group of young black kids, no more than seven or eight years old, emerged from the entrance of a boarded-up liquor shop and clustered around him. They were all wearing wraparound sunglasses and shiny black jackets.

"What you looking for man?" yelled one of them. "Crack, ice, rock, dust? We get you anything you want."

Sharrock glanced down. The kid had a strange smile. One of his front teeth had been implanted with a small emerald.

"Maybe later," he said. "Right now I'm busy, so get out of my way."

It wouldn't be a good idea to use the main entrance. Machida's car was parked right outside. He went down a side alley, then cut across a vacant lot containing piles of rubble and rotting trash. At the back of the warehouse was a loading dock which the trucks would once have used. It was locked with a rusty padlock, and the side door wouldn't budge.

Sharrock walked around to the far side of the warehouse. There was a single glassless window set in the grime-encrusted brick. With the help of a couple of conveniently positioned concrete blocks, he managed to scrabble through it and drop down inside. It took his eyes a few minutes to adjust to the gloom. What sounded like a football team of rats were scurrying about overhead and close by. The smell of rotting trash was overwhelming. Cautiously, he padded across the floor toward the front entrance, testing every step as he went.

The front of the building was where the offices had been. There was an old-fashioned, iron-grilled elevator next to the entrance. Peering up the shaft, Sharrock could see that it had stopped on the third floor. He could hear voices faintly somewhere up above. Slowly, silently, he crept up the staircase at the side of the elevator shaft. When he got to the first floor, he paused and listened again.

"What you doing, man? Looking for a long-lost friend?"

Sharrock swung round at the sound of the voice behind him. The black kid with the emerald tooth was standing in the doorway of one of the empty offices. Somehow he must have gotten into the building through the front entrance.

"Listen, I'm not looking to buy anything," whispered Sharrock frantically. "Get out of here, for chrissake."

He fumbled in his wallet and pulled out a ten-dollar bill. The kid looked at the banknote, then looked at Sharrock and shook his head. He put his hand under his jacket and pulled out a gun.

"You coming with me," he said flatly, and motioned Sharrock to carry on up the stairs.

When they got to the third floor, the kid led Sharrock to an office that was still in use. Inside, a dozen kids of roughly the same age and appearance were sitting around eating ice cream and watching hard-core porn on a portable TV. One of them was sitting in a swivel chair, his Air Jordans perched on the leather-topped desk in front of him. A small balloon of bubble gum was protruding from his mouth. In his lap, he was cradling an automatic pistol.

"Who's this guy?" he said sharply. "What's he doing here?"

"Was following the car. Caught him snooping around downstairs."

"It's a mistake," said Sharrock desperately. "I'm here with Machida. You know, the Japanese guy!"

The kid with the machine pistol gazed at Sharrock and frowned. He popped his bubble gum once, then swung his feet off the desk.

"I think this guy's lyin'," he said. "I'll get the boss." For a moment, Sharrock thought about making a break for the door, but it would have been impossible. The kids were probably all armed. What could he do? Machida would definitely recognize him this time. He could offer them money, threaten them, promise to help with whatever it was that they were doing. . . .

When the kid came back followed by Johansen, the shock almost left Sharrock dizzy. Johansen! What was he doing here! It must be some kind of bizarre mistake.

But Johansen also looked shaken.

"Max! What the hell . . . ?"

"I could ask the same. It's just the craziest thing imaginable. There was this Japanese guy, and somehow he's gotten hold of our . . ."

Sharrock's words trailed off as Machida came into the room. He gazed helplessly at Johansen, who was staring at him with those icy blue eyes.

"John, this doesn't make any sense. You're the one who's been leaking our plans to the Japanese. I don't understand."

Johansen motioned for the kids to leave the room, then sat down in the swivel chair.

"There're some things you weren't meant to understand, Max," he said slowly.

"But you set this whole thing up. Why are you leaking it, for God's sake? You said yourself it had to be kept top secret."

Johansen looked at him and gave a smile that had no mirth in it at all.

"Don't you see?" he said. "This is no leak. Machida-san here has been part of the project from the beginning."

"What do you mean?"

"You remember me telling you that our client demands total anonymity? Now perhaps you can see why. Machida-san is our client's representative here in the U.S."

Sharrock felt dizzy. The project was being sponsored by the Japanese. The whole idea was unreal.

Johansen continued.

"I'd like to let this pass, Max. I know you were doing what you thought was right. But I'm afraid that would create difficulties."

"I won't breathe a word to anyone, I promise. You can trust me completely."

Sharrock was aware that his voice was much higher than usual. Johansen was shaking his head, still smiling his mirthless smile.

Machida cut in.

"Absolutely impossible, Mr. Johansen. My people in Tokyo would not tolerate an indiscretion of this nature. I don't have to remind you of the terms of the original contract."

"Leave it to me, Machida-san. Fortunately, Max's contribution to the project was more or less complete anyway."

"That is true," said Machida, turning to Sharrock. "On behalf of my company, I would like to thank you for the efforts you have expended. Without your excellent work, this project could not have even begun."

He gave a short bow, and left the room. Sharrock was as astonished by that as by anything else that had happened. The man was actually thanking him before . . . before what?

Johansen patted him on the shoulder.

"Sorry it had to turn out like this," he said. "But there's really no other way. A contract is a contract."

He called in the kid who had been sitting at the desk.

"Take him around the back," he said. "And make it look good."

Sharrock was in a daze as the group of kids prodded and pulled him into the elevator, then out into the vacant lot. He didn't even resist when they tied his hands behind his back and put tape over his mouth. Then the kid with the emerald tooth put some white powder on a knife blade and made him sniff it. It was powerful stuff. There were white flashes in front of his eyes, and his heart started banging like a bongo drum.

Max Sharrock knelt down in the trash of the vacant lot and watched as the kid in the Air Jordans fitted a silencer to the gun. His face felt as heavy and numb as a stone, but his mind was racing with images. Johansen shaking his head, Reckard carving turkey, Machida standing up at the Nippon Society, the Japanese businessman squawking "This is an unpardonable dishonor."

The kid raised the gun barrel. "Bye-bye, mister," he said, and blew a big pink globe of bubble gum.

There was chaos that day in the financial markets. At the opening, the Dow Jones Index was hit by a heavy wave of selling from the Chicago futures market, and plunged two hundred points. The bond market collapsed. The dollar broke its recent uptrend, falling sharply against all major currencies. When the European markets saw what was happening on Wall Street, they went into an immediate tailspin. Trading was halted in Paris, and there were fistfights on the floor of the Madrid exchange. In London, market-makers simply switched off their screens and refused to answer their phones.

Billions of dollars of wealth disappeared in a matter of minutes, and the hordes of pundits who are usually ready with a thousand different explanations and excuses were suddenly at a loss for the reason why.

Regulations-san woke at five, cleared his lungs with half an hour of Noh chanting, then had his wife serve him a breakfast of two sardines, miso soup, and a banana. She placed the tray on the table, bowed once, then watched nervously as he sipped at the soup.

"Is everything to your satisfaction?" she asked in a small voice.

"It's good," said Regulations-san, smacking his lips loudly.

"I'm humbly grateful," said his wife, and returned to the kitchen to prepare her own breakfast.

They had been going through the same ritual every morning for thirty-five years now. Regulations-san had married soon after entering the ministry. He had realized that, if he was to devote himself fully to the service of the nation, he wouldn't have the time or energy for household chores. It was an arranged marriage—indeed, they had met fewer than half-a-dozen times before the wedding day—but Regulations-san had never once regretted his decision. She had been a fine wife. She never complained, had never been seriously ill. She had borne him two sturdy boys who were now married with children of their own. In those days her hair had been thick and glossy, her skin as pale as milk. All his friends had said how much they envied him. Now, she was gray, with lines on her forehead and hard skin on her hands, just as he remembered his own mother.

He glanced at the morning paper. Another trade dispute was brewing, with more of the usual demands from foreigners for export quotas, higher local content ratios, and so on. Really, the Europeans were becoming impossible to deal with! Why did they imagine they could still compete with Japanese technology? Why couldn't they stick to handbags and perfumes and things they were good at making?

He shook his head in irritation, then put the newspaper into his briefcase. There would be plenty of time to read it on the bullet train. Regulations-san had a long day of traveling ahead of him, to Kyoto and back. For the others had entrusted him with the task of explaining the situation to the old man and getting his approval for their plan of action. That was appropriate. If the others had heeded his warning in the first place, the whole horrible mess would never have happened.

It was late morning when the black limousine deposited Regulations-san at the bottom of the seventy-two stone steps that led up to the temple. Seventy-two—he felt as if he knew them all individually, their rounded edges, their shiny concavities and convexities, their moss-filled cracks. He had first climbed that stairway on a clear spring morning twenty years ago, and he had climbed it every spring since. Each year, it seemed to grow a little steeper, and his pauses for breath became a little longer.

This was the second climb of the year, which was most unusual, and he had never done it in summer before. He turned to admire the view of Kyoto stretching out below him. From this height, the strict geometry of the city was readily apparent; the long straight streets, the division into equal blocks. The capital of old Japan, he reminded himself, had been laid out thirteen hundred years ago as a copy of a Chinese city, and that is what it still looked like. Its austere formality had nothing in common with the protean jumble of modern Tokyo that he had left behind five hours before.

The insects were in full cry—cicadas and crickets buzzing like electricity. Their noise rose and fell as he went past. As he climbed higher, the air got cooler. Autumn was coming, and then winter, when the snow clouds dumped their loads on the mountaintop and icicles hung like daggers from the temple eaves. How could the old man stand the winters without any heating? Regulations-san shivered at the thought. But then the old man had been living there for almost thirty years. He was used to it by now.

The assistants were waiting at the top of the steps. They led him to the small room at the back of the temple where the old man received his guests. On the side wall was a screen painting of a leaping tiger, just a few strokes of black and white and orange. The artist, an unknown of the school of Kano, would never have seen a tiger in his life. He had painted the picture in the seventeenth century, at a time when Japan had sealed itself off from the rest of the world. In the quarter century during which

Regulations-san had known that tiger, never before had it looked so primed for destruction, so ineluctably tigerish, as it sprang through the empty air.

He sipped the thick green tea he had been brought and listened to the quiet sounds outside. Running water was trinkling into the pond. Somewhere far above, a raven was croaking. One of the priests was raking out the sand of the stone garden, obliterating any marks caused by the wind and the rain. There was the periodic *chok* of the *shishi-odoshi*, the hinged bamboo tube that filled and emptied itself of spring water with the precision of a clock.

After a while, the assistants brought in the old man's wheelchair. The operation on his throat eight years ago had made full use of his vocal chords impossible. Instead, he had a tiny microphone implanted in his throat and a small loudspeaker which one of the assistants usually placed on the table in front of any guest. At first, Regulations-san had found it disconcerting to be looking at someone whose voice emanated from an entirely different direction. Now he was accustomed to the silent lips and the harsh whisper that crackled from the machine on the table.

Regulations-san gave a brief outline of the choices they were facing. That was merely a courtesy, since the old man knew the facts already. His personal staff had been informed of everything by telephone.

"This is very serious indeed," he said when Regulations-san had finished. "I've always been worried that something like this might happen."

"It is an unbelievable stupidity," said Regulations-san. "I am almost ashamed to be Japanese. After this, the rest of the world will be laughing at us."

The old man's throat rippled with effort, and his voice was twice as loud as before.

"We Japanese worry too much about what the rest of the world thinks. That was always the problem. If we mind our own affairs with common sense, there will be no problem. My elder brother never understood that. He was a strong man, much stronger than I, but he was also a fool."

The old man smiled, and Regulations-san was startled. It was a gentle smile, almost like a girl's. There was a moment of silence, ended by the *chok* of the shishi-odoshi.

"Your plans are good," went on the old man. "You must follow them through as soon as possible. Now let me make a few small suggestions."

As he spoke, Regulations-san marveled again at his powers. The old man lived in a temple high in the mountains above Kyoto. He hadn't been down from the mountain for several years. Yet his knowledge of world affairs was incredibly detailed, and his strategic grasp as powerful as ever. He pointed out problems and suggested solutions that no one else had thought of. But then, by the age of thirty the younger Maruoka had already established himself as the most brilliant financial thinker that Japan had ever produced. His retirement into the priesthood half a century ago had been inevitable after the quarrel with Ichiro, but a generation of politicians, businessmen, and bureaucrats had subsequently benefited from his quiet but firm guidance.

When Regulations-san made his way back down the seventy-two stone steps, pausing at every eighteenth to take his breath and enjoy the view, his mind was serene. If the old man was in agreement, then the strategy must be correct. They would be able to go ahead immediately. Just as well, for there was no time to lose.

Halfway down, he stopped for a few minutes and looked out over the city. The buzz of the road was close, but he could still hear the faint *chok* of the shishi-odoshi somewhere behind him. That was impossible, of course—he was too far away. The peculiar quality of the sound was that he became more aware of it the farther he was from its source. He would still hear it as the limousine bore him down the twisting mountain road that led back to Kyoto.

That day, the convulsions that had affected foreign markets overnight spread into the Tokyo market. The dollar gyrated crazily. Gold surged, and the price of futures contracts on the Nikkei 225 stock index fell to the daily limit. Of the sixteen hundred stocks traded on the Tokyo Exchange, over half found no buyers at all, and most of the rest fell by double-digit percentages. Among the general massacre, however, the odd performance of one stock passed pretty well unnoticed. Nippon Infosystems bucked the market trend, rising sharply on unusually heavy volume.

13

:
•

As usual Toshio Iwanaga awoke at five-thirty. He dressed quickly, without disturbing the two women curled up asleep on the large circular bed. In the morning light, the resemblance between them was uncanny, much stronger than it had been last night when they had both been wearing heavy makeup.

The mother was an accomplished geisha in her mid-forties. Iwanaga had known her for years. The daughter was a seventeen-year-old apprentice geisha, with nipples like rosebuds and thighs as smooth as silk. Ordinarily, taking her virginity would have cost ten million yen, but Iwanaga was a valued customer of the house. For him, it had been half price. After plenty of sake and jokes and skillful persuasion, the mother had even agreed to his suggestion that she should join in and offer some direct tuition.

He spent an hour meditating, did half an hour's kendo practice, then ate breakfast alone. Immediately afterward, there was a phone call from Yoshimura at the Computer Center. He was requesting a five-day delay in the whole project while security needs were reassessed. Iwanaga rejected the idea out of hand, not bothering to disguise his irritation. Yoshimura was highly intelligent, and his loyalty was unimpeachable, but sometimes he was so feeble-spirited, almost incompetent. Fortunately, Terada's people had a much more businesslike attitude toward security problems.

The first appointment of the day was at nine o'clock in the secluded Meguro townhouse that Iwanaga used for especially sensitive meetings. His chauffeur drove him there in a Nissan President with smoked-glass windows.

The three Maruichi men arrived on time, bowed deeply, then gave him their progress report. It was satisfactory. London, New York, Singapore, and Tokyo had all been primed exactly as he had instructed. Silent Thunder had done everything he had asked of it. Now only the final adjustments needed to be made before the blow was struck. It would be the end of three years of meticulous preparation.

The senior of the Maruichi men was Sugaya, a man who had been under Iwanaga's instruction for ten years. His loyalty and sincerity were absolute. He asked for permission to leave the room for a moment. When he came back, he was carrying a long thin object draped in cloth. He placed it on the desk, then bowed again. "Today, sensei, we wish to mark our appreciation of your genius with a gift. It is something that symbolizes the great spirit of our common endeavor."

Iwanaga gave a short bow of acknowledgment, then unwrapped the cloth. Inside was the unmistakable form of a sword, its leather pommel scratched and worn, its body concealed in a canvas sheath. He picked it up and slowly drew out the naked blade. The crescent of steel caught the beams of the sun, and flashed fire.

"This is superb," he breathed.

He examined the mirrorlike surface of the central area, the delicate temper pattern that rippled down it like a wave, the misty white of the striking edge, still keen as a razor. The metal was alive, pulsing with different textures and shapes.

"It looks early nineteenth century," he said. "School of Masahide, possibly."

"It's by Masahide himself," said Sugaya, unable to disguise his pride and pleasure. "His inscription's right there on the tang."

"Incredible!"

Iwanaga took off his jacket, then held the sword upright at

chest height, letting it find its own balance. For a moment, he was absolutely still, his face set in a mask of concentration. Then he sprang forward, twisting and slicing in a reproduction of the kendo routine he had performed two hours before. The blade became an arc of pure light, carving the inert air into segments.

"How does it feel?" asked Sugaya.

"Absolutely weightless," said Iwanaga, beads of sweat standing out on his brow. He touched the blade against his forearm, and pressed gently. A thin crescent of blood appeared.

"It cuts," he went on. "And I felt nothing. This is truly the work of a master. Every sword has its own spirit, and the spirit of this one is exceptionally strong. Masahide must have labored over it with great love."

He gazed once more at the blue-gray steel. For a moment, he looked like a student marveling over a famous painting seen for the first time.

"A sword as beautiful as this makes me both proud and sad," he said finally, returning to his sensei avatar.

"Sad, sensei?"

"Yes. For a thousand years, the secrets of manufacture were handed down through generations of master smiths. Western swords were lumps of metal, good weapons for crude oafs to bludgeon each other with. Our swords were the highest art, the highest technology, so perfect that the common people thought the smiths were magicians."

"That is true," said Sugaya.

The other two Maruichi men nodded gravely.

"Then the Meiji Restoration came and we melted them down for scrap, sold them to foreigners as souvenirs. Thousands and thousands of ancient swords were destroyed. Only we Japanese could make weapons like this, and only we Japanese would have the stupidity to throw them away."

"And only you, sensei, can revive the culture that created the swords in the first place."

Iwanaga bowed again.

"I am deeply honored," he said. "If our movements are as silent and deadly as the strokes of Masahide's sword, we will make the whole world tremble."

When they had gone, he went through the kendo routine once more. It made him feel as if he were floating, as if the sword were making the movements all by itself and he were just being pulled along by its energy.

Noriko was a good girl, decided Kenji. She had agreed to put him up without requiring any great efforts of persuasion from him. She was also extraordinarily passionate, as the marks on his back, neck, and chest testified. When she left for work, she had a freshness in her smile and brightness of eye that he had never noticed before. She was, he suddenly realized, a good-looking woman.

He stayed in bed till ten o'clock, dozing and watching TV. It was the first time he had watched the morning scandal shows for ages. The main topic was Yumi-chan. Her love life was discussed by a panel of experts, including an astrologer, a gynecologist, and a female poet. Everyone wished her well.

At midday, he decided to call Noda to let him know what had happened.

"You were very lucky," was Noda's response. "These people would think nothing of killing you."

"What are we going to do about it? When will I be able to go back to work?"

"Relax. I've let the right people know what's going on. It shouldn't take too long."

"So there's nothing for me to do but wait."

"That's right. Though there is one thing you might be able to help me with."

"What's that?"

"Those accounts. I need the exact details of each one—the mailing addresses, the bank accounts the money was transferred to, how much went when, everything. Is there any way I can get them?"

Kenji thought for a moment. Noriko—she would be able to get all the information necessary.

"No problem," he said. "I'll be able to get you everything

you need by tomorrow."

After that, he settled back in his bed to watch Yumi-chan's first lover, a boy now studying for his university entrance exams, give a detailed description of their first kiss.

Kenji met Noriko at lunchtime in a golf driving range on the top of a ten-story office building in Shimbashi. Noriko had a good swing, much better than his own. Ball after ball was struck sweetly into the green netting at the end of the range.

"Pretty good," said Kenji. "What's your handicap?"

"Oh, I've never played on a real course yet," she said. "But Mr. Saga in General Affairs has promised to take me next month. I'm looking forward to it very much."

Saga! An oily, pretentious, smooth-talking type who was unaccountably popular with all the women. Kenji felt a rush of resentment.

"You should come with me," he said. "I'm a member of a club out in Chiba."

Kenji wasn't much interested in golf. He had bought the membership as an investment, with money borrowed from a credit company. It had cost him a year's salary, and since then prices had fallen 30 percent. He could hardly bear to look at the index of membership prices in the Tuesday newspaper.

Whack! Another perfect follow-through by Noriko.

Whack! Kenji sliced his shot badly, sending the ball careening off sideways toward the Tokyo Tower.

"That would be fun," she said. "You could teach me putting, and I could teach you how to drive properly."

Afterward, they went to a nearby jazz coffee bar. At first, Kenji thought that he could get away with giving her only the vaguest outline of what was going on. He was wrong. She refused to help him with the computer codes unless he told her the whole story. He tried to gloss over what Noda had said to him about Silent Thunder, but she was insistent. She wanted to know everything. When he had finished, she looked thoughtful.

"I know how to get that kind of information," she said. "But I need to know where to look for those unnumbered accounts.

You'll have to help me."

Kenji assumed a confidence opposite to what he really felt. "No problem," he said. "We'll do it tonight."

Mori spent the morning doing background research on Terada, Nakamura, and inner workings of the Kawashita Syndicate. Kudo knew about the structure of the organization and Taniguchi knew about its connections with big business and politicians. That was helpful, but Mori wanted something more. He needed to talk to someone with firsthand knowledge.

Mori had first come across Kunio Watanabe ten years before. At that time, Watanabe had been a brash young yakuza known for his outrageous suits and his penchant for using his fists to settle arguments. And he had a lot of arguments, most of them having nothing to do with his day-to-day business. Only the fact that he was the half brother of a senior officer in the syndicate allowed him to keep his place in the hierarchy. Then his half brother was killed in a factional dispute. There was a botched revenge attack, and Watanabe was sent up for five years. In prison, he suddenly took to writing, and his account of the yakuza world became an instant best-seller. Now he was a minor celebrity, appearing on TV quiz shows and writing a weekly column for a newspaper. Mori arranged to meet Watanabe in the back room of an eel restaurant near Tokyo station. When he arrived, Watanabe was autographing a copy of his new book for a young waitress and cracking jokes about the benefits of eel cuisine to the male stamina.

"Got a book for me?" asked Mori.

"You got to be joking," said Watanabe. "If you want a copy, there's a bookshop round the corner."

He spoke in the habitual snarl of his former profession. With his piggy little eyes half an inch too far apart, his squashed nose, and his rubbery lips, he looked like a yakuza out of a TV drama. That wasn't altogether surprising, since he had recently appeared in a couple of shows on Channel Five.

"You're getting some good reviews," went on Mori. "That was a nice one in the *Gendai* the other day."

"I know the guy. Told him I'd break his legs. He got the message all right."

Mori pretended to be impressed. The waitress's eyes opened wide. She was obviously thrilled. When she had gone, Watanabe reverted to his normal behavior, which was polite and well spoken.

"Well, what can I do for you?" he asked. "I'm always willing to help an old friend."

That was an exaggeration. Mori wasn't an old friend. Still, Watanabe did owe him a couple of favors.

"I've got two major problems," said Mori. "One is called Toru Nakamura, and the other is called Seiji Terada."

Watanabe sucked in air through the side of his mouth.

"Not the sort of problems I can get involved with, I'm afraid. I've got my career to think of. I wouldn't look good on TV without any ears and nose."

"I don't want you to get involved. I just want information. Tell me what you know about these guys, what do they dream about, what are they scared of, what makes them tick."

Watanabe was pleased to oblige. He described how Nakamura had risen to the top of the organization through psychopathic ruthlessness, sweeping aside both friend and foe. He described Terada's long rivalry with the traditionalists. He explained how the assassination of the elder Aga had split the syndicate into two separate groups, and how the senior members of the syndicate were trying to cool things down. "Aga may have been slow-moving and old-fashioned," he said. "But he knew his place in the world. He was a yakuza, and proud of it. He never pretended to be anything else. Terada's people are different. They don't know what they are, and that makes them dangerous. They don't understand the limits."

"Does the younger Aga understand the limits?"

"Of course. I know him well. We used to run around Osaka together."

"I need to meet him. Can you arrange that?"

"You! I'm not sure that would be a good idea."

"It doesn't matter whether it's a good idea or not. I need to."

Watanabe looked at him curiously. He knew better than to ask any questions.

"All right," he said finally. He opened his briefcase and took out a portable phone.

Mori got back to his office in midafternoon. There was a message waiting for him on the answering machine. The voice was friendly, super-cheerful, like a radio commercial.

"Mori-san, we've been trying to get in touch for some time now, but we keep missing you. Don't worry, we'll be in touch again soon. Until then, do try to be sensible."

This was followed by a woman's scream. Mori recognized the voice as Lisa's. Then the line went dead.

Mori lay down on the sofa and closed his eyes. In the distance he could hear a fire engine's siren, the cry of the baked-yam seller, the rumble of trucks on the expressway. For five minutes, he lay there and thought of nothing.

As Watanabe had instructed, Mori presented himself at the main Shinjuku branch of the Kawashita Syndicate at four o'clock. The office was located on the ninth floor of a newly opened building close to the station. It was a prime site. Mori happened to know that the syndicate owned a good percentage of the entire building, which was part of their payoff for ironing out a few snags of the sort that every large redevelopment scheme throws up. Some small landowners hadn't wanted to sell out. Some had wanted prices that were much too high. Some had even had the effrontery to attempt to sell to the wrong developer. The Kawashita Syndicate had offered its services, and as a result Sumikawa Real Estate had been able to complete the project without a hitch.

The reception area resembled that of an ordinary industrial company, with one important exception. It contained a pretty young girl sitting behind a desk, a Chinese vase, and a clock that gave the time in all the world's major capitals. The exception was the sheet of bulletproof glass across the entrance. It rose only after the door behind him had clicked shut and he had been amply scanned by the small video camera on the wall.

"It's Mori-san, isn't it?" said the receptionist. "We've been expecting you."

She announced his arrival into the speakerphone on her desk and ushered him into a small waiting room. Again, it was the sort of room that salarymen at any large company might use for negotiations with their suppliers. There were two armchairs separated from a smart leather sofa by a glass-top table. Opposite the door was a rack of business magazines, above it on the wall an enigmatically smiling Noh mask.

The girl bowed and gestured him to the armchair opposite the door. That was absolutely correct business etiquette. When Mori sat down, she bowed once more.

"Could I possibly bring you a drink of some sort?"

"Coffee, please. Black, no sugar."

The girl disappeared. After a few minutes, two yakuza in their mid-thirties entered the room. They introduced themselves formally and handed Mori their business cards. Kato and Sato— deputy section leaders, according to their business cards, of Dainippon Trading. They wore tiny metal badges in their lapels, just like ordinary loyal salarymen. Mori had to look quite closely before he made out the well-known diamond emblem of the Kawashita Syndicate.

"Well, Mori-san," said Sato, a tall man with a thin mustache that looked as if it needed watering. "I understand that you have some sort of business proposition to discuss with us."

"We're always interested in business ideas," said Kato. "Especially from a notable figure such as yourself."

He looked exactly the same as Sato, but without the mustache.

"I didn't realize I was notable," said Mori. "I've been trying to keep a pretty low profile."

"Don't be modest," said Kato with a slight smile. "We've heard many things about you, haven't we Sato?"

"That's right. I even came across Mori-san once when I was serving in our Hiroshima branch."

Mori flashed back to a deserted construction site in Hiroshima three years ago. A nervous meeting with a group of five yakuza.

An envelope of photographs and letters exchanged for an envelope of money. Angry words about the amount of money, insults traded. Two of them grabbing him on his way out, hauling him into a dank, urinous alley. Then the pounding of fists and knees and toecaps. Thanks to that little episode, the mayor of Hiroshima was able to stay in office, but Mori's back muscles would never be the same again.

"So you were one of those bastards."

"I wasn't actually there myself," said Sato hastily. "I heard about it from the others. You put up quite a fight, apparently."

Mori nodded curtly. Sato and Kato were starting to irritate him.

"I've come to talk to your boss," he said. "Does he know I'm here?"

"He knows all right," said Sato. "He just wants us to make sure that you're not going to waste his time. Isn't that right, Kato?"

"Certainly is."

"Tell us about this proposition of yours, Mori-san. We'll pass it on to the boss, no problem."

"You're wasting my time," said Mori, getting to his feet. "I'm not discussing anything with a couple of monkey turds like you."

Kato turned to his colleague in mock surprise.

"That's a bit rude, isn't it, Sato?"

"I don't think he understands the situation, Kato. Maybe he needs another lesson like the one he got in Hiroshima." Mori took one step behind Sato's chair, grabbed his neck in a choke hold, and lifted him off his seat.

"Listen," he hissed in the man's ear. "I don't like to be insistent, but I want to see the boss. Take me to him now."

Kato didn't budge from the armchair alongside. He looked up at Mori and shook his head in disapproval.

"You're a strange man, Mori-san. We invite you to our branch office to discuss business. We try to treat you nice and look what happens—you lose your temper!"

Mori gave a last squeeze to Sato's windpipe, then dropped him back in the chair.

"The boss," he said. "Now!"

Sato sat gulping and fingering his neck. His face had turned a fine shade of pink. Kato stood up.

"All right," he said with a shrug of his shoulders. "We were going to take you anyway. Come on, Sato. It's time to go."

There was a white Lincoln with smoked-glass windows waiting outside the building. Sato drove and Kato took the front seat. Mori had the backseat to himself. There was plenty of legroom. Cruising through the crowded Shinjuku streets, observing but unobserved, luxuriating in cool space while those outside bustled and sweated and jostled against each other—Mori could see the attraction of being a yakuza or a senior politician.

"Vivaldi or Miles Davis?" asked Kato, taking a couple of compact discs out of the compartment in the dash.

"Whatever you like," said Mori. "Where are we going, anyway?"

The chirruping of birds announced the start of spring.

"The boss is reviewing operations in Kawasaki. It won't take long to get there, will it, Sato?"

"Certainly shouldn't."

But dusk had already fallen and autumn had faded to winter by the time they arrived in the back streets of Kawasaki. There was a light steady rain, presaging the coming of another typhoon. The Lincoln purred through a neon panorama of porno video shops, pink salons, S&M clubs, peep shows, fashion massages, no-panty coffee bars, love hotels, soaplands, and strip theaters. The road surface was a gleaming sheet of purple, green, and silver.

"I suppose you control all this," said Mori.

"You could say that. We have substantial investments here, don't we, Kato?"

"Certainly do."

They stopped outside a building containing a disco called "Inferno" on the ground floor and nightclubs above. Several other large American cars were parked close by. Half a dozen clones of Sato and Kato were standing on the pavement, gazing up and down the street.

Kato said something to one of the bodyguards and he spoke into a walkie-talkie. After a moment, the reply came through.

"The boss is ready," said Kato. "He's waiting on the ninth floor."

Mori went up alone. When the doors of the elevator opened, he was confronted by three more yakuza in dark suits, one of whom was holding a walkie-talkie. Another was holding a metal detector of the type used at airports.

"Just a moment, please," he said to Mori.

He ran the head of the instrument over Mori's chest, armpits, and groin. It pinged once for his comb and once for his belt buckle.

The room that they led Mori to could have been found in thousands of hostess clubs all over Japan. It was small, snug, windowless, with a sparkling chandelier swaying in the breeze of the air conditioner. In the corner, a young man with slicked-back hair was tinkling away at a grand piano. The air was heavy with perfume.

Mori recognized the younger Aga from magazine and news-paper photos. He wasn't as thickset as his elder brother. The face was simpler and more violent. He sat on a leather couch sur-rounded by women. A tall Thai girl stood behind him, massaging his neck. On his left, a young blonde, no more than nineteen or twenty years old, was feeding grapes into his mouth. On the other side sat a Brazilian woman with the face of a movie star and skin tone of café au lait. She was giggling and pretending to be annoyed as Aga's hand explored inside the slit of her long skirt. "Girls," he said. "I want you to meet Mori-san, a famous Japanese detective. We have good detectives in Japan."

The girls smiled and waved their hands.

"They've been here less than six months," said Aga proudly. "And they understand Japanese already. This is the age of internationalization, sure enough!"

Mori nodded.

"Anyway, what do you want to talk to me about?" said Aga. "Make it quick, because I've got many problems on my mind."

"I'm sure you have. That was a bad business, what happened

to your brother."

Suddenly, Aga stood bolt upright, knocking over the blonde girl, who had been leaning against him with her hand on his thigh. For a moment, there was panic in her eyes, then she giggled nervously and backed away against the wall.

"I'll teach them," he roared. "They think they can get away with that. Killing a man like my brother—a good man, a well-respected man . . ."

He sat down again, heavily. The girls tiptoed away from him.

"My brother meant the world to me," he went on in a low voice. "He taught me everything I know, gave me my first assignment, trusted me. He was a fine man."

He was silent, gazing absentmindedly into his whiskey glass. Mori waited a moment before speaking.

"That's what I want to talk about," he said. "I have information about Terada. I know who's backing him, and I know what they're planning. It's much bigger than you think."

Aga's heavy brow crinkled into an angry frown.

"Big ideas," he roared, bashing his fist down onto the glass tabletop. "That smooth-skinned lizard and his big ideas! I've got a big idea for him. I'll crush him like . . . like . . ."

He looked around, then down at the plate of seafood on the table in front of him.

"Like a shrimp," he snarled, and stabbed down at one with a chopstick. His aim was poor, and the shrimp shot off the plate onto the carpet. Mori picked it up and put it back on the table. Aga glared at him savagely.

"Go on," he said through his crooked yellow teeth. "What ideas?"

"There's a man called Toshio Iwanaga," said Mori. "You must have heard of him."

Aga continued to glare. His eyes were bloodshot at the corners, his lips wet with spittle. Again, Mori was struck by the brutal simplicity of the man's face. It was the face of a man with no imagination at all, no capacity for abstract thought. Still, in Aga's world that was not necessarily a disadvantage. The brain of a shark is far smaller than a dolphin's, but that's no comfort to the dolphin when its flesh is being ripped from its bones.

"I know him," Aga said finally. "A man of many words, a man who cannot hide his pride. My brother did some business with him many years ago."

"Well, now he's got Terada working for him. And if what he's planning succeeds, it'll turn everything in this country upside down, your business interests included."

Aga leaned forward.

"Tell me more," he said, as softly as a woman.

Ten minutes later, Mori stepped into the elevator. Aga had believed him, of that he was sure. And he seemed to understand the urgency. It would be only a matter of time before he struck back at Terada.

Sato and Kato were waiting outside on the pavement, chatting with the bodyguards. They led him back to the car, and Kato executed a leisurely three-point turn, ignoring the lines of cars backing up in both directions.

"More Vivaldi?" asked Sato.

"I prefer something cooler," said Mori.

It was raining harder now. The neon looked smudged, darker. The pavements were congested with groups of salarymen, umbrellas aloft, nudging their way past each other. Mori settled back in his seat, his mind drifting with the horn through the opening chords of "My Funny Valentine."

The car telephone rang. Kato picked it up.

"It's for you, Sato," he said and handed the receiver over to his partner. Sato mumbled obsequiously into the phone, his head bobbing in little token bows as he spoke.

"Yes, yes . . . understood . . . yes, immediately . . . leave it to me . . . understood!"

He put the receiver down and turned to Mori.

"That was the boss," he said. "Seems like he was impressed with what you told him. He wants us to take you to the best soapland in the district. You can have any girls you want, any nationality, any number of them, any way. Lucky guy, eh, Kato?"

"Certainly is."

SILENT THUNDER 209

"Some other time, maybe," said Mori. "Right now, I've got urgent business to attend to."

Sato reached forward and turned down the volume on the compact disc player.

"The boss has invited you," he said slowly, with heavy emphasis on each word. "And no one turns down the boss's invitations, do they, Kato?"

"Certainly don't," said Kato, not lifting his eyes from the road ahead.

The best soapland in the district turned out to be a square five-story building blazing with neon. It had a large parking lot in front and the foyer of a luxury hotel, complete with waterfall, vine trellis, and female harp player. Sato stayed in the car. Kato went in with Mori and disappeared into the manager's office.

Impeccable young men in tuxedos and bow ties were welcoming the guests, mainly elderly businessmen in groups of two and three, and handing out menus. Mori took one and opened it up. The left side carried photos of the girls, together with short accounts of their hobbies, ambitions in life, and tastes in men. On the right side, in elegant gold lettering, was a list of the services on offer, with prices. The range was from forty thousand to three hundred thousand yen.

After a while, a nervous-looking man emerged from the office and introduced himself as the manager. He waved Mori into a small room with tropical fish tanks on three walls. The only other occupant was a tall, gray-haired man in an expensive suit. He didn't look up, but sat slumped in an armchair reading the *Nikkei* newspaper as if he were in a dentist's waiting room.

"Please don't hurry over your selection," the manager said politely. "If it would help, we also have a video catalog, which explains our services in rather more detail."

Mori gazed at the menu, trying to work out which item would take up the least time.

"The Sultan's Delight is highly recommended," went on the manager. "Two teenage lesbians, starting with twin-headed vibe play, then foam dance, double periscope, oral triangle . . ."

"Double periscope?"

"There's a large bath, genuine black marble. The customer sits in the middle of the bath, with a girl on either side. . . ."

The other man poked his head over the top of his newspaper. "You should try it," he said. "It's the best in all East Japan."

"It sounds great," said Mori. "But I'm afraid I don't have the time. I need to be out of here in an hour."

The manager looked slightly offended.

"Hmmm . . . Well, how about the Shogun Special? It combines maximum relaxation with maximum stimulation, all in one hour exactly."

According to the menu, the Shogun Special comprised a two-girl body-to-body oil massage, followed by "triple play." Mori nodded his agreement, and the manager disappeared.

"You should have tried the Sultan's Delight," said the other man from behind the newspaper. "Every man should try it once in his lifetime."

After a few minutes' wait, a girl in a long blue dress led Mori along the corridor, up a side elevator, and into the "soap room." It contained a large waterbed, a circular bath in black marble, just as the manager had promised, and a couch. The girl knelt down and bowed so low that her hair swept over the gleaming white tiles.

"My name is Mika," she said. "I humbly entreat your favor."

Mori nodded a greeting. Another girl came in, also dressed in a long blue dress.

"I am Emi. I humbly entreat your favor."

They both stripped off their dresses, under which they were naked, and led Mori to the couch. He lay still as they undressed him. Mika's nipples brushed across his face as she leaned over to undo the buttons of his shirt. The other girl held his leg between her thighs as she peeled off his sock.

Once in the bath, they washed him slowly, thoroughly. Emi used her crotch like a sponge, sliding soapily up and down his arm, from the shoulder to the fingertips. Mika was doing the same with his leg, pausing to bury his big toe in the hot folds of her sex. Then she moved forward, her hair falling like a black curtain over his groin. Her fingers raked lightly across his genitals, kneaded his thighs and buttocks, even nudged inquisitively into his back passage. Despite the obvious sign of arousal, which Mika was now flicking lightly with the tip of her tongue, Mori felt not lust, but a warm beneficent current flowing through his body. He lay back and closed his eyes.

"That looks like fun, doesn't it Kato?"

"Certainly does."

Mori twisted round. The two girls jumped out of the bath, as if on cue. They ran over to the couch, picked up their dresses, and brushed past Sato and Kato, who were standing in the doorway.

"What's going on?" said Mori tightly. "I'm not giving a public performance, you know."

"End of happy hour, Mori," snarled Sato. "Get out of the bath and get your clothes back on."

"You guys must be crazy. Your boss told you to entertain me, not act like a couple of peeping toms. I wouldn't want to be in your shoes when he hears about this."

Kato shook his head slowly. The hand he took out of his pocket was holding a gun.

"If you've got any complaints for the boss," he said, "here's your chance to tell him in person. He's been wanting to talk to you for some time."

There was a third man standing behind them. Sato and Kato stepped forward, and he came into the soap room. For a moment, Mori was confused. It wasn't Aga that was walking toward him, but an older, heavier man with a sadistic smile on his face. They had never met before, but the man's brutal features were instantly familiar. The last time Mori had seen them was in a photo taken in the lobby of the Seikyu Hotel.

"Sorry to interrupt," said Toru Nakamura. "But there's a lot of things for us to discuss. We've got a busy time ahead."

"These two idiots are working for you?"

"At least they've got the intelligence to see that Aga and his type are all washed up. In my book, that makes them a lot smarter than you are."

"Get moving, genius," said Sato. "You've got a lot of questions to answer."

Mori got out of the bath and pulled on his trousers and shirt. Sato came forward and grabbed Mori's shoulder. Kato had put the gun back in his pocket. Nakamura was leaning against the door, fanning himself with a menu of services. Mori saw a split second of opportunity, and seized it.

He spun in a half circle, breaking Sato's grip on his shoulder and driving his heel into the man's shin, just below the kneecap. Sato buckled, letting out a bellow of pain. Kato had his gun out again. Mori grabbed Sato by the collar and drove his head into Kato's stomach like a battering ram. Kato grunted with the impact and dropped the gun.

Someone was behind him, arm squeezing his windpipe. Nakamura was incredibly strong. Mori tried to kick backwards, but he was being lifted off his feet. Then Kato and Sato were both in front of him again, and fists were pounding into his face and chest. Mori twisted away, but the blows kept coming, each one backed with a grunt of effort. Then he was slumping on the tiles, and the fists had been replaced by knees and feet. He tasted blood in his mouth, saw it speckling the white tiles. Then there was red mist covering everything.

Kenji and Noriko waited until midnight before entering the Maruichi headquarters. The lights were off on every floor except the twenty-first and twenty-second, where the international bond and currency departments were located. There, surrounded by strict security, elite staff worked through the night, dealing directly into the European and American markets.

Years ago it had been Kenji's dream to be one of them, to sit there on high while Tokyo slept, shifting massive sums of money from market to market, from country to country. After failing the admission test twice, he had realized that it was impossible. They were looking for a different kind of employee—unquestioningly loyal and obedient, willing to sacrifice everything for the glory of the company.

The safest way into the building unobserved was up through the underground parking lot. Taking up five floors, it housed Maruichi's huge fleet of corporate limousines, composed by make according to the share of underwriting business that each auto company generated. Despite the time of night, half a dozen drivers were still on call. It was hot, and they sat in their cars with the air conditioners on, stockinged feet jammed against the side windows, snoozing or reading manga comic books. None of them appeared to notice Kenji and Noriko walking past.

The first elevator took them to the ground-floor reception area. It was dark, except for a dim light from the lamp set above the bronze bust of Ichiro Maruoka in the middle of the lobby. The play of light and shadow accentuated the deep-set eyes, the flared nostrils, the heavy mouth clamped in an expression of masterful determination. It made him look inhuman, like one of the ferocious gods that guard the gates of temples.

After making sure that no one was around, they crossed the lobby to the main elevator bank and took an elevator to the tenth floor. The computer department was deserted, but several machines were functioning through the night, recording and processing the deals being done up on the twenty-first and twenty-second floors. Screens flickered in the dark, giving off eerie green and orange glows. Disk units whirred and fax machines hummed and printers chattered to each other.

They switched on the lights just in the corner where Noriko worked. She sat down at her computer terminal and started punching in commands.

"Can I do something?" asked Kenji.

"Sure," said Noriko. "Get me a coffee from the dispenser round the corner. Milk, one sugar."

It took her about half an hour to set up a program that would seek out all the information that Noda had asked for. All that Kenji then had to do was direct her to the hidden files. She downloaded the data onto a three-inch floppy disk which she popped into her handbag. Kenji was amazed at the speed with which she accomplished the task.

She had just switched off her terminal when they heard voices outside the office.

"Quick," whispered Kenji. "Get out of sight."

They ducked down a corridor between workstations and crept

soundlessly over to the darker side of the room. The voices got closer. With a shock, Kenji recognized one of them as Rei Takeda's.

"I'll just check the printout. Wait a minute, the lights are on in here. What's going on? Suematsu, I thought I told you to maintain special security measures until the project's over!"

The familiar Osaka accent was suddenly harsh with irritation. The other voice, which Kenji didn't recognize, was confused and apologetic.

"I don't know. I'm sorry. The guys in the computer department probably forgot to turn them off."

"That's unlikely," snapped Takeda. "The guard should have been round to check that. No, it looks like someone's been in here recently."

The footsteps came up the center of the room—slowly, as if the two men were looking around them as they walked. Kenji and Noriko made themselves even smaller.

"This is strange," said the man called Suematsu.

"What's the matter?"

"The coffee in this cup. It's still warm."

"Hah! I told you so. Someone's been poking around."

Kenji bit his lip in frustration. He had forgotten about the coffee cup. Noriko had left it on the filing cabinet next to her desk.

"I'll go and see what those idiots in security are doing," went on Takeda. "You stay and check the place thoroughly. After all, the intruder might come back and finish whatever it was he was doing."

"Understood!"

One set of footsteps disappeared out of the door. The other moved slowly from one side of the room to the other. The man called Suematsu was obviously searching for further signs of the intruder's presence. Kenji squeezed himself down to the height of a wastepaper bin. They would certainly be discovered if Suematsu came over to their end of the room. And the footsteps were getting closer!

Kenji turned to Noriko in something close to desperation. For a moment, he couldn't believe his eyes. She had taken off her

T-shirt and was unhooking her bra. He watched dumbfounded as she then unzipped her miniskirt and slipped out of it.

The footsteps were just a couple of yards away now.

Suddenly, Noriko grabbed Kenji by the shoulders and pushed him over on his back. As he fell, she rolled on top of him, squeezing his legs between her thighs. The noise was too loud to be missed.

"What's that? Who's there?"

The footsteps quickened, then stopped right beside them.

"What on earth are you two doing?"

Noriko stood up, and brushed the hair out of her face. Her breasts were heaving as if she had just run a hundred-meter race.

"What are we doing? It's obvious, isn't it? We're just having a little fun. Overtime gets a little bit boring sometimes, you see."

She giggled in a way that Kenji had never heard before.

Suematsu was a short man in his mid-forties. He looked confused. He gazed at Kenji lying on the floor, then at Noriko. His line of sight fell to her heaving breasts, then down to the scanty white panties which only half covered her buttocks.

"I mean, it's really stimulating," she said, still breathing deeply. "Among all these desks and screens and printers . . . where everybody sits and works all day. . . . Come on, you must have thought about it yourself!"

Suematsu nervously fingered the knot of his tie.

"This is highly irregular," he said, his voice several tones higher than when he was talking to Takeda. "I'm going to have to take you both to the security department."

"Ooh, please don't do that!" said Noriko, in a cute-little-bad-girl voice. "I've been naughty, I know, but I can't help it. Sometimes, my desires are just too strong, you see."

"Using office facilities outside working hours without permission is strictly against company rules. This incident must be reported at once."

"That's no fun at all. I've got a better idea. Why don't you stay here with us for a while, and I'll be very nice to you, I promise."

Noriko walked up to him, put her arms around his waist, and kissed him on the side of the neck, just below the ear. One hand scrabbled at the buckle of his belt.

"Whaa—what are you doing?"

Suematsu didn't seem to be resisting much. Noriko giggled again and backed him up against a revolving chair. He sat down heavily. She pushed her breasts into his face.

"Let's all be nice to each other," she breathed.

Kenji saw his chance. He picked up a laptop computer that was sitting on a nearby desk, weighed it once in his hands, and brought it crashing down on the top of Suematsu's head. The screen splintered into a thousand fragments. Suematsu slid out of the chair and slumped onto the floor.

"Come on," said Kenji. "Let's move before Takeda gets back."

Noriko picked up her clothes and her handbag and they ran for the elevator.

Noriko's apartment was small, but it was packed with electronic gadgets. For entertainment purposes, she had a videodisc player, a double-deck compact disc player with graphic equalizer, a digital keyboard, a twenty-eight-inch TV that almost took up one entire wall, a video camera, a Walkman that worked in the shower, and a parabola antenna on the balcony. She also had a personal computer, printer, and personal fax machine.

When the information had been printed out and faxed over to Noda, they relaxed over a bottle of wine that Kenji had bought earlier in the day.

"We'd better go away somewhere tomorrow," he advised. "It won't take them long to work out who you are."

"I suppose so. That is unless poor old Suematsu gets too ashamed to tell anyone."

They both smiled at the thought of Suematsu trying to explain to Takeda what had happened.

"By the way," said Kenji a little later. "Your performance back there was really something. All that fantasy about sex in the office. How did you manage to make it up so quickly?"

"I didn't make it up," she said.

14

⋮

MORI woke to searing pains in his head, across his chest, stabbing through his legs and back. There was the taste of blood in his mouth and one of his eyes was too swollen to open more than a crack. His wrists, he discovered, were bound together behind the back of the wooden chair he was sitting in. The cords were so tight that there was hardly any feeling in his hands.

What had happened? His head throbbed with the effort of remembering. Sato and Kato. Nakamura's arm squeezing his windpipe. Being pounded with fists, feet, elbows, knees. The red mist. Then voices far away, at the other end of a long tunnel. Being hauled down a corridor, thrown into the trunk of a car. The noise of the engine starting. Then nothing.

Slowly turning his head, forcing back the waves of pain, Mori tried to make out where he was. A large room with a wooden floor. A couple of canvas-backed chairs, a gray metal desk. Light streaming in through a barred window. In the distance, the whir of a generator and a loudspeaker blaring out a calisthenic routine.

"Left elbow, yes, one, two, three. Good! Right elbow, one, two, three . . ."

There was someone else in the room, just behind his line of sight. Mori twisted his head around a little farther. It was Sato. He was sitting in a chair on Mori's left reading a manga comic book. After a while, he noticed that Mori was shifting around and got up.

"Woken up, eh!" he said, peering into Mori's face. "Thought we'd finished you at first. The boss was pretty worried, I can tell you."

Mori tried to say something, but was suddenly overcome by a wave of nausea. He retched a couple of times, and the effort sent flashes of white pain shooting across his skull. A rush of bitter liquid filled his mouth and dribbled out onto his shirt.

"Feeling bad, eh!" chuckled Sato. "Not such a tough guy now, are you?"

The retching cleared some of the mist from Mori's head. Memories of the previous evening hardened like the outlines of a Polaroid photo.

"What do you people want?" he said thickly.

"Careful, Mori. I'm asking the questions, not you." Sato rolled up the comic magazine and slapped Mori across the face with it twice. That cleared his head rather more. He checked himself over. His teeth were still there, though his upper lip was twice the size he remembered. It felt as if a couple of ribs had been cracked. The rest was just bruising. It was survivable.

"I'm going to fetch the boss," said Sato. "Don't you go wandering off anywhere now, will you?"

That would have been difficult. The only part of Mori's body that he could move with any comfort was his head. He managed to swivel the chair around slightly so that it was facing the window. He could just make out a green movement between the bars. He was somewhere surrounded by trees.

After a few minutes, Sato returned, along with Kato and Nakamura. There was someone else with them, a slim handsome man in a well-cut Italian suit of the sort that Mori would never be able to wear, even if he could afford one, without feeling ridiculous. The newcomer looked poised and relaxed, but there was something in the glance of his eyes and the set of his mouth—something cold and greedy—that gave away his profession. Mori knew him from dozens of photos in the weekly magazines that lionized the yakuza as if they were sports heroes. It was Seiji Terada, the most prominent of the "new leaders."

"Hands," said Terada tonelessly.

"Hands," repeated Nakamura.

Kato grunted obediently and produced a six-inch blade with which he cut the cords around Mori's wrists. There were deep red marks on both wrists. Mori squeezed his hands together to get the blood flowing again.

"Right," said Terada. "Have him stand up."

"Stand him up," said Nakamura.

Kato grabbed Mori by the armpits and hauled him to his feet. He swayed from side to side, fighting back the waves of nausea.

"Hit him once," said Terada.

"Hit him once."

Mori steeled his stomach muscles just in time to absorb the impact of Kato's fist. It still left him on his knees, sucking in air in huge gulps.

"That's enough," said Terada to Nakamura. "Lift him up again."

"Lift him up again."

"Sorry about that," said Terada, with a slight shrug of the shoulders. "But before we start our discussion I wanted to establish the ground rules. Meetings are a complete waste of time if the ground rules are not clearly established. Right, Mori-san?"

Terada was standing hands on hips, addressing Mori like a senior executive explaining company procedures to a new employee. He was wearing a button-down shirt that had his initials stitched on the breast pocket, silk suspenders with a wavy psychedelic pattern that matched his socks, and a pair of gold cuff links bearing the diamond-shaped crest of the Kawashita Syndicate. He was the only man in the room wearing a jacket, and he was the only one not sweating profusely.

"Now let's start from the beginning," he said. "What is the nature of your assignment? Who gave it to you, and how far have you gotten?"

Mori ran through the possibilities in his head. If they found out the truth, they would dispose of him straightaway. His only hope was to make himself more valuable to them alive.

"I'll tell you what I know," he said. "But it's not much. I'm working for a group of people who have decided to put a stop to this crazy project of Iwanaga's."

Kato glanced at Nakamura with a puzzled expression. Obviously, they hadn't let him into the details of the Iwanaga project. Terada's only visible reaction was the arching of his left eyebrow.

"Project? What on earth are you talking about?"

"Let's not play games. My employers know everything about your project that's worth knowing. They've been tracking every move that you've made. If Iwanaga thinks he can get away with something this big without people noticing, he's even crazier than everyone says."

"The sensei is not crazy," said Terada flatly. "It won't be long before his enemies learn that to their cost."

"He's going to fail. You're all going to look like fools."

"Hit him again."

"Hit him again," repeated Nakamura.

Kato seemed to take this part of his job very seriously. He gave a grunt of effort as his fist sank into Mori's stomach. Mori buckled and retched, but stayed on his feet. Kato looked disappointed. Terada passed a hand through his glossy, expensively tended hair. His voice conveyed resignation, rather than anger.

"You obviously didn't understand the ground rules, Mori-san. Your fate is in our hands entirely. If you behave in a cooperative and sensible manner, we will deal with you like reasonable men. If not, well . . ."

Terada shrugged again and glanced meaningfully at Nakamura. Mori nodded in acknowledgment. His mouth was dry, and ripples of nausea were passing through his body.

"Now, who sent you and why?" said Terada.

Mori selected his words carefully. He needed to sow the seeds of doubt in Terada's mind. He had to remain credible.

"They're top financial people, bureaucrats and bankers and so on. They've been watching Iwanaga for months, and they're determined to stop him. The police are going to move in a couple of day's time. If I were in your place, I'd get out now while you've still got the chance."

"Thanks for the advice," said Terada, with a dry smile. "But in a couple of days time, it'll be too late to make any difference. Now perhaps you could give us the names of these mysterious 'top people'? Your story can be checked out very easily, you know."

"I'm just a low-level operative," said Mori. "I've never met any of them in person. I just do what I'm told."

"The bastard's lying," hissed Nakamura.

Terada gave a sigh of disappointment. A shadow of annoyance passed over his face.

"Not good enough, detective-san," he said. "You'll have to try harder than that. Have the girl brought up here."

"Bring up the girl!"

Kato was gone for a couple of minutes. While he was away, Terada picked up Kato's comic book from the table, took one glance at it, then pursed his lips in distaste and dropped it in the wastebasket. He took a cigarette from a silver cigarette case and held it in his mouth while Nakamura lit it for him. It was a brand that Mori had never seen before, with a silver band around the filter.

Kato hustled Lisa into the room. Mori had tried to prepare himself for the worst, but he was still shocked by her appearance. She had obviously been drugged. She was wearing a factory worker's overalls with the Nippon Infosystems emblem on the front. She had a black eye and the left half of her face seemed to be swollen up. When Kato let go of her arms and shoved her into the center of the room, she staggered around without seeming to understand where she was. She didn't register Mori's presence at all.

"Let her go," said Mori. "She's got nothing to do with this."

His mind was working desperately. What did he know? What could he use? He thought back to the piece of paper he had taken from the wastepaper basket at the Computer Center. His head was aching so much. It was difficult to remember. . . .

Terada was silent for a moment. He looked at Mori, then at Lisa, then he flicked the ash from his cigarette and shook his head pensively.

"Cut off one of her ears," he said finally.

"Cut off one of her ears," repeated Nakamura.

Kato took a switchblade from his pocket, sprang the blade, and walked toward Lisa. She made no attempt to evade him as he grabbed her roughly around the neck and swept the hair off the side of her head. Mori strained to visualize the shape of the piece of paper, the lines where it had been crumpled, the names and dates. . . .

Kato tested the knife against the back of his hand, then raised the blade to the side of her neck.

"Stop!" yelled Mori. "I've got more for you. I can tell you why you're never going to succeed."

Terada motioned for Kato to pause.

"Go on," he said. "Let's see if you can do better this time."

"The bastard's lying," sneered Nakamura. "He's trying to play for time."

Kato glared at Mori. He rapped the blade impatiently against the back of his hand.

"Perhaps he is," said Terada. "But then again perhaps he's not. Let's be patient and find out. Go on, Mori-san, we're all listening closely. Try not to disappoint us this time."

Mori nodded slowly and took a deep breath.

"It's simple," he said. "The Computer Center's been infiltrated. We know your operation inside out, even down to the details of the security roster. Tanaka group at the main gate from Monday to Thursday, to be replaced by Nagatomi group from Friday to Sunday. Double strength for the Dance of the Cranes final check-through on Saturday."

His words had the desired effect. Terada's eyes widened slightly, and he brushed the tip of his tongue over his upper lip.

"It's a child's trick," said Kato angrily. "He takes us for fools."

"Have him shut up," said Terada without shifting his gaze from Mori's face.

"Shut up," said Nakamura to Kato.

Terada took a deep drag of his cigarette, then stamped it out hard on the ground. Nakamura was watching him nervously.

"Where did you get this information?" said Terada. All his

smoothness had suddenly disappeared.

"Right from the source," said Mori. "One of the programmers in the Computer Center is feeding us with information. I was there to make contact with him."

Terada nodded.

"Who is this man?" he said.

"I don't know the name. I just collect the documents from him. It's safer that way for both of us."

Terada pursed his lips thoughtfully, then took Nakamura aside. There was a good minute of muttered conversation. Kato released Lisa and looked on with obvious incomprehension.

"All right, Mori," said Terada, turning back to Mori. "It looks like we've got a job for you. Nakamura here will take you out to the Computer Center and you will identify this spy for us."

"What about the girl?" said Mori.

"She will stay here with Kato, just in case. Kato has his own unique way with women, isn't that right, Kato?"

Kato smiled modestly.

"Last month we had some trouble with a soap-girl in Osaka," went on Terada. "Kato took care of her. You may have read about it—you know, the head found in the locker at Umeda Station . . ."

Mori had indeed read about it. One of the sports newspapers had carried the story in gruesome detail. The police, he remembered, were treating it as a sex murder.

Kato shifted from foot to foot like a bashful schoolboy.

"If you attempt to deceive us, Kato will be happy to oblige again. When he's finished with the girl, the police will have work to do in five different prefectures. Now tie him up again."

"Tie him up again."

Kato pulled Mori's wrists behind the back of the chair and tied them to the chair legs. The cords felt even tighter than before. When the job was done, Terada and Nakamura left the room, leaving Kato to watch the two prisoners.

Lisa was sitting slumped on the floor in the middle of the room. So far, she hadn't even looked at Mori once. Kato walked up to her and grabbed her roughly from behind again. This time his hands slid over her breasts.

"Leave her alone, you moron," said Mori.

"We're just having a little game, Mori-san. The real fun won't come till later."

He took Lisa's hand and slipped it onto his groin.

"What about that? Feels interesting, doesn't it? That's right, go ahead. Give it a little squeeze. Good! She likes it, Mori-san. She wants to find out more."

Mori felt sick. Lisa still seemed to be in a trancelike condition, her arms and legs moving about as if she were underwater.

Kato undid the front of her shirt and started pawing about inside it.

"You're very lucky, Mori. In Kawasaki, we charge three thousand yen for a show like this. You're getting it free!"

He pulled her down onto the floor and forced her legs apart with his knee. The top half of her body was naked now. He wriggled about on top of her for a while, his hand jammed down the front of her trousers.

"Good and firm," he was muttering. "Just the way I like them."

Lisa was tossing her head about from side to side, making small groaning noises like an actress in a porno video. Her left hand, Mori noticed, had slipped into Kato's trouser pocket. Kato's mouth was moving from nipple to nipple, leaving trails of saliva across her breasts. He had forced the baggy cotton trousers down to her knees and the flat of his hand was pressing up against her groin.

Lisa's left hand emerged slowly from his trouser pocket. Between her thumb and her forefinger was Kato's switchblade.

"She's warm and wet, Mori," said Kato, pausing for breath. "She's enjoying it, all right."

He shifted his weight slightly, unzipped his trousers and pushed them down to his knees, exposing his square white buttocks. He took Lisa's right hand and guided it down between his legs. Lisa made a low half-gasping, half-purring noise.

"I wonder if she can tell the difference," Kato chuckled, turning to Mori. "She must have seen dozens in her time, hey?

Hundreds, probably!"

Lisa's other hand slipped down to Kato's groin.

"Mmmm, that's right," he said. "Easy, slowly, now just—*uhh!*"

Suddenly, Kato made a strange grunting noise, as if he was about to be sick. There was an expression of shock on his face. Then his hands went to his groin, and his whole body convulsed. When he brought his hands up to his face again, they were covered in blood. He gave a bellow that came deep from the pit of his stomach. It conveyed not just pain, but a primitive fear and confusion as well.

Lisa rolled out from under him and sprang to her feet like a cat. She had the knife in her hand. In an instant, she was at the back of Mori's chair cutting the cords around his wrists.

Kato was sitting on his knees gazing dully at the dark stain spreading over the crotch of his trousers. He looked up as Mori got to his feet. He was shivering uncontrollably.

"She cut me," he said in a broken sob.

He was sitting at just the right height. Mori took one step forward and hit him in the side of the jaw with a full-power swivel kick. Kato fell backward, the back of his head hitting the floor with a thud. He didn't move after that.

"Let's get out of here," said Mori.

Lisa nodded. She was still badly disoriented. The pupils of her eyes were huge. Mori grabbed her by the wrist and pulled her toward the door. They emerged into a brightly lit corridor with a blue strip running down the center of the floor. It was deserted, but the noise of machinery was much louder. Mori moved cautiously toward it.

On either side of the corridor, there were doors with small circular windows at head height. Glancing through the one on the left, Mori saw a couple of men in Nippon Infosystems uniforms sitting in front of a large control panel. The room on the right had a similar control panel, but no one at the table in front of it. Mori tried the door. It was open.

In the wall opposite was a window that looked out on the factory floor. It was large, probably one of Nippon Infosystems' main production bases. Several men in uniforms were wandering about among the lines of machinery, checking the video monitors mounted on each one. Conveyer belts carrying heaps of brightly colored components fed into gaping mouths and came out empty. Electronic arms picked up sheets of metal, folded them, punched holes in them, then dumped them onto unmanned carts equipped with giant optical sensors that made them look like one-eyed rats. At the far end was a loading bay where crates were being taken out of a light van and put onto a conveyer belt.

Mori tried to remember what he had recently read about Nippon Infosystems. The company had just set up a highly automated assembly plant, a place where, according to the newspaper reports, "robots manufactured robots" twenty-four hours a day. Iwanaga had claimed that it represented a new wave of manufacturing technology that no other country would be able to compete with. This had to be it.

"What are you doing here? Are you authorized?"

Mori turned round. The man who had just entered the room was tall, wearing a gray uniform and peaked cap. When he saw Mori's bruised face, he gave a start and reached for the walkie-talkie in the breast pocket of his jacket. He had no time to use it. Mori drove his knee into the man's groin, doubled him up, then hit him once on the back of the neck. He collapsed without a sound.

They stripped off his uniform, gagged him with his own socks, then used electric cord to bind his hands and legs. Mori put on the uniform and pulled the peaked cap down over his eyes.

They would have to move fast. It was only a matter of time before Nakamura and Terada found what had happened to Kato. Out in the corridor again, Lisa was walking unsteadily, her head bobbing from side to side.

"So sleepy," she kept saying. "It's a long time since I've been so sleepy."

"You've got to stay awake," said Mori desperately. "Come on, just a few minutes more."

"So, so sleepy . . ."

There was a rattle somewhere behind them. Mori looked

around for somewhere to hide. There was nowhere. He tried to pull her down the corridor by the hand, but she wouldn't budge. The noise was getting closer fast.

"Sleepy . . ."

Mori straightened her up, trying to make it look like they were a pair of ordinary workers standing around chatting. Out of the corner of his eye, he saw something appear around the corner of the corridor behind them. It was one of the unmanned carts, stacked high with wooden crates.

"Lisa, listen carefully. I want you to grab onto this thing and not let go. Do you understand?"

She nodded slowly, her eyes already half closed.

"Say if you understand!"

"I understand."

"Come on, let's do it then!"

The cart was about the size of a small car. It was moving just a little faster than a brisk walking pace. They grabbed onto the back rail, ducking behind the stack of crates, and let it lead them down the corridor.

At the end of the corridor was a closed door. The sound of the machinery behind it was deafeningly loud. Mori glanced over the top of the crates, then ducked down again. A tiny video camera above the door was moving from side to side, scanning the shape of the truck.

At that moment, the loudspeaker system crackled into life. This time, it was a woman's voice, the tone controlled and soothing.

"This is an important announcement. Will all workers please vacate the production area and take up positions for emergency procedure number four. This is not an exercise. I repeat, this is not an exercise."

They must have found Kato, thought Mori. He glanced at Lisa. Now that the cart had stopped, her eyelids were drooping again. He shook her by the shoulder and she smiled weakly.

There was an electronic hum as the door swung open. The cart waited for a moment, then purred forward into the production area, following the blue stripe on the floor.

Mori glanced from side to side. The men in uniforms had disappeared, presumably to get into position for emergency procedure number four, whatever that was. The cart went straight down the center of the work area for about thirty yards, then the blue stripe veered over to one of the machines. Mori and Lisa slipped behind the machine and watched as a giant metal claw started lifting the crates onto a conveyer belt. There they were drilled open by steel spikes that shot out from the side of the belt, upended for the contents to be removed, then lifted clear by another metal claw.

The loudspeaker sounded again.

"All workers should now have exited the production area. Will any workers still remaining please ready themselves immediately for emergency procedure number four."

Mori slid underneath the conveyer belt and edged toward the loading bay at the end of the work area, tugging Lisa along behind him by the hand. At least the noise of the machinery was keeping her awake.

The thirty yards between the end of the conveyer belt and the loading bay contained several rows of stacked crates. An unmanned crane was trundling back and forth on a blue strip on the floor, moving crates from one place to another. It would provide good cover for them to get to the loading bay.

Mori slid out from under the conveyer belt and found himself right in the path of an unmanned cart crossing from left to right. Except that this cart wasn't unmanned. Perched on the front, just behind the optical sensor, was Nakamura. He yelled something which Mori couldn't hear above the roar of the machines and his hand reached under his jacket.

Mori leaped onto the cart, pulling Nakamura by the shoulder just as the gun came free. Nakamura fired once as Mori swung him forward. The shot ricocheted off metal somewhere high up. Then they were both on the ground, rolling against the guard fence of a laser metal-cutting tool. Nakamura was holding onto the gun, but Mori had his wrist in a grip of iron. He got to his knees and jammed Nakamura's against the sharp edges of a metal block waiting to be machined. Nakamura yelled with shock and the gun clattered to the ground.

They got up. Nakamura's face was a mask of rage. He lunged forward and seized Mori in a crushing embrace. Mori felt the heat of the man's breath on his cheek. He reeled backward against the guardrail, narrowly missing one of the giant yellow claws as it groped for a metal block.

For a moment, they staggered around like drunken dancers at a karaoke bar, Nakamura's stubby fingers digging into the side of Mori's neck. Then the opportunity came. The yellow claw was swinging over for the next block of metal. Mori used all his strength to twist Nakamura into its path. The claw hovered above them for a moment as if wondering what to do, opened, then dropped onto Nakamura's shoulder. He screamed with pain as the metal pincer closed on him, then it lifted him over the guardrail and dropped him onto the machining table. The red light in the center of the control panel started to flash. Wires shot out from the side of the table and wrapped around his chest, fastening him into position. Nakamura gave out a confused roar and started pulling at the wires with his hands, but it was too late. A high-pitched whine signaled that the lasers had started. Two bright spots the size of buttons had appeared on either side of his chest, and smoke was pouring from them. Nakamura's eyes bulged and his mouth opened wide, but his scream was submerged in the loudspeaker announcement.

"Emergency procedure number four is ready to commence. The production area is now being sealed off. Will all workers please check their self-defense equipment and report any malfunctions immediately."

Mori glanced toward the loading bay. With a shock , he realized that it was only half visible. A panel was sliding down from the ceiling to block off access.

Lisa was still crouching under the conveyer belt. Mori grabbed her hand and they ran for the loading bay. The panel was coming down quickly. It looked as if they were going to be too late. They had another twenty yards to cover, and there was already only enough space for a child to duck through.

Suddenly, a red light to the left side of the panel started flashing and the panel stopped a yard from the ground. Mori could see the bottom part of one of the unmanned carts trapped outside. It was bleeping as if in distress. The panel rose a yard and the carrier scooted into the production area. Just as the panel started descending again, Mori and Lisa hurled themselves through to the other side.

There were two trucks in the bay, both with the backs open and stacks of crates beside them. A man wearing Seikyu Transportation overalls and a peaked cap was leaning against one of them eating a cup of instant noodles. He looked up at Mori and Lisa, obviously startled.

"Emergency position four," yelled Mori. "Didn't you hear?"

"I don't know anything about that," said the man apologetically. "I'm a driver. I don't even work for this company. I—"

"This is an emergency," yelled Mori. "Now get this truck around to the main gate immediately or I'll inform your department head that you refused to cooperate. Come on, get moving!"

"Understood!"

The man dropped the cup noodles on one of the crates and hurried into the cab of the truck. Mori quickly lifted Lisa into the back and got into the passenger seat.

The truck swung out of the loading bay. Outside there was a large parking lot, beyond that a wire fence about four yards high, beyond that an industrial wasteland of factories, junkyards, gasoline stands, and giant billboards, intersected by a busy expressway. Just in front of the wire fence was a small shrine framed by the gray concrete pillars of the shrine gate. Mori remembered reading how Iwanaga insisted that all employees worship at Nippon Infosystems shrines at least once a week. Dead employees and their relatives, whatever their religion, were automatically enshrined there.

"Right," said Mori. "Pull in next to the shrine gate."

The driver obeyed, not bothering to hide his irritation.

"I don't understand this company," he muttered. "Nothing makes any sense here. Nobody ever tells you what's going on."

"Just do what you're told and everything'll be fine. Now get out and check the tire pressure."

"Check the what!"

"The tires," said Mori patiently. "They have to be checked before going any farther. It's part of emergency procedure number four."

The driver looked at Mori as if he had just claimed to have taken a trip on a UFO.

"What do you mean? What on earth has the tire pressure got to do with any emergency!"

"I can't divulge that. All I can say is that our rulebook states that in the event of emergency procedures three, four, and five, all outgoing vehicles must have their tire pressures checked. So if you want to do business with Nippon Infosystems again, you'd better shut up and get on with it."

Mori adopted a tone of overbearing arrogance. The driver shook his head in despair and got out of the cab, still muttering to himself.

"Procedures . . . rulebooks . . . nonsense, nonsense!"

Mori waited until he was bending down at the right front wheel, then slid across to the driver's seat. He jammed the gearshift into reverse, gunned the engine once, and let out the clutch. The truck shuddered for an instant, as if deciding whether or not to stall, then accelerated fiercely backward.

The driver got to his feet and watched as Mori squealed to a halt within a yard of the factory wall.

"You're crazy," he yelled. "The whole lot of you. From the president down."

Mori turned the truck around and made for the front of the building. Rounding the corner of the parking area, he had to swerve to avoid a group of Nippon Infosystem employees who had suddenly emerged from a side door. There was a sound like hail rattling against the side of the truck and a bullet zinged through the open side window and exited through the roof of the cab, just above his head. Mori crouched over the wheel and put his foot down on the accelerator. The truck roared toward the main gate.

The gate itself consisted of half a dozen metal bars. It was just swinging to the shut position. There was a small guardhouse on one side, at the front of which was a sign that read "Caution—High Voltage Current." Two men in uniform were standing on either side of the gate. They had guns leveled at the cab.

Mori ducked down below the level of the windshield, held the steering wheel steady with one hand, pressed the accelerator to the floor with the other. Suddenly, the windshield shattered and the air above his head was full of glass fragments. Then there was a shuddering impact, a flash of white light, and a sound like the tearing of a giant sheet of paper. The truck bucked once, but kept on going. Mori didn't pause to look around for another two hundred yards. When he did, he saw flames leaping from the roof of the guardhouse and an empty space where the gate had been.

The truck's hood was badly buckled, and the cab was full of the smell of gasoline, but the engine still seemed in good shape. Mori used a wrench to smash out what remained of the windshield, then headed for the expressway.

It took Mori just over two hours to get back to Tokyo. He left the truck in a suburban side street, then took a taxi. Lisa slept most of the way, and by the time they arrived in the city center the effects of whatever had been pumped into her seemed to be wearing off.

"I just had the most bizarre dream," she yawned. "It was horrible. This big ugly guy was squeezing down on me, trying to rape me. You'll never guess what I did."

"What did you do?" said Mori.

"Cut the bastard's balls off. Taught him a lesson, for sure."

Then she fell asleep again, her head nestling on Mori's shoulder.

There was a doctor on the west side of Shinjuku who specialized in cosmetic surgery and sexual diseases and had a profitable sideline in supplying amphetamines to favored patients. There had been an attempt to blackmail him after one of them, a Taiwanese stripper, had been found dead in a love hotel with a syringe hanging out of her arm. After a few enquiries, Mori managed to track down the man responsible, who happened to be a close rival in the Shinjuku medical industry. As a mark of gratitude, the client had offered Mori free cosmetic surgery and sexual disease treatment for the rest of his life. Mori had yet to avail himself of either service, but now he was going to ask for a different sort of medical favor. Lisa needed a few days in a clinic where no one would ask any questions and where her presence would be kept absolutely secret.

Mori took her to the doctor's private house and explained what had happened in the vaguest terms possible. After leaving her there, he telephoned Kudo and arranged to meet him immediately.

"This is going to be the biggest break of your career," he said. "Promotion will be absolutely assured. No more chasing motorcycle gangs on rainy Monday nights. No more staking out illegal mah-jongg games. After this, you'll go straight to the top."

"That's what you told me last time," said Kudo skeptically. "And what happened? I ended up giving you information. Not only that, I even had to pay for the beers."

"This time, it's the real thing. I'm going to tell you everything I know. There's only one condition."

"One condition? What's that?"

Kudo sounded wary.

"I want to be there at the end—when the arrests are made."

"That would be completely against the rules," said Kudo.

"I know," said Mori.

In a small town in central Hokkaido, the assistant general manager of the local branch of Sumikawa Bank sat gazing into space, the financial page of the *Gendai Shimbun* open on the desk in front of him.

Tom Kono was worried. What he had just read fitted closely with the most recent information he had received from London. According to Trevor, Shimada had started to unwind his long positions on the dollar. At the same time, he was using the futures and options markets to go massively short of American and European stocks and bonds. Financially, it was an insane strategy, since he was now taking huge losses on the holdings he had previously built up, but the man seemed to have no awareness of risk at all. It was as if he were trying to create a gigantic financial snowball.

Yet massive though Shimada's trades were, they couldn't be responsible on their own for all the turbulence detailed in the newspaper. To move markets that far and that fast, there would have to be other Shimadas elsewhere following the exact same plan of action. That was hardly likely, thought Tom, but what else could explain the fact that Shimada's trades seemed to have an exponential and immediate effect on markets? The only other possibility was that the man had the sharpest sixth sense of any trader that Tom had ever heard of. And going by what Trevor had said about Shimada's dull-witted questions, that was even less likely.

Tom picked up his wooden abacus—more convenient than a calculator for adding up long rows of numbers—and was just about to start the daily chore of checking through the office expenses when one of the branch's two counter girls came rushing into his office.

"Kono-san, come quickly," she said breathlessly. "It must be something awfully important."

Tom liked Kazumi. She was the only member of the staff who didn't treat him as if he were suffering from some sort of infection. The daughter of a local farmer, she was hardworking, cheerful, and almost frighteningly healthy, but conveying information wasn't one of her strong points.

"Important? What is?"

"There's someone asking for you," she said. "He's got a big black car. With a driver. With white gloves."

Tom stepped out into the tiny customer-service area. The man who greeted him there with a generous bow could only have been in his late twenties or early thirties, but his formal manner and the stiff cut of his dark suit made him look thirty years older. He addressed Tom in smooth, confident tones. "Mr. Kono, I'm extremely honored to have this opportunity of meeting you. Your assistance in this troublesome matter has been highly appreciated by the people I represent." The middle-aged young man took a gold-rimmed business card from a pigskin card holder and handed it to Tom with another short bow. It described him as Koji Ueno, private secretary to a senior politician who, Tom recalled, had been forced from the cabinet over a financial scandal several years before.

Ueno had a soft, plausible mouth, pudgy cheeks, and a brow so shiny that it looked as if it had been polished. His hair was slicked back flat in thick oily strands. With his imperturbable sleekness and apparent eagerness to please, he reminded Tom of a sophisticated sea lion.

"Assistance?" said Tom cautiously. "I'm not quite sure I understand. . . ."

"I mean your letter. It was brought to our attention. Its contents accorded with certain of our own investigations."

"Uh . . . yes. The letter . . ." Tom replied with deliberate hesitancy. After all, this could easily be some sort of trap.

Ueno glanced around at Kazumi. She was gazing at them in awestruck silence, apparently frozen to the spot like an ice sculpture at the Sapporo snow festival. Ueno nodded his head in a mini-bow, but she just smiled nervously and stood still. He turned to Tom.

"I would be grateful if we could discuss this matter in more detail. Perhaps, if you wouldn't mind stepping out to my car . . ."

Tom paused to scrutinize the man more closely; the Tokyo University tie, the pudgy, well-manicured fingers, the strange mixture of pomposity and utter deference. No doubt about it, Ueno looked every inch what he claimed to be.

"Fine," said Tom, with a nod.

He went back into his office to get his jacket. Kazumi followed him in and helped him with it on.

"Where are you going?" she whispered in his ear while turning down his collar.

"Don't know," muttered Tom.

"When are you coming back?"

"Don't know. Maybe not for a long time."

For an instant she looked utterly crestfallen, but then she gave her usual bright smile.

"Do your best," she said.

The story that Tom was told in the car was so bizarre that at first he had difficulty in believing it. Massive coordinated manipulation of financial markets in Europe and the United States? Involving not just Sumikawa Bank, but Mitsutomo Life and Dainippon Trust and several other major institutions as well? It was beyond his wildest imaginings. Yet, as he listened to Ueno's explanation, many things began to make sense, from his own dismissal to the strange pattern of Shimada's trades.

According to Ueno, both Mitsutomo and Dainippon had undergone boardroom upheavals in the past two years. Just as with Sumikawa, control had passed from experienced leaders with strong ties to the business establishment to little-known men with no political connections. Management structures had been radically overhauled, new men brought in from outside, and power concentrated in secretive "consultative" groups that operated separately from the main board. Ueno's people had long been suspicious, and Tom's letter had alerted them to the exact nature and scale of what was going on.

"But what's the point of all this?" said Tom. "What on earth are they trying to achieve?"

"We're not sure," said Ueno. "But there must be a financial objective. After all, I don't have to tell you that when markets move around like this, the people who understand what's really happening can make a great deal of money."

Tom shook his head in incomprehension.

"But look at the cost! My bank and Mitsutomo Life and the others are going to end up making unimaginable losses. Their survival could even be threatened!"

Ueno offered Tom a cigarette. His own he fitted carefully into an ivory cigarette holder.

"That's why I'm here," he said. "The people that I represent know your reputation, and they have every faith in you. They earnestly request your further assistance in preventing this catastrophe before us."

"What kind of assistance?" said Tom. "And anyway, who exactly are these mysterious people you say you represent?"

"I'm afraid I can't reveal their identities. They are a group of private citizens with a strong interest, shall we say, in maintaining stability and prosperity."

"Whose prosperity?"

"The prosperity of the Japanese people, of course," said Ueno, sounding offended.

Tom exhaled a long stream of cigarette smoke through his nostrils and stared through the dark window glass of the limousine. The single street that constituted the heart of the small town was almost deserted. The greengrocer's tired-looking dog loped from one side of the road to the other, as it did several times an hour. A plump schoolgirl stood under the awning of the rice shop, gazing at the car as if it were an alien spacecraft. Ueno's driver was sitting at the window table of the town's only coffee bar, flicking though an ancient copy of *Thursday* magazine while munching fried noodles.

"What do you want me to do?" said Tom dully.

Ueno took an envelope out of his pocket and handed it to him.

"This is a plane ticket to Tokyo, then on to London. We want you to take charge of the situation there. Everything must be put into reverse—discreetly, with the minimum impact on the markets."

"Take charge? But what about Shimada and the new branch manager? They wouldn't stand for me coming back like that."

"Don't worry. They won't be given the opportunity to object. You will have absolute authority not just at Sumikawa, but at Mitsutomo and Dainippon too. Do you agree to help us?"

"I don't know," said Tom, shaking his head. "Unwinding those huge positions—it would be a long complicated business. . . ."

"You can have as much time as you like, all the backup you need. My people consider your participation absolutely essential. They will see that you are rewarded properly."

"I don't want to be rewarded," said Tom. "All I want is my old job back."

"That can be arranged with no difficulty at all."

Outside, the small town looked even lonelier. The fat schoolgirl had ridden off on a scooter. The greengrocer's dog had

slumped down in front of a vending machine that sold pornographic comics. Chin on the pavement, it was gazing up at them
with defeated yellow eyes. "One other thing," said Tom. "I would
like to nominate a replacement for my current job here in
Hokkaido."

Ueno looked puzzled for a moment, then shrugged and
nodded his head.

"Anything you require," he said.

"Right then," said Tom. "What are we waiting for?"

Ueno rolled down the car window and signaled to his driver.
The man pulled on his white gloves and hurried out of the coffee
bar, leaving the fried noodles half-eaten.

The last glimpse Tom ever had of Sumikawa Bank's smallest
branch in Hokkaido included Kazumi's chubby, almost perfectly
circular face at the window. He waved at her, and she waved back
with her usual broad smile. It may have been his imagination, but
it looked as though her eyes were a little shinier than usual.

15

$$\vdots$$

WHEN Seiji Terada replaced the receiver of his car phone, his natural equanimity had disappeared completely. The disastrous events at the Nippon Infosystems factory were quite beyond his comprehension. According to what he had just heard, reliable men, experienced men, highly paid men had been brushed aside by that private detective as if they were a girls' volleyball team. It was impossible! He must have had help. And that could only mean the baboon Aga!

Grim-faced, Terada steered the red Testarosa through the narrow, winding streets of the Tokyo suburb. How was he going to explain it all to the sensei! His mind reeled at the prospect. He longed to head for the open road, to put his foot down and speed away from all the mess and confusion. But instead he slowed down and checked in his mirror. He had to stay in touch with the Nissan Cima containing his bodyguards that was following at a distance behind.

Aga the neanderthal man, still refusing to accept that his time had passed! Terada chewed his lower lip in anger. Many years before, he had tried to explain rationally to the elder Aga how the Japanese crime syndicates would have to change if they were going to have a future in the twenty-first century. He had emphasized the necessity for developing new products, new strategic alliances, a whole new vision. He had pointed out how the great business leaders of the postwar era, men like Honda and Morita and Toyoda, had seized the moment and innovated fearlessly. All to no avail. Aga had sneered at his "college boy talk" and called him a traitor to the organization's traditions!

Inwardly seething at the memory, Terada eased on the brake and brought the Ferrari coasting to a halt. There was roadwork ahead, and he had to allow the opposing stream of cars to come through the single lane. A helmeted workman stood by the side of the road waving them on with his light stick. Terada glanced into his mirror again. As usual, the Nissan was right behind. After a while, the opposing stream stopped. The workman checked with his walkie-talkie, then waved them through. Impatient at the delay, Terada gunned his engine and sped forward, deliberately making the workman hop out of the way.

He first realized that something was wrong when he looked in the mirror again and saw that the Nissan was no longer there. A minibackhoe parked by the side of the road had swung out, blocking the way. Exasperated, he slowed to a crawl, waiting for the backhoe to complete its maneuver. He was so preoccupied with what was happening in his rearview mirror that it was a couple of seconds before he registered what was happening ahead. The yellow bulldozer that had been rumbling toward him on the other, cordoned-off side of the road was now veering across in front of him. He slammed on the brakes.

Two workmen jumped down from the bulldozer and started jogging toward him. Terada was about to wind down the window and bellow his anger, when he noticed their faces, sheer white with grotesquely stupid expressions. They were wearing plastic *kyogen* masks, of the sort that children wear at festivals. Then he understood. He jammed the gearshift into reverse, but it was too late. Their guns were pointing straight at him. Instinctively, he tried to duck away, but the seatbelt held him straight.

The windshield exploded into a thousand fragments. Then came a slow raking burst that had him jerking around in the front seat like a man having a fit. Then another, this time from close range, that took off the top of his head and distributed it over the back window.

Mori spent the early afternoon going through his story with Kudo's boss, a ferretlike man with nervous hands and an Adam's apple that moved up and down like an elevator. They sat on opposite sides of a gray metal desk marked with the stains of coffee mugs, between them a minicassette recorder and an ashtray heaped with Mild Seven butts.

Inspector Itoh asked several detailed questions and, despite the presence of the cassette recorder, noted Mori's answers into a looseleaf notebook in a fussily neat hand. Afterward, he made it clear that Mori was highly privileged to be allowed to accompany the police special operations group as an observer, that he should obey all instructions unquestioningly, and that he shouldn't even think about talking to anyone else until it was all over. Anxious not to get Kudo into trouble, Mori nodded politely and made noises of agreement in the gaps in his monologue that Itoh left for that purpose.

There were a couple of hours remaining before the special operations group was due to assemble. That was enough time for Mori to make the couple of calls he had in mind. He borrowed Kudo's four-year-old Nissan Cedric and drove through Ikebukuro to a run-down area of metalworking shops, cheap inns, and cinder-block public apartment buildings. He parked outside a small wooden house squeezed between a machinery yard and a concrete overpass that bore the expressway north out of Tokyo. As he got out of the car, Mori's nostrils were assailed by a thick fecal odor that seemed to rise up out of the ground. When he slammed the car door shut, a mangy bobtailed cat scooted out from between two trash cans and disappeared down the alley next to the house.

At first, Mrs. Kawada looked as if she wanted to shut the front door of the house in Mori's face.

"Leave us alone," she said in a low voice. "Can't you see we've had enough trouble already!"

"There'll be no more trouble," said Mori soothingly. "I just wanted to check that your husband's all right."

"He's doing well enough," said the woman. "He's learned his

lesson this time, that's for sure."

She stood in the doorway, arms crossed, face radiating disapproval. Somewhere behind her a baby started wailing. The vibra-
tions from heavy trucks passing on the expressway were making
the door shudder in its frame.

"Who is it?" came a young male voice from inside.

"It's that detective," Mrs. Kawada called back. "He says he
wants to speak to father."

Young Kawada appeared behind her, in his hand a small basket containing a towel and a bottle of shampoo. He was evidently
going out to the public bath. In his bright blue track suit, he
looked like a typical student getting himself ready for a date.
When he saw Mori, he gave a short bow.

"Let him in, mother," he said. "He hasn't done us any harm."

Mori left his shoes in the porch and was led up to a darkened
room on the second floor. The elder Kawada was lying on a low
bed, wearing a pair of long underpants and a stained working-
class bellyband over it. His chest was bandaged, his left arm in a
sling, and his face badly swollen. He spoke out of one side of his
mouth, without moving his jaw. Each word seemed to cost him
some pain.

"Mori. What happened . . . everything all right . . ."

"I'm fine," said Mori, sitting down on the side of the bed.
"Take it easy. There's no need to say anything."

"Be careful . . . Nakamura . . ."

"No need to worry about Nakamura anymore. That's what I
came to tell you. He was killed yesterday."

Kawada's mouth opened a fraction of an inch wider, display-
ing the bloodied gums where the front teeth had once been.

"Dead. Is it sure?"

"It's sure, all right. I was there."

"The bastard."

Mori patted him gently on the arm.

"Get well and get a job," he said. "Your family's depending
on you."

As Mori was leaving the room, the prone man called out
faintly from the bed.

"One thing . . . Mori-san . . . I've got to know . . ."

"What's that?" said Mori, turning back from the door.

"Doctor Nishida's wife . . . you did . . . didn't you . . ."

Kawada raised his hand in a fist, with the tip of his thumb poking out between his first and middle fingers. The broken mouth was distended into an expression of mirth. Mori glanced at the familiar obscene gesture, then thought of the elegant woman who went on shopping sprees to Milan and traded in her Mercedes coupe once a year.

"Not yet," he said.

The younger Kawada was waiting downstairs, leaning against the kitchen door. Mori beckoned to him.

"There's something I want to talk to you about."

Young Kawada backed away, as if he were expecting a head-butt.

"Don't worry," said Mori. "I'm just asking a favor. There are a few things I need."

When he understood what Mori wanted, young Kawada nodded respectfully.

"It won't be easy," he said. "When do you need them by?"

"Within the hour," said Mori.

Young Kawada nodded respectfully and ran up the stairs to his father's room. He came back down five minutes later.

"Father knows where to get it," he said. "I'll be back as soon as possible. Please go into our humble living room. My mother will be honored to serve you." Mori watched him wheel a bicycle out of a ramshackle wooden shed and pedal off furiously down the road.

That day the Japanese financial markets seemed to be in a schizophrenic mood. There had been another stomach-churning drop on Wall Street overnight, with the usual feedthrough to the European markets. In reaction, the Nikkei 225 Index slumped from the opening bell, driven down by waves of selling by individual investors and foreigners, and closed the morning session down eight hundred points.

In the early afternoon, the market stabilized, then soared in the final hour of trading, more than making up all the losses of the morning. Rumors circulated that the Ministry of Finance had issued "window guidance" instructing life insurance companies and banks to pour money into the domestic equity market. Since the most likely source of funds would be their portfolios of U.S. stocks and bonds, the dollar weakened further.

At first, the pace of decline was gradual, since dealers were apprehensive of central bank intervention to stabilize the currency market. Then at three o'clock a comment from an unnamed "high official" of the Bank of Japan flashed across their screens. The yen, the official was quoted as saying, was still "inappropriately weak" and the recent movement of the currency market "had full governmental support." Just twelve words, but enough to raise an instant cacophony of excitement in Tokyo dealing rooms. Ashtrays and coffee cups went flying as frantic fingers jabbed at keyboards; sweat-slippery phones were juggled from hand to neck; the air was filled with strained voices bellowing, jabbering, yelping out their desire to be aboard the simplest no-lose proposition the markets had seen for years. Within minutes the dollar had fallen another two and a half yen, the price of gold was surging, and dealers in U.S. bonds were thinking about alternative careers.

Kenji caught the news in the departure lounge at Haneda Airport. A crowd of blue-suited businessmen had gathered around one of the superlarge-screen TVs supplied by Mitsutomo Electric and were watching the news bulletin in hushed fascination. The announcer was speaking in the grave, deliberate tones usually reserved for natural disasters involving Japanese fatalities. There was a clip of frenzied activity at the Tokyo Stock Exchange, with floor traders yelling and gesticulating and losing their spectacles as they elbowed their way to the dealing counters. There was a confused, confusing comment from the minister of finance. There was an interview with a technical analyst at Dainippon Life who claimed that the dollar had broken through all important support levels and had much further to fall.

Noriko was leaning against the food counter buying some

beers. She was wearing large round sunglasses, a beach T-shirt, and black supertight stretch bicycle pants. Kenji's gaze was dragged away from the TV screen to the firm, springy musculature of her buttocks and then, when she turned, to the aggressive jut of her pubic bone. Out of the dowdy Maruichi uniform, she looked like a different woman. She acted like one as well. After last night, Kenji was exhausted.

"Here you are," Noriko said, holding out the tray.

Kenji grunted an acknowledgment. On Noda's advice, they had dressed up like a young couple off to enjoy sea, sun, and each other. Kenji was wearing a floppy sun hat and Budweiser T-shirt and carrying a Sony video camcorder. It had been a good choice. Of the other passengers in the departure lounge, half seemed to be salarymen on marketing trips and half young couples on vacation. Kenji had spotted several Budweiser T-shirts and floppy hats and one pair of bicycle pants of the same type as Noriko's. The contents, though, hadn't been anything like as impressive.

There was another thirty minutes to wait. They drank the beer and ate the hot dogs and discussed what they would do in Okinawa, a place which neither of them had visited before. So far, they had hardly been given time to collect their thoughts. Noda had insisted that they leave on the earliest possible flight, without informing friends or relatives. They had just been provided with plane tickets, half a million yen, and a hotel room in Naha under the name of "Mr. and Mrs. Tanaka" and told to get moving.

And what would happen when Noda told them it was safe to come back to Tokyo? Kenji knew that he wouldn't be going back to work for Maruichi Securities. He would have to start again, doing something entirely different. Four days ago, he had been able to envisage the pattern of the next thirty years of his life with comfortable, though often stifling certainty. Now he had no idea what was going to happen to him in the next thirty hours. The knowledge filled him with a strange, light-headed excitement.

There was just enough time for the one phone call he felt he had to make. The voice of the middle-aged woman who answered was brusque, peevish.

"Hello, hello."

"Hello," said Kenji. "I'd like to speak to Sachiko-san, please."

"Well, I'm afraid you can't. She's out somewhere, and I've no idea when she's coming back."

"Excuse me, but are you Sachiko-san's mother?"

"Yes, as a matter of fact. What do you want?"

"My name's Okada. I would like to thank your daughter for her kindness."

"Kindness? What on earth do you mean?"

"I have an incurable disease of the eyes. It prevents me from seeing well. Sachiko took the trouble to talk to me once or twice . . . she made me very happy."

"Sachiko did?"

The mother's voice sounded incredulous.

"Yes, she did. Sachiko's a truly wonderful person. I have to move away from Tokyo now, but please tell her that Kenji Okada will always remember her in his mind's eye."

When he got back, Noriko looked at him with a glow of devotion.

"Is everything all right, master?"

She used the honorific expression that old-fashioned middle-aged ladies sometimes use to address their husbands. Kenji nodded commandingly.

"Honeymoons may be important," he said. "But business always comes first. It is your duty as a wife to understand that."

Noriko nodded meekly and picked up both their bags. The JAL stewardess who checked their tickets gave her a little smile of sympathy.

As they walked through the passageway that led into the plane, Noriko turned and whispered in his ear.

"There's something exciting about airplane rides," she said. "I've always had this fantasy. . . . Wouldn't it be great to try it out?"

"Try what?" said Kenji, knowing the answer as soon as the words left his mouth.

Mori got back to the police station just in time for the planning meeting. In a dusty lecture room on the top floor, a dozen young detectives seated on benches were listening to Inspector Itoh explain how the raid on Iwanaga would be conducted. Mori stood at the back, leaning against a pile of metal chairs.

"Sit down, will you Mori," said Itoh testily. "We can't concentrate with you standing around like that."

Mori nodded an apology and took his place at the end of one of the benches.

The police had established that Iwanaga had been at the Nippon Infosystems Computer Center since the previous afternoon. They were planning to mount simultaneous raids on his private residence, the head office, and the computer center at eleven in the evening. The group which Itoh was personally commanding, and which Mori was to accompany, was to take the computer center.

From time to time, Itoh would emphasize points by tapping with a ruler at a layout diagram projected onto the screen behind him. The young detectives, busily scribbling down his comments in their notebooks, hardly even looked up. Every so often, Itoh would pause to ask, "Is that understood?"

"It's understood," came back the automatic murmur.

After a while, Mori began to get worried. Itoh's description of the evening's operation, while meticulously detailed in terms of timing and positioning, somehow managed to omit everything that was important. Underneath the morass of procedural jargon, he seemed to be saying that Iwanaga, who he consistently referred to as "President Iwanaga," could be apprehended just as simply as if he were a tax-dodging dentist or a corrupt local assembly man.

At the next, "Is that understood?" Mori put up a hand.

"May I make a suggestion?" he said.

Itoh gazed at him with vexation.

"We are always pleased to accept suggestions from the general public," he said with heavy irony. "But let's get one thing straight first. You are accompanying us on this operation for identification and information purposes only. You will not interfere with police activities and you will obey my orders at all times. Is that understood?"

"Naturally," said Mori, with the hint of a bow. "And may I say that it is a great honor for an ordinary citizen to be allowed to cooperate with you at all."

Itoh gave a watery smile.

"All right. Now what is this suggestion of yours?"

"The helicopter—it should be put out of commission as soon as we effect entry. Otherwise, Iwanaga will probably attempt to use it as a means of escape. The quickest way would be a couple of bullets in the fuel tank, but smashing the instrument panel might be a better deterrent."

Itoh shook his head sadly, like an arithmetic teacher confronted by an exceptionally dense schoolboy.

"This may be difficult for you to understand, Mori-san, but we are not a group of yakuza here. We are officers of the Tokyo Metropolitan Police Force, entrusted with safeguarding the laws of the Japanese nation. Do you suppose we can willfully damage equipment belonging to a major corporation, listed on the first section of the stock exchange? The idea is ridiculous!"

"Not as ridiculous as you'll look if Iwanaga gets away," said Mori quietly.

Itoh was unable to conceal his anger any longer. His voice went up a pitch, and a few flecks of spittle shot from his mouth.

"We are not accustomed to failure here, Mori-san. We have carried out thousands of operations like this without any problems at all. I don't believe that there is much to learn from the words of a cheap snoop such as you!"

"Perhaps not," said Mori. "But I don't think you've ever been up against anyone like Iwanaga before. I have."

Most of the young detectives had put down their pens. A couple of them were staring around at Mori with amused curiosity.

"You are disrupting this planning meeting," shouted Itoh. "That is impermissible! If you don't shut up, I'll have you thrown out at once. Understood?"

The man's face had turned the color of a pickled plum.

"Understood," said Mori with a shrug.

The rest of the meeting went uneventfully and, in Mori's opinion, uninformatively. Itoh gave each man detailed instructions about where to go at each phase of the operation, how to identify key personnel, what to say when making arrests, and what kind of materials to search for. What kind of reception they were likely to meet was simply not mentioned. After the meeting was over, one of the detectives caught up with Mori at the coffee machine. A serious-looking young man in his late twenties, he addressed Mori with hesitant respect.

"You don't really think they'll try to resist, do you?" he asked.

"I'm willing to bet on it," said Mori, flatly.

"But the man's a businessman, a company president. He'd have to be crazy to—"

"He is," said Mori, taking a sip of the murky brown fluid.

The detective raised his eyebrows.

"Have they got weapons up there?" he asked softly.

"I've only seen a couple of guns," said Mori. "But there're probably more. And watch out for Iwanaga's personal body-guards—they're trained to kill."

"Personal bodyguards? We haven't been told any of this."

The serious young face creased with concern.

"Well, I'm telling you now. What weapons have you been issued?"

"Nothing. We'll just have our pistols, and in an operation of this category we can't even take off the safety catch without asking permission from the officer in charge."

"And who decides on the category of the operation?"

"The officer in charge."

"Which is Inspector Itoh."

"That's right."

"Well," said Mori, tossing his paper cup into the bin. "It should be interesting."

The young detective nodded glumly.

They trooped down to a changing room in the basement, where they were issued heavy jeans, black turtleneck sweaters and windbreakers, and Gendai Giants baseball caps.

"I've never been a Giants fan," grumbled Mori.

"You are now," said the detective standing next to him. "Every man in this police station is a Giants fan." Mori glanced at the man's face. He wasn't joking.

Mori waited until the others had left before reaching into the inside pocket of his jacket and taking out the two packages which the younger Kawada had given him. Then he went into one of the toilet cubicles, peeled the wrapping of newspaper and string from the smaller package, and took out the four inches of black plastic inside. He weighed it in his hand. It was light. And the switch was very sensitive. Just a slight pressure from the thumb, and a quivering blade shot from the end. Thin, flexible, and curving to a sharp point, it was designed for stabbing, not cutting. Hardly the ideal weapon, but it would do. Mori rolled up the leg of his jeans, and taped it to the inside of his left calf. The larger package he put unwrapped into the inside pocket of his windbreaker, where it made a small bulge. Then he flushed the toilet and joined the others in the hallway.

"Got your cap, have you?" said the Giants fan, with a slight frown.

"I'm keeping it in just the right place," said Mori, indicating the back pocket of his jeans.

The man gazed at him in stony silence. He had no sense of humor at all.

Eight hours later, they were squatting on a heavily wooded hillside overlooking the computer center. Inspector Itoh was studying the scene through a pair of binoculars and muttering observations into a matchbox-sized radio. The twelve others were all silent—chewing gum, scratching gnat bites, or just gazing up at the splatter of constellations overhead.

Iwanaga's helicopter was sitting in the center of the open area in front of the main building, in exactly the same place as when Mori had seen it last. Lights were blazing in all the buildings, and groups of men in Nippon Infosystems uniforms were standing at the gate and in front of the dormitory building. Mori also noticed a couple of bald, kimono-clad priests standing in the shadows of the perimeter fence. They were gazing out into the forest, almost as if they were expecting something.

Mori felt a nudge in his ribs.

"Are those the bodyguards?" whispered the young detective who had approached him at the coffee machine.

"That's right," said Mori. "Remember what I said. Don't give them a second chance."

"Shut up, will you!"

Itoh swiveled round to face them, grabbing a handful of twigs to hold his balance. The result was to give a vigorous shake to the bush behind him, and there was a sudden thrashing of wings as a large black bird burst upward from it. For a moment, Itoh's face froze into a mask of comical surprise.

"All right," he hissed, after regaining composure. "It's time for Group A to move off. Group B will remain here in observation mode for the next thirty minutes. And remember . . ."

Here he stared meaningfully at the young detective next to Mori.

". . . proper procedures must be observed at all times. Is that understood?"

"Understood!"

The reply came just as automatically as in the dusty lecture room.

The plan was for Itoh and two other detectives to appear suddenly at the main gate, demand entry, and make formal arrests of the top Nippon Infosystems personnel. Then they would radio the ten others to come down and search the place. In his mind's eye, Mori was scanning an official report of the operation, recounting how Itoh courageously and almost single-handedly foiled Iwanaga's schemes. With the right media treatment, it would make him the most famous policeman in Japan. There was a fallback plan, to be used only if Itoh met with problems. Then the other ten were supposed to work their way around to the back of the computer center, get through the fence, and make straight for Iwanaga's office.

Itoh motioned for the other two to follow him down the hill. The remaining ten sat back on their haunches, watching and waiting. Down below in the computer center, the shadowy figures of the two monks were standing absolutely motionless, as if they were trying to stare right through the foliage.

"Maybe they know we're coming," muttered the young detective under his breath.

"What are you talking about! That's impossible!"

It was the Giants fan who spoke. He was glaring scornfully at his younger colleague.

"Nothing's impossible," said Mori. "Not where Iwanaga is concerned. He's got people everywhere." Itoh's second in command, a crew-cut, bullet-headed forty-year-old called Kan, motioned for them to keep quiet. He was listening in his earpiece to the position reports from the first group, who were already about a third of the way to their destination.

Ten minutes later, Itoh's group emerged from the forest onto the roadway just in front of the main entrance. After a brief exchange of words with the guards manning the gate, they were let in and ushered into the central building. Several minutes passed without anything happening. The young detective glanced at Mori and pursed his lips. Kan picked up the binoculars and started scanning the building.

"What's going on?" asked Mori finally.

"Lost contact," said Kan, tapping his earpiece. "Everything seemed to be going fine, and then just nothing."

"It's probably the building," said the Giants fan. "That concrete must be laminated with some obstructive material."

Mori looked at his watch. If no signal came through in another three minutes, the second group would have to move in.

"I doubt if it's the concrete that's being obstructive," he said quietly.

They waited, but there were no signs of activity below. Everything was bright and still.

Kan pursed his lips.

"It's not like the boss to forget a procedure," he said. "We have to assume that something's gone wrong. Everybody knows the backup plan, right?"

The response was the usual collective grunt.

"Right!"

Mori leaned over to the young detective, close enough so that nobody else could hear.

"Stick with me," he whispered. "I've got a little backup plan of my own."

Kan led them on a different route from the first group, a longer one that circled around the back of the computer center. It meant wading through thickets of brambles, edging around a precipice, then tacking down a steep slope next to a waterfall. The density of the pines provided good cover, and the slap of their footsteps on the sticky mud was lost in the rush of the water.

When they came within distance of the fence, they crept around to the area behind the dormitory building. Kan handed the Giants fan a small pair of wire-cutters, and he opened a waist-high slash in the fence.

Getting in, thought Mori, was the easy part. Even Itoh had managed that. Getting out would be a different matter.

For a moment, they remained crouching on the cold earth between the fence and the back of the dormitory building. There was perfect calm all around. No footsteps, no doors slamming, no voices. The only sound was the hum of the generator.

Kan made a circle sign with his thumb and forefinger and led off around the side of the building. One by one, the others followed. The young detective glanced back at Mori. Mori shook his head. The man hesitated for an instant, then shrugged his shoulders and disappeared into the shadows at the side of the building.

Mori waited for the searchlight to swing past, then went the other way, sticking close to the fence. Before it had completed its circuit, Mori was in the parking lot, ducking down behind a light truck.

Suddenly, there was a shouted command. Mori thought he recognized the voice as Kan's. Then came a single gunshot, followed by the rapid fire of an automatic weapon. The same voice, this time edged with panic, bellowed for the shooting to stop. The answer was another burst from the automatic.

Mori knew he had to move fast. He weaved from car to car, working his way around to the back of the central building. Now there was confused shouting everywhere. Over at the front gate a siren had been set off, and its unearthly whoop cut the air like the tormented cry of the spirit of the forest.

The layout was just as Mori remembered. The generator was located next to the fire escape, enclosed in a barbed-wire fence some six feet high. Beside it was a cyclindrical oil storage tank, with "Danger—Authorized Personnel Only" painted on it in crude white characters. Bending low, he sprinted away from the cover of the cars.

Mori didn't see the figure emerging from the shadows at the side of the building until it was too late. For a moment, the two men stood still, gazing at one another in silence. The monk was young, probably no older than twenty. His solemn, domed features regarded Mori with complete indifference. His bare feet, white in the moonlight, were splayed outward in a stance that said that Mori could not pass. Suddenly, still without uttering a sound, he lengthened the grip on the staff that he was carrying and raised it to chest height.

Mori guessed that the monk would strike for the head, and lunged low. He was wrong. With lightning speed, the monk shifted to a mid-grip and twirled the staff like a baton. The first blow caught Mori on his right shin, and the second, almost simultaneously, just above his left knee. He collapsed in a heap, his left leg completely numb.

The monk danced forward, his toes digging like tent pegs into the sandy soil. Mori rolled away just in time to avoid the downward jab to the throat, and the staff end thudded into the ground. Mori snatched at it, but missed. With his other hand, he reached under his trouser leg and tugged at the switchblade. The monk glided away to one side, almost casually wrist-flicking the staff upward against Mori's chest. For the second time in a week, Mori experienced the sensation of a rib cracking. Fighting back the pain, Mori used the chicken-wire fence to pull himself half to his feet. The four inches of black plastic were now tight in his fist.

The monk moved in for the kill, feinting to left and right. This time Mori guessed correctly. He pushed himself forward, ducking under the staff's high arc. The blow caught him on the shoulder, forcing him downward, just as he had intended. His thumb depressed the button of the switchblade. For a split second, the monk's splayed feet loomed before his gaze. That was all Mori needed. He grabbed onto a fold of kimono to steady himself. With the other hand, he drove the four inches of steel into the center of the man's foot, using his own weight as he fell to force the blade clean through and firmly into the ground beneath.

The monk's howl of agony rose to merge with the wail of the siren. In an instant, Mori wrestled the stave from the man's grasp, jabbed the short end into the pit of his stomach, then, as the monk doubled up, sent a double-fisted swing whipping against the back of his knees.

The full force of the blow jarred up to Mori's elbows. The monk reeled forward, then collapsed to the ground, the momentum of his fall freeing his pinioned foot. He reached down to tug at the blade that still transfixed his foot, but Mori moved faster, smashing the end of the staff down into the palm of the hand, which retreated immediately like a wounded animal.

The monk rolled away from Mori and rose unsteadily to his knees. For a moment, they gazed at each other in silence, mouths wide open, chests heaving with effort. Then the monk made a last desperate effort, his right hand clutching for a hold on Mori's knee, his left hand sweeping upward to the groin in a raking, tearing motion. Mori twisted to one side, and brought the smooth, rounded bar of timber crashing down on the bald skull. There was a sound like the crack of a sweetly timed baseball bat meeting the ball, and the monk went sprawling. This time he lay still, face down, arms outstretched, an inch of knife blade protruding through the sole of his foot. Mori thumped the side of his rib cage, but the only response was a muffled grunt.

Another burst of gunfire sounded from the other side of the compound, followed by an amplified voice bellowing out for the shooting to stop. Itoh must have brought a small loudspeaker with him, but it was having little effect. He was almost drowned out by the siren.

Mori knew that the area at the back of the central building could be swarming with guards at any minute. He had to move fast. He took from his pocket the other package that young Kawada had given him and swiftly unwrapped it. Under the layers of newspaper was a fat plastic tube stamped with faded characters that read "High Explosive—Property of Sumikawa Mining Corporation." No doubt it had originally been filched from one of the limestone quarries in the Tohoku region before reaching the yakuza's unofficial market for improvised weapons. It looked old and slightly squashed, but didn't appear to have been damaged. The fuse was separate, coiled in a little plastic bag. He snapped off a couple of inches, hastily attached it, and dug in his pocket for his cigarette lighter.

At first, the one-hundred-yen disposable lighter refused to spark, then when it did, the weakly flickering flame was immediately snuffed out by the breeze before he had a chance to apply it. Mori took a deep breath, gave the lighter a vigorous shake, and tried again. This time, he was successful. A tiny orange glow appeared at the end of the fuse. Mori waited just long enough to check that it had caught, then placed the device at the side of the fuel tank and sprinted back to the parking area. He just had time to duck behind the first row of cars before the shock wave of the explosion swished through the branches of the trees. The roar sang in his ears for minutes afterward.

Suddenly he noticed that the gunfire and shouts had ceased and the siren was dead as well. All floors of the building had been plunged into complete darkness, and the only light came from the blue and orange flames leaping upward from the ruins of the generator. Behind, he could make out the hole where the building's flimsy composite wall had been blasted away. For a moment, all else was eerily silent, as if there were no other human beings for miles around. Then, just as suddenly, the air was full of shouts and screams, and Itoh's megaphone was ringing out again. This time, his words were as clear as a bell.

"This is the police. Give up your weapons and come outside. Any use of weapons is a criminal offense. Come outside and sit on the ground with your hands on your heads."

Mori stood up and watched the flames pouring through the hole in the wall to seize the plastic furniture inside, shooting up the side of the building to the second floor, giving off showers of sparks that smoldered and glowed among the bushes. Within a matter of minutes, the conflagration had reached the stage of having a life of its own, no longer dependent on the point of origin. It would take some putting out now.

Cautiously, Mori made his way back to the dormitory building. It was much harder to see without the light from the windows of the central building, but he could make out groups of shadowy figures milling around the entrance, apparently obeying Itoh's instructions. Approaching the entrance, Mori saw ten or twelve uniformed men already sitting on the ground. Hands on head, they looked like schoolboys glumly waiting to be punished. They didn't look up as Mori passed.

Inside the building it was almost pitch black. The stairs were thronged with bodies, some trying to shove their way out, and some trying to stop them. It was too dark to make out the faces. Voices were raised in shouts of anger, fear, and confusion.

"Get back—your section leader commands you. . . ."

"Fire spreading above! The police are burning us out."

"Let us through or we're all going to be yakitori. . . ."

"Return to your posts! In the name of the sensei. . . ."

"Do you dare to disobey?"

"Air, I must have air. . . ."

Mori forced his way up through the crush of bodies, adding his own exhortation for good measure.

"The sensei commands us . . . we must not fail the sensei. . . ."

On the third floor, some illumination was provided by the pulsing glow of the flames eating into the back of the building. Men were hauling objects out into the corridor, trying to salvage what they could from the fire. The air was thick with the acrid smell of burning plastic.

A man with a white cloth over the lower half of his face came hurrying down the corridor with an armful of files. He shoved them into Mori's chest.

"Get these out of here," he said. "It's absolutely vital for these to be preserved."

"Understood!" said Mori smartly and took them with him up to the fourth floor, which was already deserted. Making sure that he was unobserved, he banged a window open with his elbow and tipped the files out into the night air. Dozens of sheets of paper bucked and twisted in the heat currents, and two or three soared up over the forest line like miniature kites. As he raced up to the next floor, two guards carrying fire extinguishers dashed past him, taking the steps three at a time. They didn't give him a glance.

On the eighth floor, a guard holding a rifle across his body stood blocking the way. He bent forward to peer at Mori through the gloom. Mori picked up the sweet scent of sake on his breath.

"What do you think you're doing?" the man growled. "Don't you know this is a restricted area?"

Mori glanced over his shoulder to the fire extinguisher bracketed to the wall.

"That fire extinguisher," he said. "It's required downstairs at once."

The man regarded him sourly for a moment.

"Get it yourself then," he growled finally, and motioned for Mori to pass.

Mori pulled the fire extinguisher from its bracket and freed the nozzle. It was surprisingly heavy, an old-fashioned type.

"I wonder if it still works properly," he muttered, as if to himself.

The guard turned and squinted at him suspiciously.

"What department are you in anyway? Where's your badge?"

Mori cradled the fire extinguisher with his left arm and knee and fumbled for the catch with his right hand.

"Better check it," he said with a sigh. "Just in case . . ."

"Show me your badge immediately. This is a restricted— whoah!"

A jet of liquid erupted from the nozzle and struck the guard full in the face. He dropped the gun and his hands shot to his eyes, but Mori kept on spraying. In an instant, his features were hidden in a blob of thick creamy foam. Instinctively, he arched backward, legs bowed, flapping the foam away with both hands. Mori had time to lift the body of the extinguisher back to elbow height before swinging it hard and accurately against the man's groin. There was the thud of something hard meeting something soft at speed, and the guard gave out a noise that was half yelp, half puke. He doubled up and sank to the ground, hands clutching his crushed genitals.

Mori swung the fire extinguisher once more, this time to make contact with the man's left temple. Then he covered the inert body with a large blob of foam, dropped the now empty metal tube, and raced up to the top floor.

The corridor was empty, but a flickering glow was emanating from Iwanaga's room. The door had been left a couple of inches open. Mori padded down the corridor, then stopped and listened for a full minute. Silence, apart from the thump of his heartbeat. He was on the point of going in to make a thorough search of what had been left behind, when a familiar voice called out from inside.

"Don't stand there holding your breath like a pearl diver. Come in and let me see you."

Mori pushed the door open with his toe and entered. Iwanaga was sitting on the floor in the center of the room in the *seiza* position. Before him was a low table on which were lit three long white candles of the sort used in Buddhist ceremonies. He was wearing a dark kimono which fell open at the chest and a headband carrying the emblem of the rising sun. In the dim light of the candles, the small disk looked as black as ink.

"Mori, you really are a most inconvenient fellow. The kind of man who keeps putting his nose into matters outside his understanding."

Iwanaga sounded almost amused. The three little flames danced as he spoke, imparting a red glow to his deeply etched features. His face looked harder and simpler, like the sketch of an actor's face in a movie poster.

"It's all over, sensei," said Mori. "The place is surrounded by police. Nearly all your staff have surrendered. The whole crazy business is finished."

Iwanaga arched an eyebrow.

"Perhaps," he said. "But I wouldn't bet on it. I have my contacts in high places. I have my people in position everywhere. We can wait, you know. We have been waiting three quarters of a century already."

Mori walked over to the table and knelt on the other side from Iwanaga.

"Waited three quarters of a century? What for? To get revenge on the Westerners?"

Iwanaga shook his head sorrowfully. "You have no understanding," he said. "Revenge! What pettiness of thought, what sterility of imagination! We are grateful to the Westerners. Their actions have awakened in us the awareness of our true destiny. The spirit of history."

"Yes, I know all that," cut in Mori. "I've heard the speech once already. I don't need to hear it again."

Iwanaga's lips curved into a smile of contempt, and he raised his hand in a gesture of ironic resignation. The precious stone on his finger caught the candle glow and sparkled blood-red.

"I know what you are thinking," he said softly. "You think we are just naive fanatics of the type that our country has been so excellent at producing over the ages. Not so, my friend. I am a businessman, and I have made this project the most important business of my life. Do you know the true purpose of a businessman, Mori?"

"To get rich?" said Mori.

"That is correct," said Iwanaga. "To maximize profits. That was the real purpose of our project here. We would have created more profit than any businessman has dreamed of in human history. The wealth of whole nations was there for the taking, ready to drop into our hands like ripe persimmons from a persimmon tree."

"Too bad it isn't going to happen," said Mori.

Iwanaga leaned forward, eyes shining like black jewels. Mori knew he should look away, but somehow he couldn't. The man's gaze was compelling, hypnotic.

"It still can," he said slowly. "You can help us to make it happen."

"Help you?" said Mori dully. "In what way?"

"Come with me now. We will go back to the head office

together. I have resources. I can give orders tonight that will make you so rich that you will never have to think about money again for the rest of your life. It will always be there, however much you want, whenever you want it. Do you understand my meaning, Mori?"

The voice had fallen to a soothing murmur. The unblinking eyes seemed to have grown larger, more luminous. There were tiny candle flames captured within them that rocked back and forth to the rhythm of his words.

"No, I can't," said Mori. "I don't understand your meaning. What is your meaning?"

"I'm talking about freedom," said Iwanaga in a half-whisper. "The freedom to be your real self, as you always wanted to be. I'm talking about time, making time belong to you, not to other people. No more smiling and bowing and wasting time on people you despise. I'm talking about being alive, not half dead."

Wealth, freedom, time, being alive—Iwanaga's words were swirling around Mori's brain, but somehow they didn't make sense. They were just words. With an effort, he tore his gaze away from the shining eyes and the masklike face.

"I am alive," he said. "Unfortunately for you. And freedom is something you're not going to enjoy much longer, sensei."

Iwanaga stared into the candle flames.

"You make too many mistakes," he said without looking up. "That is bad for a detective."

Mori heard the footfall behind him too late. He tried to duck away, but a crashing blow caught him on the side of his head. White pain flashed before his eyes, then he fell sideways, thumping his head against the wooden floor. When the room came back into focus, two men were gazing down at him. One was a guard holding a pistol. The other was Yoshimura. Iwanaga was still kneeling in front of the candles, completely expressionless.

"We haven't got much time," said Yoshimura, his pudgy face creased with concern. "The grounds are swarming with police. I've given instructions for the helicopter to pick us up on the roof in five minutes."

Iwanaga nodded.

"It is wise to retreat," he said. "We must not give these blunderers the satisfaction of trapping us like rats."

He stood up and smoothed out the creases in his kimono as if he were readying himself for a party.

The guard prodded Mori in the stomach with his foot.

"What about this one?" he said. "Shall I drop him into that bonfire outside, make it look like an accident?"

"Bring him up to the roof," said Yoshimura. "We may need him if the police choose to be uncooperative."

The guard grabbed Mori by the collar of his jacket and hauled him to his feet, taking care to scrape his head against the sharp corner of the desk. Mori felt the scalp rip open and the warm flow of blood.

"Careful," said Yoshimura. "We want him in reasonable shape." The guard shoved Mori out into the corridor, poking him in the back of the neck with the pistol. Yoshimura and Iwanaga followed.

They filed out onto the fire escape then climbed up onto the roof of the building. Yoshimura took the gun from the guard.

"Another three minutes," he said. "You know what to do."

The guard saluted and disappeared back down the fire escape. The three stood there in silence, Iwanaga apparently lost in thought, Yoshimura looking around expectantly. The fire at the back of the building was casting an eerie glow, and showers of sparks were shooting up into the night sky.

"They'll never let that helicopter take off," said Mori.

"Wait and see," said Yoshimura with a smirk.

A minute later, Mori heard the sound of the helicopter's blades engaging, then whirring at full power.

"Stop that at once. Leave the helicopter and sit down with your hands on your head."

It was Itoh's voice at the megaphone. His team must have been released from wherever they were being confined.

"Leave the helicopter at once and—gah!"

Suddenly there was a burst of automatic fire from one of the floors below and Itoh's voice rose to a squawk. It was shortly followed by another burst of gunfire from the other end of the building.

"Excellent," said Yoshimura, gazing at his watch.

The roar of the helicopter became much louder. First the blades then the body of the machine appeared above the edge of the roof, hovering directly in front of them like some monstrous insect. For a moment, it swayed about clumsily above them as the pilot struggled to make the tightest possible turn, then it landed just in front of the cooling tower.

"Time to leave our guests behind," said Iwanaga, walking toward it.

"What about him?" said Yoshimura, indicating Mori with his thumb. "We can't leave him. He knows too much."

Iwanaga stopped and shook his head.

"Mori is a pestilential man," he said. "Without him, none of this need have happened."

"What shall we do? Shall I dispose of him now?"

"No, that would be too dangerous. You're a lucky man, Mori. First of all, we're going to give you a lift. And then we're going to drop you off somewhere convenient."

Yoshimura gave a short chuckle at the sensei's wit and prodded Mori in the back with the gun. Iwanaga ordered the pilot out onto the roof and slid behind the helicopter's controls himself. Yoshimura pushed Mori into the seat directly behind, the barrel of the pistol poking into the side of Mori's stomach.

"Don't worry," he said. "The sensei is an expert pilot. It'll be a smooth ride. And for you, a short one."

Mori looked to one side. The man who Iwanaga had replaced in the pilot seat was standing rigidly to attention, his jacket billowing in the wind of the blades. As the helicopter lifted off the ground, he saluted sharply. Iwanaga executed a smooth one-hundred-eighty-degree turn before taking the helicopter straight up into the indigo sky. It bucked in mid-ascent as they passed over the corset of flames at the back of the building, then they were soaring high over the compound. The moon slid out from behind a bank of clouds, hardening the outline of the mountains and forest and illuminating the inside of the helicopter with a weak silvery light.

"This is a night of rare beauty," said Iwanaga, turning around to face them. "It wouldn't be complete without some music to encourage us on our journey."

Mori glanced at Yoshimura, who was nodding vigorously.

"As you always say, sensei, music purifies the soul and prepares it for new challenges. Let us have some music."

"Let us drink music!"

Iwanaga clicked a switch on the control panel, and the little canopy of metal and glass was suddenly filled with the opening bars of the *1812 Overture*. There were loudspeakers above Mori, behind him, and on both sides.

"When I was a young man," Iwanaga continued. "I hated the Russian people with a great passion. The cowardly atrocities they carried out in Manchuria were always fresh in my mind, as if they had been done to my own family. As a result, I could never bear to listen to the great Russian composers. I told myself they were showy and sentimental. Did you have the same feelings, Mori?"

"Not really," said Mori. "I've always liked Rachmaninoff."

"Ah, Rachmaninoff . . ."

Iwanaga nodded abstractedly as the swell of the music gathered around them. His raised hand rocked back and forth as if he were conducting an imaginary orchestra.

"This is not just bluster," he said over his shoulder. "There is knowledge in this music. There is suffering in it. And without suffering there can be no knowledge, no greatness. If we forget that, we will be no different from the Americans. Do you understand me, Mori?"

"I think so," Mori lied.

"Why are there no great Japanese composers?" asked Iwanaga, his tone suddenly animated. "First-rate pianists, first-rate violinists, first-rate conductors, but no composers. Why no great composers?"

Yoshimura was shaking his head regretfully. Mori said nothing. He realized that the question, like many of Iwanaga's, was a rhetorical one. The answer would follow naturally.

"Because there is no knowledge," cried Iwanaga. "Technique, yes. We have fine technicians. But no knowledge, no suffering, no greatness of spirit. We must recover greatness of spirit!"

Yoshimura was nodding now. Iwanaga turned up the volume, and the music charged forward, filling the helicopter with a thunderous vibration on the bass notes.

They were gliding low over the dark mass of the forest. Mori was able to make out the glinting waterfalls and the outcrops of bare rock as the land became more rugged and mountainous. There were no obvious landmarks, and no headlights or houselights, but Iwanaga seemed to know exactly where he was going. After some minutes, the helicopter rose over a jagged ridge, then lost speed. Iwanaga peered down through the side window.

"Here we are, Mori," he said, and lowered the volume of the music again. "This is the place where we must part company. Yoshimura-kun, please show our visitor the way out."

Yoshimura stood up and slid open the canopy door, letting in a blast of icy air. He gestured at Mori with the gun.

"Come on," he said. "I'm going to show you the shortcut."

"Just like you did to Hara," said Mori.

"It was necessary," snarled Yoshimura. "He deceived me. He deceived us all."

"That's not the way I heard it."

Yoshimura's face contorted with rage. He lowered the gun to point at Mori's groin. "I don't care how you heard it. Shut up and jump, or I'll shoot your balls off and throw you out myself. It makes no difference. No one's going to find your body up here anyway."

Mori got to his feet and moved slowly toward the open door. Iwanaga was watching intently from the pilot's seat.

"This event is regrettable," he said. "You should have taken up my offer. We could have found work for a man like you, Mori. You have persistence and great courage, which are important qualities, rare qualities."

"Thanks," said Mori, halting a couple of feet from the open door.

"Unfortunately, though, you are deficient in intelligence. That is a serious handicap."

"Sorry about that," said Mori.

"Come on, jump!" shouted Yoshimura. "We can't wait all night."

The cold wind was ripping at Mori's hair and jacket. He looked down. It was a good three hundred yards to the dense forest below. He remembered Taniguchi's photos of that jumbo jet crash on the remote mountainside—the severed hand spiked on a branch, the battered, muddied torsos—and shuddered.

He turned to Yoshimura, who was pressed flat against the side of the canopy.

"Give my regards to your wife," he said in a voice too quiet for Iwanaga to hear. "You shouldn't leave a passionate woman like that all by herself, you know. It's cruel."

"What are you talking about?" said Yoshimura suspiciously.

"Didn't you hear? I went to see her a couple of weeks back. She won't forget what I gave her in a hurry, that's for sure. And neither will the neighbors."

"Filthy liar!"

"It's no lie," said Mori. "The place with the nice Chinese vases in the front room. Bayview Heights number twenty-two, isn't it?"

"What have you been doing at my home, you bastard?"

Yoshimura's voice was cracking with rage, his eyes bulging.

"Something you ought to thank me for. She was pretty near insatiable. And what sharp teeth, eh, Yoshimura-kun!" Mori put a hand to his groin and gave a lewd wince. Yoshimura stepped forward and made a savage swing of the gun barrel at the side of Mori's head. Mori saw it coming well in advance and ducked away, twisting Yoshimura's wrist forward and down. The gun clattered to the floor. For a moment, Mori was lurching in the open doorway, his left hand clutching at nothingness, his right hand pulling Yoshimura with him.

"Dispose of him, you fool," yelled Iwanaga.

But Mori pulled away from the edge just as Yoshimura swung with his free hand. Their two bodies came together in a clinch and they swayed back and forth like drunkards.

"Out!" Iwanaga was bellowing. "Shove him out!"

With a deep grunt, Yoshimura shoved forward, sumo-style. Mori took a step back, allowing his opponent to gather momentum, then yanked him sideways by the jacket against the side of his own upper leg. Yoshimura's center of gravity swung away from his legs and suddenly he was hanging out of the side of the helicopter, one hand scrabbling at the sleeve of Mori's jacket.

"No! I'm falling! Sensei, help me!"

"Where is your dignity?" roared Iwanaga from his seat. "Death is a friend. Embrace him with dignity."

"Sensei," yelped Yoshimura, his white face sinking back into the empty air, the fingers of his left hand locked around Mori's wrist.

But Iwanaga turned to the controls of the helicopter and maneuvered it into a sudden rolling tilt, jerking the tail sharply downward. The momentum sent Mori reeling inward against the seats. Yoshimura's grip was broken. There was a brief scream, which sounded laden more with outrage than terror, then nothing.

"No dignity," said Iwanaga, staring out into space. "Death is the most important moment in a man's life. It must be faced with dignity."

Mori picked up the gun from the floor behind the seat.

"All right," he said. "Let's get going back to the compound."

"I don't think that's necessary," said Iwanaga flatly.

"Aren't you forgetting something?" said Mori. "I've got the gun here."

"I am aware of that," said Iwanaga. "I am also aware that you cannot pilot a helicopter."

"What is the connection?"

"You cannot impose your will on me, Mori. I will not allow it. I will continue to my destination."

"Stop playing games, Iwanaga. Turn this thing around now or you'll go the same way as your faithful retainer."

Iwanaga turned and gazed at Mori full in the face.

"You try to threaten me?" he said with surprise. "That was another of your mistakes. You make too many mistakes!"

He returned to the controls, turned up the volume of the music to earsplitting levels, and put the helicopter into steep dive.

"What are you doing?" shouted Mori.

"I'm teaching you the most important lesson of all," Iwanaga shouted back. "How to die with dignity."

The overture was charging to its climax, complete with crashing cymbals, the peal of bells, and the roar of cannons.

"Stop!" yelled Mori, but he couldn't make himself heard above the sea of sound.

They were dropping fast, the dark shapes of individual trees now distinct, now some of their branches. Right until the last moments, Mori thought Iwanaga would pull out of the dive. But then he saw the left hand flailing around and the head rocking from side to side, lost in the thunderous rhythms. The man was oblivious to all else but the music.

Mori glanced down and saw a silvery gleam coming from a large gap in the forest. They were hurtling down over a spread of water, probably one of the deep volcanic lakes common in the remote mountain regions. It was now or never. Mori rolled across the floor to the open door, and used his feet to push himself clear of the helicopter. For a few seconds that seemed like an eternity, he was spinning and tumbling between the moonlit sky and the dark water below. He just managed to make his body into a ball before the water rushed up to meet him.

There was an explosion in his ears, a shock that jarred every bone in his body, then blackness and icy cold all around. For an instant, he was unconscious, a block of stone plummetting endlessly through the depths. Then, he was semiconscious, struggling to hold his breath as the pressure squeezed his skull like a vise. Then he was fully conscious, thrashing his way upward, ears pounding, eyes popping, and finally breaking above the surface as the breath burst from his lungs.

He did so just in time to catch the flash of light and "crump" of the explosion. It looked like the helicopter had crashed on the other side of the small densely forested ridge that rose directly from the edge of the lake.

Mori struggled to the side of the lake and collapsed on the soft reedy ground there. He was breathless, freezing cold, and bleeding from the nose, and his left ankle had taken a bad knock. After a while, he stripped off his clothes, wrung them out, and put them on again. Then, he hobbled toward the ridge, forcing his way painfully through the thick undergrowth.

It took him some twenty minutes to reach the top of the ridge, from where he could see the small fire where the helicopter had crashed. Another fifteen minutes and he was down alongside it. The machine was badly mangled. The propeller had been twisted off, the paintwork blackened in the fire, and all the windows shattered. There was a smell of burning plastic in the air, and a few flames were still licking around the tail. Mori peered inside, half expecting a gruesome sight of the sort that Taniguchi regularly photographed for *Thursday* magazine. It was dark, and the fumes and heat were making his eyes smart, but one thing was obvious. The helicopter was empty.

He spent the next ten minutes hunting through the undergrowth around the wreckage in case Iwanaga's body had been thrown clear by the impact. He found nothing. After a while, he sat down a little way off and watched the tiny flames dying. The night was quiet, almost windless now. Gradually, the moon faded behind a convoy of clouds and the darkness thickened. It didn't take him long to fall into a heavy sleep.

Mori was awakened by the sound of voices. He had an excruciating headache and his mouth was parched, as if he had the worst hangover of his life. The sun was already hot on his face and the air was filled with birdsong. Where had the birds come from, he wondered idly? There were so many of them, so many thousands, making so much noise. Had they been hiding in the trees, watching him all night?

"So Mori, here you are. Having a well-earned sleep, eh?"

The sarcastic voice was instantly familiar. Mori squinted up into the sun. Itoh was staring down at him, a group of detectives by his side.

"What's happening?" mumbled Mori weakly. "Where's Iwanaga?"

As he spoke, the throbbing in his head got worse and a wave of nausea welled up within him. The burning feeling on his cheeks, he realized, was not caused by the sun. He was running a high fever. "That's what we want to ask you, my friend—it was you who helped him to escape. After disobeying my express orders, causing massive destruction of private property, and endangering the whole mission. If I wanted to, I could have you locked up for the next ten years!"

Itoh's voice was trembling with anger.

"I think Mori acted bravely. Without him, there might have been many more casualties. He tried his best."

It was the young detective who had befriended Mori in the police headquarters.

"Shut up, you fool! This man is dangerous and untrustworthy. For all we know, he was in league with Iwanaga all along! Take him back to headquarters for interrogation!"

But this time the young detective was not going to be browbeaten into submission. He spoke with the slow calm purpose of a man who has weighed his words.

"It should be clear to all of us here that many difficulties were caused by not paying attention to Mori's analysis of the situation. We could have averted the many basic errors we made."

There was a moment of silence as the full weight of the heresy sank in, then two other voices muttered agreement.

"That's right."

"We should have paid attention."

Itoh's mouth opened and closed like a goldfish gulping for air.

"Enough of this," he spluttered finally. "Let's get him out of here."

"Iwanaga," said Mori, as the Giants fan grabbed him by the armpits and hauled him to his feet. "He must be around somewhere. You've got to stop him."

"Don't you worry about that," said Itoh gruffly. "Just leave it to the professionals."

"That's right," said the Giants fan, giving Mori a hearty thump between the shoulders. "We professionals are used to cleaning up the mess that interfering amateurs leave behind."

Mori rocked back and forth dizzily. The wave of nausea was welling up inside him, his stomach quivering uncontrollably.

"That's good to know," he grunted, and snatched the Giants

cap from the man's head and held it to his mouth.

The Giants fan gazed at him in horror.

"What do you think you are doing? No, stop . . ."

But it was too late. Mori's stomach was heaving like a boat in a storm, and his mouth was disgorging great clots of puke, streams of bile, filling the cap till it sank with the weight.

"Thanks," he said, wiping his mouth. "I feel better now."

Then he sank back to the ground and welcomed the sensation of consciousness melting away.

16

.
.
.

I T was the week after the meteorological office had officially
declared the end of summer. In due obedience, the beer gardens had all closed down, the swimming pools had been
drained dry, and the cicadas had turned down the volume. The
sun still blazed down at midday, but the humidity had gone, and
air conditioners were no longer necessary in the evening. Tokyo's
army of salarymen had put away their short-sleeved shirts for another year, and the office ladies were already sporting knee-length
leather skirts, ankle boots, corduroy berets, and other items from
this autumn's fashion mandate.

Everything was back to normal, or so it seemed. The Gendai
Giants were on their way to winning the Central League pennant
for the third year in a row, and the Seikyu Lions had the Pacific
League sewn up. The yen had returned to a gently rising trend
against the dollar. Ishizaka had suddenly withdrawn from the
contest for the premiership. In his place, the party had chosen the
leader of one of the mainstream factions, a crinkle-faced, somno-
lent old racoon dog of a politician, renowned for his command of
factional intrigue and creative fund-raising techniques. A new
series of trade disputes had broken out, and the new prime minister had promised the Americans and Europeans that he "would
make all due efforts to establish the necessary consensus for
preparing an appropriate response."

Some stranger things were happening too. The Ministry of

Finance's decision to "recommend" the breakup of Maruichi Securities had sent shock waves through the business world. After all, "excessive concentration of financial power" was not a problem that had previously given the molders of Japan's economic policy much cause for concern. The weekly magazines were full of rumors and conspiracy theories. The most popular was that an unholy alliance of the banks, the U.S. Treasury, and Yamamura Securities, Maruichi's deadly rival, were behind the ministry's startling move.

The takeover of Nippon Infosystems excited almost as much comment. Conventional wisdom had long held that hostile takeovers were unsavory Western affairs that could never happen in Japan. Since only small proportions of listed companies' shares are available to be traded on the stock market, the rest being safely stowed away in the hands of friendly financial institutions, it was hard to see how a predator could succeed. When a little-known American company made a formal bid for Nippon Infosystems, conventional wisdom merely chuckled at its temerity. The chuckles were replaced by stunned silence when Japan's major banks, insurance companies, and pension funds voted almost unanimously to accept the terms of the offer.

One fine evening, Wheels-san and Heavy Industry-san entertained a Midwestern senator and his wife at the Bunraku puppet theater. The play was a tale of illicit love, conflicting duties, revenge, and suicide. Wheels-san had seen it performed a dozen times before, but still he found the climax, when the unhappy lovers throw themselves into the stormy sea, unbearably affecting. The main puppetmaster, a man who had been rewarded for his prowess by the title of "Living Cultural Treasure," handled the hero with such consummate tenderness, such deep understanding of passion and fate. He achieved greater depth than any human actor that Wheels-san had ever seen.

Afterward they took the senator and his wife, who had spent most of the performance asleep, to a restaurant where they could eat American steak. Compared to Kobe beef, with its lusciously marbled texture, the meat was almost inedibly coarse, but the two

Japanese did their best to chew their way through it. The senator wanted to talk about soybean contracts, donations to the state university's new Japan Center, and investment credits for the expansion of the auto factory that Wheels-san had established five years before. Heavy Industry-san wanted to talk about American politics.

"That was a great surprise about Senator Reckard, was it not?" he asked. "Our Japanese politicians would never retire from political life at such a young age. In fact, most of them retire only at their funerals!"

He gave a short bark of laughter.

"It was a real bolt from the blue," agreed the senator. "I would guess there's probably much more to it than meets the eye. All the usual rumors have been going round—drink problems, women problems, money. . . . But I don't suppose you're interested in all that."

They saw the two guests back to their hotel at an early hour. The senator's wife was leaving in the morning for a shopping trip to Hong Kong, and they had already promised to take him somewhere more interesting the next evening. There would be plenty of opportunities then for more intensive information-gathering.

After depositing the Americans at the New Otani Hotel, Wheels-san and Heavy Industry-san went together to a geisha house in Kagurazaka. After a few drinks and a few games, they dismissed the women.

"The plan is proceeding smoothly," said Heavy Industry-san. "Soon, everything will be back to normal."

"That's right," said Wheels-san thoughtfully. "Still, I wonder if it's good to leave so many of them at liberty. They're dangerous men."

"It's better this way. We can't let wind of what happened get out to the public, or to our trading partners. That would be absolutely disastrous. And anyway . . ."

Heavy Industry-san shrugged his shoulders and drained his cup of sake. Wheels-san waited for him to finish the sentence, but he said nothing.

"Anyway what?" asked Wheels-san finally.

"After all, they weren't doing it for their own benefit," said Heavy Industry-san, with a strange kind of softness in his voice. "They were doing it for the good of Japan."

Wheels-san looked at Heavy Industry-san closely. There were ten years between them, and a lot more besides. Heavy Industry-san often talked with nostalgia about the coup attempt of 1936, of the camaraderie of that snowy night in Akasaka.

"Maybe so," said Wheels-san. "But it's a different world now."

"That's true," said Heavy Industry-san, without much enthusiasm. "It's a different world."

They finished their drinks and called out for the women.

Twelve thousand miles away, Tom Kono was also draining a glass of beer. It was two o'clock in the afternoon in London. Tom was leaning against the bar in his favorite pub finishing off a pint of his favorite real ale and listening to Trevor explain what made the Liverpool soccer team so unbeatable.

"Excellent individual players, of course," Trevor was saying. "That goes without saying. But none of them is irreplaceable. It's the culture of the team that counts, the systems, the coordination. . . ."

"You make it sound more like a company than a soccer team," said Tom.

"That's exactly the point. Liverpool's like a well-run Japanese company, just like Sumikawa when I joined it."

"And now Sumikawa's more like Everton, right?"

"Not that bad. More like Notts Forest, I should say. Brilliant manager, plenty of energy and hustle, but still not a class team. Lacking the killer instinct."

They finished their drinks and made their way back to the office. In the old days, Tom would never have gone to the pub at lunchtime, but now he had plenty of time on his hands. After several weeks of painstaking work, he had managed to unravel the financial cat's cradle that Shimada and the dealers at Mitsutomo and Dainippon had left behind. All that remained now was to sell out the huge positions that were left without disturbing the markets. And to do that would take months, if not years.

Back in his office overlooking St. Paul's, Tom reflected on his conversation with Trevor. It was true that Sumikawa Europe no longer commanded the respect that it had in the past. There had been too many management changes, too many good people had left. As acting branch manager, it was Tom's responsibility to restore the sense of teamwork that had made the operation so successful in the past. He had made a start by promoting Trevor to chief dealer and giving him free rein to bring in the best people he could find. Tom had also abolished all distinctions in status between local and Japanese staff and made it plain that jobs and salaries would be dependent on ability, not on seniority, education, or nationality. Already, the office had a friendly, relaxed atmosphere that would have infuriated ex-Branch Manager Yamaguchi. But there was no longer any reason to worry about what ex-Branch Manager Yamaguchi would think. He was safely ensconced in his new ten-year posting—as Deputy Manager of General Affairs in Sumikawa's smallest branch in Hokkaido.

Outside, the weather had suddenly deteriorated. Tom had walked back to the office bathed in the effulgent autumn sunshine, but now the buses and taxis had their lights on and the great dome of St. Paul's had turned a darker shade of gray. Tom stared out at the sheets of rain that came sweeping across the towers and spires and skyscrapers of the City. He had never felt more at home in his life.

On the lonely mountain overlooking Kyoto, a shadow flitted up the seventy-eight stone steps that led to the ancient temple. It moved swiftly, softly, without disturbing the raindrops on the twigs or rousing the wood pigeons in their nests. When it reached the top of the steps, it paused for a moment, faded into the background while a young priest emptied a bucket of water from a window, then moved noiselessly over the gravel courtyard to the empty porch. There was no more than an instant of light as a door slid open and shut.

The shadow moved slowly through the temple's inner precincts; into corners, underneath staircases, behind doors. It passed through the incense smoke and chanted sutras, and not one of the priests raised his eyes from his devotions. It nosed into the kitchen, where a vegetable stew was bubbling away in a big copper cauldron. It slipped down the cold, wooden corridors without making a creak.

Finally, it came to a small, windowless room where an old man sat reading a book under a flickering yellow lamp. When it slid through his half-open door, he looked up and smiled. The shadow was absolutely still.

"I thought you might come," came the wheezing voice from the loudspeaker on the table. "I've been thinking about you a lot recently."

"I'm surprised you can bear to think of me at all. After what has happened, you should fear me."

Strange gulping sounds emerged from the loudspeaker. The old man's toothless mouth was wide open and his chest was moving up and down. It took him several moments to recover.

"Forgive my laughter. It's just that you sound the same as when my brother first brought you here. An angry, impetuous little boy."

"This is not a joke, uncle. You have made yourself my enemy."

"Idiot! Have you learned nothing?"

"I have learned enough about you. You have destroyed me just as you destroyed my father."

"My brother destroyed himself. He was a brave man and a strong man, but also a fool. I warned him about you. On his deathbed, I implored him to entrust your education and spiritual training to me. Instead, he chose to leave you with your foster parents, and look at the result. You have no moderation, no humility, no self-knowledge at all. It is sad."

"What use are moderation and humility in times like these? The spirit of Japan is under unprecedented attack."

"The spirit of Japan? Hah! Your nonsensical schemes have done nothing but harm our country's interests. You stimulated anti-Japanese elements in foreign countries, even tried to bring them to political power. What on earth did you think you were doing?"

"It was necessary, uncle. This parasitic relationship with the Americans must be broken by any means possible. Under my plan, the Americans would have done most of the work for us. And in the resulting crisis the people of our nation would have rediscovered their true identity. Japan's destiny cast anew by the will of ordinary Japanese—that was always my father's dream."

The old man shook his head. He looked tired. When he spoke, his voice had faded to little more than a metallic croak.

"You talk about your father as if he were a god, yet he cared nothing for you at all. He begot you in a geisha house, had you taken from your mother at birth, never once acknowledged you as a member of the Maruoka family. Forget him! You won't be free until you do."

"I was born a Maruoka and I will die a Maruoka. If my father hadn't been hounded to his death by the Americans, he would have recognized me for what I am. Everything that I have accomplished, everything that I planned—it was done in the true Maruoka spirit. That is something that you appear to have forgotten long ago, uncle."

The voice quavered defiantly, like an angry adolescent's. The old man bent forward in his seat. In the flickering candlelight, his face looked as hard and old as a rainbeaten stone carving.

"What do you know of the Maruoka spirit?" he rasped, the words interspersed with deep sucks of air. "Your absurd schemes have disgraced our name!"

The rasp became a hacking cough, and the cough a wheezing paroxysm.

"Uncle! Are you all right? Shall I call for help?"

The answer came between deep, shuddering breaths that had the candle flame dancing like a demented spirit.

"Go from here! Never let me see you again. You are not worthy of your father's name."

The air was fractured by a strange cry, a mixture of rage and pain and despair, and then the shadow dissolved into the night. It took several minutes for the old man's breathing to return to normal. When it had, he wiped his eyes with a small cloth he kept in the sleeve of his kimono, picked up his spectacles, and turned his gaze to the book on his lap.

Soon the only sound left was the *chok* of the shishi-odoshi, endlessly emptying itself and filling itself.

Three weeks later, when the mountainsides had turned vermillion, copper, and gold, a farmer's wife was busy stacking rice bales in a dried-out paddy. She looked up to wipe her brow and saw the man walking past.

He was dressed, she remembered later, in ragged shirt and trousers, like an itinerant peddler, and had a hunter's peaked cap pulled down over his face. She called out a greeting, but he ignored her and carried on up the mountain path.

Later on, just before dusk, a couple of hikers glimpsed him much higher up. By then, he had left the path and was forcing his way through the thickets of brambles that covered the final stretch up to the peak. They noticed the long thin object wrapped in canvas that he was carrying. They thought it was probably a hunting rifle.

They were the last human beings to see Toshio Iwanaga alive. Having reached the mountain peak, he found a flat rock that suited his purpose and sat down in the lotus position, facing due east.

By midnight, the mountain was silent except for the occasional hoot of an owl. The air was bone-chillingly cold, but Iwanaga did not move an inch. He didn't even glance up at the naked sky, the silver sliver of moon, the milky way like a streak of semen. He sat there staring at nothing, thinking of nothing, preparing himself for nothing.

Dawn came quickly, hardening the dim silhouettes of the mountains, gently brushing away the thin layer of mist that hung over the valley below. Larks, thrushes, and finches raised the morning chorus. They were joined by the enfeebled creaks of the few remaining cicadas and crickets. In a farm far below, a cock was crowing.

Iwanaga waited until the red eye of the sun had risen fully above the horizon. He had chosen his spot well, for the unmistakable shape of Mount Fuji could be seen directly below it.

Indeed, for a moment it looked as if the sun were perching on Fuji's summit, like a giant football.

He picked up the canvas-wrapped object he had brought with him and set it on his lap. Slowly, deliberately, he took out the sword and held it in front of him. The steel rippled and flashed. Again he marveled at how well it balanced . . . like a dancer, like a beautiful woman making love. Masahide was truly a genius!

He pointed the tip at the center of the sun, flicked his wrists over, and, without taking his eyes from the peak of Mount Fuji, drove the steel deep into his belly. The pain came like a long-lost friend. It was happiness to greet it. He began breathing deeply through his nose. His eyes were swimming. Yet something wasn't quite right. He gave a frown, as of disappointment, and wrenched the blade free. Intestines were bulging out through the wound, and his hands were dripping with blood.

He steadied himself, then plunged the blade in once more. This time it was exactly right. He felt an ecstatic gratitude for the waves of agony that were surging upward in an unstoppable tide. He shuddered violently, then gave a sigh of satisfaction that seemed to go on and on forever as all the breath and life that was in him rushed to escape.

Iwanaga slumped sideways onto the rock. The birds got noisier. The stain of the sunrise spread across the horizon, linking north to south.

The rice harvest was finished by the time Mori took the rickety old train up through the mountains to the tiny fishing village facing the Japan Sea. The paddies were wastes of burned stubble, and the tractors had been put away until next year. The trees, though, were hanging with mikan oranges and ripe persimmons, and all along the water's edge there were squid hanging up to dry, like thousands of white socks on a washing line.

The village itself seemed even smaller and quieter than he remembered, and Mr. and Mrs. Hara older and more wrinkled. They took him back to the wooden house on the hill and offered him green tea and seaweed crackers and listened to what he had to say. When he told them how her son had died, old

Mrs. Hara smiled and nodded.

"I'm glad he didn't inconvenience anyone after all," she said in a low voice.

Mori kept his explanation to a minimum. The murder, he said, was, the result of a dispute with a group of criminals who had since been arrested. The two men directly responsible were both dead.

"He wasn't the type to get into quarrels," said the old man, shaking his head.

"He fought for what he thought was right for Japan," said Mori. "That was why they had to kill him."

"It's a strange world, Mori-san. People quarrel about things that make no sense at all. I went up to Tokyo once—for the graduation ceremony, you see. I don't like that place at all. They've got everything that's unnecessary, and the things that are really necessary—why, they're not there at all."

"Now, father. Mori-san doesn't have much time left. . . ."

It was obviously a monologue that had been gone through many times before, probably, thought Mori, with young Hara sitting where he was sitting now, nodding sympathetically and pretending to agree.

"You can't get good crab meat," complained the old man, as if his trip to Tokyo had taken place last week. "It doesn't smell fresh at all."

Old Mrs. Hara shot him a look that quieted him at once and returned to questioning Mori about the story of her son's death. Mori answered as he could, without mentioning Yoshimura or Silent Thunder or Iwanaga's crazy plot.

When the time came to leave, Mrs. Hara took out an envelope with his name written on it in her old-fashioned hand and bowed low before him.

"We are humbly grateful for all you've done," she said. "Please honor us by taking this small thing."

Mori shook his head gravely. They had already paid his bill, and what he had just told them certainly wasn't worth a bonus.

"It's very kind," he said, bowing low in return. "I can't accept this. It would be against the rules of our association."

The old woman looked confused, as well she might.

"Wait a moment," said the old man. "I have something for you, something you really need. You must take it with you to Tokyo."

Before Mori could say anything, he hurried off into the kitchen, from where there soon came the sound of a hammer banging in nails. When he returned, he was carrying under his arm a wooden box about the size of a small suitcase. He handed it to Mori with a look of eager anticipation on his face, and Mori knew that this time he couldn't refuse.

They drove him the few miles down the coast road to the station, past the persimmon trees, the gravestones between the rice paddies, fishing boats being hauled up onto the sand, groups of solemn, dark-faced schoolboys playing marbles by the side of the road. Who knows, thought Mori, one of them might be the next Hara, to play with currencies and interest rates one distant day with that same utter absorption. The train was waiting at the station, the engine muttering quietly to itself. As before, the carriages were mostly empty. There were no whistles or buzzers, no bellowed loudspeaker announcements. The train just gave a heave and a sigh, then slowly rattled forward down the long line that led back to the condition that Mori called reality.

Old man Hara walked down the platform next to the carriage window, waving his leathery old hand. His wife was walking three paces behind him.

Mori waved back, then the train picked up speed and left the platform, the station, and the little village behind.

He looked down at the wooden box on the seat beside him. A faint scraping sound was coming from somewhere inside it. The old man had told him not to open it until he got home, but his professional curiosity was getting the better of him.

He pulled at the lid, but it wouldn't budge. The nails had been banged in tight. He took a small claspknife from his pocket and tried to prize open a gap to look through.

It wouldn't yield, no matter how hard he forced it. Determined to have his way, Mori stood up, bent over the box, and leveraged downwards with all the weight in his body. For a moment nothing happened, then suddenly the lid sprang free and skidded across the carriage floor.

Mori stumbled forward onto the seat, tipping the box over sideways, then fell to his knees. There was a roaring sound as the front part of the train rushed into the tunnel.

When Mori looked up, the biggest crab he had ever seen in his life was a couple of inches from his face, its tiny stalk-eyes fixed on him with grim determination. The roaring got louder and closer, then everything went black.

Afterword

In the 1920s, the world came to Paris. In the 1950s and 1960s, the world came to the United States. In the 1980s, the world came to Tokyo. My first (nonfiction) book, *The Japanese*, was written in the mid-1980s, and tried to express a personal view of the tremendously dynamic political, economic, and social phenomena developing in Japan at that time. Since then two things have happened. First, foreign-produced studies on the nature of Japan and the Japanese have become a minor growth industry, with a new product on the market almost every month. Second, the pace of change in Japan has accelerated, making many perceptive comments invalid by the time they are published. Indeed, one of the serious flaws in the work of the revisionist school of criticism is that the Japan they are criticizing has already ceased to exist. Naturally, the Japan that does exist now has many features worthy of comment as well, but by the time they are recognized and analyzed, they will have disappeared, to be replaced by something else.

Japan is changing, as always. This writer is changing too. Analysis, categorization, and prescription no longer seem the most suitable way to express the range of experiences and potentialities present in the concept of "Japan." In a novel, the pretense of objectivity is no longer necessary. Impressions, even distorted and exceptional ones, have their own inherent validity. Probably many readers of the Japanese edition of this book found the "Japan" that exists in these pages utterly different from their own "Japanese Japan." Similarly, the "America" that is depicted is unlikely to be recognized by many Americans. Nonetheless, both versions must be included among all the possible "Japans" and "Americas" that exist in the world's imagination. In that sense, they have reality.

Tokyo, with its love hotels, karaoke bars, and "intelligent buildings," is itself a fictional city—assembled from the collective consciousness of the human tide that sweeps through it every day. An Englishman from the nineteenth century who arrived in modern London (or an American from the turn of the century who arrived in modern New York) would find many surprising features, but he would recognize the city as his own. On the other hand, a visitor from Meiji Japan would find Roppongi, Harajuku, and Shinjuku no more familiar than Mars. That sense of artificiality and impermanence—particularly present in the city's erotic life—is something that distinguishes Tokyo from the other great cities of the world. As the German film director Wim Wenders puts it, "Living in Tokyo is like being in someone else's dream."

I spent the 1980s working in the maelstrom of one of the greatest bull markets in history. The Tokyo stock market is a place where the border between truth and fiction is indefinable, and often irrelevant. Many of the experiences and stories accumulated over the years appear in this book, but modified, blended, and exaggerated. Many ordinary characters are based on people I have met—colleagues, friends of friends, and so on. Much of the action goes on in places that I have actually visited. As the Russians used to say of their history books, "It's all true, except for the facts."

The world economic and financial system has internationalized at an extraordinary pace over the past two decades. Decisions taken in one country often have a dramatic impact on people living a continent away. Unfortunately, however, the political cultures of individual countries have not managed to internationalize to the same extent. The French government cannot do anything that would alienate French farmers, who make up a tiny proportion of the total population. The U.S. government is worried about using Japanese integrated circuits in its high-tech weapons. As the Gulf crisis showed, Japanese political culture is still obsessed with its own "uniqueness," apparently unable to take any hard decisions without outside pressure.

In the 1990s, the world economy is unlikely to be as robust as in the 1980s. Recessions and continuous slow growth will put increasing pressure on governments to attend to the demands of domestic pressure groups. Economic nationalism is on the rise even though the idea of a nation as an economic unit is fading. Protectionism—disguised as the creation of economic blocs—is now at its strongest in a generation. In the United States and Europe, Japan is seen both as the enemy who must be resisted and as the exemplar whose economic success story shows that trade barriers, industrial policy, market intervention, and so on do actually work. At the same time, the disappearance of the Soviet Union has created the conditions for a nonideological, pre-twentieth century conception of national interest.

Japanese people sometimes ask me what can be done about this state of affairs. The answer is simple. Historically, the free trade system has been supported by the nation that benefits the most from it—Britain in the late nineteenth century, the United States after the Second World War. The United States and Britain demonstrated their support for the system by example. They opened their own lucrative domestic markets, which then became a powerful bargaining tool for enforcing the same behavior on others. Japan, now the biggest beneficiary of the free trade system, must develop the political will to do something similar. And for that it needs strong and effective political leadership. When my Japanese friends hear that, they often look rather depressed.

As the stock market proverb goes, "the higher the mountain, the deeper the valley." Since the beginning of 1990, when I started writing this book, the financial and economic environment has changed entirely. The weakening in the Tokyo market now under way will doubtless be as memorable and far-reaching in its consequences as the bull market that preceded it. I know that the original of Kenji in *Silent Thunder* is having quite a difficult time. Recently, he joined a small investment advisory firm as a fund manager, but the market quickly turned against him. Nearly all the stocks he bought are 10 to 15 percent down on the purchase price, and he is wondering how he is going to explain that to his new boss. I told him he should have followed my recommendations, not those he heard from his old colleagues at "Maruichi." His golf swing has improved quite a bit though, and he tells me he is going to get married to Noriko early next year.

I happened to meet Mori in a small yakitori place I sometimes go to after work. We drank half a bottle of Suntory White together and discussed baseball and women. Lisa, he told me, had gone off to Okinawa with a twenty-five-year-old trumpet player, who played fusion music, not even proper jazz. It didn't seem to worry him—in fact, he seemed slightly relieved. As usual, I ended up paying the bill. He thanked me and said that he was now working on something really big—a complex and bizarre series of incidents that could decide Japan's fate in the twenty-first century. When it had all been cleared up, he would give me the whole story and I could do with it what I liked.

A kind offer, but before that I'll see how much interest people show in his previous experiences. With the great bull market long gone, everyone is under pressure, myself included.

This book was written in accordance with a suggestion by Kodansha Ltd., and could not have been completed without the active support and encouragement of executive editor Mitsuru Tomita.

Peter Tasker
Tokyo, 1992